Praise for Lisa Wingate's

Dandelion Summer
Winner of the 2012 Carol Award for Women's Fiction
from the American Christian Fiction Writers

"An old man's haunting memories and a young girl's dreams merge in Lisa Wingate's absolutely unforgettable story of hope and reconciliation."

—Sherryl Woods, *New York Times* bestselling author of *Beach Lane*

"*Dandelion Summer* is a rare gem of a book. It's a story of two unlikely allies on a journey to find their Camelot, but it's so much more than that. It's a story of missed opportunities and new beginnings, of understanding the past and creating dreams, of aiming for the stars even when you doubt that the stars are within your reach. It's a story beautifully told, with richly drawn characters that will squeeze your heart and make you want to laugh and cry at the same time. Like dandelion seeds, J. Norm and Epie will take root in your heart and stay with you long after you've closed the last page."

—Karen White, *New York Times* bestselling author of *The Beach Trees*

"A gripping and beautifully told story that crosses generations and reminds us it is love that changes our world. With both startling insight and humor, Lisa Wingate tells a story that takes the reader to the moon and back to the human heart. *Dandelion Summer* has a compassionate and lyrical heartbeat you won't want to miss."

—Patti Callahan Henry, national bestselling author of *Coming Up for Air*

Beyond Summer

"*Beyond Summer* is beyond good. It's great! Lisa Wingate's tale of three women from disparate backgrounds and how they join together to survive corporate greed is a cautionary tale for our times. But it is also a story of women's love for each other and their families and the consequence of that love. Out of hardship comes growth and out of desperation, friendship, and out of unasked prayers come answers."

—Sandra Dallas, *New York Times* bestselling author of *True Sisters*

continued . . .

"If you are looking for a great book this summer, be sure to put *Beyond Summer* on your reading list. The characters will find a place in your heart. I didn't think I would ever find a book that came close to *Tending Roses*, but *Beyond Summer* might have matched it."   —*The McGregor Mirror* (TX)

"A timely story about finding strength and wealth in the most unlikely of places."   —*Booklist*

The Summer Kitchen

"The consistently engaging and popular Wingate delivers a warmhearted and genuinely inspirational story of tragedy and hope."   —*Booklist*

"Their lives intersect and are changed in profound ways. As always, Wingate's stories are uplifting . . . dealing with matters like friendship, grace, and the power to make a difference in others' lives."

—*The Beaumont Enterprise* (TX)

A Month of Summer

"With her signature gentle spiritualism, Wingate sheds light on the toll that aging and disease take on families as she launches a new series with broad appeal."   —*Booklist*

"*A Month of Summer*, with characters we love and plot twists that surprise us, teaches us that it's never too late to open our hearts."   —*Southern Lady*

A Thousand Voices

"Wingate paints a riveting picture of the Choctaw Nation as one woman searches for the family she never knew. Heartfelt and revealing, Wingate's latest proves that she's a rising star in the world of women's fiction."

—*Romantic Times* (Top Pick)

"A delightful, heart-wrenching story written in first person with captivating characters, *A Thousand Voices* is sensitively told and masterfully written. It will capture the imagination of readers from the first page . . . not to be missed . . . a perfect 10."   —Romance Reviews Today

"Lisa Wingate provides a warm character study of a fully developed individual seeking her roots."   —*Midwest Book Review*

Drenched in Light

"Heartfelt and moving, enriched by characters drawn with compassion and warmth."
—Jennifer Chiaverini

"Another winner."
—*Booklist*

The Language of Sycamores

"Heartfelt, honest, and entirely entertaining . . . this poignant story will touch your heart from the first page to the last."
—Kristin Hannah

"An excellent storyteller who knows how to draw readers in quickly and keep them turning the pages, laughing one minute and grabbing for a tissue the next."
—*Lubbock Avalanche-Journal*

"Wingate presents another one of her positive and uplifting books . . . tales in the midst of turmoil that are inspirational without being preachy."
—*Booklist*

Good Hope Road

"A novel bursting with joy amidst crisis: small-town life is painted with scope and detail in the capable hands of a writer who understands longing, grief, and the landscape of a woman's heart."
—Adriana Trigiani

"Wingate has written a genuinely heartwarming story about how a sense of possibility can be awakened in the aftermath of a tragedy to bring a community together and demonstrate the true American spirit."
—*Booklist*

Tending Roses

"A story at once gentle and powerful about the very old and the very young, and about the young woman who loves them all. Richly emotional and spiritual, *Tending Roses* affected me from the first page."
—Luanne Rice

"You can't put it down without . . . taking a good look at your own life and how misplaced priorities might have led to missed opportunities. *Tending Roses* is an excellent read for any season, a celebration of the power of love."
—*El Paso Times*

Novels by Lisa Wingate

The Blue Sky Hill Series
A Month of Summer
The Summer Kitchen
Beyond Summer
Dandelion Summer

The Tending Roses Series
Tending Roses
Good Hope Road
The Language of Sycamores
Drenched in Light
A Thousand Voices

The Texas Hill Country Trilogy
Texas Cooking
Lone Star Café
Over the Moon at the Big Lizard Diner

A Month of Summer

Lisa Wingate

NAL
ACCENT

NAL Accent
Published by New American Library, a division of Penguin Group (USA) Inc.,
375 Hudson Street, New York, New York 10014, USA
Penguin Group (Canada), 90 Eglinton Avenue East, Suite 700, Toronto,
Ontario M4P 2Y3, Canada (a division of Pearson Penguin Canada Inc.)
Penguin Books Ltd., 80 Strand, London WC2R 0RL, England
Penguin Ireland, 25 St. Stephen's Green, Dublin 2, Ireland
(a division of Penguin Books Ltd.)
Penguin Group (Australia), 250 Camberwell Road, Camberwell, Victoria 3124, Australia
(a division of Pearson Australia Group Pty. Ltd.)
Penguin Books India Pvt. Ltd., 11 Community Centre,
Panchsheel Park, New Delhi - 110 017, India
Penguin Group (NZ), 67 Apollo Drive, Rosedale,
North Shore 0632,New Zealand (a division of Pearson New Zealand Ltd.)
Penguin Books (South Africa) (Pty.) Ltd.,
24 Sturdee Avenue, Rosebank, Johannesburg 2196, South Africa

Penguin Books Ltd., Registered Offices:
80 Strand, London WC2R 0RL, England

First published by NAL Accent, an imprint of New American Library,
a division of Penguin Group (USA) Inc.

First Printing, July 2008
10 9 8 7 6 5 4 3 2 1

 REGISTERED TRADEMARK—MARCA REGISTRADA

LIBRARY OF CONGRESS CATALOGING-IN-PUBLICATION DATA:

Wingate, Lisa.
  A month of summer/Lisa Wingate.
    p. cm.
  ISBN 978-0-451-22403-3
  1. Women lawyers—Fiction. 2. Fathers and daughters—Fiction. 3. Older parents—Fiction. 4. Dallas
(Tex.)—Fiction. 5. Domestic fiction. I. Title.
PS3573.I53165M66 2008
813'.54—dc22   2007049711

Set in Adobe Garamond · Designed by Spring Hoteling

Printed in the United States of America

To Memaw and Grandaddy Hutson,
who remind us
that true love is not found
only in a brief moment of passion
but in a lifetime of
little moments
spent together

ACKNOWLEDGMENTS

I can't drive away from Blue Sky Hill without leaving behind a little love letter to the many people who helped bring this neighborhood and its residents to life. First and foremost, thank you to my brother-in-law, Vance, and my sister-in-law, Stacy, for helping me to discover the neighborhoods growing and changing in the shadow of downtown Dallas. Thank you for contributing many setting details and for driving me around, and around, and around the streets of Lakewood, patiently holding up traffic while I snapped pictures. Thank you also to Larry and Martha Mayo for answering a plethora of real estate law questions over lunch at Johnny's, and to Elaine Morley for providing legal details pertaining to Rebecca's work as an immigration attorney. Without your input, this story would be incomplete.

A round of heartfelt gratitude goes out to the wonderful group of nursing home personnel, who do difficult jobs every day as nurses, therapists, administrators, and home-care workers. Thank you in particular to Candi Adcock for sharing lunch, information, and your incredible coworkers. Thank you also to Janice Boyd for reading the manuscript. All of you are the angels who, like Mary in the story, see not only aging bodies but also the vibrant human beings who need and deserve love and dignity.

A long-distance thank-you goes out to my friend Jennifer Magers for excellent proofreading and help with technical issues regarding nursing home care. Thank you also to my online scrapbooking girlfriend, Teresa Loman, for helping to bring the SCRAPS page of Lisawingate.com alive with the wonderful DSP online scrapbook pages. My gratitude also goes to the Web genius and talented writer Donna McGoldrick for expert maintenance of Lisawingate.com and to computer guru, friend, and encourager extraordinaire Ed Stevens for helping with Internet presence and for telling me all about the dream life in the little ski village of Zermatt. Thank you also to my mother and mother-in-law for never-ending encouragement, help with proofreading, and companionship in book travel. Thanks also for being the wonderful grandmas who sweat through hundred-degree baseball games and take part in penguin huddles at subzero football stadiums wherever the Wingate boys are playing. Wonderful grandmas are the glue that holds a family together.

A big thank-you goes to the fantastic people at New American Library, who design the beautiful covers, edit the text, catch the mistakes, and bring these stories to readers. Books, like people, do not develop in a vacuum. Each becomes a combined product of the dedicated efforts of many. My heartfelt gratitude goes in particular to Kara Welsh and Claire Zion; to my editor, Ellen Edwards; and to my agent, Claudia Cross of Sterling Lord Literistic. Here's to the many roads we've traveled on the way to Blue Sky Hill, and the many yet to come.

Last, thank you to readers far and near, because without you I'd just be a slightly off-base Texas girl who still plays with imaginary friends. Thank you for sharing these journeys with me, for recommending the books to friends, for sharing your own news, and views, and e-mails. Your friendships create meaning in these stories and meaning in my life. I hope you'll find blessings in this trip to Blue Sky Hill.

Peace be the journey, now and always.

A MONTH *of* SUMMER

CHAPTER 1

Rebecca Macklin

During an anniversary trip to San Diego, I stood on a second-story balcony above a Japanese garden and watched the gardener comb a bed of red gravel and gray stone with a long wooden rake. Shaded from the rising sun by a wide straw hat, his body arched against the tidal breeze, he patiently drew intricate curves and swirls, which the tourists walked by without noticing. From their vantage, his work would go largely unappreciated, but he seemed unfettered by this fact. He kept at his task with a certain determination, a resoluteness—as if he knew each stone, knew where it must go, exactly how it must lie to complete the proper picture. A leaf blew into the garden, and he danced across the gravel on the light, silent feet of an acrobat, removed the leaf, then repaired the damage with his rake.

On three separate days, I stopped to observe the gardener. Each time, the pattern of stones was different. One day a running swirl of ocean waves, one day a sunburst of rays originating from a single center, one day a series of concentric circles, as if God had touched down a fingertip, rippling the crimson sea. A leaf drifted from overhead, landed in the center, and the gardener left it.

How did he know? I wondered. *How did he know that this time the leaf was meant to stay?*

Taking up his tools, the gardener strolled away, and disappeared down the boulevard, a small man hidden beneath the shadow of his hat, at peace with what remained.

I had always wished to be like the gardener, to see the larger canvas, to know which leaves should go and which should stay, to be at peace with the stones left behind.

Unfortunately, I was not.

They haunted me.

I combed the gravel of my life again, again, again, creating artificial shapes, patterns that became habitual, yet felt incomplete.

Perhaps I was always waiting for the leaf to fall and complete the picture.

But when it did, I didn't recognize it.

At first.

It drifted downward in the form of a plane that had been circling Dallas for what seemed like an eternity before dropping through a March thunderstorm to find the runway. By then, the pilot had confessed that we'd been burning off fuel on purpose, due to a malfunction in the plane's braking flaps. He would still be able to land using wheel brakes and ground spoilers, he assured us, but we should assume the crash position, just in case. The flight attendant demonstrated the procedure, then we began our descent, hugging our knees, the guy beside me praying under his breath and me fumbling for the air sickness bag, thinking, *I hate flying. If I survive this, I'll never get on a plane again. I'll drive. Everywhere.*

In the back of my mind, I remembered Bree, the law clerk who'd given me a ride to the airport, saying, "You know, Mrs. Macklin, statistically flying is much safer than driving."

"I don't care," I told her. "I'd much rather travel by car, where I can be in the driver's seat. If they'd let me *pilot* the plane, then I'd like flying."

Bree giggled, the sound too light and childlike for her tightly

French-twisted hair and trying-to-impress dark suit. "Control is an illusion," she offered. "I've been reading *Ninety-Nine Principles of Everyday Zen*, and that's the first one. You can't achieve Zen until you relinquish control of the universe to the universe."

Glancing at the visor mirror, I tucked a few strands of dark hair behind my ear and met the red-rimmed hazel eyes of a woman who was tempted to say something sharp, world-weary, and cynical. Why were young law clerks always seeking the deeper meaning of life in self-help books? "Be careful what you buy into, kid," I advised, as Bree pulled up to the curb in the airport drop-off zone. "A good lawyer can't afford to be Zen. You'll get mugged at the negotiating table." *By the way, are you sleeping with my husband?*

Bree laughed again.

She could be, I thought. *She's beautiful. . . .*

I closed my eyes as the plane bounced against the runway, then went airborne again, and I saw Bree's face. Then it faded into the face of the woman lounging at a sidewalk table with a fresh frappe from my favorite Santa Monica coffeehouse. The woman smiled at Kyle, her long blond hair lifting in the saltwater breeze, her eyes sparkling. She slid a hand across the table and into his, while I sat in the right turn lane, not four miles from our home. Hadn't it occurred to Kyle that I might pass by, driving Macey to school? Didn't he wonder what would happen if I saw? If Macey saw? Macey would know exactly what was going on. Southern California kids aren't stupid. Even nine-year-olds understand what it means when a married man is sitting in a sidewalk café with an ocean view, in broad daylight, holding hands with a client.

Fortunately, Macey was looking out the other window, her head jiving to whatever downloaded song was playing on her iPod.

The light turned green, and I drove away, my hands shaking on the steering wheel, the café scene playing over and over in my mind until it seemed like a bad movie rather than reality. One of the hazards of living within proximity of the movie capital of the world. Everything seems like fiction. Even your own life.

Macey reached for the door handle as I pulled to the curb to let her out. I tapped her on the shoulder, and she turned back to me, tugging out her ear buds. "Bye, Mom." She leaned across the car and hugged me, her long, honey-brown hair, her father's hair, tickling my shoulder. "Have a good trip."

"I will." Closing my eyes, I held on to her until finally she wiggled away. "Be a good girl, Mace. You've got your routine down, right? Isha's going to pick you up from school every day except Wednesday, because that's her day off." *Thank God for the new au pair.* "Dad's supposed to come get you on Wednesday." *What if he's sleeping with the au pair, too?* "Kendalyn's mom will give you a ride to school in the mornings, and to gymnastics Tuesday and Thursday, and—"

"And on Friday—if you're not back by then—Grandma and Grandpa Macklin pick me up, so I can stay with them at the beach for the weekend, and on Monday afternoon—if you're still not back—I'm riding to dance class with Pesha, but Pesha doesn't do dance on Wednesday, and Wednesday's Isha's day off, so this Wednesday, Brooke Strayhorn's mom is gonna stop by for me—Brooke's annoying, you know. All she talks about is video games—but anyway, after Dad drops me at home, if he has to go back to work, I'm supposed to lock up and stay in the house until they come to get me for dance class. Don't answer the phone. Don't answer the door. Stay inside." She swiveled her head, blinked at me over her slim shoulder, then smiled. "I've got it, Mom. Don't worry about me, okay? I'm not a baby."

I touched the side of her face, smoothed a hand over her sun-lightened hair. "I know, sweetheart. You're amazing."

"Moh-om," she sighed, rolling her gaze toward the window to make sure no one was watching. When the coast was clear, she leaned over and gave me a quick kiss. She hauled her backpack off the floorboard, then stepped onto the curb, turned around, and hip-butted the door shut in one efficient movement. I sat a moment longer, watching her disappear, thinking how wonderful she was, how confidently she moved, her body tightly muscled from gymnastics and dance, preteen gangly and still filled with girlish confidence. *Why isn't she enough?* I wondered. *Why aren't she and I, a beautiful home, a thriving law practice, enough for Kyle? How could he put everything at risk? How could he risk destroying her? If he leaves, she'll blame herself. No matter what we tell her, no matter how many of her friends' parents she's seen get divorced, she'll think he left because she wasn't good enough.*

That reality sank over me like the salty mists of a cold winter day, ached with the dull familiarity of an old injury newly awakened. A part of me knew how it felt to see your father walk out the door and never look back.

Watching Macey bound up the marble stairs, her steps buoyant and light, I had a dawning awareness that, somewhere in the hidden recesses of my consciousness, I'd been waiting for this to happen. I'd been waiting for the day Kyle would leave, and the world would come crashing down around us, and Macey would walk up the courthouse steps one at a time, suddenly a tiny adult. . . .

The plane bounced against the runway again, and across the aisle a little Hispanic girl screamed, then tried to unbuckle her seat belt and crawl into her mother's lap. *Macey wouldn't do that,* I thought. *Macey would have more sense. She'd handle this like a pro.*

Hugging my knees, I hung on as the plane careered down the runway as if in slow motion, the moments stretching and twisting as the mother pulled the screaming girl back into her seat, pinned her daughter's flailing hands, curled her body protectively over the little girl's.

Outside, the engines roared and the brakes squealed, the plane fishtailing back and forth. Over the noise, the mother sang close to her daughter's ear—a lullaby in Spanish.

I would do that for Macey, I thought. *I'd fold myself over her and sing to keep her calm. She would probably think I'd lost my mind.*

"Mom," she'd say. "Chill out. It's gonna be all right. I saw this on an episode of *CSI*, and they got the plane stopped right before it fell off the runway. It was so cool. . . ."

For a perverse instant, I wished Macey were with me, sitting in the middle seat, where the bald man in the rumpled suit was bent over his knees.

If it weren't for Macey, I wouldn't care whether we made the landing or not. . . .

It was a startling thought, and as soon as it came, I pushed it away, stomped it down and buried it under piles of more practical mental dialogue. *Of course I'd care. Of course I care about my life. It's just been a strange week. Too many plates spinning off-kilter at once.* Even as I thought it, I wanted to close my eyes and never come in for a landing—just glide, and glide.

That's crazy. If a client said that to you at the office, you'd tell her she needed to go see somebody, maybe consider taking a mild antidepressant. It isn't normal to want to check out of your own life.

Is it?

Combing back a curtain of tangled hair, I pressed my palms over my ears. Seconds stretched out endlessly, until finally I felt the motion around me slow, the plane lurch up, then down, then turn to the left in what was obviously a controlled maneuver.

I took a deep breath and crawled back into my own skin. A glance out the window told me we were veering toward a taxiway, passing fire trucks and airport emergency vehicles deployed for our landing. The crews waved as we went by. Overhead, the speaker crackled and the pilot came on, his voice calm and self-assured.

"Ladies and gentlemen, our apologies for the bumpy landing. We'll be taxiing to the gateway, expecting arrival at the gate in about . . . uhhh . . . six minutes. Sorry for the slight delay, but we welcome you to Dallas–Forth Worth."

A flight attendant began reading off connecting flight numbers and gates, and passengers glanced at each other with bemused expressions, thinking, no doubt, as I was, *Were we huddled, only moments ago, in crash position, or did I dream that?* The frantic thoughts of the past half hour seemed ridiculous now. Beside me, the bald business-man cleared his throat and straightened his suit. He glanced at his watch, as if to say, *What—you thought this was a real emergency?*

Gathering my belongings, I prepared to bolt as soon as we came to a stop at the gate. As the plane shuddered into place, I popped out of my seat and hurried past six rows of seats before the aisle became crowded with passengers taking luggage from the overhead bins and waiting for the door to open. In first class, a male flight attendant was mopping his forehead and assisting an elderly woman who'd boarded with the handicapped passengers during the stopover in Houston. Hands shaking, the woman clung to his arm as he helped her gather her purse and move down the aisle.

I steeled myself for a slow exit. What I wanted to do was run past them, push my way through to someplace that wasn't vibrating under my feet. Logic whispered that getting off the airplane wouldn't solve the problem. The whole world was shifting, everything folding and faulting, threatening to crack.

I should call home, I thought, then realized there wasn't any point. Nobody would be there, except possibly Isha. Macey would be gone to gymnastics, and there wasn't much chance that Kyle would be home at four fifteen. He probably wouldn't answer his cell phone, either. This evening, he would stay at work late, checking and double-checking lucrative corporate real estate contracts and preparing for pending mediations—burning the midnight oil. Isha would put Macey to bed, and Kyle would wander in whenever he finished up at the office.

What if all those nights he said he was busy at the office, all those times I surrendered to exhaustion and went to bed alone, Kyle was really burning the midnight oil somewhere else? What if his tendency to let the cell phone roll to voice mail after hours wasn't because he didn't want to be interrupted in his work, but because he wasn't alone? There was a time when I would have been in the office enough to know what Kyle was working on, but the past year of seeing to the Santa Monica boutique left to me in my mother's will had caused me to do much of my work via dial-up. In some vague way, I knew that the office wasn't the only place where distance had seeped in, but I'd convinced myself it was part of the cycle all marriages went through. Things got busy, life got in the way, you drifted for a while, then reassessed, decided to work harder, refocus, and come back together. . . .

What if Kyle had decided to move on, instead?

The exit line started progressing toward the front of the plane, and I watched passengers ahead of me sag with relief as they stepped onto the jetway. Behind a young mother, the elderly woman traded the attendant's helping hand for a small three-wheeled walker, then politely shooed the attendant away, insisting she didn't need a wheelchair. A frustrated businessman squeezed past me, hemming me in beside the woman.

"Well, that's it. I shoulda taken the bus up from Houston," she said, gazing toward me as we started up the jetway. "If God meant human beings to fly, he'd of given them wings."

"I'll second that," I replied, and we smiled at each other, briefly linked in the kinship of survivors. I fell into step beside her, the need to hurry seeping out of me as I considered baggage claim, car rental, and what lay beyond—just across town now, rather than safely across the country. Only a short drive away, in the once trendy, then down-and-out, and now rapidly revitalizing area just east of downtown Dallas, was my father's house. *Our* house, once upon a time, before everything changed.

For the past thirty-three years, it had been *her* house, *their* house. A place where I was supposed to spend a month of my summer vacation each year, according to the custody agreements. The plan met its end before lawyers and judges could ever rehash the wisdom of sending a twelve-year-old girl for summer visits in a house with the *other woman and her mentally off son*, as my mother put it. I didn't put words to it at all. I just sat down in the entryway of my mother's boutique and refused to go. My mother was pleased that I was firmly on *her* side. My father didn't fight it. I knew he wouldn't.

Victory is sometimes painful. In a hidden corner of my heart, I needed him to fight harder, to care more, to prove he loved me more than he loved *them*. That vague disappointment grew into a bitterness that made it easy to write "Return to Sender" on birthday cards and Christmas gifts I knew *the other woman* had picked out. It prevented my showing interest in my father's Alzheimer's diagnosis at seventy-three. When *she* wrote to me, I wrote back and told her to do whatever *she* thought was best. Hanna Beth was his *wife*, after all. Making appropriate arrangements was her concern. She'd asked me to come several times as the last two years slowly peeled layers from his memory. I declined, not always politely. She urged me to make peace with him while I could. I responded that I felt no animosity about the situation—it simply was what it was. She asked if there was anything she could do to convince me to come before it was too late. I admitted, quite frankly, that I didn't think so.

I was wrong. When you're notified by the police that your incapacitated father and your adult, but mentally challenged, stepbrother have been alone in a house for three weeks, and Social Services is one complaint away from taking over, you have no choice but to get involved. Hanna Beth Parker had suffered a stroke and landed herself in a nursing home at the worst imaginable time.

"That's the baggage claim there," the woman with the walker said, pulling me back to the present. I realized I'd been strolling down the

corridor with her—not interacting or offering my name, just matching her slow pace, as if we were together. She must have thought that
was strange.

"Oh, yes, I guess it is," I agreed, angling with her toward the exit
to the baggage area. "Sorry. I was a million miles away."

Craning sideways, she studied me as I held open the door. "I could
see that." She concentrated on moving her walker across the threshold,
then added, "But don't worry. I was watching out for you, just in case
one of them international criminal types might come along, or such."

"Good thing," I said, hiding a smile, not sure whether she was
kidding. My mother had always been on guard in busy public places
like airports. She'd watched too many TV crime shows and read the
plethora of Internet forwards about potential schemes used by mug-
gers, kidnappers, and human predators of all types. She'd always complained that work often took me to downtown LA, *where no place was
safe*. Even in Santa Monica, the *homeless problem* made her uncomfortable, because *you could never tell about those people*.

"Thank ya, sweetie." The woman with the walker paused to turn
her wheels toward the luggage carousel, then shifted directions with
her body.

"My pleasure," I said. The twang in her voice dredged up some
old memory I couldn't quite put a finger on. There was an unhurried
cadence to the words, as if she tasted each one carefully before letting
it out. My mother would have called it *gum chewing*. She said people
in Texas talked like they had wads of gum in their mouths. After years
of living all around the world, following my father's job in the petro-
leum industry, she'd been less than thrilled when, the year I turned
twelve, we ended up in Dallas, my father's hometown. As always, my
father was a man ahead of his time. He foresaw trouble ahead for oil
families living in the Middle East, so he took a position in the corporate office. He was nothing if not a good businessman. Even Mother
could never deny that fact.

"The pilot did a darn good job," the woman with the walker said, pausing to grab her dangling purse handle and attempt, with shaking hands, to hook it over the arm of her walker. Her wallet, brimming with credit cards and a thick checkbook, was about to fall out. My mother would have had a heart attack.

"I'm just glad to be off the plane." I hovered for a moment, watching her futilely reach for the purse handle. Would my retrieving it embarrass her? "I guess the emergency landing wasn't such a big deal after all."

Using an umbrella from the front basket of her walker, she deftly hooked the purse strap and hung it back in place. "It's a bigger deal than people probably think. My brothers flew supply planes back in World War Two, so I know a little bit about such things. 'Course, with short runways overseas, you either got the plane stopped or you went in the drink. With these long runways, you got more space, but you got bigger planes, too. Lots heavier. Our pilot today was a crackerjack."

"That's good to know." But it really wasn't. I didn't want to believe that we'd come close to potential disaster.

Luggage was starting to pop onto the carousel, and my companion gave it a concerned frown.

"Is someone meeting you here?" I asked. No matter how good she was with her umbrella handle, she couldn't lift bags off the conveyor.

She checked her watch. "My grandson, but I guess he's got held up in traffic. He's a doctor. Busy man. My husband and I raised him after my son died. I come up from Houston to visit him every few months, get my medical tests done, hang around the facility and read to the patients. This time I'm gonna have a little of that orthascotic surgery—that's why I had to fly in, instead of drive. Got to have a ligament repaired in my knee before I can drive again." She looked around the room a second time. I tried to imagine what kind of a grandson would leave his elderly grandmother, in need of arthroscopic knee surgery, at the mercy of strangers and unable to get her luggage off the carousel.

But then, the anonymous concerned citizen who had contacted the city police on my father's behalf was probably thinking the same thing about me. "Can I help you get your luggage? I have a cell phone. We could try to call—"

She cut me off with a quick hand chop. "No. No, now I'm fine. I'll just go over there and get me one of them good-lookin' skycaps to grab off my bags, and I'll wait for my grandson. He'll come. You don't worry yourself over me, all right?"

"All right," I said. "You're sure?" I found myself wanting her to say no, wishing she would provide a distraction from my impending trip across town to the nursing home to see Hanna Beth.

"I'm fine, sweetie, just fine." The woman started toward the waiting skycaps. "I'm not as helpless as I look. I know judo. Anybody gives me any trouble, I'll smack 'em in the kazongas with my umbrella." I blinked in surprise, and she glanced back over her shoulder, giving a saucy one-sided smile. "Soon as I get this darned leg in better shape, it'll be, *Look out, world, here comes Ouita Mae Barnhill.*"

I stood for a minute watching Ouita Mae Barnhill disappear into the crowd and wishing I had her certainty about the outcome of the next few days. Finally, I stepped up to the baggage claim, grabbed my suitcases, and faced the fact that, willingly or not, I had arrived in Dallas.

As March went like a lamb into April, I was returning thirty days early, thirty-three years late, for my month of summer.

CHAPTER 2

Hanna Beth Parker

Every day at noon, Claude passes by my door, his slippered feet shuffling across the linoleum as he pulls his wheelchair along. He stops and tells me about the food in the dining room, as if that might entice me to get out of bed and walk down the hall. On rainy days, when the world outside the window is melancholy and dim, he talks about trains.

Claude drove lumber trains down in the Piney Woods of East Texas. He has the cloudy eyes of a poet when he describes the scent of steam rising off the engine, casting a gossamer mist over everything for just a moment until the train reaches speed. He tells me this story over and over because he can't remember that he recounted it yesterday, the day before, the day before that. Life, he says, if he stays long enough to become philosophical, is a journey by train. Outside the window, the scenery is rushing by. If you look away for even an instant, something passes uncaptured. Far in the future, when you leaf through the photo album of memory, your finger, aged and crooked, will rub lightly over that empty space, and you'll wonder, *What might have been there?*

In your daydreams, you'll return again and again, try to open your eyes for that single moment, but you can't. This is the science of regret, according to Claude.

Life is a journey by train, and the engine's always at speed.

Don't close your eyes, even for a moment.

After World War II, Claude drove the trains that took the Jewish people home from the concentration camps. He should have known that sometimes the scenery outside is so ugly there's nothing to do but close your eyes for as long as you can, and pray for traveling mercies.

I wanted to tell him that, but I couldn't. Each time he repeated the story, all I could do was lie there and listen, until finally the young nurse's aide, who wore her hair in a bun and dressed in long skirts and tennis shoes, found him. "Is he bothering you?" she'd ask sweetly, then adjust my pillows and smooth my hair while my eyes followed her movements. She'd smile sadly as she turned away, took Claude's wheelchair handles, and said, "Come on, Mr. Fisher. Let's go find you something to do. She needs her rest so she can get better."

Had the doctors really told her I would get better, or were those nervous words only filling empty space during that uncomfortable moment when she pictured herself in my place? Occasionally, even the young look at these aging, crippled bodies and see the weathered wrappings of once-vibrant human beings—people who lived and loved, worked and dreamed. They see that you can be standing at the clothes dryer folding laundry one minute, planning a trip to the grocery store, thinking about what to cook for supper, and considering what sort of flowers you might plant in the beds this spring. And the next minute, you can be sprawled awkwardly on the floor, unable to move, realizing that a flower bed may have been an impossible presumption.

No one wants to imagine a moment like that. To imagine it is to realize the fragile nature of life. I know this, of course. I should know it better than most, but sometimes, I have been guilty of oversight.

Lying in the nursing center, I had time to consider the truths of my existence. The train had slowed to a crawl, a limp, if you will, like the Little Engine That Could, chugging up a long, steep hill, puffing out the mantra, *I can, I must, I will, I can, I must, I will.*

I can get better.

I must get better.

I will go home.

On my very first night here, after transferring from the hospital to the nursing center, I made up my mind that I would not die in this place. I *must* not. And that was that. I'd decided about the issue, and I have always been a determined woman. Some might call me stubborn, but I prefer to think of myself as resolute.

I would have told those things to Mary, the young nurse's aide, if I could have, but my mouth wouldn't form the words, and besides, Mary was always in a hurry. With a demanding job and two little boys, the oldest barely school age, and their father bringing them to the nursing center parking lot promptly at four thirty, on his way to work, she didn't have time to dally. Her young husband was always unhappy if Mary wasn't finished with her shift and waiting out front for the boys, but generally, she was.

I watched them out the window, when I could get my head turned far enough to see. The boys were cute little things. The younger one, a towhead with a quick, stocky body, reminded me of my Teddy at that age. I often wished Mary would bring the little fellow inside for a minute. There's no tonic for sadness like a child's smiling face.

The day Mary stopped by my room after four thirty, even though her family was waiting in the parking lot, I knew something had happened. The nagging fear that had been inside me since I came to consciousness in the hospital rose to the surface. Something was wrong at home. I'd known, as my days in the hospital and then the nursing center ticked by with painfully slow progress, that this moment might come. Even the most trusted hired help cannot be expected to forever manage the care of a dear man who remembers the history of every significant World War II battle but cannot recall how to write a check;

and a boy who knows the names of each flower in the garden and every stray cat in the neighborhood, who lives in the body of a man, but does not always remember to look both ways before crossing the street.

Mary hesitated in the doorway. "I wasn't sure if they told you that the administrator had a call from your daughter . . . uhhh . . . Rebecca, I think she said."

No! I cried, but only a faint gurgle, a senseless sound, came from my lips.

Mary seemed to guess the meaning. There was no telling how much the staff knew about our family situation. "She should be here soon. I just didn't want you to be . . ." She searched for a word, then finished with, "Surprised."

My hopes, which had kept me chugging uphill hour upon hour, sank, and the fire went out of me. I'd hoped for many things these past weeks, but Rebecca's arrival wasn't one of them. My problem was not so much a lack of faith that peace could be made with Rebecca one day. Over the years, and particularly since Edward's illness, I'd sent letters to her, urging her to visit her father while there was still time—while a bit of that strong, silent man remained.

My pleas went unheeded. Now, I wanted them to remain so, at least for the time being. I couldn't let our lives fall to the mercy of this stranger, this angry young woman with Edward's dark hair and hazel eyes, but her mother's fine, aristocratic features and her mother's view of past events. I couldn't continue to lie here, unable to defend Edward and Teddy, unable to explain the truths of our family history.

Mary appeared to recognize my desperation. She crossed the room and squeezed my hand. "The physical therapist should be here in a bit, Mrs. Parker. You're the last one on her list today. You work real hard and do everything she tells you to do, so you can get better, all right?"

Don't cry, I thought. *It's useless to cry.* But like everything else in my body, my tear ducts no longer listened to my wishes. My eyes welled up, and my vision swam behind a wall of water. Mary reached for a tissue. "Don't worry. It'll be all right." Mary always spoke in such pleasant ways. She never rolled her eyes, or huffed, or grumbled under her breath. She never shared in the gossip and complaining that took place among staff members when they thought we couldn't hear. She just came and went in her white sneakers, her long denim skirt swishing heavily around her ankles. She was an island of quiet goodness in a sea of frustration and uncertainty.

After checking her watch, and then the window, she dried my cheeks, then slipped a hand under my legs, lifted my knees, and fluffed the pillows there. As she threw away the tissue, she noticed the romance novel a young volunteer with the book cart had left after reading to me the day before. Her brows drew together, then she frowned and reached for the half-empty soda the volunteer had left on the table. "Looks like this needs to be thrown out." Picking up the bottle, she discreetly turned *Pirate's Promise* facedown.

"I'll see you in the morning." She angled her head so that she could look at me eye to eye, but her gaze wandered back to the book, taking in the miniaturized picture of the pirate and his lady in a wild embrace. Sometimes, when I gazed at that picture, I thought of Edward years ago. I was never as buxom as Marcella, the countess with the long red hair, but Edward was every bit as handsome as Gavin, the pirate captain. Gavin was a striking figure—the type to set a young woman's heart aflutter. . . .

Flushing, Mary turned away from the picture. "Better?" she asked.

Yes, I said, and attempted to nod, but my head jerked sideways, and the sound came out as a distorted moan, "Eh-eeeh-ehhhsh."

Mary smiled at the pathetic attempt. "That was good. You've been practicing."

"Eh-eeeh-esh."

"Did you show your physical therapist?"

I willed my head to one side, then let it fall back to center as the answer rushed out harshly, "Ohh-ohh-ooo-oh."

Mary sighed. "You should. She'd be so happy. It's progress."

"Pffff," I blew out, then turned my face away as the door clicked open and the PT came into the room in the squeaky nurse's shoes that always announced the beginning of our daily torture sessions. As far as I could tell, Gretchen was never *happy* about anything.

"Good afternoon, Mrs. Parker." In Gretchen's deep, gruff voice, even the greeting sounded like a command. *Have a good afternoon, or else.* "Any changes?" she asked, looming at the foot of the bed and taking in Mary from head to toe, then frowning.

"Nothing," Mary replied, and squeezed my hand as Gretchen cracked her knuckles and lowered the window blind, shrouding the room in the necessary dungeon-like darkness. Mary gave my arm a last reassuring pat, then skittered out the door like a kitten ducking under the fence to escape a scrappy, pug-nosed mutt.

Gretchen pulled her cart around to the bed and pushed up her sleeves, then reached for the blanket. As usual, I cringed when she drew it back. Even after weeks in the nursing center, being helped with the most basic of functions, these small losses of dignity were still hard to accept. I understood now why Edward sometimes became angry and resentful about his disease. It was humiliating, incredibly frustrating, being unable to do things you once took for granted.

I reminded myself, as always, that pride would not make me well. Turning toward the window, I tried to focus on something else, something far from here, as Gretchen went to work, bending and stretching, lifting and turning parts of my body I couldn't feel anymore.

Through the broken slats in the middle of the blind, I could see Mary arguing with her husband on the curb. He pulled out his wallet, showed her it was empty, then threw up his hands. Perhaps he had a short fuse today because she'd been late coming out to get the boys.

I hoped that was not the case, being as she'd stayed to comfort me. Her husband was young, like an overgrown teenager in his unkempt, overly long hair, sloppy jeans, and loose-fitting T-shirts. He made a strange picture next to little Mary, with her modest skirts and her chestnut hair pinned in a bun. I wondered how the two of them had come to be together.

Then I reminded myself that love sometimes has a mind of its own. I should know that, if I knew anything. . . .

Something wrenched in my leg, and I heard myself moan. The sound surprised me.

"Starting to feel that," Gretchen observed matter-of-factly; then I watched her lower my left leg to the bed and take up my right. I focused outside the window again. Mary's husband was gone. Mary had scooped up the littler boy, and they were waving good-bye to him. I guessed the argument was over.

Mary paused by the row of neatly trimmed forsythia bushes, and together she and the boys studied something on one of the branches. A caterpillar, perhaps, or birds building a nest. I closed my eyes and thought of all the times I'd done those things with Teddy. The most perfect moments of my life were those simple, quiet ones spent watching butterflies comb the flowers, or observing ants parading in a line across the driveway, or capturing fireflies and laughing as the cage of Teddy's tiny fingers lit up.

I tried to picture Teddy's hands, tried to draw closer to him, to Edward and home—away from this place, away from Gretchen's grunts and heavy breaths, away from the scents of antiseptic and perspiration, away from my own body.

I'd almost achieved it, almost left the nursing center behind by the time Gretchen finished poking and prodding, moving and stretching. As she gathered her things and finally walked out the door, every part of me ached—the parts I could feel, and the parts I couldn't, which made no sense. How could there be pain in useless limbs I couldn't control? Was it only a figment of my imagination? Was my mind making me feel the way it seemed I should, after being twisted like a pretzel? Then I wondered if I was getting better. I needed to heal, to miraculously recover before Rebecca arrived. Perhaps this new pain was a sign of returning function. Perhaps I could will it to happen, just because these were desperate times.

Gazing through the broken place in the window blind, I imagined a sudden healing, and wished I could see the rest of the parking lot and the lawn beyond. Gretchen always closed the blind. She was probably afraid that if anyone passed by, they'd call the police, or the investigative reporter on News 9, and she would be turned in for torturing helpless, infirm people.

I pictured Gretchen in handcuffs, trying to avoid TV cameras, pursued by a hoard of reporters with microphones, as the police dragged her out the doors.

I heard myself laughing, an odd, chugging sound like an old car sputtering on a cold morning.

I was instantly sad. That wasn't my laugh. That wasn't anyone's laugh. It was only a strange, uneven, embarrassing tangle of noise. I wanted my laugh back. Edward always loved it. I suppose I did, too, but I'd never thought about it. You never imagine that you'll wake up one day, unable to do such a simple thing as laugh, missing such a basic part of who you are.

Claude passed by in his wheelchair and noticed that the window blind was down. "Well, hey there, Birdie. Who come along and closed the drape?" He always called me Birdie. I wasn't sure why, because my name was there on the door.

Claude went on talking as he scooted himself across the room, his feet shuffling, then slapping with each step, like the flippers of a seal, pulling its body along behind. "Why'd they close yer window blind, Birdie? That's no good. You won't be able to see if someone drives up." Bracing a hand on his chair, he stretched upward, his legs folding under his weight like wet toothpicks, the chair teetering dangerously on one wheel as he tried to reach the little plastic pole that would swivel the blinds open.

If the nurses came by and saw him doing that, they would have a fit.

"Ooh-oh-o-o," I forced out, watching the wheelchair tilt further to one side. I could picture him collapsed on my floor.

"Don't worry. I can get it." He extended his thin fingers as far as he could, still six inches from the plastic pole.

"Nnnooo-o-o," I said again, the word so clear it shocked me. Claude glanced over his shoulder, still teetering above his chair. Hope soared in a part of me that had been hopeless, and I felt momentarily triumphant. *You'll fall*, I added, but the words were just gibberish. It sounded like "Ooogllall."

I closed my eyes and started to cry.

"Don't cry, Birdie," Claude soothed, and I heard him sink back into his chair. "We'll just pull this cord and raise up the whole thing. That'll work." I heard the slats slapping together. Sunlight flooded the room and blanketed the bed, turning my eyelids yellow and soft pink. I imagined that I could feel the sun, warm and soothing on my legs. I imagined the sunlight melting away the lingering twinges from Gretchen's ministrations, strengthening muscles, repairing nerves.

For a moment, I thought I could feel it.

"Well, blame it!" The light faded, and I opened my eyes. Claude was struggling to raise the blind again. "Darned thing's broke. It won't lock in up there." He sat holding the cord. "Guess I could tie it to my chair, but then I'd probably forget and take the whole shebang with me when I go." He grinned at me, his faded blue eyes twinkling. "Back in the day, I'da hopped right up there and fixed it, but I guess for now I can just sit here and hold it awhile. Reckon that'd be all right, Birdie? Say, did I ever tell you I was over fifty years with the Angelina and Neches Railroad? Drove them lumber trains back and forth to Chireno in Nacogdoches County, down in the Piney Woods. . . ."

A tickle began in my stomach, and I couldn't help it, I started to laugh. For a fraction of a second, it sounded like my laugh, then it turned back to the chugging sound. I let myself keep laughing anyway.

Claude glanced over his shoulder, bemused. "You see something out . . ." He paused to check outside the window. "Well, would ya look at that? Ole Gret's got a flat tire, way down to the other end of the lot. Reckon that's good cause for a laugh."

From where I was lying, I couldn't see the end of the parking lot because of the forsythia bushes, but I laughed anyway.

"Looks like she's gonna change that thing herself," Claude went on. "Probably won't have any trouble. She'll just haul that car up with one hand and slap the tire on with the other. You ever wonder if she's *always* been a woman?"

I coughed and gasped, then choked on a swallow of air.

"Well, she's got the jack, and she's a-lookin' for a place to put it. I could give her some ideas about that."

My body convulsed with laughter, until somewhere in the melee of strange sounds I heard an occasional fragment of my own giggle. A sense of joy, and hope, and possibility spun around me.

The blind zinged downward suddenly, banging the windowsill with a thunderous smack. "Oh, darn, I think she seen me watching," Claude gasped. "Come tomorrow, she'll fold me like a paper wad, chew me up, and spit me out."

Peeking carefully through the broken slats, he continued the play-by-play of the activity outside. When Gretchen finally drove off, he began the train story again. "Did I ever tell you I was over fifty years with the Angelina and Neches Railroad? Drove them trains down in the Piney Woods. . . ."

Somewhere far into the forests of deep East Texas, where the smell of pine, coal smoke, and fresh-cut lumber was thick in the air, I fell asleep. I dreamed I was on the train, the windows open, the breeze caressing my cheeks, the sun high and hot. At the front of the car, Teddy was just a little boy, pretending to drive. Teddy loved mechanical things of all kinds. Clinging to the window frame, he stood on his tiptoes, trying to see out.

"Be careful," I said, but he couldn't hear me. Stretching my arms, I tried to move closer, but I was trapped in my seat, pinned by something heavy and solid I couldn't see. "Come sit with Mommy," I pleaded, but the engine and the wind were too loud. The train rushed faster. Teddy inched higher, pulling himself up on the window frame.

"No, Teddy. Don't do that. Get down," I called, careful not to startle him, remembering the time I'd hollered at him for climbing impossibly high in a tree at the playground. When he saw me below, he let go and fell all the way to the ground. It was the first time I'd ever allowed myself to fully comprehend that Teddy might never be able to see to his own safety. How could a child almost eight years old not understand that a fall so far would be dangerous?

My dream moved suddenly to the playground. I was running toward the tree, watching Teddy's body smack the branches, falling, and falling, and falling, while I remained powerless to stop it. My legs were leaden, refusing to move normally. "Teddy, no!" I cried. "No!"

"Mrs. Parker . . . Mrs. Parker . . ." A voice came from somewhere in the distance, luring me away from my struggle to reach Teddy. "Mrs. Parker . . . It is all right. 'Tis all right. You are having a dream, missus. Wake up."

I can't, I thought, fighting to get back to the park, but it was slipping away as Teddy fell. *I have to reach Teddy. I have to help him. Can't you see he's in trouble?*

The voice called to me. "Wake up. 'Tis only a dream, missus."

Dragging my eyes open, I saw the second-shift nurse, Ifeoma, standing above me, checking my chart. "You cried out in your sleep just now. Do you feel pain?" she inquired in the thickly accented English of her home country, Ghana.

"Noh-oh-o-o," I answered, trying to make the sound emphatic, even though a part of me wished she would bring a sedative, so that I wouldn't hear the moaning of the patient down the hall, the nurses clanging by with their carts, the clock softly ticking away the hours.

Ifeoma paused to reposition my body, then straightened the coverlet, something she didn't normally do. "Your daughter is here, missus. She is in the administrator's office just now."

The muscles in my legs tensed, or maybe it was only my imagination. A soft groan passed my throat. Ifeoma raised a brow, then efficiently smoothed a last wrinkle from the cover before turning to leave the room. "I am certain she will come to you soon." She left the door partially open, in anticipation of a visitor.

I wanted to rise from the bed, go over and close the door, tell Rebecca that she wasn't welcome, wasn't needed. Why, after all these years, did she have to come now, when I was like this? I couldn't possibly face her in this condition.

CHAPTER 3

Rebecca Macklin

All the self-assurances that I was ready to face Hanna Beth Parker couldn't stop my heart from hammering as I prepared to enter her room. Despite the fact that I was an adult now, and she was elderly and powerless, my fingers froze on the door frame, and I stood unable to move forward. I was the twelve-year-old girl waiting beside my mother's car on the curb of what had been my front yard, *our* front yard. My life lay scattered in pieces on the lawn—bicycle, antique French-white desk and chair, the frame to the four-poster that had once made me feel like a princess but now seemed ridiculous. Boxes of clothes and dolls, various paintings, vases, carvings, and dishes from our time in Iran and Saudi. My mother had claimed those exotic treasures in the divorce, and my father hadn't argued. He felt guilty, no doubt. He deserved to feel guilty. A forty-two-year-old man who suddenly ditches his family for a woman ten years younger should feel guilty.

Hanna Beth came onto the porch unexpectedly. My mother stiffened, swiveled toward Hanna Beth with her mouth slightly agape. She hadn't imagined that we'd drive up and find *the woman* already there, already settling into *our* house before the transport company had even finished removing *our* things. But it figured that *she* would be there, on the porch gloating. She'd won, after all. She had my father, our house, our life. She had everything. It figured that she would be the one supervising the movers. My father was probably at work, safely detached.

My mother swept past Hanna Beth, went into the house without a word. Hanna Beth didn't follow, just stood out of the way by the railing. She was smaller than I'd anticipated, not the formidable enemy I'd pictured. Her slender, willowy body was clothed in a lightweight sundress too summery for the early March day. She was beautiful, with large brown eyes and auburn hair that hung in ringlets down her back. The dress swirled around her long, slim legs as she walked. The workers took note, passing by with their boxes. She stood uncertainly at the top of the stairs, the sunlight glinting on her hair, outlining her form beneath the fabric.

At any other time, in any other place, I would have liked her, admired her beauty, the way she moved, her steps silent and graceful, like those of a dancer, unassuming, as if she wasn't aware of the picture she made standing there in the yellow dress. She held a flowerpot in her hands, and there was dirt on her hem.

She was planting flowers in *our* garden. I hated her like I'd never hated anyone. I wanted to dash across the yard, throw open the back gate, and rip the flowers from the ground one by one. I wanted to shred them into tiny pieces, destroy the roots, poison the ground, so that nothing could ever grow here, so that Hanna Beth could never make a beautiful life in this big house, while my mother and I were moving to an apartment in Santa Monica, California, a place I'd only visited on occasional vacations to see my mother's family.

Teddy came out the front door, pushing one of the moving dollies, making the men laugh, because, even at fourteen, he was clumsy with it. Spotting me by the curb, he let the dolly fall upright, then waved and hollered with a big, stupid smile, like he was trying to catch someone's attention from a half mile away. I was glad my friends were in school, the street quiet. Before his mother could stop him,

Teddy dashed down the steps and started across the lawn in a gangly, lumbering run, still waving. "Hi, Bek-ty, hi, Bek-ty. Bek-teee, hi-i!"

Hanna Beth bolted after him, catching up as he reached the car. I'd backed away, grabbed the door handle, uncertain, afraid.

Hanna Beth took his flailing hand, encircled it with hers, calming his frenzied movements. Patting his fingers, she smoothed tangled blond hair from his forehead. He tipped his chin toward her, and for just an instant he looked normal, like the boys I went to school with. But if Teddy had been in my school, he would have been in the *special* class—the one they kept hidden off the end of the gym, where they taught things like making ham sandwiches and buttoning your own shirt.

"Rebecca, this is Teddy," his mother said, and smiled at me like she was making a presentation. "Teddy's been very eager to meet you. We both have. We're very much looking forward to your coming this summer." The words were proper, crisp. She sounded like a teacher, which she was. She worked as a live-in at the *special* school a few miles away, where brick buildings from another era crouched behind a rusty iron fence. The kids I hung around with made jokes and told Frankensteinian stories about deformed children locked in the basements when we passed by that place. My father frequented the coffee shop across from the gates, which was how he'd run into Hanna Beth, a little over six months ago, now. By unfortunate happenstance, they'd renewed an old acquaintance, initially formed in childhood when Hanna Beth's father worked for the oil companies. He wasn't an engineer like my father and grandfather, just a rig manager. Her family lived *off* Blue Sky Hill, in the neighborhoods of small three-bedroom bungalows the residents of Blue Sky Hill thumbed their noses at during dinner-party conversations. Hanna Beth and my father had always known each other, and when they crossed paths in the coffee shop, they knew each other again, and our lives were ruined.

"I got f-owas," Teddy said, his face contorting as he worked out the words. "Plant in f-owas deep." He nodded earnestly, making the motion of digging a hole, and putting in a seedling, then flailing his free hand toward the backyard. "Wanna see?"

I yanked the door handle so hard it ripped through my fingers, bending the nails backward. I didn't care. All I wanted to do was get away, get into the car and lock the door, lock *them* on the other side of the glass.

Hanna Beth didn't protest, but just stood there holding Teddy's hand, looking sad. Turning him away, she started toward the house. He smiled and waved cheerfully over his shoulder, too stupid to understand what was happening. "Bye, Beck-tee, bye-eee! Have fun!"

I hated him.

I made up my mind that he and Hanna Beth might have everything else, but they wouldn't have me. The courts could do their worst—lock me in jail, throw me in juvenile hall, line up custody orders from here to California—but I wasn't coming back to Dallas this summer, or any summer. It wasn't as if my presence in *his* house, in *their* lives, would be missed. My father and I had become strangers who passed in the hall. I doubted he would fight to enforce the custody agreement. He proved me right, of course.

Now Hanna Beth's stroke had accomplished what thirty-three years and a court order could not. I'd come back.

Unfortunately, the pain had traveled with me across the country, across the years, and as I stood outside her door, it was as fresh and as much a part of me as it had been that twelfth summer. It stabbed as sharply now as then—like a chronic injury, reawakened by a careless movement, a sudden strain caused by the burden of picking up something too heavy. Its intensity surprised me. I'd expected, in this adult body, safely entrenched in a life that was completely separate from that of Hanna Beth and my father, to be able to maintain a comfortable detachment, a reasonable objectivity. Instead, I wanted to lock myself away someplace quiet, and nurse the raw spot until it stopped burning.

In the midst of that realization came a new one. Was this what lay ahead for Macey? Would she stand outside a door someday, halfway through her life, a grown woman with a damaged little girl inside? Would she feel for Kyle what I felt for my father? Would her confident smile, her openness, her self-worth slowly diminish until she found trust a struggle, faith a chore? Would she always feel vaguely inadequate, unworthy, as if she had to prove something, to be more than she was, because no one could love her just for herself?

I didn't want Macey to feel those things. *I* didn't want to feel them. *You're forty-five years old, Rebecca, it's time to grow up,* I told myself. Some part of me sensed that, as much as I didn't want to admit it, closure of a sort might lie beyond the door, in Hanna Beth's room.

Taking a deep breath, I steeled myself and stepped through the opening.

The room was quiet, with a stale, medicinal smell. I moved into the alcove between the bathroom and the wall, let go of the door. It creaked partway closed behind me, then hung ajar. I paused at the sound, waiting to see if she would say something, ask who was there. It occurred to me that she probably couldn't. The nursing center administrator had referred to her as having suffered a stroke in the brain stem, resulting in a coma of short duration. She was making progress since being transferred from the hospital to the nursing center, but she would require ongoing rehabilitation in a supportive and low-stress environment. The administrator looked pointedly at me when she said the words "supportive" and "low-stress," letting me know she suspected that our family situation wasn't conducive to either of those things. The remainder of our discussion was clinical, to the point, yet I walked into Hanna Beth's room expecting to find a formidable enemy—the beautiful woman in the yellow sundress. In my mind, Hanna Beth was unchanged by the passage of time. She was still that ethereal, but devastating vision.

When I turned the corner, the woman in the bed was small—a pale, white form, wrinkled and twisted, bleached out like a paper doll wadded up and left in the sun. She seemed as much a part of the bed as the sheet and coverlet themselves, as if she'd been there long enough to have been absorbed by those inanimate objects, to have taken on their characteristics.

Her face was turned toward the window. I moved to the foot of the bed to see her, to allow her to see me, to take her in and satisfy a morbid curiosity as to whether anything remained of the person I remembered. Perhaps if the answer was no, I could look at her objectively, consider her predicament, my father's, and Teddy's as if they were strangers, caught up in a tragic circumstance for which there seemed to be no easy answer.

Her eyes were closed. She didn't react as my toe bumped the wheel of the bed, rattling the frame. Apparently, she was sleeping.

A disproportionate sense of relief washed through me. Resting my hands on the railing, I stood observing her, trying to see Hanna Beth Parker, but I couldn't. This was merely an old woman, her silver hair in a disarray of tangled curls against the pillow, her skin nearly translucent, her face hanging slack. Her arm, bent and curled, dangled off the bed, pinched between the mattress and the security rail in a way that looked uncomfortable. I should have moved it, picked it up and tucked it in with her, but instead I stood frozen, maintaining a safe distance.

She's just an old woman, I told myself. *She's harmless, powerless. Helpless.* Stepping around the end of the bed, I leaned closer, hesitated, afraid that if I touched her, if I bridged the space between us, repositioned her hand, something unexpected, unwanted, might happen. Jerking away from the bed, I stepped back, then turned, started toward the door. An old man passing by in a wheelchair stopped to peer into the room.

He smiled at me. "Hey, there. Looks like we got a visitor here. You Birdie's daughter?" He nodded toward Hanna Beth.

I shook my head, stepping aside as he struggled to move through the doorway. The metal rim of his chair collided with the frame in a resounding clang. I was aware that the noise might wake up Hanna Beth, and then I would be trapped here with her, this stranger blocking the escape route.

"I was just on my way out," I said, pushing the door fully open so that it caught on the rubber stopper.

The man nodded, craning to look at me as I fidgeted, unable to slip between his chair and the wall. "You Birdie's daughter?" he repeated, with an amiable smile.

"No, I . . ." Suddenly the air in the room, Hanna Beth's presence, the scent of stale linens, bedfast bodies, and antiseptic was too much. I couldn't think. "Stepdaughter," I said finally. I'd never in my life, not even in my mind, used that word to describe my relation to Hanna Beth. In my mind, there was no relationship between us. "She's my father's wife."

The man nodded. "Oh, well, ain't that nice? She don't get many visitors. Used to be a gal stopped by—her housekeeper, I think—but I never did get to talk to her, really. She ain't been here in a while, though. I'll bet Birdie's real glad you come."

A hot, uncomfortable flush pushed into my cheeks. "She's sleeping, I think."

He peered past me. "Hmmm? Well, that could be. Them physical therapy sessions can sure wear a body out. They got a big German gal does the work here. Got arms like a scullery cook and looks like some of them nurses the Luftwaffe had in their secret hospitals, back in the big war. I was in the army at the end of it—drove them trains after VE Day. I ever tell you about that? I started out runnin' them trains after the war, and when I come home, I got on with the A & NR Railroad, down in the Piney Woods. Drove them lumber trains for fifty years. Good life back then, bein' a company man. Not like it is for young folks now." He paused as a woman in a long denim skirt and a flowered scrub top passed by, leading two little boys by the hands. Rolling the chair backward slightly, he turned to intercept her. "Well, how-do, Mary-not-contrary. Why are you still here this evenin'?"

The young nurse's aide—*Mary*, her nametag read—glanced at me apologetically. "Waiting on a ride home with Dottie, Mr. Fisher. She doesn't get off until seven."

Mr. Fisher scratched his chin, frowning at the two boys who were eyeing him and the chair with interest. "Thought I saw your husband come by a while ago. Don't he usually take the bus from here and leave you the van?"

Mary shifted self-consciously, her gaze darting toward the window, then back. "We had a little mix-up with the van, that's all." She jostled the boys' hands, as if she were trying to bolster them. "It's okay, though, we got to eat in the cafeteria, didn't we, guys?"

The older boy nodded shyly, and the younger one yawned, rubbing his eyes. He looked like a child who ought to be home slipping into a warm bath, putting on a fluffy sleeper with feet in it, and snuggling into bed.

Mr. Fisher ruffled the boys' blond hair, then pointed at Mary. "Those are fine young fellas. I bet you're mighty proud, havin' a pair of handsome boys like these."

They looked up at their mother, and she smiled down adoringly. "I sure am, Mr. Fisher."

"They got names?" Mr. Fisher rolled his chair back a bit more, allowing me an exit path. I took advantage of the opportunity to step into the hall.

"Brandon and Brady," Mary answered, indicating first the older boy and then the younger one.

"Guess I should shake your hands, then." Lifting his arm from the wheelchair, Mr. Fisher greeted Brandon, then Brady. The conversation seemed to run out temporarily, then Mr. Fisher waved a thumb toward Hanna Beth's room. "Y'all ought to go on in and say hi to Birdie. Bet she'd like to see these fine-lookin' boys. I opened her blind in there for a while, earlier on. Nurses shouldn't shut them things where a body can't even see the sun. Sunshine is a healin' force. Kills germs, too. Back in the army, if we didn't have any other way to get the vermin out of our bedrolls, we'd air 'em out. Works pretty good."

Mary glanced at me, clearly wondering who I was. "Rebecca Macklin," I said, extending my hand.

Mr. Fisher seemed to recall my presence. "Well, land's sakes, pardon me. This is Birdie's daughter. She just come to see her mama." He turned from me to Mary. "This is Mary. She's your mama's nurse aide during the day." He held a hand beside his mouth. "Best one here, but don't tell the rest I said so."

Mary and I exchanged greetings.

"Excuse me for not standin' up." Mr. Fisher patted the wheelchair, and I blanched. Swatting my arm, he laughed. "That was a joke, hon. One thing essential around here is a sense of humor. Ain't that so, Mary?"

Mary nodded indulgently, recapturing the boys' hands as Brady wandered toward the door to Hanna Beth's room. "We all need to have your attitude, Mr. Fisher."

He gave a throaty chuckle, squinting down the hallway. "You know, when I was a young chap, my pap told me no matter where you are, keep your face to the light and the shadow's gonna fall behind you. I always remembered that. There's light somewhere in every situation." Rubbing a hand across his five o'clock shadow, he pointed at Mary. "I ever tell you I drove them old steam trains after the war? I bet these boys would like to hear about that."

Brady perked up. "Ohhh, I wike twain," he breathed. "I got Thomas twain."

Mr. Fisher turned his attention to Brady. "I seen that show down in the TV room just the other day. They was some kids visitin' their grandma, and they watched it. Reckon if we could go check? Maybe we could find it on TV." Mr. Fisher and both boys turned to Mary expectantly.

I took advantage of the chance to exit the conversation. "I was just on my way out," I said to Mary. "But I'd like to talk with you about Hanna Beth's condition, when we have the chance."

Mary focused on me, ignoring Brady, who was trying to pull her toward the commons area. "I'm here every day . . . but you might want to talk to her attending physician or the physical therapist. I'm just a nurse's aide."

"Don't let her kid you," Mr. Fisher interjected. "She's the one does all the work around here."

Mary stumbled forward, both boys tugging her hands. "Boys!" she scolded.

I waved her away. "No, it's fine. We can talk another time."

"It was nice meeting you," she said, then followed Brandon and Brady down the hall, her feet dragging, unable to match their enthusiastic pace after a long day at work. I knew the feeling. Many was the day I worked late wading through the latest Immigration Services e-mail bulletins, filing with Immigration Court on behalf of internationals in imminent danger of deportation, or facilitating visas for multinational corporations impatient to import foreign executives, software designers, and engineers. At the end of an extended day at the firm, I arrived home feeling a sense of accomplishment, only to be quickly mired in parental guilt because the au pair had fixed Macey's supper, helped her with her homework and her bath, then put her to bed. Part of me was glad the house was quiet, the sofa waiting for me to crash, but part of me realized I'd missed the evening with my daughter. We hadn't talked about what happened at school, or who'd been in trouble in the lunchroom, or how gymnastics or dance had turned out that day. *Having it all* was part of the modern myth, the self-inflicted curse that tried to swallow working mothers in a pit of guilt-induced exhaustion.

I'd finally settled for the reality that you could have all of one thing, all of the other, or some of both. Macey was an incredible kid—secure, well-adjusted, smart, with aspirations of becoming a biochemist or Olympic gymnast. It was hard to argue that we hadn't struck a functional balance. I was glad I wasn't in Mary's position, stuck at work without transportation, trying to see to the immediate needs of two young children when my mind and body were tapped out for the day.

As I left the nursing center behind, I wondered, just briefly, if Hanna Beth had felt the push and pull of that struggle. What must life have been like for her? Before she married my father, she was a single mother, teaching at the institutional school, struggling to raise a developmentally challenged son in some tiny faculty apartment on campus. Did she worry about Teddy when her time and energy were taken up with caring for the monumental needs of students more severely handicapped than he? Did she feel that she should be spending more time with her own son, that she couldn't teach at the school and give him everything he needed? Was that why she quit her job as soon as she married my father? Was that the reason she took my father away from us?

I'd never, ever considered the difficulties of Hanna Beth's life. Even now, thinking of it felt like a betrayal of my mother, of our family before Hanna Beth. Our lives were good then, privileged. Happy.

My mind slipped back in time, and I lost my way temporarily, drove through the urban streets of Deep Ellum, where old speakeasies and the black jazz clubs of the Prohibition era were being converted from abandoned, run-down buildings into trendy restaurants, art galleries, and nightclubs. When I was young, in the days before downtown revitalization, my mother avoided those areas assiduously. She was uncomfortable even with the aging neighborhoods around the Blue Sky Hill area—where the home my grandparents built with oil money had been passed down to my father. Mother filled out applications to transfer me to a private school with other kids from the privileged bubble of Blue Sky, drove to Highland Park to shop, and tolerated the surrounding neighborhoods as an inconvenience of this temporary location for our family.

It turned out to be temporary in a way she hadn't anticipated.

In the years I had been away, Deep Ellum, Uptown, and Lakewood had clearly undergone death and resurrection. The streets were now an odd combination of old buildings renovated to contain upscale loft apartments and shops, and new construction on streets where Prairie and Craftsman-style homes built in the thirties and forties had been bulldozed to make room for McMansions and condominium complexes suited for urbanites seeking an uptown lifestyle.

Driving along Greenville, I passed by Vista Street without recognizing it at first. The huge blue gingerbread-encrusted house that had always marked the turnoff was gone. A quaint shopping center and matching condominium complex stood in its place. I looped around in the parking lot, thinking that if my mother could have seen the condos, she would have been shocked. One of her comforts in leaving the house to my father and Hanna Beth had been her conviction that the entire area was *going bad*, and eventually even the property on Blue Sky Hill would be worthless. It was probably better that she'd never known about the resurgence in the shadows of downtown. Such knowledge would only have goaded her.

Memories assaulted me as I continued up Vista Street to Blue Sky Hill Court. I could feel my childhood wrapping around me, changing me, taking me back to those months before the divorce. I wasn't driving, but riding in the back of my parents' car, traveling from the airport, seeing for the first time in recent memory my own country. The trees, the grass, the hedges and flower beds with their bright colors were startling, the humidity oppressive after the years I'd spent in the desert.

Even compared to our fairly luxurious accommodations in Saudi, the neighborhood on Blue Sky Hill was impressive, my father's house at the end of the road awe-inspiring, with its expansive lawn, wraparound porches, tall wrought-iron fence, and high leaded-glass windows. I could recall visiting my grandmother there, playing in the third-story attic and the garden house in the backyard, and walking down to the wet-weather creek to watch minnows swim and dragonflies skim the water.

That first day back in the States, as we stopped in the driveway, I bolted from the car and ran through the grass, feeling that I was finally home. The sensation enveloped me once again as I rounded the corner and the house came into view at the end of the street. After the long day of travel, the wild storms of emotions, the unanswered questions, Blue Sky Hill felt like a sanctuary.

As quickly as the sensation developed, it faded. This wasn't the home I remembered. The house in general lacked the meticulous care of years past. The window frames needed cleaning. The screens were rusted and torn. Around the garage doors, the wooden trim had sunbaked to a crackle, and high on the eaves, long strings of peeling paint hung from the attic dormers. A triangular piece of the leaded glass had fallen out, and no one had bothered to cover the hole.

Resentment swelled inside me as I rolled up the driveway, then parked and turned off the engine. How dare Hanna Beth allow the house, *my grandparents'* house, to disintegrate into this condition. If my father was no longer able to attend to things, she should have hired people. My father had investments, royalties in various oil and gas wells, undoubtedly a healthy pension from a lifetime of corporate employment. It wasn't as if he couldn't afford to hire help. Stepping onto the driveway, I felt oddly possessive of the house, as if it were my duty to set the place to rights.

In the wake of that impulse came the cool grip of reality. I had no idea what awaited me inside. My only information came from a short phone conversation with a Dallas police officer. According to him, Teddy had been found at a DART station, lost and out of money after wandering on and off buses and light rail trains all day, trying to navigate his way to the hospital to find his mother. When the police brought him home, they found my father, half dressed, asleep in a cold, dark house with the stove burners on full blast because he couldn't remember how to turn on the heat.

After spending some time sorting out the situation, the officer had tracked down my contact information in Hanna Beth's address book. He called, somewhat impatient by then, and told me they'd had complaints more than once about my father and Teddy wandering lost in the neighborhood, and if something wasn't done, Social Services would be forced to take over.

The complexity, the impossibility of the problem struck me as I walked toward the front porch, where all those years ago Hanna Beth had stood in her yellow dress. Why was I here? What was I going to do? What *could* I do?

Around me, the day was dimming, which seemed appropriate. The shadow of the house overtook me as I climbed the steps, gathered my courage, then knocked on the door. No one answered, so I rang the bell. I could hear movement inside, see a shadow through the glass, but still the door did not open. The form in the darkness behind the frosted window was brown-haired and broad-shouldered, not my father's.

"Teddy?" I leaned close to the door, closed my fingers over the knob. "Teddy, it's Rebecca . . . Rebecca Macklin. Open the door. . . ."

CHAPTER 4

Hanna Beth Parker

I'd been a coward, pretending to be asleep when Rebecca came into the room. I knew it was wrong, and wouldn't solve anything, but still I couldn't force myself to open my eyes and greet her. Perhaps it was pride. After all these years, I did not want her to see me this way. I was much like a little child, like Teddy when he was young, thinking that if he put his hand over his eyes I wouldn't be able to see him. Foolish notion, but somewhere in me there was the thought that I couldn't let her know how bad off I was—that if she knew she would close up the house, pack Edward and Teddy off to some sort of facility—perhaps even this one—and then return to her life in California.

The thought of Teddy in a place like this, languishing with the infirm, unable to enjoy our walks, to feed the fish in the creek and the stray cats, to spend hours in the garden, was unbearable. A change of location would destroy what was left of Edward. The familiarity of the house on Blue Sky Hill Court, the consistency of our routines, was the thread that kept him from slipping off into a place so vast, and dark, and deep that neither of us wanted to consider its bottom. It was impossible to imagine the day when this strong, handsome man, this beautiful soul I'd loved since I was a child, wouldn't know me. It was impossible to picture my life without his witty jokes, our home without his shoes by the front door (even though he knew I

would complain about it), my bedroom without the flowers he sometimes spirited from the garden and left on my pillow. Being ten years
younger than he, I always supposed there would be a day when I
would experience, once again, life without him. I always knew vaguely
that something would eventually have to be done for Teddy. But not
yet. Not so soon. It wasn't time.

My mind cast a net into the sea of despair. Why was this happening? How could God, whom I'd faithfully worshipped in church until
Edward became too ill to go, whom I'd trusted when it grew clear that
Teddy was not like other children, to whom I'd poured out my prayers
for my son, allow this to happen now? How could He leave me at the
mercy of the one person who resented my very existence, who had no
way of understanding the events that had transpired those many years
ago? How could Rebecca return now, when I lay here unable to move
or speak, unable to accomplish the most basic human functions, unable to tell her the truth?

I pulled up my net before it could become too heavy, before
the catch of impossible questions could drag me under. I could hear
Claude Fisher's voice again outside the door. I thought of him telling
Mary and Rebecca that the key to every situation was to keep facing
toward the light, to look for the possible good. I'd always found that
to be true, but now the darkness seemed too vast for such an optimis-
tic notion.

In the hall, Claude was saying good-bye to Mary and the boys,
promising that tomorrow he would tell them more about the trains.

My door swished open, and Mary's quiet footsteps followed. Poor
thing. She was probably worn to a thread by now. I wondered about
the problem with her husband and the car.

She stopped by my bed, picked up my arm, which I didn't know
was dangling, and tucked it back in beside me. She was wearing the
old blue button-up sweater she always put on when she was on her
way out. She looked too weary for a girl in her early twenties.

"That's better, huh?" she said, folding back the sheet and pulling it up under my chin. "I hope the boys didn't make too much racket out there."

"No-ooo." The word was surprisingly clear.

Mary smiled. "Being quiet isn't exactly their best thing."

"Baaa-shin." This time I managed little more than an unintelligible groan. I'd wanted to ask her to bring the boys in, just for a minute, so I could see them. I felt the usual pang of frustration at not being able to communicate something so simple.

Mary didn't seem to notice. "Your daughter was here while you were sleeping. She seems nice."

I didn't answer. Perhaps it was best that I couldn't. Someone as sweet as Mary could never understand the kind of family strife that separated us, or the anxiety I felt at our coming back together.

Mary gazed down at me, her thoughts seeming to drift. "They've reduced your medications some, so you might not sleep quite as soundly at night."

I blinked, because I didn't have the energy to attempt another word.

Mary hovered a moment, seeming reluctant to leave, even though her eyes were drifting shut. She gave the covers a final check and patted my arm through the blanket. I hoped she and the boys didn't have far to travel home. I closed my eyes so she wouldn't feel as though she had to remain at my bedside.

There was a faint, familiar scent on her hands—baby lotion, perhaps, or powder-scented wipes. A childhood smell, the link to a memory, a happier time. I drank it in, grabbed the line and pulled it closer, imagined that it remained after Mary left. I imagined that I was cuddled on the sofa with Teddy when he was tiny. I'd almost conjured the feel of his little body curled so perfectly against my chest, when something clanged in the hall, pulling me from my reverie.

Outside in the corridor, two nurses were talking about the new incontinence therapy program.

"Okay, no," one was saying. "The probe looks kind of like a tampon, only it's metal and it has a wire attached to it. The one end of the wire has the probe, and the other has the little connector that plugs into the computer. You know, like your digital camera plugs in with."

"Ohhhhhh . . . ," the other nurse answered. "Well, then what happens?"

"The patient goes into the bathroom and inserts the probe, then you plug it into the computer and try to make the little birdie fly by squeezing the Kegel muscles. The harder you tighten the pelvic floor, the higher the birdie flies."

"You're kidding," the other nurse said.

I groaned to myself, hoping that my pelvic muscles came back on their own as I recovered. If Gretchen arrived tomorrow with a metal probe and a laptop computer, I was going to rise from my bed by sheer force of will and walk home.

"If you don't like birds, you can use a fish," the first nurse added. "You make the fish swim faster on the screen."

"That's just weird."

"It's really pretty cool, and it works. All of us in PT had to use it during training. Rosie and I are good. I can make that fish swim a hundred miles an hour."

The response was a moan. "Oh, stop. This is what y'all are doing during those lunchtime training sessions? Sitting around making the birdie fly?"

"We're thinking of putting some money in a pool and hosting the incontinence Olympics."

"You people in PT have waaaay too much time on your hands."

"Hey, if you can't have fun with incontinence training, what can you have fun with?" The two of them laughed together. "Oh. Oh, I've got to tell you this one. The other day we had our first set of test patients. So we give them the probes, explain everything, and send them into the bathroom to insert. This one poor little lady stays in there forever, and when she finally comes out, she has the *wrong end* in."

"The part with the computer plug on it?"

"Yeah. Poor thing."

"All right. That's it," the second nurse said. "I've had all the retention and elimination I can stand. I'm going to get something to eat."

They parted ways in the hall, and I lay there wanting to laugh. I imagined flying birds and animated fish, metal probes and rows of nurses competing in the incontinence Olympics. Gretchen took the field, towering over all the other competitors. She was wearing a fishing hat, carrying a lug wrench in one hand and a glistening stainless steel probe in the other. Just before the gold medal ceremony, a door slammed down the hall.

I listened to the rhythmic beep of an oximeter; the occasional clang of metal on metal; the rattle of a gurney passing by as a patient was transferred, probably back to the hospital; the wailing of the moaning woman, who cried out repeatedly that she was dying and needed help. The ones with dementia seemed more restless late in the day, as if they were anticipating the night ahead, when the lights would dim and the hallways would empty of visitors. When night fell, it was easy to feel vulnerable, lost in this large, cold place. At night, I was like a child in a dark bedroom, afraid to close my eyes, sensing hidden threats in the shadows.

I didn't want to die in a place like this, and I didn't want to live in a place like this. I didn't want to be alone.

Evening light crept in around the edges of the window blind. I focused on that, listened as ambulatory patients moved down the hall for game night, and thought of an old poem:

Oh far away, do smile at me, at me,
In swells of rose and deepest blue,
Await my sleep to carry me,
Away to the shores of a moon-bright sea . . .

I wanted to let sleep carry me away, back to the days when we children from the houses off the hill rode our bicycles to the park in Blue Sky—back to the days when I stood by the old iron fence and watched a tall, broad boy with striking hazel eyes and thick, dark hair. He smiled at me, and I fell in love, but I was just a girl, and he a teenager, practically a young man. My father worked with his father. I made it a point to see him again. . . .

A phantom pain in my legs pulled me from the memory. The sensation was akin to a charley horse, but throughout my legs, dozens of charley horses, a thundering herd, running at top speed.

My teeth chattered and my breath came short with the pain. *It means something,* I thought. *It means I'm getting better.* One wish in a long line of wishes that began when I fell to the laundry room floor and lay crumpled there with something dripping into my mouth. I didn't know where I was, or what was happening. The liquid tasted salty and thick. I thought it might be blood.

I prayed as I was fading away. *God, please, don't let Teddy or Edward find me here dead. Not now. We're not ready.*

When I finally came to in the hospital, I gathered that days had passed, and the doctors had been waiting for me to regain awareness. After that, it was anybody's guess. I heard words like "coma," "brain stem," "subarachnoid bleed," "impaired function," "aphasia," but in my mind I was back in the little hospital in College Station, forty-eight years ago, when, after fainting behind the wheel of my car on my way to freshman classes, I hit a telephone pole and was taken to the hospital, where my parents were informed of two things: I'd lost a great deal of blood, and I was pregnant. The doctor discussed the pregnancy with my family, and the fact that, if the fetus did survive, there was no way to predict what effect the trauma, blood loss, and medications would have. There was also no way to know how the pregnancy might hamper my recovery. There were treatments and medications they couldn't use because of the fetus. He intimated that a loss of the pregnancy might be for the best. I was young, unmarried. Children should be years in the future for me.

As the doctor left the room, my mother stood in the corner, weeping. My sister, Ann, agreed with the doctor. My father was silent. He only looked at me in a scornful, disappointed way that hurt more than anything he could have said. Eventually, he would want to know, of course, who the father was—how, when my parents had worked so hard to provide a college education for me, I could have done such a thing, why I hadn't told them.

My mind was a fog that had nothing to do with the accident. I pretended that, with all the stresses of spring semester, I hadn't known I was pregnant. But the truth was that I had. The truth was that I'd been stalling for time since just after winter break. I'd been hoping, praying, waiting for an answer that had finally come just before the accident. The letter had been brief, to the point, communicated through his family lawyer, and unmistakably clear. He denied responsibility for this pregnancy, and I should not attempt to contact him again. If I had a baby, I would be having it on my own. If I chose to raise it, I would be raising it on my own. That idea would trouble my stern, old-fashioned Catholic parents as much as anything. Errant Catholic girls were occasionally known to quietly go off to *special places*, disappear for six, seven, eight months, then return as if nothing had happened, rejoin normal life with little more than an occasional backhanded whisper to mark the passing of those months, the creation of a life.

As I lay in the hospital, the options, the repercussions, went through my mind in a flash. I'd caused all of this. It was my fault.

I wondered if losing the baby would be my punishment.

Years later, when I realized Teddy wasn't like other children, when he missed the developmental milestones, failed to attain normal speech, and fine motor control, I wondered if my sins had been visited upon him. When he grew up unable to do the things other boys did, I felt cheated, cursed. When I sat by his hospital bed on his fifteenth birthday, after a group of neighborhood boys pushed him off the little bridge by the park, I felt blessed beyond measure. As big and strong as he was, Teddy hadn't fought back. He thought the boys were his friends. He didn't want them to be in trouble. He didn't want to hurt anyone. There was nothing in Teddy but goodness. Evil and the reasons for its presence in the world were beyond the realm of his heart's comprehension.

I wondered where he was now—if Rebecca would go to the house and find him there, if she would be kind to him. More than anything, I wanted to be there, to protect him, if need be, from her.

CHAPTER 5

Rebecca Macklin

A series of dead bolts, security chains, and locks clicked this way and that as Teddy attempted repeatedly, unsuccessfully, to disengage all of them at once. The locks were an odd conglomeration of antique hardware and new brass units, which appeared to have been freshly installed. Sawdust had coated the door and collected in the corners of the threshold. I touched a finger to it as Teddy tried to solve the puzzle again, then pulled on the door, meeting the resistance of at least one dead bolt.

With each failure, his movements grew more frantic, and he muttered instructions to himself, occasionally calling out, "Jut a minute, A-becca. Jut a minute, okay? Don't go way, A-becca. Don't go way. Okay, A-becca? I gone open the door. I gone open the door. A-becca?"

"I'm still here." I laid a hand on the glass as the muscles in my neck stiffened with frustration, and a vague tightening sensation pinched at the base of my skull. The beginnings of a migraine wouldn't be far behind. I needed to get to the hotel room I'd reserved, dig out the bottle of the medication the doctor had prescribed last month, and lie down where it was dark and quiet.

I will not have a migraine, I told myself, even though, after a year of suffering, I should have known that refusing to be afflicted with something as ridiculously inconvenient as migraine headaches didn't make them go away. Sometimes the body takes on a life of its own.

Was that how Hanna Beth felt, lying in her bed at the nursing center? Did it seem as if her own body had betrayed her? Was that how my father felt as his memories began to fade? News of his decline came in a letter disguised in a Christmas card—a package bomb, of sorts. A stealth attack that went undetected until Macey, gleefully opening a stack of Christmas mail as we drove to gymnastics, held up a card with a painting of a cardinal in the snow, and asked, "Who's Hanna Beth?"

"Never mind," I said, then snatched the card away and tucked it between the seat and the console. "That's someone you don't know."

Macey shrugged and returned to the stack of mail.

I drove on, wishing Macey hadn't torn the envelope. I wanted to send it back unopened, as usual—to prove I had no interest in making contact.

But the card, now freed of its innocuous wrapping, tugged at the fringes of my vision, until finally in the parking lot outside Macey's gym, I slipped a hand between the seat and the console and pulled it out. I read Hanna Beth's letter, her warning—almost two years ago now—that time may soon run out.

I threw away the card, unburdened myself of it as I walked into the gymnastics studio. The words lay on my mind, conjured a vision of my father coming in from work with his briefcase, stopping to pluck a daisy from the pot by the door, hand it to me, and pat my hair. "How's my girl?" he said. The memory wound through my senses, a muscle tightened in the back of my neck, and my head began to compress with the new and blinding sort of headache I'd experienced intermittently since reaching my mid-forties.

I willed myself not to have the memory or the headache. *Ultimately, it's not so much what life deals you as what you choose to own that matters,* a spiritually searching law clerk had once said to me. She'd heard it on a talk show.

As Teddy tried the locks again, I thought of tall, suntanned Susan Sewell, sitting at the sidewalk café with Kyle. I didn't want to own that reality, either. I'd forced it from my thoughts most of the day, made it misty and unreal, like a scene from a movie you fall into so deeply that you mentally insert yourself for a moment before realizing it's just a story. Those are only actors. This is not your life.

This could never happen to you.

My mother said that to a girlfriend on the phone as we sat in a Dallas hotel room making plans to move the rest of our things out of my father's house the week after all the paperwork became final. *Well, you know, Carla, I never thought this would happen to me, but you can't be too sure. Watch yourself—that's all I can say. You think you know somebody. You think you're a good wife, and you're doing all the things a good wife should, and then boom, you're on your way to California to live in your parents' guesthouse until you can figure out what comes next. It can happen faster than you think. A woman can't afford to be pie-in-the-sky these days. A woman has to be practical, watchful. . . .*

My mother went on, warning our younger ex-neighbor, whose daughter I'd babysat while she and her husband went with my parents on dinner dates, never, ever to be too trusting of her husband, to be *gullible.* Was that what I'd done? Had I been gullible, believing Kyle was spending so much time at work because my absence, while seeing to my mother's affairs, had increased the workload around the office? Was I naive to believe that planning a surprise anniversary trip to San Diego could bridge the distance? When we were together in San Diego, the distance became concrete, developed sharp edges that sliced through our conversations, brought up difficult subjects . . . why was Kyle spending more time than ever at the office, why was I still hanging on to the boutique?

"It's been a year," Kyle pointed out. "It's time, Rebecca."

"It's not that simple, Kyle. There's a lot to deal with." How could I explain what I couldn't understand myself? Letting go of the shop was like letting go of my mother. I knew Kyle wouldn't understand that line of reasoning—in fact, he would resent it. My mother had always been a barrier between us. In his view, she was overly dependent, a purposeful interloper in our relationship. In her view, he was too demanding, too slow to understand that, as a divorced woman with no other children, she would naturally rely on me for advice in business contracts and financial dealings, for help and care and comfort when her lupus flared up and periodically caused debilitating symptoms.

Kyle did his best, but the truth was that my mother was hard to deal with. Now that she was gone, it was tough for Kyle to accept that so much of my time was still consumed with her affairs. Part of me wanted to keep the boutique, as my mother had desired, so that the thriving shop she had built from nothing could one day be passed on to Macey.

Part of me was afraid to even mention that possibility to Kyle. Both of us knew I couldn't keep spreading myself so thin.

On the anniversary trip, we made love to keep from talking. The big things remained unsettled, but by the time we came home, we were laughing about little things, joking, flirting, enjoying each other. It felt good. It felt like we were finally moving into a cycle of recovery.

You think you're doing all the things a good wife should, and then boom. . . . It can happen faster than you think. . . .

Maybe those words had been in the back of my mind all along. Perhaps that was why I'd always been in such a hurry to cram everything—a career, a child, a house, vacations, lessons and activities for Macey—into what felt like a limited amount of time. Perhaps that was why I could never relax and just . . . be. Even during our vacations, I felt the need to keep busy with tours and activities, to do everything before time ran out.

What if Kyle was tired of it? What if he was tired of the boutique, the lingering guilt and grief that made me hold on, my driving need to be good enough—a good enough daughter, wife, lawyer, mother? What if Kyle was tired of it? What if he was tired of me?

Behind the door, Teddy was getting emotional, muttering and sobbing about the locks, occasionally hollering for my father, "Daddy Ed." Wherever my father was, he wasn't answering. I had the fleeting thought that something might have happened to him. What if he'd wandered off, and Teddy was alone in the house? What if my father had suffered a heart attack, a fall, an accident of some kind? Would Teddy know what to do?

I felt a surprising stab of panic, like nothing I'd expected to feel. For years I'd been prepared for a letter, a note, a communiqué from an estate lawyer, telling me my father was dead.

I grabbed the lower doorknob, tried to twist it, to push open the door. On the other side, Teddy turned the locks frantically, sobbing, "A-becca? Don' go way, A-becca. Don' go way. A-becca?"

"Teddy!" I snapped, trying to calm the torrent of words, to stop the frenzied click of dead bolts locking and unlocking, and Teddy yanking the door, pulling and rattling it until it seemed the frame would give way. "Teddy, listen! Is there another door? Is there another way you can let me in? Is there another door, Teddy?" The racket stopped, the shadow receded from the window, and everything went silent. "Teddy?" I called. "Teddy, are you there?"

No answer came from the house. I leaned close to the frosted glass, tried to see through to the other side. Nothing but misty white shapes.

At the end of the wraparound porch, where an attached garage with an overhead apartment had been added in the fifties, one of the doors creaked, then started upward, the motorized opener squealing and grinding as the heavy wooden door bounced along, the panels bowed and off-kilter, in need of repair. I left the porch, skirting the overgrown bushes.

Teddy emerged from the garage. "A-becca! A-becca! Hi-eee!" Beneath an uncombed mop of salt-and-pepper hair, he smiled broadly, giving a buoyant, joyful grin that was nothing if not genuine.

All I could think of was moving day, thirty-three years ago, when he ran across the lawn waving and calling my name. I wanted to retreat to the car again and close the door.

I backed up a step in the driveway, threw out my hands without thinking. When Teddy reached me, he grabbed my fingers and held them in his, oblivious to the barricade. "Hi-eee, A-becca," he said, shaking my arms up and down so hard that I stumbled sideways and a twinge pinched in the back of my head. "The policeman say to Daddy Ed, A-becca gone come." He squinted hard, thinking back, apparently. A network of wrinkles formed around his eyes, and it seemed strange for them to be there. I took him in fully for the first time, a man in his forties, a big, broad-shouldered boy with a two-hundred-pound body and the cautionless way of a child. "That wud yed-terday, I think. Yed-terday. The police give me ride in po-lice car." His eyebrows shot upward with surprising enthusiasm. "Policeman say, 'We gotta call somebody, Teddy. Who we gone call?' And I say, call A-becca. She my sit-ter. My sit-ter in Cal-forna. Tha's a long, long way." Pursing his lips, he shook his head and frowned, suddenly somber. "A long, long way, and she can't come see Daddy Ed. If the police say it, you gotta come, though." Loosening his hands from mine, he raised a finger into the air. His eyes met mine, just for a moment. "You all-way gotta do what a policeman say."

I slipped my hands behind my back, afraid he would grab me again. *She my sit-ter.* For thirty-three years now, they'd been telling him he had a sister, and I didn't come to visit because I lived too far away? Why would they do that? Why would they foster in him the expectation that I would one day arrive here, and we would somehow share a normal family relationship? "Teddy, where is Daddy Ed?"

Teddy glanced toward the garage door, now hanging crooked with a colony of mud wasps nested in the corner. "Oh, he sleepin'."

Disquiet tickled the corner of my mind. How could anyone sleep through the yelling and the racket of Teddy trying to open the door? "Teddy, how long has Daddy Ed been asleep?" He seemed confused by the question at first. "Teddy, how long?"

Teddy backed away, intertwining his fingers against his chest, worrying the front of his soiled Ford Trucks T-shirt. His smile went slack, and he blinked rapidly. "I don' know." He ducked his head almost imperceptibly, waited for me to say something.

"Did he get up this morning?" I stepped around Teddy and started toward the house. "Did he have lunch with you?" I had a vision of Teddy alone in the house with my father's body, like something in a horror novel or a sad news report.

"We got pea-nit butter jelly—me 'n Daddy Ed got pea-nit butter jelly for lunch—I know how to do it." Teddy mumbled the words in a string without punctuation. He followed me across the threshold into the cloakroom, where coats hung neatly on hooks, and shoes were lined up underneath the long wooden bench I remembered from my childhood. A mountain of dirty clothes lay piled in front of the dryer and scattered on one end of the floor, as if someone had started to do the laundry, but then forgotten. Something had mildewed in the washer. I could smell it from across the room.

"Where's Daddy Ed, Teddy?" I moved through the open area, pushing away the assault of memories. I used to hang my coat on the ornate metal hook by the English oak umbrella stand. The coat was red wool, my favorite. My father's golf cap hung directly across from it. I liked his hat being there. The hooks were empty now, except for a mangled umbrella covered with the dust of disuse and ready for the trash.

"He in here," Teddy said, and led me into the hallway. "He in the chair. He sleepin'. He got some pills sleep. He got some pill."

My level of anxiety ratcheted upward. "He took sleeping pills? Teddy, did you give him pills?"

Teddy curled his fingers against his chest again, pulling absently at his T-shirt. "No, no, A-becca. I don't touch no pill. Mama say, don't touch no pill. No pill."

I slipped past Teddy, then hurried down the paneled wood hallway, the conglomeration of family pictures a blur as I passed my father's office, the master bedroom, the small maid's pantry that my mother had used as a sewing room. It was filled with plants now, mostly tiny starts potted in all sorts of unconventional containers— cooking pans, Tupperware bowls, drinking glasses, discarded cups, and take-out containers from various restaurants.

Rounding the corner into the living room, I saw my father crumpled in a recliner by the fireplace. The memory of him there, in that place, in a chair like this one, was strong as I crossed the room. Standing over him, I laid a hand on his arm, touched his wrist and felt a strong, steady pulse, listened to his breathing. He stirred slightly, and I backed away, unwilling to be within reach, to be found touching him if he woke up. I wondered if he would know me. Hanna Beth had left a message on my answering machine a year ago, warning that he was growing worse. My mother was in the hospital at the time, suffering from active lupus and end-stage renal failure. By then we knew that, after years of triumphantly and repeatedly forcing her lupus into remission, this battle would probably be her last. A final and telling rejection of my father seemed like one last thing I could do to please her.

She wouldn't like it that I'm here, I thought, standing over my father's chair. *She wouldn't like this at all.*

I backed away another step, felt an intense sense of guilt, then repulsion, toward him, toward this place. The room was stacked with newspapers, muddy gardening clothes, dirty dishes, shoes, socks, glasses with lumpy, soured milk, pizza boxes with the leftover sauce dried black, and bits of cheese, hard and green with mold.

The combination of scents in the air was nauseating, dizzying.

I looked at my father, at what was left of him, a shrunken shadow of the tall man I remembered, the man who lumbered down the hall with long, confident strides, his cowboy boots thundering on the hollow wooden floor. He was the John Wayne of my childhood. A presence always larger than life.

The pill bottle was lying atop a tumbling pile of manila file folders on the table next to him. I picked it up, read the quantity prescribed, and counted the pills inside. The bottle was mostly full. He was probably fine.

He smelled. Bad. His hair, once almost black, now silver, was slick with oil, his clothes dirty and rumpled, his face covered with the uneven patches of a stubbly beard. On his left cheek, the hair grew around a crescent-shaped scar left by a tile that fell from a rooftop in Saudi. The roofer slid down his climbing pole, rushed to my father and sank to his knees, babbling in some other language. My father only squinted up at the roof, then took out his handkerchief and pressed it over the blood. He said something in Arabic, then we walked to our car and drove to the hospital for stitches.

I always wondered what he'd said to the man who'd crouched at his feet.

Teddy shook his head as I turned away from my father's chair. "Mama say don' touch the pill." His eyes darted toward the bottle in my hand. "Don' touch the pill. Don' touch no med-sin. Them look like candy, but it's bad."

"It's okay, Teddy. I'll take care of it."

"Daddy Ed get mad. He get real mad." His fingers braided and unbraided under his chin. "Mama say no."

His physical size, the rising degree of anxiety, sent an uncomfortable sense of vulnerability prickling over my skin. What if he became violent? Was he capable of it? "It's okay, Teddy. I saw your mom today. She and I agreed it would be best if I took care of the pills for now. I bet when your mom's here, she takes care of the pills, doesn't she?"

Teddy's frenzied movement stopped. His blue eyes welled up and spilled over. "I wanna see Mama."

Something tugged inside me. I thought of Macey—how she would feel if she were separated from me and couldn't understand why. "We can't right now, Teddy. She's sleeping." The last, last thing I was prepared to do was put Teddy in the car and try to take him to the nursing center today.

Teddy sniffled, and wiped his nose on the back of his hand. "The bus won' go see Mama. I ask the man, say, I gone see Mama. She at the hop-sital. But the bus won' go. It won' go. I ride the other one, and the other one, but all the bus don' go see Mama."

"Is that why you were on the buses yesterday, Teddy? You were trying to get to the hospital?"

"Daddy Ed wan' Mama," Teddy went on. "Kay-Kay say she gone take me see Mama, but she don' come no more. She don' come. Kay-Kay don' come. . . ."

"Teddy, who's Kay-Kay?"

Teddy blinked, surprised. "Kay-Kay, she make good cookie for Daddy Ed. She give Daddy Ed pill . . . clean the floor, washin' clothes. . . ." He stretched out the words, pantomiming the actions as he talked. "And the win-dow, and the jelly on the plate. . . ."

"Okay, so you have someone who takes care of you?" Relief flooded through me, although, judging from the condition of the house, she wasn't doing her job. "Where does she live?"

Teddy shrugged.

"Do you have her phone number?"

Another shrug.

"Do you know her last name?"

Teddy shook his head, then said, "She jus' Kay-Kay."

Tucking the pill bottle in my pocket, I blew out a long sigh, then surveyed the stacks of mail and papers around the room. Somewhere in all of that, there was probably a checkbook, a bill from a home health agency, or a maid service that would allow me to track down this Kay-Kay.

Right now, the tightening in my head was growing, and nausea had begun to rock my stomach. I needed to get to my hotel, take some medication, and beat it down. "Okay, Teddy. I have to go check into my room, get my suitcases out, and rest for a little bit, but I'll be back later. I'll bring some take-out food to eat, and maybe by then Daddy Ed will wake up. We'll try to find Kay-Kay and get her to come, and that will make things better, okay?"

Teddy crossed the room to the entryway and headed for the wide wooden staircase. "Here you room, A-becca. It all set. All fix, all set."

"No, Teddy, wait." Before I could stop him, he was bounding up the stairs three at a time, his heavy footfalls echoing through the cavernous entryway and into the living room. "Teddy . . ." The pounding in my head grew louder. Pushing it aside, I started up the stairs. From somewhere overhead, I could hear furniture squealing across the floor in the first room on the left. The room that used to be mine. When I came to the door, Teddy was trying to straighten the blanket on a bed. Various bookshelves and a sewing table—probably Hanna Beth's—had been scooted to the edges of the room, and the bed, a desk, chair, and dresser formed an off-kilter arrangement in the center.

Teddy finished smoothing the blanket and placed the chair carefully under the desk, then smoothed his hands along the chair back, as if he were making sure no dust had settled there, that everything was perfect. The realization struck me like a splash of water, unexpectedly warm, yet inconvenient. Teddy had prepared this room, my room, for a homecoming. There was even a little-girl picture of me on the desk, one my mother had taken in the instant I jumped from the edge of a hotel swimming pool and sailed toward the water.

I moved into the room and picked up the picture. I could remember the moment it was taken. I was jumping toward my father, into his outstretched hands, just beyond the frame.

In the photo, I was looking at him, buoyant with anticipation, confident he would catch me before the water pulled me under.

I set the picture down, turned it away, so I wouldn't have to look at it. Memories like that one, memories in which my father was an integral part of my life, in which I adored him, were the enemy. I'd learned from my mother that in cultivating anger, in nursing disdain, it was always more productive to stack up the negatives, to remember all the times he had disappointed me, failed me, chosen other things, other *people* over me. I'd created a past in which his leaving was only one more transgression in a long string of failings—something that was to be expected, eventually, considering the kind of person he was.

The swimming pool picture didn't fit neatly into that accounting. It was easier to set it down facing the wall.

Teddy didn't notice the picture; instead, he was looking at me, taking in my expression, his smile slowly drooping. He searched me, seeking some sort of approval, some hint of affection. "There a other room." He flailed a hand toward the doorway across the hall. "This A-becca room, but there a other room." He glanced around at the furniture, making plans to move it.

Pinching the tightness in my forehead, I tried to figure out how to explain to him that I couldn't stay here. "It's a nice room, Teddy. Thanks for getting it ready, but . . ."

His face lifted. Turning clumsily, he started toward the door, his bulky body shuffling from side to side. "You gone sit down. I gone get the suit-cate. Jus' a minute. Jus' a minute."

"Teddy . . ." The protest was wasted. He was already clomping down the stairs, each impact booming through the house. I stood with the room swirling around me. I'd waited too long to take the migraine medicine.

Rubbing my forehead, I turned off the glaring overhead light and sank onto the edge of the bed. The soft, pink glow of sunset bathed the room, as down below the garage door closed, and Teddy came up the stairs again, my hanging bag bumping along behind him, the metal hanger making a high-pitched *ping, ping, ping* that felt like the squeal of a dentist's drill. Lying down on the edge of the bed, I closed my eyes.

Teddy came in with my suitcases, muttered, "Ssshhhh." I heard him carefully arrange my bags on the floor before he tiptoed from the room and quietly descended the stairs.

I grabbed my carry-on, pulled out the migraine medicine and a water bottle, took a pill, and lay down again.

I thought of the swimming pool picture, remembered jumping from the edge, taking flight over the water, then landing in my father's arms. . . .

When I awoke, it was dark outside. The tide of pain in my head had receded, conquered by the medicine, or sleep, or both. A crocheted afghan lay loosely over my body. The desk lamp cast a soft glow. On the floor beside my suitcases, a peanut butter and jelly sandwich lay on a cake-and-punch plate next to a glass of iced tea. The tea was settling into a filmy mixture, clear on top, brown on the bottom, with swirls of bleeding color in between. *Heterogeneous solution,* I thought, momentarily flashing back to the worksheet Macey had brought home from class yesterday. She'd missed *heterogeneous solution.* Kyle came in early for family dinner night, and we talked about heterogeneous solutions, so Macey wouldn't miss the question the next time. Kyle had always been the science whiz in the family.

I realized I hadn't even called home yet, and I checked my watch. It would be after ten thirty there. Grabbing my cell phone, I turned it on, then dialed the number. Isha would be in her room next to the garage by now, off duty. Macey would be in bed, sound asleep. Kyle would be dozing on the sofa, watching the news with a Diet Coke and a bag of mini rice cakes. He'd changed his snacking habits lately, trying to get in shape. I'd thought it was a great idea, something we could do together—focus on eating right, maybe get up early some mornings and go to the gym or take a run down on the beach like we used to before the business, and parenthood, and life got in the way. Now I wondered if there was something sinister behind Kyle's new focus on fitness.

The phone rang three times before someone picked up.

"Hello?" Macey's voice was drowsy and thin, not her usual businesslike, adult-in-training phone greeting.

"Mace? How come you're answering the phone so late, sweetheart? Where are Dad and Isha?"

"Isha's asleep. Dad called and said he was going to be late, so she stayed up here and watched a movie with me. She fell asleep. She snores, by the way. Not a really bad kind of snore, but just a little whistly kind of snore like Grandma Macklin does. It's funny. We rented *The Princess Bride*. It's really good. I think we should buy a copy. I told Isha probably we could just keep this one. The movie store has that deal where if you find a movie you like, you can buy their copy for a used price. I told Isha—"

"Mace, why are you up watching a movie at"—I checked my watch to be sure—"almost eleven o'clock on a school night?"

Macey went temporarily mute. Through the phone lines, across thousands of miles, I could see the wheels turning. "It was a really good part, and I didn't want to turn it off. It's almost over now, though."

"Isha let you start a movie after eight o'clock?" Even though Isha had only been with us a couple months, of all the au pairs we'd had she was by far the best about sticking to the rules. For a twenty-two-year-old, she was extremely mature and detail-oriented. Macey liked her, as well, so she was a perfect fit.

"Huh?" Macey was stalling. When she knew I wouldn't like the answer, she usually asked me to repeat the question, so she could have more time to process. Smart girl. "Macey, why were you starting a movie after eight o'clock? Even if Isha didn't tell you not to, you know better."

"Oh, we started at seven," Macey was quick to set me straight. "She said I could skip reading time, but just for tonight because I was kind of sad that you were gone and all. Tomorrow I can read double to make up for it. I read some in the car going to gymnastics today, too. I'm halfway through Harry Potter, and I just got it a week ago. Mrs. Nagle says that's really good. She hasn't ever had a fourth-grader read Harry Potter so quick."

She paused long enough to take a breath. Part of me wanted to reach through the phone and hug her for saying she missed me. Tonight I needed someone to miss me. Another part of me felt the compulsion to cross-examine, to make my point about breaking the rules. "If you started the movie at seven, why is it still on?"

"Huh?"

"Macey, you heard me."

She gave a huge, dramatic sigh. "Isha fell asleep before it was over, and it wasn't quite bedtime, and there was this one *really* good part I wanted to see, like, just in case you said we couldn't buy the movie and Isha had to take it back tomorrow? I went back to find that part."

"And it took an hour and a half?" The picture was becoming clearer. Poor Isha. If Kyle came home and found Isha asleep and Macey watching a movie at this time of night, he'd go ballistic.

"No." Macey sighed again. "I forgot to turn it off. I didn't mean to, but it's really good, and—"

"Macey . . ." I stopped her. "You didn't *accidentally forget* to turn off the movie. You wanted to stay up and watch, and so you *chose* to do that, even though you knew you weren't supposed to. Just because Isha didn't stop you doesn't make it all right. You know the rules, and it's your responsibility to follow them. Aside from that, you made a commitment to Isha to go to bed when the movie was over, and you didn't keep your promise." Glancing toward the hallway, I thought of the unspoken commitment that had brought me here. "We all have to do things we don't want to, just because it's right. Learning to do those things is part of growing up, part of being a responsible adult."

"I know," Macey huffed, as in, *I've heard this speech before. Would you like me to quote it for you?* "I'm sorry." The happy jingle in her voice was gone, replaced by a defeated, remorseful monotone that said, *Well, darn, I messed up again.*

I felt the inconvenient tug of empathy, of being in her place, listening to my mother's oft-repeated lecture about people who don't keep commitments, who don't stick to the rules. Such people grow up to be unstable, starry-eyed dreamers who flit off from their families and start entirely new lives, and think everyone ought to forgive them for it. . . . "I just don't want you to be tired during school tomorrow, Mace."

"I know." The answer was sullen, the undertone unmistakable. She didn't feel like chatting with the fun-killer anymore.

"We'll talk about the DVD when I get home."

"Okay."

Weary, lonesome tears prickled behind my eyes. I found myself wanting to keep her on the phone, even though it was bedtime. "Did you have a good day?"

"Yes." The simple answer was Macey's way of sulking—a passive-aggressive protest.

"Some details, please."

"It was okay. The social studies test was easy. Coach Kara was sick, so we didn't do much in gymnastics. We stopped to get subs on the way home. I bought a foot-long for Isha and me. She had to pick off the olives because she hates olives. I did my homework. Dad called and said he'd be late, and so Isha and me went out to get a movie."

"Isha and I." The correction was out of my mouth before I thought about it.

"Isha and I," she repeated with an exaggerated yawn. "I guess I better go to bed."

"All right." Part of me wished she would launch into some long-winded story about school, or gymnastics, or going to the movie store with Isha.

"Night, Mom." Macey yawned again.

"Good night, sweetheart. Go to bed now. Wake Isha up and tell her she can head on to bed, too. Tell her to check the doors and turn on the alarm first." *You'd think your father could have come home, considering that he knew I was out of town tonight.* "I love you."

Macey didn't answer, and I felt loneliness closing in around me.

"Night," she repeated.

"Sweet dreams, Mace." My voice quavered, and despite knowing better, I felt myself falling down the slippery slope of coercion and preteen emotional blackmail. "Listen, about the movie. Just go ahead and tell Isha I said you can keep it. It sounds good. Maybe we can watch it when I get back."

"Cool!" Macey squealed. "Thanks, Mom. You'll really like it. I love you."

I love you. Even though I'd just bought them with a DVD, the words felt good. They were the salve I needed. "I love you, too. No more late nights, okay?"

" 'Kay, Mom. Bye."

I said good-bye and hung up, then sat on the edge of the bed feeling vacant and exhausted. Picking up the sandwich plate and tea, I studied the partially open door. The hallway was dark, the house quiet. There was no sound of a TV, or anyone moving around. I set the sandwich and drink on the night table, stood up, then crossed the room and peered out. At the end of the hall, the bedroom door, open earlier, was closed now, the threshold dark underneath. I tiptoed out, descended the stairs, and went through the entryway to the living room. The chairs were empty, and my father was snoring in the master bedroom. I walked to his door, looked in, saw him lying in the king-sized bed with his back turned toward the wall. On Hanna Beth's side, a nightgown lay neatly atop the covers. My father's arm was stretched over it. I stood watching, not knowing how to feel. Had Teddy told him I was here? Did he understand?

Finally, I went to the kitchen, rifled through the refrigerator, the pantry, the cabinets. The shelves were bare save for bags of macaroni, beans, flour, and rice. On the counter were two loaves of bread and a jar of peanut butter. When I opened the refrigerator, the stench was overwhelming, even though it was empty except for a jar of jelly, something molding in a casserole dish, and a cache of rotting produce in the vegetable drawer. My stomach rolled over as I closed the door, then stood looking at the piles of dirty dishes in the sink, on the countertops, on the breakfast table. Every dish in the house must have been used.

Bracing my hands on the counter, I let my head sag forward. There was no way I could sort this out tonight. I needed to go to sleep, attack the problem in the morning, figure out . . . something.

I couldn't imagine what *something* might be.

CHAPTER 6

Hanna Beth Parker

I heard a thunderstorm rumbling in the distance and thought of Teddy. Teddy hated thunderstorms, especially at night. I hoped that, at home, he was sleeping soundly.

The first muted rays of dawn were peeking through the window when Betty, the third-shift nurse's aide, came to clean the bed and change my sheets. Betty was heavyset and less than five feet tall, with a scraggly graying bouffant that added several inches to her height. The bouffant was so tall and thin that when she entered with the hallway light behind her, the hair formed a translucent web of tangled strands. As she approached the bed, the hair solidified, so that she seemed to grow taller the closer she came.

As usual, Betty couldn't be troubled with niceties. She yanked back the covers, rolled the top sheet into a wad and threw it in her laundry cart, then shoved me roughly to one side, slid a plastic pad under me, ripped off the adult diaper, wrinkled her nose and scowled at the mess.

"For heaven's sake," she grumbled as she rolled me over again, so that I collided with the rail hard enough that I felt it. Wadding the pad into a ball, she tossed it into the trash, replaced the bottom sheet, then changed her gloves, checked her cart for something, and walked out the door, leaving it hanging open so that people in the hall could see everything. A man pushing a laundry cart passed by, and I pressed my eyes closed, heat rushing into my face.

"Git outa here," Betty snapped as she whisked in with another disposable undergarment, letting the door remain ajar. Without looking at me, she grabbed my arm and measured my pulse, then glanced down at my body, said, "Looks like we're dry now," and slapped on another diaper. Covering me with a new top sheet and blanket, she grunted as she folded the corners, propped up my knees with pillows, and slightly lowered the head of the bed.

"Stinks in here," she muttered, and pulled out a large white spray bottle. A cloud of aerosol followed her as she pushed her cart toward the door.

In her wake, I tried to catch the scent of Mary's little boys, but all that remained was the antiseptic. Outside in the hall, Betty hollered at Claude Fisher. Apparently, he wasn't supposed to be up and around this early. Betty wanted to know how he'd gotten out of bed. She'd put him back once already. He told her he was old, not an invalid, and she instructed him to go back to his room.

Claude returned to his room next door, and I closed my eyes again, trying to find the scent of little boys as the aerosol cloud faded. There was nothing. No trace of sweet-smelling memories.

In my legs, the charley horses were running wild. Betty had whipped them into a frenzy, and I felt as if I might lose my mind. I wanted to scream, but I knew all I'd manage was an unintelligible groan. A wave of helplessness and loneliness and misery swept over me. I wanted to be home. I wanted life to be normal again, but I didn't think I had the strength to get from here to there. It was too hard, too far uphill.

I started to weep. I couldn't do this. I couldn't. It would be easier to die right now and be done with it.

"Hey, Birdie, don't cry." Claude's soft voice came through the darkness, through the haze of pain, a focus point of light, drawing me out. "I got somethin' for ya. Watch this."

Catching a breath, I blinked away the blur and watched him shuffle across the room, dragging his chair to the window. Soft pink light poured in as he raised the blind, then secured the cord with three pushpins. "Stole these from the bulletin board. Betty's picture kind of slipped down behind the CPR chart. I reckon they'll find it one of these days." Sitting back in his chair, he admired his handiwork and grinned mischievously. "Birdie, just look at that sunrise. Ain't that a promise to behold?"

I turned to the window as much as I could. Outside, the sky was ablaze with shades of amber and crimson, amethyst and rose against pure turquoise blue. The clouds that had dimmed the light and threatened rain had passed over, creating a dazzling panorama of shape and color, a glistening shore filled with possibilities.

I was reminded of something Edward said to me once, when we climbed the scaffold of an old drilling rig and, together, watched the sun descend. *The most beautiful sunsets begin with the passing of a storm. . . .*

Edward was always such a wise and sentimental man. He would not have shown that side of himself to others, but he never hesitated in opening it to me. We were always safe with each other. Watching the sun awaken, I imagined I was sitting with him on the patio, enjoying a summer morning, fresh mugs of coffee steaming into the air. I knew how the garden would smell. I drank it in, felt the dew in the air, tasted the faded scent of night-blooming jasmine as it turned shy in the early light.

By the window, Claude sat silent, as if he were imagining something, too. Finally, he excused himself, saying he'd better take his usual stroll before breakfast. He smiled and patted the edge of the bed as he went past, leaving me to watch the dawning sky alone.

The sunrise had come and gone by the time Betty returned. She breezed into the room, then repossessed the pushpins and lowered the blind. "Who the heck did this?" she grumbled, making it clear that the blind, and everything else in the room, myself included, was too much trouble.

"Nnnoooo," I protested as she closed off the sky, relegating me to a narrow view of the parking lot through the broken slats.

Betty glanced over her shoulder, seeming peeved that I had some speech returning. "Hush up, now. You better rest. You're set for a swallow study today. That oughta be somethin' to look forward to." The blind fell the rest of the way to the windowsill with a slap, and Betty muttered to herself, "Just what I need—one more off-the-peg tube and on mush. Like I got all day to sit around and spoon-feed people." An irritated puff of air escaped her lips as she yanked the covers back over my legs. "G'night, Irene," she said on her way out the door, and I listened as her spongy white shoes squeaked out of earshot.

I lay wondering if Rebecca would come again today. Had she gone to the house to see Teddy and Edward? If so, I hoped Edward was having a good day. On good days, he didn't mind new people. Evenings were not his best time, though. It was as if the Aricept and his other medications wore off by evening, leaving him confused and restless, wandering the house but unable to remember why. Sundowner's syndrome, the doctor called it. Kay-Kay would explain all of that to Rebecca, of course. . . .

Maybe, if she could convince Rebecca to help her, Kay-Kay would bring Teddy and Edward to the nursing center to see me. It was probably too much for Kay-Kay to accomplish on her own and that was why she hadn't brought them to visit already. I hoped that was why. I hoped Edward's state hadn't worsened. If he was worse, surely Kay-Kay would have come to tell me. When had Kay-Kay last been here? Or had she been here? Had she come since I'd been transferred from the hospital? It was all such a blur—the time in the hospital, the time here. The days slid together like spills of wet paint, drab colors swirling and mixing until they formed a quiet gray. I remembered Kay-Kay standing over my bed, telling me everything was all right at home, promising she would take care of Teddy and Edward.

I hoped she had the dishes cleaned up, so Rebecca wouldn't see the place a mess. Kay-Kay could be a little lax about the dishes sometimes. . . .

For a moment, I was back in the kitchen. My kitchen. I was home, and I could clean up the dishes myself. . . .

The door opened, the sound forcing me back to the nursing center. Claude came in with a new supply of pushpins. He raised the blind and secured the string to the wall again, carefully pressing in the pins. "Gret's picture fell off the bulletin board, so these wasn't bein' used." He sat back and again admired his work. "Reckon she'll notice?"

I imagined Gretchen's picture in the dusty crevice behind the CPR chart. It was a wickedly pleasant thought.

Glancing over his shoulder at me, Claude blinked in surprise. "Why, Birdie. I think you're smilin'. 'Course, that out there's somethin' to smile about. Hear all them birds singing? Every bird in the air's come down to join the choir."

I breathed deeply of the new day and listened to the birdsong in the Bradford pear trees outside. My mind slowed, my body relaxed, and the tightness Betty had left behind ebbed away.

"Silver linings." Claude leaned forward to take in more of the sky. "Normally, it'd be *red sky in the morning, sailor take warning*, but I seen mares' tails out there last night, and there's even a few this mornin'." He pointed out the window, but my view was limited. "See them high, thin ones that start at a little tip and whisk upward into the last of the pink? Mares' tails. The mares are runnin' happy this mornin'. They got their tails flying up in the wind. Farmers know what that means. When the mares' tails point down, watch out, but when they're runnin' up, good day ahead. My pappy always watched the mares' tails." Rolling his chair back, he turned to me. "Why, Birdie, I believe you got the prettiest smile I ever seen."

Dimly, I could feel movement tickling my lips. I wondered if Claude was flirting with me, but the thought seemed foolish, considering our present situation. Aside from that, he had to be well over eighty, far older than me, and I was a married woman.

Claude swiveled the wheelchair and returned to contemplating the sky. "My pappy believed in working smart and working hard." He paused to take a hankie from his pocket and wipe a disemboweled fly from the window glass. "He was forty-eight years old when I was born. My folks'd long since give up on ever having kids before they had me and my twin sister. My mama nearly didn't make it through the birth, and the doctors thought we wouldn't make it, either. Back then, they didn't have all the medicine like they do now." A chuckle slipped past his lips and he patted his stomach, which was thin and sunken like the rest of him. "As boy children go, I was a pretty poor disappointment, kinda scrawny, but my pappy never let me know it. He loved us both, just like we was strappin' and perfect."

Claude went on with the story about the farm where he grew up. I heard it only dimly. I was thinking of Edward, and what a good father he'd been to Teddy. He'd never made Teddy feel any less than perfect. It was sad that Rebecca didn't know that part of her father. I'd so tried to discourage him from giving her up to her mother, but he let it happen out of guilt, as a form of penance for leaving Marilyn. There was so much Rebecca didn't know, so much she didn't understand about her father and the events of that year.

Claude was rambling on about the trains when Ifeoma walked in. I was glad it was she and not Betty who discovered him. Ifeoma must have been working an extra shift, which she often did. As far as I could tell, she was a single gal with no family to go home to. I supposed she needed the money additional work could provide. Perhaps she sent it back to someone in Ghana.

Bracing her hands on her hips, she frowned, towering over Claude like a parent correcting an errant child. "You are not to be here, Mr. Fisher."

Claude smiled up at her like she'd said something nice to him. "I was just telling Birdie about my trains." He watched her expectantly as she circled the wheelchair and grabbed the handles. "Ifeoma, did I ever tell you about my trains?"

"Maaa-ny times." Ifeoma sighed, turning him toward the door. "Out wit'cha now. You cannot go about waking all the others—do you hear?"

Putting his feet on the footrests, Claude folded his hands over his stomach and sat back for the ride. "All right, but if Nurse Betty ain't gone home yet, just put me in the closet 'til she leaves."

"Betty must complete her work," Ifeoma defended. "She has no time to chase around an old man."

"If she wouldn't be so hateful to me, I might not hide from her," Claude protested. "I don't never hide from you, Ifay. Back in Buffalo River School, my first-grade teacher had a sayin'—Squawking bird's unwelcome soon no matter the color the wing, but songbird, plain gray, is welcome long as she sings, and sings, and sings."

Ifeoma rolled her eyes, her habitually formal posture softening slightly. "In Ghana, we have also a saying—Old rooster, he loud on the fence, quiet in the stew."

Hooking a finger in the neck of his robe, Claude loosened it like a hangman's noose. "That's a good sayin', too. If you give me my medication, Ifeoma, I won't even fuss."

I heard myself laughing before I felt the muscles contracting, puffs of air lifting me off the bed.

Ifeoma raised a brow at me, surprised. Her full lips parted into a wide, slow smile that was dazzlingly white against her mahogany skin, and she threw her head back, laughing as she went out the door.

I listened as the sound drifted away. It was good to hear someone laugh with abandon, a real laugh, not the forced, controlled kind reserved for places where no one is supposed to be too happy. The picture of her smile stayed with me as I turned back to the window, watching the third-shift staff go home and the day shift come in. I waited for Mary to arrive. She and her little boys would ride the DART bus in at seven. They'd get off at the stop out front, then wait until the day-care van came at seven thirty. She was late today. The bus came and went, and then the day-care van, with no sign of her. She'd never been late before.

Ifeoma came back in and took care of providing my breakfast through the peg tube, and I surmised that she was covering for Mary. As efficient as Ifeoma was, I wanted Mary. The prospects for the day would be dimmer without her.

When Gretchen showed up with her cart, her brawny form blocking the light from the hall, the prospects dimmed further yet.

"You're first on the list today," she informed me brusquely. From her box, she whipped out the wide leather therapy belt she used to move people around. "I hear you been holding out on me. Let's see what you can do." There was axle grease under her fingernails.

I jerked my leg away as she came closer. The movement surprised me.

Gretchen was pleased. Her pale gray eyes sparkled with enthusiasm for her work. "Well, lookie there. That's something new." After lowering the bed, she grasped the belt between her hands and stood over me like Dr. Frankenstein about to flip the switch and illuminate his helpless creature like a Christmas decoration. "Betcha there's more where that came from."

"Don't let her whup ya, Birdie," Claude's voice came from the doorway.

Gretchen glanced over her shoulder. "When I need your opinion, I'll ask for it, Fisher. You better head on back to your room now. I got some special exercises planned for you today."

I had the vague sense that Gretchen was trying to make a funny, and I started laughing again.

Gretchen squinted one eye and peered at me through the other. "Mmm-hmm. Well, look at this. A cheerful patient. I love a cheerful patient." She cracked her knuckles in preparation and closed the window blind. She held the pushpins up, studying them for a moment, then glanced speculatively toward the doorway before tossing them into the corner, where someone could step on them later. "Let's see what else we can do, shall we?"

Our session began whether I wanted it to or not, and within a half hour, Gretchen had explored every inch of my abilities. We'd discovered that some motor control was coming back in my right leg, and I could squeeze the fingers of my right hand a bit. At least Gretchen said I could. I couldn't feel it, really. The fiery muscle cramps started, and I closed my eyes, groaning.

"Looks like we've got some involuntary muscle activity here," Gret observed. "Feel like you've got kind of a charley horse in there?"

Kind of? I thought. *Kind of?* "Eeeehhhsssh," I groaned.

"That's good." Gretchen was delighted. She began kneading my leg between her brawny hands like a long, white lump of dough. The pain ebbed with amazing speed, and for a short while Gretchen and I were on good terms. Then Gretchen grabbed the therapy belt, yanked me onto my side, and pulled me into a pro wrestling move similar to the ones Teddy watched on TV.

"Aaahowww," I moaned.

"Gotta keep those muscles stretched," Gretchen said, then propped me high on the pillows and slipped off the therapy belt. Without a word, she packed up her tools and left the room. If I never saw her again, it would be far too soon. Even as that thought crossed my mind, however, there was a sense of accomplishment, a still, small voice telling me that finally this work and suffering were leading somewhere. These were baby steps, but they were steps.

Mary came in as I was recovering. She looked exhausted, her eyes red-rimmed and puffy. She forced a smile when she realized I was awake. "I hear you're doing well today."

Yes, I thought, and the word came out, "Essshhh." I was disappointed with the sound of it.

Mary smiled again. "See. That was better."

"Eeeyyye?" I wanted to ask why she'd been late this morning, why she looked sad.

She didn't understand, and I experienced the usual moment of irritation at being unable to communicate. I wanted to comfort her, to be useful for something.

"You look good today," she said, moving the pillows on the lower half of the bed, changing the position of my legs. She took the brush from the nightstand to comb my hair. "How about we fix your hair? You've got such pretty hair, Mrs. Parker."

I wanted to tell her she had beautiful hair—thick, in a glossy, chestnut color. It was a shame she kept it wound up in a bun like that. She was a lovely girl, even in her plain, unassuming clothes and with no makeup.

A noise from the doorway caught her attention, and she glanced up, surprised as the door pushed open wider and her little boy slipped through. The top of his head crossed my vision as he bolted to her, holding up a piece of paper with a Magic Marker drawing on it.

"Mama. Wook! Twain-twain!" he squealed, tugging at her skirt and trying to show her the drawing. "Man make twain. Woo-ooo-woo!"

Mary scooped him up, blushing and stepping back from the bed. "That's a pretty train, Brady, but you're not supposed to be in here. You're supposed to be in the TV room until the day-care van comes. Where's Cindy? She said she'd keep an eye on you."

"Her in da pod-dy," Brady replied, unabashedly.

Mary frowned toward the door. "Where's Brandon? Why isn't he watching you?"

"B-andon talk the twain man."

"Mr. Fisher?" Brady shrugged, and she explained, "The man you met last night? The one who told you about his trains?"

Brady nodded vigorously, then swiveled in her arms as his brother skidded through the door. "Brady, you stupid! You're supposed to stay down there!" Brandon's high-pitched voice echoed around the room and escaped into the hall. A few doors down, the moaning woman called out in response.

Mary silenced Brandon with a finger to her lips, then set Brady down and turned to me, her cheeks red, her eyes nervous and fearful. "I'm sorry, Mrs. Parker . . . I really apologize . . . I . . . we had a mix-up this morning and missed the early bus. The day-care van's coming back to get them. Brandon's going to be a little late for school, huh?" Laying a hand on Brandon's head, she forced an encouraging smile and turned him toward the door.

Down the hall, the moaning woman wailed for help, and Brady's eyes grew large.

Mary reached for his hand. "Come on, guys."

I wanted to tell her to wait, not to take the boys away. "A-aaate," I heard myself say, and my hand jerked toward Brady's picture. I tried to conjure the name for the thing that pulls a train, but the words were a jumble in my mind. "Tss-eee?"

Mary squinted, trying to make sense of me. I moved my hand toward the paper again.

"Tss-eee," I repeated, growing hopeful.

Brady clutched his chubby hands around the bed rail, wrinkling the paper as he climbed up like a little boy on monkey bars. "Her wanna see twain," he interpreted, his bright eyes turning my way with a look of eureka.

"Yeee-sssh!" I cheered, suddenly triumphant.

Mary smiled indulgently. "Just for a minute." She glanced toward the door. No doubt she had work to do, and she was already behind from being late this morning.

Hooking an elbow on the railing, Brady tapped my arm and began describing the parts of his train engine. That was the word— "engine." I felt another small burst of victory. I wouldn't lose that word again.

I soaked in the little-boy scent of Brady, the feel of his nearness, the precious ring of his high voice. He was a very bright boy. He knew a lot about trains. Perhaps Mr. Fisher had given him an education.

Claude appeared in the doorway, finally. "Well, there you boys are. Y'all disappeared on me," he said, and wheeled himself into the room.

We were all gathered around the picture, and Brady had shin-nied in next to me, when Dr. Barnhill, whom I remembered from my stay in the hospital, came by. He frowned sternly, surveying the commotion.

Mary scooped Brady off the bed, blushed, and steered the boys, then Mr. Fisher, toward the door. "Sorry, Dr. Barnhill," she mumbled, slipping past him.

"Mary." His reply held little intonation, then he turned to his charts.

"Morning, Doc!" Claude called back.

"Good morning, Claude. How's the pacemaker doing?" Dr. Barnhill answered without looking up.

Claude's hand made a hollow sound, thumping his chair. "Right as rain, Doc. I ain't had a single spell since it got put in. You should of seen me dancin' down the hall while-ago."

Dr. Barnhill chuckled and shook his head as he turned to me. "Looks like you're feeling well enough for visitors, Mrs. Parker."

"Yyy-eeesh!" I answered, and Dr. Barnhill smiled again.

CHAPTER 7

Rebecca Macklin

In the morning, I awoke suspended in time. Blinking against the slanted light, I took in the deco-style ceiling fixture, with its ornately filigreed brass arms and the Tiffany globe of hovering dragonflies. As a child, I'd loved to lie in bed late and watch the sun trail across the ceiling, giving life to the dragonflies. I imagined them like the Skin Horse and the Little Wooden Doll—living beings trapped in suspended animation, awaiting freedom with breathless anticipation.

Watching them again, I felt my childhood self, like a spirit lying atop me, her form relaxed, comfortable, unhurried, her fingers resting loosely against the pillow. I slipped into the memory, and my body was small and wiry, like Macey's—bold with life, with confidence. Fearless.

I'd almost forgotten her, the spirit that floated like a gossamer mist over me now, the girl who lived in this place. She died the summer I turned twelve. She took on fear; she took on the pain of rejection, anger, guilt, self-recrimination; the idea that, if she'd been a better girl, a better daughter, there wouldn't be so much dividing. Dividing possessions, dividing money, dividing family. Dividing her.

Eventually, the dragonflies were only bits of colored glass.

I can't let that happen to Macey, I told myself. *I can't let her take it onto herself.* Even as the thought traveled through my mind, I realized that part of me had been preparing for this day for seventeen years, since Kyle and I met at a convention in San Diego. He was a young lawyer with a Pepperdine education, and I was a hotel concierge, working my way toward a law degree, even though my mother thought it a ridiculous idea. She wanted me to enroll in retail design classes and take over the shop. But at twenty-eight, after having dropped out various semesters to nurse her through lupus flares, I wanted a life of my own, now that her illness had gone into remission. I wanted to be independent, to become something so substantial that even my father would have to stand up and take notice. My success would be proof that I didn't need him, after all.

When I met Kyle, I was attracted to him because he was nothing like my father. Where my father was always reserved, a quiet man, a brooder and a thinker, Kyle was outgoing, a charmer, a people person. He was tan and athletic, a California boy with honey brown hair and the most incredible blue eyes. I was so struck by him the day we met that I knocked over a cup of coffee and doused his briefcase while trying to give him directions to Coronado Island. He just smiled and asked if he could buy me another cup. I said yes, and we spent three hours that evening talking in a café, watching the sun descend over the ocean. After that, I couldn't think about anything but him, and even though my mother tried in every way to prevent it, we flew to Lake Tahoe and got married on a mountaintop four months after we met. For years afterward, my mother pointed out the impetuousness of that decision. Such rash choices usually lead to disaster, she said.

I was determined to prove her wrong. I made up my mind that Kyle and I would have the perfect life. We could achieve it if we worked hard enough. He took a job with a firm, found his way into the lucrative arena of real estate law. Brokering big-money corporate deals suited him, and he was good at it. I finished law school, passed the bar, and moved into immigration law, which seemed a perfect fit for me, after having lived overseas as a child. When I found out I was pregnant with Macey, we made plans to take on a partner and start our own firm so we could spend more time together, perhaps cut back the workload a bit to accommodate the demands of parenthood. Shortly after the firm was formed, Macey came along with wispy blond hair and her father's blue eyes, to complete the picture.

The perfect picture. Why wasn't that good enough for Kyle? Why wasn't *I* good enough?

The cell phone beeped in my purse, warning that the battery was low. What would Kyle say if I called right now? What would he say if I confronted him about the scene in the café?

Deep in my head, an old, familiar admonition warned that I should be practical, careful, not do anything until I was home. *Never, ever trust a man to do the right thing, Rebecca,* my mother advised. *A woman can't afford to be pie-in-the-sky. A woman has to look after herself. . . .* She always followed up with the assessment that, if she'd been smart, she would have hired a better lawyer during her divorce, gotten more. She would have taken the house on Blue Sky Hill. She would have sold it to one of the salvage companies that bought old houses in decaying parts of town, and plucked out the valuable items—stained glass, ornate doors, fixtures, tin ceilings, trim work, wooden floors, expansive mantelpieces—then left the carcasses behind for demolition.

If only she'd been smarter about the divorce, she would have watched that house come down, rather than seeing Hanna Beth move into it.

She'd be livid if she knew you were here, a voice whispered inside me again. *She would hate every part of this.*

Sitting on the edge of the bed, I raked my hands into my hair, combed it back and looked toward the hall, listening for sounds. There was another peanut butter and jelly sandwich plate by the door, with a glass of tea, the ice cubes still fresh this time. Apparently, Teddy was up.

The rhythmic sound of hammering in the backyard caught my attention, and I walked to the window. Teddy was on the red stone patio, clumsily hammering three boards together to make a bench. When he finished and set it upright, the bench was uneven, one leg longer than the other. It listed to one side like a sinking ship as he picked up several potted plants and put them on top. The backyard, a neatly manicured maze of paths and gardens, was filled with an odd conglomeration of lopsided scrap-lumber potting benches. Tiny plants grew in everything from wineglasses to discarded restaurant cups and cutoff soda bottles.

I stared in amazement as Teddy placed potlings on the newest bench, then wiped his hands on his pants, picked up his tools and disappeared into the tiny garden house beneath my grandmother's pecan tree. Family legend said that she'd removed a planned sunroom from the blueprint of the house, so as not to destroy the tree.

Surveying Teddy's menagerie beneath the sprawling shade of the pecan, I wondered if he had always spent his days building benches and filling them with makeshift pots. Where did the plants eventually go? Right now, the backyard was overrun with Teddy's creations.

I considered the question as I took my toiletries and clothes to the bathroom, showered, and dressed. The overhead fixture had burned out in the night, but the light from the long oval window was suffi-cient. Pulling my damp hair into a clip, I felt almost prepared to take on the day, to face my father. In the mirror, I saw in myself his hazel eyes, his dark hair. My mother always claimed those characteristics came from her family, but we both knew they didn't.

What would my father see when he looked at me? Would he see the forty-something woman with my mother's face, her nose, her lips, her high, arched brows, but his eyes, his thick, dark hair? Perhaps he wouldn't recognize me at all. Perhaps I would come as a shock to him, a strange woman descending his stairs.

The idea was unsettling, frightening. Teddy said my father became angry sometimes. If that happened, how would I handle it? What would I do? I had no experience in dealing with an Alzheimer's patient. If he was confused enough to get lost in his own neighborhood, to take sleeping pills in the middle of the day, what else would he do? What had happened in this house since Hanna Beth was taken to the hospital?

Bracing my hands on the counter, I gripped the edges, trying to contain my unhelpful imagination. The first thing, the *very* first thing, I needed to do today was track down this Kay-Kay, find out why she left, and get her to come back. After that, the house needed to be brought into a livable condition, and groceries purchased. Hopefully by then, after talking with Kay-Kay and Hanna Beth's caretakers at the nursing center, I could figure out what should happen here in the long run. The sooner I cleaned up the mess and made some sort of arrangements, the sooner I could return home and try to figure out my life.

Even though it seemed a ridiculous waste of time, illogical in so many ways, I stayed at the mirror long enough to put on makeup. I wanted my father to see me looking my best. Or perhaps I was only delaying the inevitable. When I was finished, I went back to the bedroom and laid everything carefully atop my suitcase—folded, ready for a quick exit.

Gathering my courage, I descended the stairs slowly, one step at a time, craning to look around the arch, to see if anyone was at the bottom.

The entry hall and the living room were empty, illuminated only by natural light from the windows, the house impossibly quiet. I checked the kitchen, then walked through the French doors onto the patio. The air smelled good this morning, fresh with the feel of spring, and sweetly scented by the dampness of a vine growing on the trellis by the chimney. The plant was in beautiful shape, obviously well cared for and painstakingly pruned. Maybe someone came to tend the flower beds—a yard man or gardener. Maybe whoever cared for the yard could help me find Kay-Kay.

"Teddy?" I called, weaving through the menagerie of planting benches toward the garden house. "Teddy, are you in there?"

He came out with a seedling cupped in his hands. Passing through the undersized door on my grandmother's miniature gingerbread creation, he ducked and turned sideways. "Hi, A-becca. Good morning, good morning, good morning!"

It occurred to me that Teddy held none of the resentment toward me that I held toward him. I felt a sense of guilt, a vague unwanted regret for all the nights I'd lain in bed hating him. "Thanks for the sandwich." I nodded over my shoulder toward my room.

Teddy squinted at the window. "It's ohhh-kay." He stretched the word in the middle, staring upward until he lost his balance and stumbled off the stone path. He pointed into the pecan branches near my room. "It a dove, got a nest in the tree. Mourn-ind dove." Curling his lips, he made a birdcall that was so lifelike it caused a bird to answer from somewhere in the hedge near the fence. "There she id," he said with satisfaction. "There mama bird. Jus' like the book *You My Mother?* I got that book." He turned toward the house, seeming to have forgotten the seedling plant in his hands, and decided instead to search for his copy of Dr. Seuss's *Are You My Mother?*

"I'm sorry I slept so long last night. I really meant to pick up a pizza or something," I said, wondering what should come next.

"I like pizza." Teddy's brows rose, his eyes broadening with anticipation.

"I'll order some later. It looks like you're about out of groceries." Which was an understatement. My father and Teddy were surviving on two loaves of bread, a jar of jelly, and a tub of generic peanut butter, as far as I could tell. And that brought up another question—how could anyone walk out and leave them in this condition?

"Kay-Kay bring the gross-ries." Teddy looked toward the bay windows on the breakfast nook, as if he expected her to appear there any moment.

Clearly, Kay-Kay hadn't brought groceries in a while. "Teddy, do you know how to get in touch with Kay-Kay? Where she lives, or her phone number? "

Teddy's fingers began kneading the plant roots, sending a shower of potting soil over his tennis shoes. He shook his head, his expression narrowing with apprehension.

"I'm not mad," I interjected quickly. "I just thought I should probably call her about the groceries."

"Kay-Kay bring the gross-ries." The anxiety in his hand movements increased until pieces of root drifted downward with the soil.

"Oh, I know," I rushed out, once again vaguely aware of his size, his strength, the fact that I had no idea what he was capable of. "I thought probably I could call her and see when she's going to come with the groceries. Maybe I could pick up some extra things. Did she bring you the bread and peanut butter and jelly?" I clung to the momentary hope that someone was visiting regularly, providing food, at least.

Teddy shook his head. His shoulders sagged forward, and he blinked rapidly. The mother in me recognized that body language. He looked like Macey caught in the act and searching for an explanation that wouldn't get her grounded.

"Did someone else bring the peanut butter and jelly?"

Teddy shook his head, still hooding his eyes.

"Did Daddy Ed buy it?" Another negative response. "Did you buy it?" The nearest grocery store was miles from here. There was a car in the garage, but surely Teddy wasn't allowed to drive it. Surely my father didn't drive anymore.

Teddy began weeping, his shoulders shuddering with wracking sobs. His hands closed over the plant, crushing it.

"It doesn't matter," I soothed, feeling nervous and inadequate. "It doesn't matter, Teddy. Don't worry about—"

A crash from the house, the sound of a door hitting the wall and reverberating, brought me up short. "Marilyn! Mar-i-lyn!" My father's voice was the deep baritone I remembered from childhood.

Teddy dropped the plant and the soil, turned and ran toward the garden house. Tripping on the stoop, he fell through the door in a pile, then scrambled forward on his hands and knees and disappeared.

"Mari-lyyyn!" It occurred to me suddenly that the name my father had called out was my mother's. The realization was bizarre, unreal, something my mind couldn't process at first. Why was he in the house screaming for my mother, of all people? "Mari-lyyyn!" The call was fearful, panicked, demanding a response.

Adrenaline rushed like an electrical current through my body. I ran across the patio, threw open the back door, found my father crouched beside the coffee table, throwing piles of magazines, dirty dishes, and rotten food onto the floor in a frantic search for something. He batted a glass of soured orange juice across the room and it shattered against the heavy oak fireplace, spreading shards of glass, droplets of juice, and chunks of mold over the hearth and into last winter's ashes.

"Stop!" I heard myself scream. "What are you doing?" I was on top of my father, grabbing his arm before I'd registered the thought that, even now, he was a large man. "Stop!" I hollered again. "Stop it!"

Rocking back on his heels, he swiveled toward me, blinked as if my presence surprised him. I backed away, slowly straightening as he stood up.

"You're . . ." He paused, let his arms, loose-skinned and thin compared to the strong arms I remembered, hang at his sides. His head tilted as he took me in, his eyes sharpening with a look of recognition. "There you are."

After thirty-three years, it wasn't how I'd pictured our reunion. "Hi, Dad." It wasn't what I'd imagined I would say, either. I'd imagined something with more drama. I'd role-played this moment so many times, but never this way.

He leaned forward, grabbed my shoulders so quickly I didn't have time to react. "You're here." He gasped out the words with a long sigh, pulled me close in a hug I didn't return, but didn't push away. His body sagged against mine, as if he had been waiting for me for a very long time. I felt his ribs and collarbones beneath his loose white undershirt. He seemed only half the man I remembered.

"I'm here." A lump rose in my throat. My emotions were twisted inside, indiscernible. In some little-girl part of myself I didn't want to acknowledge, I'd always dreamed that my father would be glad to see me—that he'd wanted to continue fighting for contact with me, but Hanna Beth wouldn't let him. I knew better, of course. If my father had really wanted me, he would have insisted that the custody order be enforced. Instead, he sent the checks on time, paid for my health insurance until I was of age, and otherwise let go. If it weren't for monetary considerations and the birthday cards my mother helped me send back unopened, he would have ceased to exist in my life.

He moved his hands to my shoulders again, pushed me back hard enough that I stumbled, and he held me up. His attention darted around the room, then fixed on me. He whispered, "Marilyn, *those people* are here again. They've taken my pills. They hid them somewhere."

Breath rushed from my lungs, and I stood in a hollow, airless shell, caught between logic and the strange reality of this decaying house, in which my father called me by my mother's name. Was it really possible that he didn't know who I was? That his mind was so clouded, so tangled in the past that he believed he was talking to my mother? His eyes pleaded for me to understand, to respond. "What . . . what people?"

His glance flicked back and forth, checking the corners. Leaning around me, he peered into the darkened kitchen. "*Those people.* They went all through the house last night. They've taken my pills." He put his face close to my ear. "They say things about me, you know. It's not true. None of it's true."

His fingers squeezed my shoulders tighter. Nervous perspiration dripped down my back. When I'd watched him sleeping last night, crumpled in his chair, old and harmless, I'd assumed I could handle him, take care of his needs, figure out what had to be done here. Now it was clear that I'd had no real concept of the problem. Had things been this way before Hanna Beth went to the hospital, or had they become worse since she left? How could she possibly have taken care of him, like this? "There's no one here." I'd intended the words to be firm, but instead they trembled. "It's all right. Let's just sit down a minute."

His nostrils flared, and he shook his head vehemently, then glanced toward the window. "I *saw* one of them in the backyard. I didn't tell him anything."

"That was Teddy."

He gave the name no reaction, other than to release me and cross to the opposite side of the room. "They eat all the food. Now, they've taken my pills." Turning unsteadily, he lost his balance and collided with the door frame. "They ate the bread last night. There's an empty wrapper."

"Teddy and I ate the bread." Surely, faced with enough logic, enough reality, he would emerge from whatever world he was in, and step into the one in which I needed his help. "I'll buy some groceries today. Let's not worry about the bread. I need to know how to get in touch with Kay-Kay. Do you know where I can find her phone number?"

He pushed off the door frame and went to the entry hall without answering. I clung briefly to the hope that he was going after an address book or list of contacts. His footsteps passed over the ceramic tile, then echoed across the ladies' parlor in the front of the house. "See there? There's *their car* in the drive."

"It's my car." Taking a deep breath, I started through the entry hall. "I parked it there. It's my car. No one's here but me."

My father moved the heavy velvet curtain aside, peeking through the parlor window. "There's one of them on the lawn. He'll steal things. They always steal things. They hide things. They hid the car keys."

Thank goodness, I thought, and the reaction was almost comical. On the heels of that thought, there was sadness, a full realization of my father's plight. This man who had traveled the world, who loved antique cars and flew small planes as a hobby, couldn't even drive anymore. He didn't know where he was, *when* he was. He was seeing imaginary people out . . . A movement on the lawn caught my eye. I pulled the curtain back. There *was* someone on the lawn—a power company employee, with a van.

The reason for the house being dark, for the lights not working in the bathroom, the refrigerator not humming in the kitchen this morning suddenly became clear. I hit a light switch. Nothing.

"Stay here," I ordered, and rushed to the front door, struggled to open the host of locks, then dashed across the lawn.

By the time I reached the curb, the meter man was getting back into his van. He rolled down the window when I knocked. "Excuse me. Our power is out this morning."

He twisted to look at the clipboard on his dash. "Power's been turned off for nonpayment, ma'am. You'll have to go down to the office to get it turned back on." He wasn't rude exactly, just matter-of-fact, as if he dealt with this situation often.

"You can't turn off the power," I protested, desperation pounding in my ears. "My father's wife has been in the hospital. He has Alzheimer's. He probably doesn't know how to pay the bill. Please. I'll give you a check right now."

He held up both hands, palms out. "I can't help you, ma'am. You'll have to go down to the main office. I just do the meter work. I'm sorry, ma'am."

Without waiting for an answer, he pulled away, and I stood on the curb, exactly where I'd been thirty-three years ago. I wanted to do now what I'd done then—climb into the car, drive away, leave Blue Sky Hill and never look back.

CHAPTER 8

Hanna Beth Parker

The day-care van delivered Mary's boys to her at the end of her shift, rather than their father bringing them. Mary didn't linger, letting them pick flowers from the bushes or catch grasshoppers, but packed them into the faded minivan her husband had left in the parking lot earlier. She drove away, seeming in a hurry.

For three days, Mary didn't come back, and neither did Rebecca. With the passage of each day, I felt a deeper foreboding. Sleep might have been a refuge, but each time I closed my eyes, I dreamed of taking Teddy, just a toddler, to the seashore down at Galveston, where Aunt Rae, my father's sister, lived in an old beach house my uncle Hugh built before he died. In the dream, Aunt Rae threw her arms wide and hugged me. Her love wrapped around me like a favorite coat, warming away the chill of loneliness that had lingered since I'd chosen the scarlet path of unwed motherhood.

Teddy toddled to the top of the dune, excited to explore the beach and the wide expanse of curling water.

"I guess we're heading to the beach." Aunt Rae started after him, turned her face toward the sun, gazed out over the water and sand. Aunt Rae had always been beautiful, red-haired and olive-skinned, with full lips and a stunning smile. She looked like my father. I could see him in her face, and it was almost as if he were there, watching the grandchild he refused to acknowledge scamper toward the shore.

Putting on her sun hat, Aunt Rae laughed. She had my father's laugh. I longed to hear that laugh again, to win it from my father's mouth, but I couldn't give up Teddy, no matter how strong my father's archaic belief that the respectable thing would have been to give my baby to a family with two parents, not to condemn him to a life that would always be marked by the untoward label given to fatherless children. When I wouldn't sign adoption papers, my father pleaded with me to at least divulge the identity of Teddy's father, so the man could be compelled to do the right thing. I couldn't tell him that Teddy's father had married someone else, that the communiqué from his family lawyer had made his choice perfectly clear, sealed his decision without ambiguity. He was committed to his fiancée, to their planned life together. He didn't want me, and he didn't want Teddy.

In the dream, I looked up suddenly, noticed that Teddy was too far out in the surf. "Teddy, come back!" I called, but he couldn't hear. "Teddy!" I tried to stand up, and the sand sank beneath me. "Teddy!" He was toddling farther and farther out into the water, mesmerized by the foamy waves, cautionless as always. The water lapped at his waist. A wave caught him, splashed over his chest and knocked him from his feet. He came up, turned toward the watery horizon, skimmed his small hands across the surface and started outward again.

"Teddy!" I fought to rise, clawed away the earth, but there was only more sand. "Teddy!" I screamed.

"Mrs. Parker . . . Mrs. Parker. I'm here. It's all right. It's okay."

I dragged open my eyes, focusing on Mary's face. "Mmmaarrry." The word surprised me. I wondered if she was part of the dream, too. She'd been away so long.

"Hi." Leaning over my bed, she fixed the pillow and moved my hair out of my face. Up close, her eyes were strained, her smile weary. "You've gotten a lot better these last few days. You were talking in your sleep, and I could understand you. I hear you've had good therapy sessions, too. Gretchen was really proud of you, and the speech therapist just bragged and bragged on how well you're doing. I'm sorry I haven't been here. I had . . ." She paused, looked away. "Brandon's asthma's been acting up and the after-school day care wouldn't take him." I could tell there was more to Mary's absence, something significant.

I feared the case to be the same with Rebecca. If it hadn't been for Claude coming now and again, complaining about Mary being gone and mentioning that he, too, wondered why Rebecca hadn't returned, I might have thought I dreamed her visit. The clearer my mind became in the present, the more the past weeks seemed unreal. Sometimes, just waking up, I felt as if it were all a dream, as if I could step from bed, and walk to my garden, and begin spring planting, just as normal as you please. The illusion never lasted long, particularly with Gretchen's daily sessions, and new visits from an occupational therapist, and the girl with the VitalStim swallowing machine helping me to eat ice cream and other mushy substances. In the afternoons, there was also a speech therapist. She showed me picture cards—scissors, computer, doll, sandwich, knife—and I tried to deliver the words from my brain to my mouth, and to remember what each item was used for. Not an easy task, but she insisted that I was improving.

Mary seemed to agree, but even so she frowned. "You look a little upset this morning."

"Drrreeemm." The word came out surprisingly easily, so I tried again. "Dreeem-um."

Mary nodded. "Your brain's healing. It's a good sign."

Despite her encouragement, I felt uneasy, uncertain. Underlying everything was the concern about what might be happening at home. What if, at this very moment, Rebecca was making plans to close up the house, making *arrangements* for Teddy and Edward? Surely, Kay-Kay would not allow such a thing without a fight, without coming to me. Kay-Kay had been devoted to Edward's care for over a year, ever since it became a problem to leave him at home while I went to the grocery, the bank, the doctor's office. Kay-Kay kept the house running, assisted with the cleaning, the gardening, frequently stayed overnight for no extra pay when Edward was having a difficult evening. Kay-Kay had seen us through so many difficult days. She wouldn't let Rebecca waltz in and change everything.

Mary raised the bed and repositioned my legs. She forced a smile, but her face was lined with worry that made her look like an old woman in a girl's body. "Did your daughter come back to visit? I'm sorry I wasn't here to talk to her."

"Nnooo."

Mary concealed her surprise, then changed the subject. She unwound a cord from the safety rail and slid the remote under my hand on the bed. "Let's try this. I bet you might be able to get the bed to go up and down, maybe even operate the TV." She moved my fingers onto the buttons. I felt it dimly, like a sensation underwater. "See, this square one is the TV, then beside it is the channel button, then under that, the remote control for the bed. Feel that? The little triangles for up and down? Under that, the rectangle is your nurse call button."

"Nooo." I pulled my hand away. I didn't want to talk about the television. I wanted to know why Rebecca hadn't come back. I wanted someone to find out, to tell me.

Mary assumed my frustration was centered around the feeble workings of my fingers. "Don't worry about it. Just keep trying. You can do it."

"Rrrr-beeeck." The ability to produce a decent semblance of the word, such a simple thing, gave me a quick sense of triumph. "Rrrr-beeek-uh?"

Mary cocked her head to one side, deciphering the sound. "Rebecca?" she said finally. "Your daughter?"

"W-aare?" I asked. "Gen-boo?" The last word was a disappointment. I was trying to ask if Mary could find out where Rebecca was, why she hadn't come back.

Mary's eyebrows, arched like a little china doll's, drew together. "K-ul. K-ul R-baa." *Call Rebecca, call Rebecca, call Rebecca.* My fingers clenched in frustration. My breathing sped up until my throat became dry and I fell into a fit of coughing and choking.

Mary grabbed the cup from the bedside table, dribbled a few drops of water into my mouth with the bendy straw. "Ssshhh," she whispered. "Don't try so hard. It'll come. Stress makes things worse, that's all. I think you better rest now, Mrs. Parker. I'll be back again later." After tucking the sheet around me, she moved toward the door.

I didn't want her to go. I wanted her to call Rebecca, to call Kay-Kay, to find out what was happening at my house. I willed my hand to move to the remote, to lay over the button. My arm jerked, then moved, my fingers landing on the remote. The TV blared to life, and Mary jumped back, then threw a hand over her chest.

"Oh, my gosh," she breathed, lowering the volume, then returning to the bed with a triumphant smile. "You did it, Mrs. Parker. Good for you!" She moved my finger to the channel button. "There, now you can watch what you want, and you won't be bored." She patted my hand, then started toward the door again, adding, "Good for you."

I rested my wrist on the sound button, pushed down, and the TV blared again.

Mary turned in the alcove, braced her hands on her thin hips, quirking an eyebrow. "Well, Mrs. Parker!" she said, shocked and a little aggravated. "You're going to have us both in trouble." She crossed the room again and reached for the remote.

I rolled away, dragging it with me.

"Mrs. Parker!" Leaning over the bed, she recovered the remote and turned off the TV, sounding as forceful as I'd ever heard her.

"What in the world has gotten into you? You are going to have to calm down." She tied the remote to the bed rail, out of reach, then helped me onto my pillows again and fixed the sheet.

Desperation welled in my eyes, spilled over. Mary's face became tender. "It's all right, okay? Just try to relax and we'll talk again later. There are some volunteer readers in today. I'll ask one of them to come by and read to you for a while. It's good for your language processing. How would that be?"

I lay back on the bed and closed my eyes without answering. My legs had started to ache and burn, and I was suddenly exhausted. I didn't have the energy to continue trying to make myself understood.

"Ssshhh," Mary soothed. "Just rest." She slipped away on silent feet, assuming I was drifting off to sleep. Instead, I stared out the window, tried to conjure a plan to make her understand. Nothing came to mind.

Sometime later, the squeal of the door hinges told me I had a visitor. I turned away from the window, hoping it was Rebecca. Instead, Mary was coming back, pushing a woman in a wheelchair. The woman, her hair plaited in a thin gray braid behind her head, her face weathered and wrinkled, looked older than me, but her manner, the upward tilt of her chin, her brightly colored Bugs Bunny sweat suit, testified to a spunkiness that even the wheelchair couldn't camouflage. Any other time, I would have wanted to know her, but right now, I wasn't in the mood for guests.

"Oh, good, you're awake," Mary said as she wheeled the woman around to the side of my bed and parked the chair. "Mrs. Parker, this is Ouita Mae Barnhill, Dr. Barnhill's grandmother. She's here with us, healing up from a little surgery and doing some volunteer reading to keep busy. Dr. Barnhill thought you two might enjoy spending time together."

I wanted to tell Ouita Mae that I wouldn't be much company,

but perhaps the lack of words was a mercy, considering my mood. In truth, it was kind of her to read to me, particularly when she was just healing up from surgery. Clearly, Dr. Barnhill came by his caring ways naturally.

Mary gave me an encouraging smile as she exited the room, leaving the two of us alone.

Ouita Mae sighed, reached for the book on the table. "You probably don't really want company," she said matter-of-factly, opening the book to the place where my last volunteer reader, a student from SMU, had tucked in a scrap of plastic from her soda bottle label as a marker. "I didn't want company after I had my stroke. I couldn't talk, nor anything, and I hated having people see my face saggin' and my hands curled up. I looked lots worse than you, by the way. You don't look bad a'tall, sweetie. Of course, you're younger than me, so you'll heal up in no time. I was eighty when I had my stroke. Left side." She held her hand in the air between us, turning it over and back. "You can't tell it now, though. Don't let this chair fool you, either. That's just because I had this orthoscotic surgery day before yesterday. I got some problems with my legs, but I usually get around pretty good."

"Ooooh," I said, and for the first time in weeks, the hope I'd been fostering grew and radiated warmth. If Ouita Mae Barnhill could come through a stroke and return to a normal life, so could I.

Clearing her throat, Ouita Mae slipped her reading glasses onto the end of her nose and turned her attention to *Pirate's Promise*. "I like a good love story with a happy ending," she remarked, then began reading aloud the story of Gavin and Marcella's star-crossed romance. When we reached a scene in which Gavin and Marcella could no longer resist the attraction between them, she paused after the first kiss, skimmed ahead, and said, "This don't leave much to the imagination. Reckon it'll do to say that, even though his pirates raided her father's ships and caused her daddy to lose all his money and die a broken man, she's sure got a thing for him, and she can't keep herself from it. He ain't lookin' for a woman, but he hasn't ever seen one like her."

I couldn't help myself. I laughed.

Ouita Mae smiled at me. "Makes me think of bein' young, lookin' at a boy, and feelin' the kind of love that takes your breath away. You know, I got a sweet little neighbor girl who's twenty-four. I've known her since she was born. She's been dating the same boy off and on since her junior year of high school. After all these years, they decided they ought to get engaged, start planning a wedding. A part of me was sad to see it, a little. I'm afraid she'll just get married, go on through life with the fella that seems safe and easy, and she'll never feel the kind of passion that Marcella's got for Gavin." Misty-eyed, she turned to me and added, "You know?"

"Yeeesh," I whispered, because I did know. I had that kind of passion for Edward. Even now, I felt incomplete without him near.

Ouita Mae rested her chin on her hand and sighed, then returned to the story. In her relaxed, slow-paced East Texas accent, the tale of Lord Winston's plot to steal Marcella from her pirate lover and force her into marriage took on an entirely new flavor—a bit like hearing John Wayne read Shakespeare. Occasionally, Ouita Mae paused to insert comments that made me laugh. I let my worries go and just enjoyed her company.

By the time she closed the book, the lunch trays were being delivered, and in the hall, ambulatory patients were moving to the cafeteria. I was surprised that so much time had passed. "If that Lord Winston isn't a sorry lot. He's got Gavin and Marcella gettin' along about like two alley cats in a tow sack," she said, as she set the book on my night table. She braced it against the lamp so that the pirate's picture was facing outward. "Thought you might want somethin' to look at." Winking at me, she turned her chair around. "I'll come back tomorrow, and we'll find out what happens next."

"Aaann-ooo," I said, which didn't sound much like *thank you*, but Ouita Mae nodded, patting my foot as she wheeled her chair past.

"Don't you think a thing of it, y'hear?"

Mary poked her head in the door. "You ready to go down to the dining hall, Mrs. Barnhill?"

I beckoned Mary to the bed, moving my arm in a clumsy, sweeping motion, then letting it fall to the mattress.

Mary crossed the room and stood by me, glanced at the pirate on the book's cover, and blushed. "Did you need something, Mrs. Parker?"

"K-ul Rrr-buk-uhhh."

Mary sighed, inclining her head sympathetically. "I'm sorry, Mrs. Parker. I don't know what you're asking for. Want me to turn on the TV?" She picked up the remote.

"K-ul Rrr-buk-uhhh," I said again.

Mary lifted her hands helplessly. "I'm sorry."

"Oh, for heaven's sake." Ouita Mae paused halfway to the door. "It's clear as day. She wants you to *call Rebecca*."

Mary's face lifted with understanding as Ouita Mae disappeared down the hall. "Call Rebecca," she repeated. "I'm sorry, Mrs. Parker, I should have gotten that."

"Yesssh," I repeated, relieved that finally I'd communicated. "K-ul R-buk-uh."

Mary's look of excitement quickly faded. "Mrs. Parker, they've been trying to call the contact number in your file for a couple days now, and it's not a working line." Fidgeting with the water glass, she frowned. "They don't have any way to get ahold of your family."

They don't have any way to get ahold of your family. The reality of the words struck a hard blow. All my previous joy flew from the room like a sweet scent before a storm. Why would our phone have been disconnected? How? Much of the recent past was foggy in my memory, but years ago, Edward had arranged for all of our monthly bills to be drafted automatically from our bank account. We'd had a disagreement about it, because I was afraid the bank's computer might fail to pay on time. Edward laughed and said that computers don't forget things, people do. There was no way our bills could have gone unpaid.

Unless Rebecca had changed things. Unless, as I feared, she was closing down the house, moving Teddy and Edward . . . where? What if this was her final revenge for my taking her father from her all those years ago? Having heard only her mother's side of the story, she probably had no reason to feel charitable toward Edward, or toward me. At twelve, she was powerless, but now, all the power rested with her.

The idea tensed the pit of my stomach, tying a hard knot of fear. I grabbed Mary's hand on the railing. "Myeee hhh . . ." I couldn't form the word house. *My house. My house. My house.* "Myeee hhhow." *That isn't right. That's not right.* I turned my body, tried to reach for the TV remote.

"Mrs. Parker, what are . . . the TV?" Mary took the remote and turned on the television. "All right, tell me when you see something you want to watch."

I waited while she flipped through the channels. A commercial came on, something about vinyl siding. "Hhhow! Hhhow!"

Mary turned to the screen, took in the picture. "House?" she muttered, then, "House! Your house?" Her lips parted in a silent *Ohhh.* "Mrs. Parker, you can't go home right now. You have to stay here until you're better."

"Nnno." The sound was louder than I'd expected. It filled the room "Yyyou ugg-go." We'd practiced *stop* and *go* in speech therapy, thank goodness. I punched my hand clumsily toward the screen again.

She considered the words for a moment, like a contestant trying to solve a puzzle. "You want me to go home?"

My hand fell against the railing, my arm exhausted by the effort. "Yyyyou hhhowt uggg-go. Myeee."

"You want me to go to your house?"

"Yesh," I breathed, and let my head sink to the pillow. "Yyyou ugg-go."

Mary drew back, unsettled by the dawning realization of what I was asking her to do—something far beyond the scope of her job. What choice did I have but to ask, to plead with her? There was no one else. There was only Mary, with her wide jade-colored eyes and her soft heart, who might understand that I needed to know what was happening to Edward and Teddy.

Without Mary, I was helpless.

CHAPTER 9

Rebecca Macklin

The days were passing in a blur of phone calls and visits to utility companies, cleaning the house and throwing out all the rotten food, hours spent digging through piles of mail, both opened and unopened, which my father had randomly combined with paperwork from the file cabinet in his office and stacked in odd places. There seemed to be no pattern to his actions, only a determination to protect various pieces of information from *those people*, who came and went silently, rummaging through the house, moving things, hiding bills beneath the paint cans in the garage, stealing the peanut butter and tucking it under the bathroom sink with the spare toilet paper. When I brought home groceries on the first day, half of them disappeared before the next morning. My father insisted that *those people* had come and eaten the food. I found hamburger rotting under his bed two days later. If he didn't take his sleeping pill in the evening, he moved through the rooms at night, turning the lights on and off, sometimes talking to *those people*, sometimes threatening them, sometimes hiding from them.

He wanted to be sure that I, Marilyn, didn't listen to anything *those people* said about him. They told lies. They wanted him to be fired from his job. In the evenings, when his delusions reached their height, he was certain that Teddy was one of *those people*. He screamed at Teddy, tried to make him leave the house. Teddy ran upstairs to his bedroom, turned out the lights, and stayed, no matter what time it was. My father had trouble navigating the stairs, so Teddy was safe there. If he turned out the lights and kept silent, Daddy Ed would eventually stop hollering from the entry hall.

Teddy had developed an amazing set of coping mechanisms for dealing with the increasing dementia. He'd learned to get up early, make peanut butter and jelly sandwiches for breakfast, eat quickly, leave a sandwich by my father's chair, then go to the backyard, where various stray cats waited for crusts of bread and Teddy's tender attention.

For whatever reason, my father wouldn't enter the backyard, so Teddy could remain there unmolested, except for an occasional back-door rant, during which Teddy hid in the garden house. When Daddy Ed slept in the afternoons, Teddy came in, made sandwiches again, took one, left one by the chair, then went back outside. In the evening, he sneaked inside and hid in the coatroom or the maid's pantry until my father went to bed. On windy nights, he carried seedlings with him in his makeshift pots and put them inside where they wouldn't blow over. He was preparing for spring planting of the flower beds, convinced that growing the plants and readying the flower beds would make Hanna Beth come home.

Watching him work outside, I felt a nagging sympathy and an intense sadness. Teddy knew everything about plants—how to grow them, how to nurture them, how to prune the rosebushes and thin the iris bulbs—but he couldn't understand the events taking place inside the house. He couldn't comprehend the severity of his mother's condition, or the fact that raising a multitude of seedlings wouldn't bring her back. He was convinced that if he kept planting, she would come. When she did, he was certain she would fix Daddy Ed, and things would be normal again.

If only the problem were that simple. After three days of house-cleaning, sneaking the gas man in to relight the pilot lights on the stove and furnace, replacing pieces of the cable box, which I later found hidden in a kitchen drawer, and arranging for the electric service, I felt as if I'd been dropped into some strange docudrama about the monumental problems facing the elderly and mentally ill.

The difficulty of caretaking, an issue I'd only considered in the context of my mother's lupus, became increasingly clear. In my mother's case, there were shop workers and a live-in maid to help her. Even on her worst days, I knew she was in good hands when I couldn't be there with her. When I returned, she would be peacefully reading a book or watching TV in the apartment above the shop, or she'd be downstairs rearranging displays and showing customers the latest goodies from the garment district. Her surroundings would be immaculately clean, everything in order, sweet-smelling, despite the collection of prescribed medications, exotic essential oils, and herbal remedies on the counter.

When I left the house on Blue Sky Hill, even just to go to the closest grocery store, to the electric or gas company offices, or to the bank in a futile effort to gain access to my father's accounts, I had no idea what I would return to. I left Teddy behind in hopes that if something happened, he could handle it, but the truth was that Teddy was even more lost than I was.

On the third day, the utilities finally in order, the television fixed, and stashes of rotten food cleaned out, the house took on a vague sense of sanity. My father found the television both mesmerizing and calming. The old reruns on TV Land were a particular comfort to him. They fit neatly within the time period into which his mind had slipped. He'd decided that we had just returned from Saudi.

"There you are, Marilyn," he'd say, when I walked through the living room. "Shouldn't Rebecca be coming in from school?"

There was a strange satisfaction in his asking about me. The sensation came, unwanted, then flew away when I reminded myself that he wasn't really thinking about me, just remembering the past.

Teddy didn't fit easily into his recollections. After trying repeatedly to explain who Teddy was, I finally gave up and started telling him that Teddy was the gardener. Trying to force the current reality on my father only caused him to become agitated, loud, and aggressive.

Teddy was happy to be the gardener, as long as the house remained relatively peaceful and the TV in his bedroom was working again. He came in and out the back door of the garage and typically sneaked up the stairs when my father wasn't looking.

After three days of intermittently searching for information about my father's doctors and medications, calling pharmacies listed on aging prescription bottles, and talking to administrators at Hanna Beth's nursing center, I was beginning to wonder if my father had ever received any supervised medical treatment for his illness. The drawers in the kitchen and master bath contained a hodgepodge of prescriptions, filled at different times by various online pharmacies—strange, considering that there was no computer in the house. When I logged on to the Internet with my laptop and Googled the attending physicians listed on the bottles, they hailed from locations throughout the United States and Canada, even Mexico. As far as I could discern, he hadn't seen a local doctor in well over a year. The last prescription authorized by a nearby doctor was for Aricept, an Alzheimer's medication. I called Dr. Amadi's office and explained my father's situation.

"I don't have your name as an emergency contact in your father's file," the receptionist informed me. "I can't give out his medical information."

"May I bring him in for an appointment?"

"Yes, ma'am. When did you want the appointment?"

"Tomorrow."

"Ma'am, we're running three weeks out on appointments."

My frustration bubbled up and poured into the phone. "You don't understand. I need to bring him in *tomorrow*. His wife is in the hospital, and he has been alone in the house. I have no idea what medications he's been taking, or should be taking, and he can't tell me. He's confused, and he's seeing things that aren't there. I don't know how long he's been this way, and there's no one I can ask. I *need* to bring him in *tomorrow*."

"Ma'am, our files show that we haven't seen Mr. Parker in well over a year. I don't have any record of a request for a transfer of his files, but he *must* have been receiving treatment somewhere else."

I paused, rubbing clammy palms on my jeans, struggling to keep my desperation from spiraling out of control. I was tired of uncertainty and fear, tired of getting the runaround from utility companies, tired of the bank refusing to allow me to access my father's accounts, tired of trying to produce order from insanity, alone. "I don't *have* any more recent information. I need to bring him in *tomorrow*. This is an emergency . . . *please*."

The receptionist sighed. "I can squeeze you in at ten thirty."

Relief opened my lungs. "We'll be there. Can you tell me where your office is located?" As I jotted down the information, a new problem crept to the forefront. So far, I hadn't seen my father leave the house. My contact with him had consisted of trying to mollify his outbursts, keep him calm—either sleeping or watching television—convince him to take in regular meals when he wasn't hungry, and reassure him that *those people* had left the house. I had no idea what might be involved in getting him into the car and to a doctor's office.

After hanging up the phone, I went in search of Teddy. At least he was aware of Hanna Beth's routines, and some information was better than none. He would know how often she took Daddy Ed out of the house, and how she accomplished it.

I looked for Teddy in the backyard, then in his room, the kitchen, the garage. Finally, it became clear that he was gone.

My pulse raced faster and faster until it thrummed in my ears, and I felt dizzy. I paced back and forth in the entry hall, looking out the front door, checking up and down the street, alternately walking to the living room and making sure my father was still settled in front of the TV.

An hour passed, then another twenty minutes. My father fell asleep; I stood on the front steps, trying to decide what to do. In the days I'd been there, Teddy hadn't left the yard. He'd asked me repeatedly to take him to see his mother, and I'd told him I couldn't until I had things straightened out at the house. What if he'd grown impatient and decided to try the DART system again? What if he was wandering around town on buses and light rail trains, alone, lost, at the mercy of anyone he might happen across? It was already almost five o'clock. What if darkness fell, and he was still out there?

I checked the living room again, then grabbed my purse and car keys. Hopefully, my father would sleep until I got back. If not, there would be trouble. When he awoke in the early evenings, he was always confused, his paranoia heightened. If I, Marilyn, wasn't there to redirect his attention with some supper and then more TV, he started wandering the house, looking for *those people*, and hiding various items in secret places.

Please, God, please, please, I muttered under my breath, hurrying to my car. The plea, the prayer in my head surprised me, but at the moment there was no one else to ask. *Please keep him quiet until I get home. Please let Teddy be all right.*

The muscles in my neck and arms stretched tight as I started down the block, gripping and ungripping the steering wheel. From the driveway of a neighboring garage house that was probably a rental, a dark-haired man with a ponytail watched me. Glancing toward my father's house, he took an art portfolio and a briefcase from his car and turned away.

I pulled to the curb, rolled down the window, and called out, "Excuse me. Have you seen a man walk by? He's tall, salt-and-pepper hair? He was wearing a yellow T-shirt and jeans."

The neighbor swiveled his head in my direction, keeping his body pointed toward the garage door, showing a silent reluctance to get involved. "Just got home," he said, then hesitated a moment, checking up and down the street. "Sorry."

"Do you know anyone else who might have been around today—any of the neighbors I could call?" I pressed.

He shifted a step closer, seeming to consider the request, then pushed the car door shut. "I just moved in a couple weeks ago. You might ask at the shops down on the corner of Vista." Satisfied to have pointed me in another direction, he tucked the portfolio under his arm. "If I see him go by, I'll tell him you're looking," he added, then disappeared into the garage.

I wondered if he was the one who'd called the police about Teddy and my father.

I continued down the street, rounded the block, turned onto Vista again, drove past the shops at the corner of Vista and Greenville. I asked about Teddy at the convenience store, where the clerk claimed to have seen him in the past but not today. I continued winding through the neighborhood streets, past quiet houses, past a creek and an overgrown park with playground equipment rusty from disuse, down a few blocks to the border of Blue Sky Hill, where small, bungalow-style houses lined the edges of neighborhoods my mother would have referred to as *unsavory,* or *off-hill,* which meant pretty much the same thing. In front of a flamingo pink Prairie-style house, two women who looked out of place in the low-rent district were locking up after an estate sale. I pulled over and asked them about Teddy. They said he'd walked by earlier and stopped to take some empty foam cups from the trash pile out front.

"He didn't hurt anything," one of the women added as she watched me from behind the old woven-wire yard fence. "He just took the cups and went on down the block."

I thanked her for the information, then sat trapped in a moment of uncertainty before finally turning toward home. Maybe Teddy had come back by now, and in any case, I didn't dare leave my father alone any longer.

At the condominium construction site on Vista, workers were packing up their tools for the day. I pulled to the curb as they loaded equipment into a pickup truck. "Have you seen a man pass by here?"

One of the construction workers, a short muscular man with long corn-rowed hair and cinnamon-brown skin, leaned close to the car and grinned, displaying a row of gold-capped front teeth. "You lookin' for any man, or someone in particular?"

I ignored the obvious undertone. "Tall, salt-and-pepper hair, big shoulders, kind of overweight. He had on jeans and a yellow T-shirt, probably green tennis shoes."

The construction worker laughed, shrugged, unscrewed the top of his thermos and poured the contents onto the ground. "Lotsa people pass by here."

A second worker, a redheaded guy who looked no more than eighteen years old, ambled toward the car, rolling up an extension cord.

"He walks kind of . . ." I tried to think of how to describe Teddy's lumbering gait, his mannerisms. Over the years, my mother had turned "mentally challenged" into a curse word. I couldn't apply that term to Teddy anymore. "He has . . . health problems. He's not supposed to be out alone."

The redheaded man slapped his coworker on the shoulder. "She's talkin' about the dude that gets the scrap lumber—the dumb guy." Turning to me, he pointed down the block. "Last week, he come by here wanting to trade a plant in a McDonald's cup for my san'wich. I seen him hangin' out by the school after that. I figured maybe he was lookin' for scraps there." Dusting off his hands, he frowned. "I ain't ever seen him cause nobody no trouble. He's just kinda slow—you know, like retarded and stuff."

His partner jabbed him playfully in the arm. "Yeah, he ain't the only one, Rusty."

"Shut up, Boomer," Rusty answered, then turned back to me. "You a social worker or somethin'?"

"No, he's my . . ." *Stepbrother* still wouldn't roll off my tongue. Old habits die hard. "I'm taking care of him. He left the house without telling me."

Boomer blinked, his mouth dropping open. "Dang, I figured he lived under a box or somethin'. There's lots of them street people down by the bridge."

There's lots of them street people. . . . I pictured Teddy wandering lost among the homeless. My emotions swung violently, and a prickly, tear-filled lump formed in my throat. "I don't know if he can . . . find his way home. I'm not sure . . ." *Of anything.* Even though it was completely unlike me to get emotional in front of strangers, my voice trembled. I let my head fall back against the seat. What now? What next?

"Hey, lady, chill out." Boomer touched the window frame, then pulled his hand away. "The dude goes by here all the time. He'll come back. He . . ." Pausing, he looked down the street, shading his eyes. "That him?"

Slapping the car into Park, I leaned out the window. The figure materializing in the distance was, unmistakably, Teddy. He was walking carefully, carrying something in his arms, cradling it like a baby. As he came closer, I made out the torn remnants of a Wal-Mart sack strung around a collection of dirty foam cups, empty aluminum cans, and fast-food containers. On top of the pile, he was balancing a loaf of bread and a jar of peanut butter, holding them with his chin.

When I stepped onto the curb, he called, "Hiiieee, A-becka!" To the construction workers, he added, "Hiiieee!" He almost lost his cargo, then clumsily wrapped his arms and body around it, bending lower and lower, until he was limping along with his legs pressed together, his collection trapped between his arms, chest, and thighs. "Hiiieee!" he said again, smiling crookedly upward when he reached us.

"Guess ya found him," Rusty observed.

Boomer bent down, resting his hands on his knees and squinting at Teddy's cache. "What'cha got there, dude?" Glancing back at Rusty, he grinned wryly. "You got some good paper cups and stuff?"

Teddy nodded with enthusiasm. "Yeah, I got cups. 'N pea-nit butter. It's good."

Boomer caught the peanut butter jar as it rolled off the stack. He stood up, and Teddy's brows knotted as he craned to keep the jar in sight.

"You gonna make you a sandwich?" Holding up the jar of peanut butter, Boomer grinned at Rusty, then examined the generic label.

"Yeah, a sam-ich," Teddy answered. "Good sam-ich."

"I bet that is go-o-ood sam-ich," Boomer mocked with a sarcasm to which Teddy was completely oblivious. "You gonna make me one?"

Teddy, still struggling to contain his bundle of trash, hesitated, then answered, "Oh-kay." He prepared to set down his treasures and fish out the bread, so he could make sandwiches on the sidewalk.

Rusty chuckled, then glanced at me, and noted the rising fury in my cheeks. He snatched the peanut butter jar from Boomer and handed it to me. Taking in Teddy's confused expression, he leaned close to Teddy and added, "He don't want a sandwich. He's just . . . kiddin' with ya, dude."

" 'Kay," Teddy replied pleasantly, then looked sideways at me, and said, "He kiddin', A-becca. He just kiddin'."

The familiar sense of humiliation—the one I'd felt standing on the curb at twelve, hoping my friends couldn't see Teddy running across the yard—swallowed me whole, and all I could say was, "Get in the car, Teddy." Without waiting for an answer, I opened the back door, threw in the peanut butter jar, and waited while Teddy wrestled through with his bundle. His shirt was covered with soda stains, his hair stiff and sticky, having dried with soda in it.

The door reverberated as I slammed it shut. "Thanks," I spat to the construction workers as I yanked open my door and got in. How many times had Teddy passed by here, and how many times had they teased him like this? Who'd given Teddy the bread and peanut butter, and what did he have to do to get it? The question was sickening.

Rusty leaned toward the door, thumbing over his shoulder toward Boomer, who had returned to cleaning up their equipment. "He don't mean nothin'."

I didn't answer. I couldn't. I put the car in Drive and left the condominiums behind. We'd gone down the block and turned onto Blue Sky Hill Court before I could talk. At the end of the street, my father's house, nearly hidden behind thick hedges and the high iron fence, seemed quiet. Hopefully, my father was still sleeping inside. "Teddy, you can't wander off without telling me." It felt strange to be talking to an adult, someone two years older than myself, in the mommy voice I used with Macey.

" 'Kay." Teddy began gathering his things in the backseat, blissfully unaware of the storm still rising within me. Drawing in a cleansing breath, I pulled into the driveway, parked the car and turned around. If it had been Macey in the backseat, the next line would have been the one that reminded me of my mother and began with *Young lady* . . . "Teddy, I mean it. You can't go out of the yard without telling me."

"Hooo-kay," he singsonged, while scooping cups and used food containers into the broken Wal-Mart sack. "I gone put dirt in the pots." He fingered the cups, his concentration focusing there. "In the pots."

I wondered if he'd heard what I'd said, if he'd understood it. "When you need things, you have to let me know, and we'll go buy them at the grocery store. No more wandering around the neighborhood picking up trash."

"My pots," he muttered without looking up.

"Pots," I ground out. "No more going out for pots, or food. We'll buy that stuff at the grocery store. If you need bread or peanut butter, you *tell* me, and we'll go *buy* it."

Teddy pulled the bread into his lap, suddenly aware that I was upset. His mouth trembled, and his fingers twisted into the bread wrapper. "The lady gimme it. The lady did."

I wondered who *the lady* was, but now wasn't the time to ask. "I understand that," I said, swallowing my swirling anxiety, trying to remain calm. I took a deep breath, counted to ten. "I'm not mad, Teddy. I'm not mad at you, okay? We just need to have a . . . a promise between us, okay? You don't go away without telling me. Ever. Not for any reason." Surely Hanna Beth didn't allow him to wander the streets at will.

"Ohh-kay." Nodding solemnly, Teddy frowned at the smashed bread and began trying to fluff it up again.

Leaning my cheek against the headrest, I considered the next mountain to climb. "Teddy, do you and Hanna . . . ummm . . . your mom ever take Daddy Ed to the doctor? I need to take Daddy Ed to the doctor tomorrow, so we can get his medications straightened out."

"Kay-Kay take Daddy Ed." His answer came amid the squeak of foam and the crinkling of paper as his trash bundle collapsed, and he gathered it again. "Kay-Kay take Daddy Ed in the car."

Kay-Kay again. It figured. The mysterious Kay-Kay, who had apparently bailed out on Teddy and my father, leaving them to starve, or worse.

In the backseat, Teddy was silent, his attention focused out the window. "A-becca?" His voice broke the silence as I reached for the keys to turn off the engine.

"Yes, Teddy?"

"Don't go way wit-out telling me. Ever." It was one of the clearest sentences I'd ever heard Teddy put together—a deliberate, concerted repetition of my words.

"That's right, Teddy. I don't want you to leave the yard without telling me, all right?"

"A-becca?" Teddy leaned forward, laid his hand on the seat, his pile of cups falling to the floor, unnoticed. "*You* don't go way wit-out telling me."

His gaze met mine, and suddenly I realized Teddy wasn't the one who'd failed to understand—I was. His eyes searched me, read me, waited for an answer. All at once, I understood. He wasn't making a promise, but seeking one.

"I won't go away without telling you, Teddy," I whispered, then laid my hand over his on the seat. Something inside me pulled and tugged, broke free and stretched. I felt a connection to my stepbrother that was deeper, more tender, than anything I'd imagined possible. "I won't. I promise."

We remained a moment longer, the two of us held together by a bond I hadn't prepared for and couldn't file neatly into the framework of my life. Teddy's hand turned and enclosed mine, a warm, tender circle holding me fast as the sun drifted low behind the towering trees of Blue Sky Hill.

Finally, he pulled away, turned around, and looked behind us in the driveway. "Got comp'ny," he said, and I glanced back as a rust-spotted minivan pulled in. It stopped, and a woman in a blue sweater and a long denim skirt got out, looked tentatively at the house.

Teddy opened his door, waving and saying hello as he scrambled to gather his treasures in the backseat. I turned off the engine and exited, hurrying to catch her before Teddy could. *Social Services* ran through my mind. Had the man next door called someone?

The visitor came closer, and I knew I'd seen her before, but I couldn't pin down the location. The airport, maybe? The bank? The electric company office? My time in Dallas was a collage of frantic activity, everything running together in a watercolor of impression and emotion that felt like it had lasted weeks rather than days. The last time I'd talked to Macey—last night? this morning?—it felt as if I'd been away from her, detached from her daily routines, forever. Kyle had called about negotiations with a potential new partner for the firm—was that yesterday—and I couldn't believe the negotiations were still ongoing. Kyle had laughed and reminded me that I'd only been gone a short time.

The woman in the driveway smiled timidly, smoothed her hands over the front of her skirt, then pulled her sweater modestly over her thin hips. Her gaze darted uncertainly toward Teddy's clumsy exit from the car, then back to me. She seemed embarrassed, apologetic, sorry to be bothering me. "I don't know if you remember me . . ." She paused, her eyebrows arching upward over timid green eyes, then lowering again when I didn't answer. "I'm Mrs. Parker's CNA. We met the other day when you came to visit her?"

A thunderbolt of anxiety boomed inside me, emanating from something instinctive and moving outward, slowing until I was conscious of a sudden breeze rustling the iris beds, a bird calling overhead, a frog croaking in the ditch. My mouth went dry, my pulse thready. "Is she . . ." I glanced over my shoulder. Teddy had dropped the peanut butter jar and was trying to fish it out from under the car. "Did something happen. . . ? Is she all right?" I couldn't imagine any reason for the nursing center to have sent someone here other than to deliver bad news. What would I tell Teddy? What would I say to my father?

"No, no, she's fine." The woman reached toward me apologetically, her name tag peeking from under the sweater as the front fell open. Mary. I remembered her now. We had talked in the hallway.

She had two little boys. The man in the wheelchair was going to tell them a story about trains. . . .

She put her hand on my arm as if she thought I might teeter off my feet, and she would catch me. She hardly seemed strong enough to catch anyone. Her fingers were thin and small, her wrist pale and fragile-looking. "I'm sorry. I didn't mean to scare you. Mrs. Parker's doing really well. They've reduced her meds, and she's making great progress with her therapy." Releasing my arm, she pulled the front of her sweater closed again and stood holding it together. She glanced toward her van, seeming concerned as Teddy walked down the driveway to investigate her vehicle. "I would have called, but the number listed on Mrs. Parker's form was disconnected, and there wasn't another number in her file—just the address." She continued watching the van as if she were afraid Teddy might jump in and drive off with it. "I didn't want to show up here without calling, but Mrs. Parker asked me to come. She insisted on it, actually." Teddy circled her vehicle, and she craned to see around the other side.

"The utilities were disconnected when I got here," I explained. "No one's been paying the bills." It felt good to tell someone that, to vent, even a little. "My father has Alzheimer's, and Teddy's not . . . capable." I nodded toward Teddy, who was studying the inside of her van like a zoo patron looking into an exhibit. What in the world was in there? "They had a caretaker here, apparently. Someone named Kay-Kay. I think she may have lived in the apartment over the garage, but when I arrived there was no one here. Do you know anything about her? I've searched the house and the garage apartment, and I can't find any contact information."

Mary caught a few wispy light reddish-brown hairs and tucked them into her thick bun. "A woman came to see her a couple times—kind of heavyset, black hair, maybe about fifty? I thought she was a relative, but then Ifeoma, the second-shift nurse, told me the woman said she was a maid, and Mrs. Parker's husband had asked her to check on things at the nursing center, because he was housebound and couldn't come visit. When the maid stopped showing up, the speech therapist tried to see if Mrs. Parker could give us the woman's name or phone number by using an alphabet board, but she couldn't do it. After a couple of tries, it was too upsetting for her, so they left it alone. It's pretty normal for stroke patients to get stressed over things they can't remember or can't sort out, especially early on. I've only been at the nursing center for a couple months, so I didn't ask too many questions. I figured Mrs. Parker didn't have anyone other than her husband and the housekeeper—until the administrator said you were coming. Then I found out about the police, and that she had a son living here also. Some of the workers were talking about it at lunch. By then, nobody had come to visit Mrs. Parker in a while."

I let out a frustrated sigh. "I can't figure out what's going on. Whoever this Kay-Kay is, she seems to have dropped off the face of the earth."

Teddy was tapping on the window of Mary's vehicle, leaning close to the glass.

Mary backed up a step, her face narrowing with concern.

"Teddy, don't do that," I called. "Leave her car alone."

Teddy motioned to the interior with his handful of cups. "There a boy and a other boy! Two boy in the car!"

Mary moved protectively toward the vehicle, scanning the windows. "They must've woken up. I probably better go before Brady has a fit. He hates the car seat. Mrs. Parker just wanted me to . . . check if everything's all right here. She really needs you to come see her."

"Wait," I said, jogging to catch up with her. "Can you stay a few minutes? I wanted to ask you some questions about Hanna Beth." She frowned, and I added, "I'd invite you into the house, but it's still kind of disorganized." *And my father's in there, doing heaven knows what.* "We could sit in the backyard. There's plenty of room for the kids to run around."

Mary hesitated on the path, studying Teddy, me, the house, trying to assess the situation before getting her kids out of the car.

"Please." I realized I was practically begging. I needed help. I needed to talk to someone, and Mary was here. She had at least some knowledge of Hanna Beth's condition, of what we could expect going forward.

Mary unfolded her arms, let them fall to her sides. "The boys haven't gotten to run around outside in a while." She focused on the van, where the older boy was trying to open the dented sliding door. The younger boy was hidden in a car seat, his hands flailing in and out of view as Teddy played hide and seek through the glass. I could hear him squealing gleefully as we came closer.

"I'll get them," Mary said. I waited on the sidewalk while she unloaded the boys and introduced them. Teddy said hello with his hands still full of rescued trash.

"Teddy is Hanna Beth's son," I interjected, as Mary took the boys' hands and we walked around the side of the house.

Mary nodded. "Hi, Teddy," she said, and there was a kindness in her voice that made Teddy beam.

"I got pots." He nodded toward the trash bundle. "I got a bird nest. Mockin' burr . . . Mockin' bird. Sings good. Wanna see?" He pushed the back gate with his body so we could pass through.

"I think I need to talk to Rebecca," Mary answered, "but the boys might like to see the bird nest." She jostled the boys' hands, and they looked up at her. "Do you guys think you could be really quiet and look at a bird nest? No touching, because then the mommy won't come back."

Brandon slipped from her hand, but the smaller boy, Brady, paused, still clinging to her. "Wiw da daddy come back?"

Mary smoothed his hair tenderly. "Just be careful, okay? Don't touch." She sent him toddling after his brother, following Teddy across the yard. Teddy paused to set his trash bundle on a planting table near the garden house. Bending close to the boys, he pressed a finger to his lips, then pointed toward a large crepe myrtle by the fence. Together, they tiptoed off like adventurers on safari. Mary stood watching, her gaze taking in the collection of seedlings and homemade potting benches.

"Please, have a seat." I motioned to the patio table and chairs. "Can I bring you a glass of tea? I need to check on things in the house." It sounded ridiculously formal, considering the situation.

"Don't go to any trouble." Mary moved to the patio table and balanced on the edge of a chair, her knees together, hands folded primly on her lap. I left her there and slipped through the back door. My father had awakened and wasn't in his chair. I could hear him in his office, slamming drawers and moving papers. He often spent hours in there, rearranging files and furniture, putting documents and old newspapers into stacks that made sense only to him. No matter how many times I tried to tidy up, the house was in a perpetual state of disarray.

At the moment, he seemed to be occupied where he was, which was probably just as well, as he had no view of the backyard from there. No telling how he would react if he saw Mary sitting on the lawn chair. He might decide she was one of *those people.*

I was purposefully quiet as I went to the kitchen, poured two glasses of tea, then returned to the patio. Mary had relaxed somewhat, leaned against the armrest. At the far end of the yard, Teddy and the boys were squatted down by the patch of butterfly bush that was just beginning to bloom. A squirrel ran across the fence overhead. Teddy pointed it out, and Brady clapped his hands, squealing.

"Thanks for letting them play," Mary said. "They needed to get out and run around. I promised I'd take them to the park, but

I haven't had—" She aborted whatever she'd been about to say, and finished with, "Time. It's kind of a drive to a nice park. The one by the hospital has a lot of bad people in it."

"Thanks for staying to talk to me." I handed her a glass of tea, then sat down. "I need to find out more about Hanna Beth's condition."

She shifted uncomfortably. "You might want to come in and talk to her doctor. I'm just an aide. Dr. Barnhill could tell you more than I can."

"I haven't been able to get away from the house." The answer came out more sharply than I'd meant it to. The next thing I knew, I was spilling the entire story of my arrival, the trouble with the utilities, the mysterious Kay-Kay, the mess inside the house, Teddy wandering off this morning.

Mary listened and nodded, leaning closer to my chair, seeming to share the unpredictable swells of frustration and desperation.

When I finished, she appeared to be at a loss. "I'm really sorry."

I slashed a hand in the air, embarrassed. If this had been a deposition, I would have been the witness who cracked and spilled my life story all over the negotiating table. My body felt rubbery, as if I'd run a marathon and burned up every ounce of fuel. "I didn't mean to unload all of that. I'm just . . ." My voice cracked, my emotions so much closer to the surface than usual. What was wrong with me?

I took a deep breath, swallowed hard. "I'm sorry," I said again, gathering my thoughts. "I have to make plans . . . going forward." I tried to imagine what those plans might be. "I need to know about Hanna Beth . . . when . . . whether she'll be able to come back here. If I hire help for them—someone to come in during the days, maybe someone to stay in the garage apartment full-time—is it possible that she'll recover to the point of living here again?"

Mary nodded. "I think so . . . she's doing really good."

"How soon?"

She shifted uncomfortably, stopped to watch Teddy and the boys capture a caterpillar by the fence. Teddy let it crawl on his hand while the boys watched. He pointed and explained something and the boys leaned closer.

"You really might want to talk to Dr. Barn—"

"I will, but I want to know what you think." I knew I was being less than polite, interrogating her, trying to get the answer I wanted. I needed someone to tell me that Hanna Beth would recover, miraculously return home and take over.

Mary knew what I was asking for. Twisting her hands nervously in her lap, she looked away, fine strands of hair catching the sunlight, teasing her cheek. "When she does come home, she'll need a lot of help. She'll need someone here full-time."

It wasn't the answer I wanted.

Mary turned her attention toward the house, studied the apartment over the garage, and frowned contemplatively.

CHAPTER 10

Hanna Beth Parker

The evening seemed to stretch on forever as I waited to see if Mary would return with news of my house, Teddy, and Edward. My mind tensed with anticipation when the door opened, but it was only Ouita Mae, stopping by to see if I wanted to watch *Wheel of Fortune* and read a bit more about Gavin and Marcella.

"Yesss," I said, and was pleased with how clearly the word came out. When I opened my mouth, there was never any telling.

"Wonderful!" Ouita Mae clapped her hands, then turned on the television, and steered herself around the bed. "This chair," she grumbled, as she tried to get situated. "I'll be glad to get back on my feet. I spent enough years of my life cooped up in a darned wheelchair."

"Uhhh?" I inquired, and she blanched, as if she'd forgotten she was talking to a woman flat on her back in bed.

"I had an accident years ago that gave me some trouble."

"Eeennn?" I asked, then concentrated and tried again. "W-ennn?"

"When?" It was nice that Ouita Mae could understand me. She must have had some practice at it. Resting the book in her lap, she watched the first puzzle come on the TV screen, and her attention wavered. "A saddle horse fell with my daddy and me when I was just little, broke me up pretty good. Over the years, these old legs haven't been quite right. Lots of surgeries, and I was never gonna run any marathons in my braces, but the doctors gave me many good years on my feet. Sometimes I think that's why Phillip decided to be a doctor instead of a cowboy, like his granddad wanted him to be."

"Guuud dr-toc," I said, then snorted at the bungled word.

Ouita Mae understood. "Yep, he's a good doctor, if I do say so myself." Leaning close to the bed, she raised an eyebrow and added in a whisper, "But just between you, me, and the fencepost, I could stand to see a little less doctorin' and a little more romancin' from that boy. All these cute nurses making eyes at him all the time, I keep thinking he'll find some nice girl, settle down, and make me a great-grandma—but it'd be like my own grandchild, being as we raised that boy. I'd like to bounce a little one on my knee again before I kick the bucket."

"Mmmm," I said, and nodded. "Mmmeee, tuhh." I'd tasted firsthand the bittersweet of knowing I would grow old without the pitter-patter of tiny feet in my house. After Teddy's difficult birth, the doctors had told me I'd probably never have any more children. At least for Ouita Mae, there was still hope for a crop of great-grandkids. "Mbeee tu-sun." It was a poor imitation of *maybe soon*, but Ouita Mae gathered the meaning from the unspoken language of lonely old women.

"It better be soon," she said. "I'm not getting any younger. Rate I'm goin', Phillip's babies and I'll be in diapers together."

I laughed—a sound something like a donkey braying. Ouita Mae slapped my arm, said, "Oh, Lordy, I'm sorry about that," then she laughed with me. I was struck by how good it felt to have a friend, a woman who understood how I felt. Over the years on Blue Sky Hill, there hadn't been much time for that sort of thing. In general, other ladies weren't interested, or it was awkward. I couldn't blame the neighbors, the church acquaintances, the mothers from the school PTO, the wives of Edward's coworkers, with whom I was expected to socialize. How could it be anything but awkward, sitting at the company picnic, the park, the playground, talking about grades, music lessons, cheerleading, boyfriends, girlfriends, scholarships, college, romance, marriages—all the things that go into the making of a life? How could they help but feel they were hurting me by bringing up those milestones, by indirectly pointing out that Teddy's future would be different?

It was good to be here with Ouita Mae, chatting as women do. I had the strange thought that I was glad I'd ended up here, that I wasn't at home, where Edward's state was fragile, and Teddy occupied himself in the yard talking to birds and plants, and the neighborhood was changing—the old folks selling out, new homes and condominiums going in for busy families who came and went without time or interest in socializing.

I wasn't lonely here. . . .

As quickly as the thought came, I banished it. Of course I wanted to go home to Edward and Teddy. Of course I did.

I turned my attention to the puzzles. Teddy loved *Wheel of Fortune.* He liked to watch the letters turn around and try to name them. Edward always guessed the puzzles long before I could. He was a whiz with words and always had been. Even now, he could figure out the puzzles most of the time.

I imagined Edward and Teddy curled up in the living room watching the show, and it was almost if we were together. I heard Teddy laughing and counting when one of the contestants made a good supposition, and several letters lit up at once. Each time that happened, Teddy clapped and cheered.

"Oh, good one!" Ouita Mae said, and I heard Teddy exclaiming, *Good one, Mama! Good one!* Ouita Mae counted the letters just like he would have. "Five. My goodness. Five." I heard Teddy cheering, *Five. Five. Got five!*

When Ouita Mae solved the final puzzle of the night, I heard Edward's voice, just as if we were all there together.

"Well, let's see what's goin' on with Gavin and Marcella." Ouita Mae turned off the TV and opened the book, relaxing against the back of her chair, tipping her chin up so she could see through her bifocals. "These love story books have changed since back in the day. I have to say, this one's sure got me hooked. I always did like history and sailing ships . . . and pirates, of course. That Errol Flynn. I'd of married him, when I was a girl."

"Ohhhh," I mused in agreement, and she smiled, scanning the pages before she found our stopping place and began reading.

The ship was passing through a storm with Gavin and Marcella clinging to the rails. In Ouita Mae's voice, the story quickly began to find a breath of its own.

"Well, Lordy, I got to turn the page for sure, now," she said as we finished the chapter. "That's interesting stuff about what a science it was to use the sextant to navigate ships. I guess if your navigator took dysentery and died like theirs did, it pretty much would be the end of the world. Good thing Marcella learned all about using a sextant, growing up in that fishing village with her uncle." Her tone added a hint of melodrama that made me giggle deep in my throat.

Ouita Mae's lips twisted to one side in a reluctant, wry smile, and she leaned closer to me. "She oughta know that a man's mind ain't clear when his sextant's involved, though."

I blushed, and my stomach convulsed around a puff of air, and the next thing I knew, I was laughing again.

Ouita Mae shook a finger as if I were the naughty one, then she tipped back her head, squinted through her glasses, and went on reading. Marcella spent the next chapter letting the ship drift off course, too proud and stubborn to admit to Gavin that she was merely a ladies' maid, the daughter of a fisherman, rather than the heiress he thought he'd kidnapped. By the time we'd traveled the pages of missed connections, Ouita Mae was tired, and so was I.

"Oh, these silly young girls." Setting down the book, she pulled off her glasses and rubbed her eyes. Without the thick lenses, her eyes were so dark I couldn't see the centers. Her grandson had her eyes.

"Yeeesh," I agreed. If I hadn't been so stubborn, so determined that I could take care of myself, I wouldn't have let Teddy's father slip away all those years ago, after the letter came. He was out of the country then, working his first job with a fledgling oil company, beginning to make a success of his life. There were plans for him—an engagement to the granddaughter of a senator, a level of society my family could never attain. I didn't blame him, in a way. Those who lived on Blue Sky Hill didn't mix with those who lived off. I should have known that, should have kept it in my mind, when I left with him after working a late-night shift in one of the stores of Highland Park. It was pure chance that we crossed paths there. He was shopping for Christmas gifts, and I was working while home from college on Christmas break. We hadn't seen each other in years, but I was smitten with him, as always, and this time I was not a girl ten years younger, too young to be of interest to him. I was a woman, old enough to know what I was doing.

The letter from his family lawyer pointed that out in no uncertain terms—the pregnancy was my doing. Edward wanted no contact with me. Even years afterward, I'd wondered—if I'd written to Edward a third time, a fourth, a fifth, however long it took. If I'd insisted on hearing from him personally, if I'd made certain those were his words rather than the words of his family, would things have been different? If Edward had been there when I went into early labor with Teddy, if he'd insisted we go right to the hospital, would Teddy be different?

On the heels of that thought, there was always the guilty question—how could I wish for something other than what was, when I loved Teddy so much?

Ouita Mae sighed, as if she sensed my sudden melancholy. Resting her chin on her hand, she let the glasses dangle off her finger. Her regard wandered far away, found the window, took in the stars.

It occurred to me that Mary hadn't returned to tell me about her visit to my house yet. She'd promised she would. I'd lost track of the time while Ouita Mae was reading.

"It's funny the things you wish you could go back and do different."

I almost didn't hear Ouita Mae at first. My mind was elsewhere.

"It's little things sometimes, you know?"

"Mmmm," I agreed. Little things. Like a second, third, fourth letter you could have written. A swallowing of pride that might have changed everything.

"I think about those things." Ouita Mae sighed again, her face suddenly solemn, contemplative, a little sad.

"Mmmm."

She laughed softly in her throat. "There was a boy once. I don't know why that came to mind just now. I don't know why that boy still comes to mind at all. It's not like I haven't had a good life, a good marriage. We had our son, and then when we lost him, we had Phillip to raise. I wouldn't trade him for anythin' different. . . ." She glanced my way. Our eyes met, and I knew. I understood that feeling of regret, the sense that there was a moment when the paths divided and you chose one over the other.

Ouita Mae went on with her musings. "I guess readin' about Gavin and Marcella made me think about it. The day I laid eyes on that boy was the first time I ever did believe in love at first sight. I was sixteen. I was helping take the cattle to the Tom Green County Livestock Auction for sale day. My daddy'd made me a special saddle, so I could ride just like anybody else. When I was riding, my mama would let me wear pants, of course. I sure did love those sale days, because I could ride into town on that big paint horse, and strangers in for the cattle auction wouldn't even know I wore braces. It felt good, you know, being like everybody else." She laughed again, shaking her head, then turned back to the window, her thoughts focusing on the past. "There was a new boy there one day—a tall boy, and, lands, he was something to look at. He'd brought some livestock in for the sale. All the girls wanted to catch his eye, but he was looking at me." Tossing her chin up, she laughed. "Oh, Lord, I felt like Cinderella at the ball. I felt like the luckiest girl in Tom Green County. That boy had the bluest eyes. He smiled at me, and we laughed, and joked, and flirted. We sneaked out behind the barn, sat there in the shade with the horses shoulder to shoulder. He leaned over and gave me my first kiss, and I was sure I'd just fell in love."

A sigh wound through me. When I saw Edward in Highland Park that day, I fell in love so hard that nothing else mattered.

"You know, and it's a funny thing," Ouita Mae went on. "I sat on my horse all day, even after my skin was raw, because I figured if I got off, that boy would see me hobbling around on my braces, and wouldn't look at me the same way anymore. Toward evenin', we girls went down to the swimmin' hole, and oh, mercy, I was glad to get off the horse and take those braces loose. I remember, I was sitting by the edge of the pool. I'd tossed my braces over by a tree, and I was just letting the sun cover my skin. I heard a horse nicker, and I looked up, and that boy was riding past on the road. He glanced my way, and all I could think was to turn around and hide my legs in the water until he went on by."

Her lips made a soft *tsk-tsk-tsk* as she turned her wheelchair and started out of the room. "I found out later that boy was staying with family in town and helping his daddy sell off some livestock because, back home, his sister had the polio." She paused, looked over her shoulder at me, the creases fanning out around her eyes. "He ran off and joined the service a few days later, and I never saw him again. Ever since that day, I've wondered what might of happened if I hadn't hid my crippled legs in the pool." Her voice trailed off, barely a breath exhaled, as if the story were yet unfinished. As she disappeared into the alcove, she added, "I always thought, if that boy died in the war, maybe it was my fault."

She disappeared out the door and left me musing over the story of the girl at the pool, whose split-second decision could have changed everything. The hardest thing about the road not taken is that you never know where it might have led.

I was looking out the window, contemplating the idea, when I heard Mary and her boys outside in the hall. She was trying to shush them.

"Mrs. Parker?" she whispered, opening the door slightly. "It's Mary, are you sleep—" She didn't have time to finish before the door pushed wider and her little one slipped through. He ran in carrying a seedling in a Dixie cup—a geranium just growing its first mature leaves, the ones that would distinguish it from other seedlings.

"Wook! I got p-want. Wittle baby p-want!" he babbled, as he skidded around the corner of my bed and held up his treasure.

I was swept to the brink of happy tears in the space of an instant. I knew they'd been to my house. The Dixie cup had an awkward scribble on it. Teddy's marking for *geranium*.

I sank against the pillow, overwhelmed with emotion, flooded with relief. At home, Teddy was planting flowers, just as always.

"I'm sorry, Mrs. Parker." Mary tried to snatch up the little boy, but he stiffened in protest, still struggling to climb the rails and show me the plant. His brother grabbed his shirt to pull him down. "Brandon!" Mary scolded in a hush. "Brady, ssshhh! Get down."

"Nnno," I protested, motioning toward the plant. "Sssee." I wanted to see the cup, to touch Teddy's creation, feel his hands on the seed, on the soil. How many times over the years had we done that together?

Mary lifted Brady up, and he leaned toward the bed, stretching out his arms like a child waiting to be held.

"Ere." I moved my hand beside me, glanced at the empty spot on the mattress, then back at Mary. "Here." The word, usually an impossible jumble, came quickly in my excitement.

Brady lifted his legs over the rail, then folded them underneath as Mary set him beside me. "I got p-want," he repeated, holding the cup close to my face. I could smell the rich, damp soil, the bit of fertilizer Teddy would have sprinkled on top, the water he'd delivered faithfully, carefully. Teddy always understood that tiny plants were tender, that they had to be nurtured and protected.

Brady's chubby finger stroked the emerging leaves. I knew Teddy had shown him how to do that. "J-mam-y-yum," he said.

"G-rain-yum," his big brother corrected.

"Geranium." Mary pronounced the word slowly, so the boys could hear all the sounds.

"Teddy gimme," Brady said, holding the plant close to me again.

Mary repositioned his hand. "Don't put it right in her face, sweetheart. She can see it. Mrs. Parker is Teddy's mom. Did you know that?"

Brady's brows twisted together as he tried to make sense of the idea that even grown boys had mothers. "Him big." His eyes narrowed skeptically.

"He's all grown up, Brady," Brandon chimed in, resting a hand on the rail and yawning, then looking toward the door as if he were ready for something more entertaining. "Even big boys have mommies."

Brady turned back to me with a new level of admiration, now that I was Teddy's mommy. Little children always loved Teddy. In stores, he talked to the babies and made the crying toddlers smile. At the park by the creek years ago, he'd helped the landscaping crew tend the flowers, letting the children plant with him and watch the seeds come up. I'd never seen him so excited to get up and go somewhere each day. Someone complained anonymously, because Teddy wasn't a certified city employee, and that was that. Shortly afterward, the park was fenced off and locked up, undoubtedly slated to eventually become part of a condominium complex.

Brady's shoe pressed the remote as he wiggled closer to me. The television came on, and both boys turned to it.

"Mom, they got my channel here." Twining an arm through the rail, Brandon leaned against the bed and focused on the TV. "Hey, it's Zaboo Mafoo!"

"Boo Foo!" Brady cheered, wiggling closer to me so he could see the screen.

Mary laid a hand on Brandon's head. "Boys, we have to go. We just came to tell Mrs. Parker we went by her house and everything was all right." The last words were hesitant, and she hooded her eyes, as if there were more she wasn't telling me.

"Mom, pleeease," Brandon whined, his head falling sideways against his shoulder. "I love this one."

On television, a long-armed puppet made to look like some sort of monkey caught a tiny green snake, carried on a conversation with it, then kissed it on the head.

"Eeewww!" Brady squealed, scooting closer to me. "Teddy catch w-izard."

"Lizard," Brandon corrected.

"Come on, boys." Mary moved her hands to Brandon's shoulders to turn him toward the door.

"I like this part," Brandon protested, shrugging her away.

"We need to go."

"I don't wanna get back in the car." Brandon teetered on the edge of a temper fit.

"Brandon . . ." Mary's voice was firm. She glanced at me with a mixture of apology and embarrassment. I knew how she felt. I could remember being in exactly her position, disagreeing in public with a whiny, tired child, hoping things didn't descend into anarchy.

"Nnnooo!" The word was out of my mouth, and I was waving toward the TV before I had time to consider that old women shouldn't interfere in young women's parenting. "Www-ach. Tay . . . sss-tay."

Brandon looked from his mom to me, hopefully, his hand still on the rail, his attention drifting toward his show.

I turned to Mary apologetically. I didn't want her to be angry with me. No doubt she needed to get her boys home to bed, but I wanted her to stay, to tell me everything that had happened when she'd gone to my house. I wanted her to describe every minute, so it would be as if I were there again. I wanted Brady to snuggle his little body under my arm, warm and wiggly, just the way a little boy should be.

Mary's face grew sympathetic, a look I knew so well these days and normally hated, but if sympathy would prompt her to stay, then so be it. She let go of Brandon, then sat on the edge of the chair and tucked her hands under her legs, as if she didn't know what to do when she wasn't working. "This *is* a good one." She glanced toward the TV, and Brandon grinned.

"Yesss!" he cheered. He grabbed the other chair, scooted it over by the bed, and sat down, never taking his eyes off the TV. Suddenly an electronic zombie, he tucked up his legs, crisscross.

"Myeee hhhow?" I said, and stretched my hand toward Mary. The hand, crossing my line of vision, distracted me for a moment. I didn't know I could move it that well. "Myeee howt?" I said again.

Mary took Brady's plant and set it on the nightstand. Brady snuggled against my arm, having forgotten there was anything in the room but the TV.

"Rebecca told me to let you know she's taking care of things. She didn't want you to worry," Mary said finally. "She said she would come by as soon as she could. We stayed a while and the boys played in the yard. You have a beautiful yard. Teddy showed the boys some bird nests and things. They really had fun, and—"

"Well, look at who all's in here." Claude Fisher's voice boomed from the doorway. "Land's sakes, Birdie, you havin' a party again and didn't invite me?"

The door smacked against the wall as he rolled his wheelchair over the threshold.

I guessed I was having a party after all.

CHAPTER 11

Rebecca Macklin

Dr. Amadi decided to put my father in the hospital for tests and ob-
servation. He was shocked by the amount of weight loss since the appointment a year ago, and equally taken aback by the severity of the
dementia. Twelve months before, my father had been lucid enough
to carry on a conversation, discuss his medication options, understand that the progression of Alzheimer's disease was a very individual
thing. He was concerned about his disease laying further burdens on
Hanna Beth. He was worried about Teddy's understanding of what
was happening. He was pragmatic, determined to control his diet,
sell his golf cart, and start walking the course, on the theory that a
healthy body would prevent decay of the mind.

"This was a *year* ago?" I asked, as Dr. Amadi and I stood in the
hall talking, while my father waited inside the examination room
with a nurse. Somehow, my father had decided he was in for broken
ribs, an injury he'd sustained after a load of oil field pipe fell from a
transport trailer when we were living in Saudi.

I could hear him on the other side of the door telling the nurse
about the accident as if it had just happened. She was patiently playing along as she tried to convince him to put on his clothes.

Dr. Amadi checked his file again. "Yes. It has been . . . thirteen
months. We have not seen him since that time," he answered in the

rhythmic cadence of a thick Indian accent. He was a small man with a dark birthmark on his left cheek, and brusque, matter-of-fact mannerisms my mother would have hated. She never liked doctors who kept everything on a clinical level, who couldn't find time to chitchat about her emotional state, her various dreams, intuitions, herbs, and visualizations that had always, she was certain, forced her lupus into remission.

"Do you know why he hasn't been in since then?" I asked, thinking, *Why was this man, diagnosed with a progressive disease, allowed to slip off the radar?* According to the records, Dr. Amadi had been my father's and Hanna Beth's doctor for several years.

He gave me a cool look, perceiving criticism, perhaps. "One would assume they had chosen to consult a geriatric specialist."

Without his files? I tamped down the question. The fact was that, right now, I desperately needed Dr. Amadi's cooperation. "They've had some kind of home care provider. Most of his recent prescriptions were filled online."

"I see." Raising a brow, the doctor wrote something in the file and frowned. "I will need a list of everything he has been taking."

"I don't know what he's been taking," I admitted, impatient with the cat-and-mouse game of who was responsible for my father's care. Bad daughter? Bad doctor? What did it matter now? "I've just come into town, and with my father's wife in the hospital, there isn't anyone to tell me. I'm doing the best I can to get a handle on the situation."

"As are we all." The doctor made one last notation, then turned away and started down the hall. "We can admit him to the hospital for a day or two and correct his medications. Then we will know more. The nurse will give you the paperwork you need, if this is the way you would like to proceed."

I didn't argue. After the Herculean effort of getting my father fully dressed this morning, into the car, and to the doctor's office, I was ready to agree to almost anything. All along, my father had been intensely worried about *those people*. He wouldn't go out the front door, because *those people* had put locks on there, and they knew when he tried to open them. He wouldn't go out the back door, because *those people* peered in from behind the privacy fence. Sometimes they gathered on the patio and talked about him. They tried to get him fired from the company. They said he'd stolen money from the pension fund—a miniature Enron scandal.

I'd finally pulled the car into the garage and convinced him that *those people* were not in there, and we could slip into the car secretly and drive away without being noticed. The dementia being what it was, I couldn't bring Teddy along with us, so I'd left him home, after making him promise he wouldn't wander off while I was gone. All morning long, I'd been subconsciously checking my watch, counting the hours, worrying. What if Teddy forgot his promise? What if something tempted him into going on another walkabout? What if he was gone when I got home?

I can't keep doing this, I thought. Pausing by the door, I braced a hand on the frame. *I can't keep doing this. I can't. It's insane.* I'd awakened feeling sick this morning. Sick, and tired, and mildly dizzy. Exhausted.

I went to tell the nurse to proceed with the admission paperwork. At least in the hospital, my father would be safe. Without him constantly moving stuff and hiding it at home, I could work on returning the place to a reasonable state of organization.

Dr. Amadi's nurse was matter-of-fact and efficient. She let my father believe he was going in for the broken ribs he'd suffered in the oil field accident. He liked the nurse because she was young and attractive. By the time all the paperwork was finished and I took him two miles down the street to the hospital, everything was in order. They'd given him a mild sedative to help him make the transition calmly.

He was falling asleep, exhausted by the day, when a nurse and an orderly helped him into his hospital bed. A queasy feeling oozed over me as they unwrapped an IV needle. I stepped into the hall, walked down a few doors, and sank into a chair in the mini-lounge by the elevator. It was only four thirty, but every muscle in my body was throbbing, my lungs filled with medicinal-smelling air, my mind racing with details. Hanna Beth was just a few miles down the street in the nursing and rehab center. Mary had told me she was doing better, regaining some language. Maybe she could explain why there was no recent record of my father having received treatment from a doctor. Maybe she could tell me how to reach Kay-Kay. Then again, maybe the questions would be too stressful for her. The nursing center administrator had repeatedly cautioned me not to expect too much, warned me that Hanna Beth's symptoms could worsen under stress.

My cell phone rang, the sound seeming unreasonably loud in the marble corridor. I dug the phone out of my purse and opened it quickly.

"Rebecca Macklin."

There was a pause on the other end, during which I heard Kyle telling one of the clerks to pull a file for him. I entertained the temporary notion that he was wondering about me. Amid the recent craziness, I hadn't called home in two days. Except for one short conversation with my paralegal yesterday and a text message bedtime kiss to Macey last night, California and the office seemed a million miles away.

"Sorry about that." Kyle came back, still using his all-business voice. "What can I do for you?" His mind was elsewhere, clearly.

"You called me, Kyle."

"Oh, Rebecca, sorry." I heard the squeal of his chair as he got up, probably to close the door. "I need to tell you something before you hear it thirdhand."

A rapid pulse bolted into my throat. I imagined him calling to tell me, via cell phone, that he'd been having an affair, and word was out, and he was leaving me—us. I wouldn't be able to handle it. I couldn't hold up under one more catastrophe.

"I meant to call you earlier, but I got tied up in a meeting." His voice had the mollifying tone he employed to give skittish clients a false sense of security just before he served up a dose of legal reality, the don't-panic-but-the-bridge-is-out-and-the-brakes-are-gone voice. "I didn't want you to hear it from Macey first."

My God, Macey knew? He'd involved our daughter? I gripped the arm of the chair, squeezed hard. "What's going on, Kyle? Just tell me."

"Don't panic."

"Don't pacify me," I snapped. The words echoed against the sterile white walls, and an elderly couple strolling with an IV stand glanced my way. I turned toward the wall, rubbing my forehead and shielding my face. "Just tell me, Kyle."

"Everything's been taken care of. There's nothing for you to do. . . ." I pictured the purposefully calm facial expression that would come along with that artificially sedate tone. To emphasize the fact that there was nothing to panic about, he would rock calmly back in his chair, twirl a pencil in his fingers, look out the window, his sandy brown hair falling neatly over his collar as he surveyed the ocean in the distance. In that light, his eyes would be blue, like the water. If I walked past his office door in a moment like that, I would think that he looked perfect for the cover of *Forbes*—an accomplished man surrounded by the markers of success, oozing self-confidence. I admired that about him. He'd grown up the brilliant, athletic golden boy, the caboose baby with loving parents and older siblings admiring his every move. He was always secure in his position, as a good lawyer should be. "It's already handled, all right?"

What's handled? A divorce? A separation? A tender reconciliation during which you confess to temptation and I attempt forgiveness?

"Macey had a little accident in phys-ed class this morning. She doesn't want to admit to the details, but as nearly as I can gather, they were in the gymnastics room, and Macey was showing off for the other kids, doing flips off the beam without a spotter. She landed on the edge of the mat and popped a tendon in her ankle."

I felt sick. "Is she all right?" I pictured my daughter lying in some emergency clinic alone while Kyle was in meetings. Why was he still at work?

"She's fine. I told you everything is fine." Clearly, he'd caught the insinuation that he couldn't handle the situation on his own.

"Where is she? Who's with her?"

Kyle huffed into the phone, as in, *If you'll just shut up and let me talk*. . . . "She's home now. Mace's going to be out of commission for a little while. She has a temporary brace on the ankle. The doctor will put a walking cast on in a couple days, when the swelling goes down. Mace is actually kind of excited about it. She's never had a cast before. She called me to ask what color I thought she should get."

My mind whirled through the barrage of information—popped tendon, doctor visit, swelling, temporary wrap . . . Macey would miss the state gymnastics meet in two weeks. How did she feel about that? She'd been working for state all year. "You let Isha take her to the doctor?" How could he send our daughter to the emergency clinic with a twenty-two-year-old au pair? What was he thinking?

"My parents came up and took her." He said it as if it made all the sense in the world that someone else would bring our daughter to the emergency room. "It was Macey's idea. She knew I had to meet with a client in LA today."

My chest clenched at the idea of my daughter lying in the school nurse's office with a popped tendon, trying to make herself less trouble to her father. The day compressed around me. Air wrenched from my lungs in a sob, and I stifled it with my hand. "I'm coming home." I'd have to hire somebody here. Now. Today. I could pay from our bank account until I gained access to my father's funds, either through Hanna Beth or a power of attorney.

Where would I find someone who was willing to clean stacks

of mail and newspapers, and patrol for rotten food underneath the beds and inside the closets? How could anyone be expected to deal with Teddy hiding in the backyard, my father wandering the house at night, *those people* coming and going without warning? How would it affect Teddy if I left? What about Hanna Beth. . . ?

"Macey doesn't want you to come home." Kyle's reply stopped the whirling in my mind. "She knew you'd say that, and she told me to tell you that Grandma Macklin is going to stay with her for a few days, so she won't be alone."

A pinprick stung somewhere in my mother's heart. Macey didn't feel she needed me there? Nine years old, and she was already making her own arrangements? "Where's Isha?"

Kyle hesitated, and I sensed another bomb about to drop. "I fired Isha last night. She left this morning."

"What . . . wait . . . Kyle, what are you talking about? Isha's been great so far. Macey adores her. Why in the world would you fire her, especially when I'm out of town?" I tried to imagine what he could possibly be thinking. "She's over here on a work visa, Kyle. Without her job, she'll be deported."

"I found her another job." He paused to thank Bree for bringing him a set of depositions, then told her she'd done a good job. I listened intently, trying to decide if the tone conveyed friendly office conversation or something more. I pictured Bree, fly-away ringlets of hair sailing in the window breeze as she drove me to the airport. She was twenty-four, gorgeous, gullible, a teenager rattling around in a woman's body, in a man's world. What man wouldn't be attracted to that? "I had a client who was looking for someone to watch her kids," Kyle went on. "She's going back into the real estate business now that her divorce is settled, and she needed someone who could be there at odd hours. Two little girls. Isha's a perfect fit."

"You *gave* our au pair to one of your *clients*?" I thought of Susan

Sewell, the blonde in the café. Kyle was handling property issues in her divorce case. . . .

Kyle huffed into the phone. "I didn't *give* her away. I'd already fired her, so I did the nice thing and found her a new job. I think she'll get along fine at Susan's house."

Susan. Susan Sewell. Susan . . . who now had Macey's au pair.

I wanted to demand answers, to say, *I saw you in the café holding hands, smiling at each other, intimate, like it wasn't the first time. What's going on, Kyle? I want the truth.* . . .

Instead, some legally savvy defense mechanism I'd inherited from my mother was warning, *Not now, not now. Don't tip him off that anything's wrong. You can never trust a man to do the right thing.* . . . Another part of me, the emotionally raw and exhausted part, was saying, *If it's true, I don't want to know. Not right now.* . . . "Kyle, if the problem with Isha was bad enough to fire her, why would you recommend her to someone else? Especially someone with young children. If she's not doing her job . . ."

"She'll do fine at Susan's. Don't worry about it, all right? It's handled. My mother is going to stay here for a few days until Macey's back on her feet. I've already called the agency and they're sending information on a couple of au pairs they have available. If none of that works out, they can provide a temp nanny until we come up with the right person."

I swabbed my forehead, trying to wipe away the images of Kyle interviewing new au pairs, and his mother helping in the decision. As much as I loved Kyle's parents, his mother would pick somebody like Mrs. Beasley—a sweet, cookie-baking, coddling, bun-wearing nanny who would tiptoe around behind my back, giving Macey snacks she wasn't supposed to have, letting her stay up late to read stories and play board games and instant message with her girlfriends, just like Grandma Macklin did.

"Kyle, you can't leave me with *it's handled*. What happened? Why did you fire Isha? You never had a problem with her before."

"Why do you always have to harp on things?" The frustration, the disgust in Kyle's tone, jerked me back against the chair like a sudden slap. That was the bitter, sharp-edged voice couples shot at each other from across negotiating tables during divorces. "Why can't you just trust me to handle it? I'm not an idiot. I don't need a manager, Rebecca."

"I'm not trying to *manage* you, Kyle." As usual, he was attempting to put me on the defensive, to imply that the problem was *me* and my unreasonable need to control things. I hated it when he intimated that all of our marital disagreements stemmed from my having trust issues due to some Freudian reaction to my childhood—as if *he* was perfect because he came from an ideally intact family with two parents who never fought about anything, at least not in front of people. "Pardon me if it seems strange that I want to know what's going on at home. I'm sure if it were you, you wouldn't give us a second thought." I winced as soon as the harpoon went out. I could feel it spiraling toward the target. A fight wouldn't accomplish anything. I didn't want to hurt him. I wanted . . . I didn't know what I wanted. "I'm sorry. I didn't mean that. I'm just . . . tired."

"I understand that, but I . . ." Whatever he was about to say, he held it back. I heard the chair squeak, the office door close. "I know that what you're doing down there is hard. I wasn't even going to tell you Isha was gone, but Macey had her accident, and I knew she'd want to call you tonight, so I figured I'd better bring you up to speed first."

"What *is* going on, Kyle?" I hated it when he kept things from me just because he didn't want to deal with my reaction and the discussion that would inevitably follow. "I'd rather just know. What happened with Isha?"

Someone knocked on his office door and he paused to answer,

sign something, and close the door, while I waited on the line, imagining everything from Isha letting Macey watch R-rated movies, to leaving her alone in the house, to having a lover's spat with Kyle and threatening to reveal the truth.

"Last night when I came home, she was waiting in a negligee with an open bottle of wine. It didn't leave much to the imagination."

"Isha?" I said slowly, trying to imagine dewy-eyed, bubbly Isha, who still got down on the floor and played Barbie Fashion Show with Macey, doing something so calculating and misguidedly sophisticated. "Are you sure you didn't misunderstand? I can't picture Isha doing something like that."

"There wasn't any misunderstanding it." Kyle's answer was toneless, flat. "I know a play when I see one."

How often do you see one? "I just never thought . . ."

Kyle laughed ruefully. "Don't be naive, Rebecca. These girls come over here and they don't have a dime in their pockets. It's no surprise that some of them figure it'd be easier to marry a living than to make one."

"What did you tell her? What did you say?" The scene materialized in my mind, the details remaining misty.

"I told her to get dressed, and we'd talk about her job. Nothing happened, if that's what you're asking." The last sentence was light, disturbingly frivolous, as if he couldn't imagine my thinking he would actually be receptive to her offer. In some strange way, that was comforting.

Pride, or a sense of self-preservation, kept me from digging any deeper. The world underneath me seemed to be shifting faster than I could catch my footing. I was teetering on the edge of something big and black and ragged. I wanted him to reassure me, to say, *Of course I would never do that, Rebecca. I wouldn't do that to you, to Macey. You two are my life. We have a good life. Together. I love you.*

Instead, he laughed into the receiver. "What do you think I am, stupid? Can you say 'sexual harassment lawsuit'? I got her out of the house as fast as I could."

"I guess that's wise. What did you tell Macey?"

"She thinks Isha got a better job offer." I heard the electronic chime of his laptop firing up in the background. "She's a little burned about it, but on the other hand, she doesn't think she needs a nanny anymore. She'd rather have her driver's license and a car."

"Very funny. And she does need a nanny."

"Yeah, I guess." Kyle didn't sound convinced.

"I don't want her coming home to an empty house. She's too young. There are too many nights when you're tied up at work and I'm busy dealing with issues at the boutique." Why was he always in such a hurry for Macey to grow up, to push the parameters of childhood and be a third adult living in the house? Why did family life, raising our child, seem so insignificant to him—just another task to complete, a case to settle before moving on to the next stage of development.

"Don't get me started about that stupid store," he ground out, making clear, once again, that he thought it was high time I divested myself of the place. "Your store manager had some problem with a shipment yesterday. I told her *not* to call you, just do whatever she thought was best. It's always something there."

My head started pounding, my thoughts throbbing with things I wanted to say but couldn't. The store was an argument that seemed insignificant now. "I'd better go. I'm at the hospital. My father's doctor wanted to check him in for a few days."

"It's that bad?"

"It's really bad. He's having delusional episodes. He gets agitated." I wanted to tell him everything, to share with him all the difficulties of the past few days, all the challenges ahead. I wanted to empty myself of all the tightly packed frustration, to lean on him and have him hold me up the way I would have when we were newly married and starting the firm together—before resentments and defense mechanisms created distance between us. When had our lives become so separate that it seemed unnatural to share significant events, to bolster and support each other?

Kyle's computer chimed again, an indication that he'd already moved on to other things. "Sounds like the hospital's a good idea." The words were robotic and distracted. He was reading something while he was talking to me.

I didn't answer. There seemed to be no point.

"You might wait awhile to call Macey," he went on. "Mace is feeling fine, but the pain medicine they gave her at the emergency clinic made her sleepy, and she's taking a nap. Hopefully tomorrow she'll feel well enough to do her homework. The doctor doesn't want her to go back to school until she has the permanent cast on."

"I'll call her later." I ached to be sitting on Macey's bed, stroking her hair, watching her sleep. She had to be heartbroken about missing the state gymnastics meet. Kyle's mom would never understand how important it was. Neither would Kyle.

"Talk to you later, then," he said absently. No time for useless sentimentalities like *I love you* and *I miss you.*

I said good-bye and closed the phone, sighed, and sat there with it folded between my hands, the battery warm on my palms. How had my life become such a mess? My time divided until I was shortchanging everything—my career an unsatisfying rush, my daughter a miniature adult running her own life, my father a stranger living halfway across the country, my husband a dispassionate voice on the other end of the phone?

What would he have said if I'd asked about the scene in the café? Would he tell me the same thing he had about Isha—that it was an unwelcome flirtation, something he hadn't asked for and had quickly rejected?

He wasn't rejecting it the moment before the stoplight changed and I drove away. . . .

Maybe he didn't care if I knew. Maybe he'd been out with Susan in broad daylight on purpose, hoping I would see and confront him and the deceptions would be over. Could seventeen years of marriage really mean so little to him? Could *we*?

What if nothing was going on? If I talked myself into trusting my husband, would I become one of those ridiculously blind women who sat at the negotiating table, finally accepting what everyone else already knew—the kind of women my mother bitterly criticized after her own divorce. *Trust your instincts*, she would have said. *A woman can't afford to be naive. . . .*

Letting out a long sigh, I laid my head back against the wall and closed my eyes. I could feel the plaster vibrating as the elevator hummed upward. I concentrated on the sound, trying to let the simple, meaningless white noise eclipse everything.

I needed to get back to the house, make sure Teddy was all right. . . .

I needed to go by the nursing center, check on Hanna Beth. . . .

I needed to call Macey in a little while. . . .

Poor Macey. . . .

I pictured her asleep in her bed, her long, honey brown hair falling in soft strands against the pillow, her lips pursing slightly as she slept. I loved to watch her sleep. . . .

The picture fell away. Everything fell away.

Peace, finally. . . .

The clang of a metal tray jolted me upright. My muscles were stiff and leaden, and I sat blinking, trying to get my bearings. I was in a hospital corridor. There was a woman in a wheelchair across from me. I knew her from somewhere.

My mind hopscotched, trying to make the connection. She was familiar—the gray hair in a thin braid down her back, the quick dark eyes nestled among loose skin and a thick fan of lines.

She smiled. "You were out like a hound on a hot day." Even her voice, the slow, lazy Texas drawl, was familiar.

"I must have drifted off for a minute." I glanced at the giant clock hanging on the wall like a piece of modern artwork. It was ticking toward six. "Oh, my gosh." I pulled my cell phone out and double-checked the time.

The woman nodded. "You been here awhile. You were sleepin' sound."

"I can't believe I did that," I said, glancing around.

Shrugging, the woman closed the magazine in her lap. "I imagine you were tuckered. I just hated to leave you here, sound asleep with your purse layin' out like that. You might wake up, and it'd be gone." She motioned to the floor, where my purse was lying partially spilled by my feet. It must have fallen when I drifted off.

"I'd of picked those things up for you, but if I tried to get down there, it'd be my luck my grandson would come and see me, and ring my neck. I just had orthoscotic surgery a few days ago. This is my grandson's hospital."

"We met in the airport." I pointed a finger at her, the memory rushing back. The flight seemed weeks ago.

"We did," she affirmed. "I never forget a face."

"Small world."

She laughed under her breath. "Not so," she said, still smiling. "I told you I'd be here."

CHAPTER 12

Hanna Beth Parker

Mary told me that Rebecca would be coming to visit, but the morning passed and there was no sign of her. Mary said she'd probably gotten busy, what with the house to take care of, but I knew there were things Mary wasn't telling me. I worried about those things as the afternoon hours crept by. Gretchen was quick with my therapy session, seeming in too much of a hurry to linger. Ouita Mae didn't come to read to me. Dr. Barnhill stopped in and told me his grandmother wanted me to know she was busy with some appointments at the hospital.

"I hear you and my grandmother have been keeping each other company," he said, and smiled.

"Yye-sss." I was concentrating on making my words more succinct, but the speech therapist had advised me not to expect too much too soon.

Dr. Barnhill smiled indulgently, his hand resting on the rail, his dark eyes taking me in. "It's good you're keeping her busy." His pager beeped, and he stepped away from the rail, glancing down to check it.

I wanted to tell him that, as much as I treasured his grandmother's company, he should be certain to take some hours away from the hospital and enjoy her while he could. Someday, she wouldn't be here any longer, and he'd have all the time in the world for other things.

Over the years, as I'd watched other parents try to keep up with their busy children, I'd realized how fortunate I was to have Teddy. Yes, there were milestones in other children's lives that Teddy would never attain, but in Teddy's world, there was always space for me. His eyes always lit up when I walked into the room.

I couldn't communicate all of that to Dr. Barnhill, and he was headed out the door anyway.

I lay listening to the silence, disappointed that Ouita Mae and I wouldn't be reading about Gavin and Marcella today. When Ouita Mae read it, the story whisked me back to the days of pirate ships on the high seas, into the body of a young woman falling in love. It felt good to relive those feelings, to remember how I'd felt about Edward all those years ago. Throughout my girlhood, when our paths crossed at the park or the pool or our fathers' company picnics, I was smitten. I sometimes rode my bicycle up Blue Sky Hill Court, past his house, in hopes of seeing him. When we came across each other again, that winter break I was home from college, I felt as though I were Cinderella keeping company with Prince Charming. I imagined that he lingered around the store where I was working because he wanted to spend time with me, because he enjoyed laughing about the old days. When I was finishing my shift, he invited me out for a bite. After we ate, we drove down to the lake and talked about his time in graduate school, his new job with a small oil company, his plans to make good on his first big job in South America. I imagined the exotic life we could have together. I wouldn't stay stateside, as my mother had. Married to an executive, I would travel the world, live in unusual places with names my parents couldn't even pronounce.

The plans we make are so much smoke and illusion, like a magician's trick we convince ourselves to believe until the veils are cast away, and we see clearly that God has painted a different picture. In so many ways, I would never have become myself if not for those years of working at the institutional school and raising Teddy on my own.

Even after decades of having Edward to provide for me, love me, take care of me, that determined young woman was inside, reminding me of my own strength. Without her, I probably would have given up and died on the laundry room floor.

Closing my eyes, I drifted back, remembering how it was to be young and vibrant, the future spread out before me like a buffet of choices. I hadn't made all the right ones, but in the end, my years had been full and happy, fortunate.

I was thinking of a family vacation to Disney World when I heard Claude come into the room. I opened my eyes, and he was looking out the window, watching Mary get her kids off the day-care van and put them into hers. They didn't go anywhere, just sat there, all three in the front seat.

Claude realized I was watching, too. "Thought I'd caught you sleepin', Birdie," he said. "Reckon they're telling their mama all about their day at school. They're sweet boys."

I lifted my head off the pillow so I could see better. It looked as though the boys were having a snack in the car, which was their afternoon routine lately. I was worried that I hadn't seen their father come by since the day he and Mary were fighting. He might have started a new job or some such, but I feared he was gone. Mary looked tired these days, ragged and frail. Did Claude know anything about it? I'd heard Mary's boys in his room this morning, visiting with him before the day-care van came. He helped them get their packs on and sent them out the back door when the van arrived. Mary must have been busy elsewhere.

Claude didn't have Mary and the kids on his mind this evening. "I ever tell you about my trains?" he asked.

"Ye-es," I snapped. The tone surprised me. I was in a mood, after looking for Rebecca all day and coming up empty.

Claude drew back, then chuckled under his breath. "Reckon I did. I forget things sometimes."

I felt like a poor neighbor and an ungrateful friend. I hoped Claude wouldn't decide to leave.

He just stared out the window. "I don't mean to talk your ear off. You get old, and when you live by yourself, all you got to talk about is doctor visits, your Social Security check, and things that happened a long time ago. You forget that folks don't want to hear all that stuff." The sadness in those words made my heart sink low. I'd never heard him sound so melancholy.

I concentrated very hard on forming words. "Yeeewww he . . . hewwwp . . . eee." The end of the sentence wouldn't come out. *Me. You help me.*

He smiled again and winked at me. "Ah, Birdie, you're a light," he said. "You, and Mary, and those boys make this place livable." He paused to think. "And maybe Ifeoma, but I gotta have a little more time to figure her out. She's got a little boy back in Ghana, but the daddy didn't want her to keep him because his skin ain't light-colored enough. I asked her one day if she had a family, and that's what she told me." His fingers drummed the arm of his wheelchair. "Ain't that a sad thing?"

"Ye-esh," I murmured, and in my mind the picture of Ifeoma began to change into something soft and sympathetic. I felt a sense of kinship, the bond of mothers raising children in a world that judged by appearances.

Claude tapped the glass with his fingertip. "It's hard to understand people sometimes, ain't it, Birdie?"

"Yes." A single, perfect word.

He laughed softly. "My daddy used to say that working with mules could teach you a lot about dealin' with people. I ever tell you about my daddy workin' those mules?"

"Nnno."

Claude seemed pleased. He'd found a new story to tell. "To work a mule, you got to try to figure him out, you know. A mule's slow, and he's stubborn in the bridle. If you whip him too much, he's like to lay right down on his belly, harness and all. You can't get a mule up if he don't want to get up. You got to work *with* a mule, not against him. A horse won't do them things. Good horse will labor 'til he drops over dead, if you whip him hard enough. He'll work fast, or slow. He'll come light in the bridle. Mule's got a mind of his own, but that's because he's smart—comes from the jackstock in him. In the wild, a burro don't have the speed of a horse, so he's got to be intelligent. He's got to think his way out of trouble. He's always thinkin', lookin', cogitatin' things over in his mind. Bird flies up, or a car goes by, he ain't gonna panic and bolt like a horse would. He's gonna think things through, just like he's gonna think you over when you put a harness on him. You do him wrong, he don't forget it. My daddy was like them mules. He never did forgive me for joinin' the army without permission. Reckon I deserved him being mad. It was a bad thing I done, runnin' off like that when he needed me."

I tried to imagine Claude Fisher ever doing a bad thing. It was a hard instance to picture. Then I thought of my own father, how bitter he was when he sent me to the home for unwed mothers, and then I chose to keep Teddy. I wasn't trying to hurt him, but when I awakened and saw my baby boy, my heart fell into those eyes. I knew I couldn't give him up. I knew I would do everything I could to give him a good life.

I had no idea how difficult that would be.

I wasn't trying to hurt Rebecca or Marilyn when Edward and I found each other again, all those years later. I wanted Teddy to have his father. I yearned to be able to give Teddy a safe, stable home in which to grow up, to provide for him the extra help that might eventually make the difference between an institution and a good life. New treatments, new therapies were being discovered all the time. I wanted Teddy to have those things, but I couldn't afford them. Between working and raising Teddy, I didn't even have time to research the possibilities. I knew Edward could give us a better life. But I never desired that Rebecca suffer for it. I'd hoped to explain that to her, make her see that her father and mother were divorcing because of choices that were made, lies that were told, a deception that had festered. I didn't want Edward to lose his daughter because of me. I didn't want Rebecca to lose her father.

The wounds we cause, while unintentional, still bleed.

"G'night, Birdie." Claude rolled past my bed, headed for the door. "You have sweet dreams, there."

"Oooo-oo," I said. *You, too.* The muscles in my face and jaw were tiring, going slack. Talking was always harder in the evening.

Claude's wheelchair stopped squeaking at the threshold. "I saw Ifeoma workin' her way down the hall. Maybe if I hurry out, she won't come in here and get onto me again." With a sly laugh, he added, "I'm still winnin' her over with my charms. She ain't such a dry patch of ground as she wants folks to think."

I watched his shadow disappear from the doorway light, then turned toward the window again, thinking that I should enjoy the view before someone came in and took the pushpins away again. Outside in the hall, Ifeoma captured Claude. She warned him that if he didn't stop bothering people, she was going to lock him in his room. Claude just laughed.

Mary came up the hall on her way to take one of her boys to the bathroom. Claude asked if she and the boys wanted to go to the TV room for a while. No doubt he was hoping Mary would rescue him from Ifeoma.

Ifeoma inquired as to Mary's reasons for still being at the nursing home, now that the day shift was over. Mary said her car wouldn't turn over, and she was waiting for a friend to come and jump-start it. She told Claude good night, and that she'd better go outside and wait for her friend. The boys were disappointed to miss the TV watching.

I wanted to tell her to let the boys come in and watch television with me, but they were already headed down the hall. Ifeoma took Claude back to his room, admonishing him to stop wandering the corridor.

Claude tried to make a joke of it. "You know I'm just lookin' for you, Ifay," he said, but Ifeoma wasn't amused.

"I have no time for your nonsense, old rooster. You must not bother the others, or I will give a shot in your tail, and put you to sleep."

Claude laughed. "Ifay, you sure know how to break a man's heart."

She snorted, walked out his door, and disappeared down the corridor with long, nearly silent strides. Claude's roommate, a bedfast man whose mind had failed before his body, moaned.

"It's all right, Herb. She don't mean anything by it," Claude soothed. A few minutes later, Claude switched on his TV and turned the sound up loud. His wheelchair squealed as he opened his window, then called Mary's kids over from where they were playing in the grass by the car. They stood at the window, watching Claude's TV like customers at a drive-in movie, and Claude turned the sound up a little louder.

If Ifeoma comes by again, I thought, *there's no telling what she'll do to him.*

I fished my remote from under the covers and turned my TV up loud, too, so maybe Ifeoma wouldn't notice his. The boys stood at the window, the glow illuminating their sweet faces. I fell asleep watching them watch the TV.

In the morning, I awoke smiling. I remembered the boys at the window and imagined I could hear them laughing. As I opened my eyes, the laughter remained, and I knew it was real. I looked around the room, trying to make sense of it. The first rays of dawn were breaking outside. It was before seven, yet. After so many days of watching, I knew exactly what time the sun rose. My blind was still up, and I couldn't remember having been awakened last evening when Betty arrived on her shift.

The little giggle came again, seeming to originate from somewhere within the walls and float around the room. I wondered if I was imagining it, after all. Perhaps my mind had finally gone round the bend.

"Ssshhh," someone whispered from inside the wall. "Ssshhh."

I cocked an ear in that direction.

"It tick-ewll," a child's voice whispered back.

The sound was coming from Claude's room, drifting through the air-conditioning system from his bathroom vent to mine in the early-morning silence. The mild night had caused the air system to hush its constant attempts to regulate the temperature.

"Ssshhh, we have to be quiet in here, remember?" It was Mary's voice.

The shower came on, and Brandon said, "It's too cold."

"Ssshhh," Mary answered. "Here. That's better. Hurry, sweetheart."

I heard them moving around in the bathroom, the water turning off and on. In the hallway, Betty's squeaky shoes passed by.

"Mornin', Betty." Claude's voice seemed close. He must have been sitting in his doorway. "My lands, but don't you look bright-eyed and lovely this mornin'. Fine day out there, ain't it?"

A high-pitched, sarcastic laugh traveled the corridor. "What're you doin' up so early, Fisher?"

"Scared to sleep late," he replied.

Betty grumbled and moved on.

I heard Claude chuckling to himself. He sat in the hall awhile longer, then his chair scraped against the jamb as he pushed back into his room. He knocked on the bathroom door, whispered something I couldn't hear.

"Almost done," Mary's hushed answer came through the vent. "Here, Brandon, just put these back on. Brush your teeth real quick, let's . . ."

The air-conditioning system fired up, and I couldn't hear the rest. I leaned over in my bed so I could see out the window. As dawn eclipsed the streetlights, Mary and her boys hurried from the building and disappeared into the parking lot. The boys were still in their pajamas, carrying little backpacks, their hair freshly washed and still wet. Mary was dressed in her long skirt and scrub top for work, her hair hanging loose and damp down her back.

I kept watch out the window as the nursing center came to life, Betty working her way down the hall, the breakfast trays coming around, ambulatory patients proceeding to the cafeteria.

When it was time for the day-care van, Mary was on the sidewalk with the boys, now dressed and ready to begin their day at Brighter Horizons Child Care Center.

I heard Claude next door in the bathroom, turning the water on and off. Betty came by and knocked, demanding to know what he was up to.

The bathroom door lock clicked as he opened it. "Doin' a man's business," he replied. "Already got myself all washed up and ready for breakfast, too. Thought I'd save ya the trouble. Used up the towels, though. I spilt some water and wiped it up the best I could."

"Mmm-hmm," she replied suspiciously. "Don't be gettin' in the shower alone, Fisher."

"No, ma'am," Claude replied. "I just parked my chair right by-side it. Worked out real good, and . . ." The air system clicked on again.

Outside, Mary hugged her boys tight, put them on the day-care van, then stood combing her long hair and twisting it into a bun.

The truth became clear, as I watched. Mary was bathing her children in Claude's bathroom and getting ready for work on the sidewalk, not because she'd had some schedule mix-up with her husband, or because the van needed a jump-start, but because she didn't have anywhere else to go.

CHAPTER 13

Rebecca Macklin

In the middle of the night, I heard someone in the house crying. My first thought was of Macey—that she'd had a bad dream and was afraid to get out of bed and come to my room.

"Mace?" I mumbled drowsily, but no one answered. I opened my eyes and reached for the button on the bottom of the terra-cotta night lamp beside the bed, but it wasn't where it was supposed to be. My fingers settled, instead, on a ruffled, ballerina-style shade, the lace covering crispy and old. *I'm in a hotel*, I thought, fumbling for the switch.

My eyes adjusted to the ambient glow from the streetlights outside. The thick wooden blinds and the heavy, ornate window trims clarified my surroundings with sudden focus. I rolled over and checked the windup clock on the desk across the room. Four thirty.

I listened for the noise, wondering if I'd only dreamed it, or if, a thousand miles away in California, Macey was in pain, and through some invisible connection only mothers understand, I was feeling it, hearing her sob. I'd called home three times last evening, but Macey was out cold from pain medication. Finally, I'd lain awake thinking about her, about everything, tormenting myself with hypothetical scenarios. What if Macey awakened in the middle of the night, and Grandma Macklin couldn't hear her from the guest room? A freight train could run through the house, and Kyle wouldn't wake up. What if Kyle wasn't even there? He could tell his mother he had an over-night business trip—she'd never know the difference.

The questions swirled again as I listened for the sound. I sat up, feeling dizzy and disoriented. Unsteady on my feet, I started toward the bathroom. The sound came again, a long, sniffling sob, but not a child's. I stepped into the hall, then traced the noise down the dark-ened stairs. As I turned the corner to the living room, I saw Teddy on the sofa, his body curled awkwardly around the white crocheted throw that had been draped over the back of the sofa. Sobbing, Teddy rocked back and forth, his face buried in the folds of the blanket.

"Teddy?" I whispered. He'd been fine last night. I'd explained to him that Daddy Ed was in the hospital for a few days so the doctors could straighten out his medicines and help him feel better. I'd let him listen in while I called the hospital and checked to be sure every-thing was all right. Teddy and I had ordered a pizza and watched part of a movie together. The evening was peaceful. I'd fallen asleep on the sofa. When I woke up, Teddy was carefully covering me with the white afghan and getting ready to go to bed.

Now he was clenching the blanket and weeping, his body trem-bling in spasms of grief.

"Teddy, what's wrong?" I crossed the room, sat down on the cof-fee table, slipped my hands between my knees. Even in April, the house was cold at night. The thin cotton pajamas, which would have been perfect in Santa Monica, felt like ice against my skin. "Teddy? Did you have a bad dream?"

Teddy continued rocking, his sadness spilling into the blanket. I had no idea what to do. What would Hanna Beth do if she were here?

"Hey, it's all right." I leaned closer, tried to see his face under the thick, tangled mop of hair. He needed a haircut. "Can you tell me what's wrong?"

His breath wheezed inward. He shook his head, gathered the edges of the blanket closer to his body and hunched over the bundle, stroking the fringe in a slow, repetitive motion.

I sat helpless, watching him. "Did your mom make this?" I asked, finally. "The blanket—did your mom crochet it?"

He didn't answer, just continued rocking. "Teddy, is this your mom's blanket?" When Macey was younger, if I was away overnight, she went into my room, took my pillow off the master bed, and slept with it. For the past year or so, I'd noticed that when I traveled and came back, my pillow was still in place. "Are you lonesome for your mom? Is that what's wrong?"

His sob formed into words that disappeared into the blanket. Stroking the damp tangles away from his cheek, I leaned over so I could see him. "Teddy, it's okay to miss her. Of course you miss your mom. I know it's been hard without her here, but . . ."

"I wan' Mama," he sobbed. "I wan' Daddy Ed home."

I was struck by the fact that, even after the torment my father had put Teddy through these past weeks, Teddy wanted him here, with us. "Teddy, sometimes people have to go to the hospital for a little while when they're sick, so the doctors can help them get better. Remember? We talked about that last night?"

Teddy pushed farther into the sofa pillows, away from my hand. "Nobody don' come back. Mama don' come. Kay-Kay say, 'I goin' hop-sital, Teddy,' and Kay-Kay . . . and Kay-Kay don' come . . ." The words disintegrated into a sob that shook his body. His shoulders quaked until the bones seemed to rattle beneath his skin.

A lump of emotion rose in my throat. I thought about what it would be like to be Teddy—confused, alone, first his mother, then his caretaker, and now Daddy Ed gone. The world was crumbling around him, everything changing, and he was powerless to stop it, unable to predict where it would end, unable to understand the time, and distances, and complications involved.

I laid my hand on his shoulder, felt the quaking tide of grief, felt myself sink into it, understand it. Life could be normal one day, and in a split second, everything changed. For now, there was only pain and fear, and a desperate fight to stay above the flood.

"It's okay, Teddy," I whispered. "We'll figure it out. I promise we'll figure it out." Leaning close, I rested my chin on his shoulder, then slipped onto the sofa and sat beside him. "Don't worry. I'll take care of things. They'll come home. They'll come home." How could I promise that? What if I was wrong? "It'll be all right." Would it be? Could I make it all right? What would *all right* look like?

Bending forward, Teddy lowered his head into my lap the way Macey sometimes did when she'd suffered a dose of preteen heartbreak at school. Hanna Beth's blanket fell over my knees. "I wan' Mama." Teddy's voice was a whisper of pain, the hoarse, tender outcry of loneliness. "I wan' Mama. I wan' Mama."

"I know you do," I whispered. "I know you do." I slipped my arms around him and curled over him, cradling him, cradling my own wounded spirit. "We'll go see your mom in the morning," I promised. "We'll go see Hanna Beth."

I awoke on the sofa, covered with the white afghan. Teddy was gone. On the coffee table, a peanut butter and jelly sandwich and a glass of milk sat waiting. I could hear Teddy down the hall in his plant room, talking to the seedlings.

Sitting up, I caught the scent of peanut butter, and my stomach rolled over. With all the emotion last night, I didn't feel like eating anything. I hid the sandwich in the bottom of the kitchen trash and poured the milk down the drain, so as not to hurt Teddy's feelings. There was something incredibly tender and sweet about the fact that he never made a sandwich for himself without making one for me.

My cell phone started ringing before I was halfway up the stairs. I hurried the rest of the way, turned the corner to my room, and grabbed the phone off the nightstand. Answering, I sat down on the bed, still feeling logy and off-kilter.

"Hi, Mom." Those two words washed over me like the cool, salty ocean breezes of home.

"Hi, sweetheart, how's my girl? I tried to call you last night, but Grammy said you'd taken your pain medication and you were out like a light all evening."

"I just woke up," she said in her drowsy just-out-of-bed voice. I loved that voice. I could picture her sitting on her pink bedspread, her soft brown hair tussled on the pillow. I knew how she would smell, how it would feel if I snuggled in and wrapped my arms around her. She would lay her head against my chest and burrow into the crook of my shoulder.

I pictured her slim, knobby ankle wrapped in a temporary brace, and sadness slid over me. I hoped Kyle had come home last night to tuck her in, that he'd hung around this morning long enough to talk to her about her leg, maybe bring her breakfast and comfort her. "I'm sorry I wasn't there yesterday."

"Mom, it's not that big a deal." Macey was business as usual, surprisingly chipper, considering. "They're gonna put a walking cast on it in a couple days, and the doctor said then I can do everything— except maybe go to the beach, because of all the sand getting in it, and dance and gymnastics . . . but I don't know . . . I didn't want to go to state all that bad, anyway. I think I'm ready for a break from gymnastics."

"Mace, you love gymnastics." I pictured my little girl in her leo-tard and sweatpants, up in the game room for hours on end, all the furniture pushed to the edges so she could practice walkovers and stride leaps, doing handstands against the wall and holding them as long as she could to build her upper-body strength for tumbling passes, watching the Olympics on DVD and dreaming of being there one day. "You've always loved gymnastics."

"I know." She sighed into the phone, then hesitated in a way that indicated something important was coming next. "It's just that . . . well . . . you know I'm always going to gymnastics and stuff, and I don't get to just, like, hang out with my friends, go shopping and stuff like that, y'know? I think maybe next year in school I want to do junior drill team."

The last words came rushing out as if they'd been saved up for a while. *Drill team?* I thought. *Where the girls dress in short skirts and dance like mini NFL cheerleaders? That? My little girl?* "Well, Mace, that takes a lot of time. Are you saying that you want to give up gymnastics and do drill team instead?" I had a sense of being out-of-body, as if someone else should be standing here having this conversation with an emerging teenager.

"Yeah . . . I mean . . . I guess so . . . for a little while." She sighed again, and I could picture her sitting there picking at the white strings on her coverlet, finally finding the courage to level with me, long-distance. "Drill team's cool, Mom. Hardly any of my school friends do gymnastics anymore."

"So now we're picking our activities based on what our friends do?" The words sounded harsh, like something my mother would have said. Was I always so quick to dismiss Macey's opinions?

She went silent. "I dunno," she muttered finally, sounding defeated. "I just thought about it. . . ."

I pictured the trophy shelf on her wall, crowded with ribbons and medals and tiny golden statues of miniature gymnasts in beautiful poses. I remembered taking her to her first gymnastics class when she was four, just a baby with her chubby legs, her round stomach not yet the slender waist of a girl, her head still too big for her body in the pink leotard. It wasn't long before the coaches singled her out, saw potential. Years of training, of competitions and exhibition performances followed. When I missed a meet because of work, Macey and I reviewed the tapes later, reliving her triumphs and tragedies over popcorn and root beer floats.

Now all of it might be coming to an end. I wasn't prepared. Her life was moving on. I wanted to go back to every competition, every exhibition performance I'd missed, every fragment of her childhood I'd let slip by, and be there in person.

"Mom?" Macey probed the silence tentatively, like a surrendering soldier raising a white flag. "It's not a big deal. I mean, I was just thinking about it, but Coach Kara would probably have a fit anyway. She thinks I can make elite, and—"

"Mace." I stopped her from doing what I'd always done with my mother, bending to her will, then resenting it later. "Just give it all some good thought, okay? We'll talk about it when I get home, but it's your decision. I want you to do what you want." The words trembled with emotion. Too many things were changing at once. Too many things ending, beginning, turning blind corners.

"Mom, are you all right?"

I held the phone away from my mouth, trying to quell the rush of conflicting emotions.

"Mom?"

The last thing Macey needed, lying at home with an injured leg, was to hear me falling apart, long-distance. "Yes, honey, I'm fine. I just miss you, that's all. I'm sorry I wasn't there with you at the emergency clinic yesterday, and that I'm not there today to take care of you while you're home sick."

Macey coughed into the phone. "Moh-a-om. I'm not a baby. I can handle it."

Even though the comment was meant to reassure me, it stung. "I know you're not a baby. I'd just like to be there with you, that's all."

"I'm fine, Mom. My leg doesn't even hurt that much today. Grammy's, like, driving me crazy about it. She won't let me get out of bed. I told Dad she doesn't have to stay after I get the walking cast on. I can stay here by myself in the afternoons."

"No, Macey, you can't stay there by yourself."

She huffed a frustrated snort. "Did Isha put the moves on Dad?"

"Macey!" My voice exploded into the room and echoed down the silent hallway. Blood drained from my face and I had a sudden attack of vertigo. "That's . . . that is inappropriate. Why would you say something like that?"

She didn't answer right away. No doubt she was calculating damage control. "I heard Dad and her talking. It's no big deal."

What did you hear? Tell me what you heard. I wanted to probe her, get an eyewitness account, but I knew that would be wrong. "I don't really know what happened. I wasn't there." It felt strange to be defending Kyle, giving him the presumption of innocence, especially considering what I'd seen in the sidewalk coffee shop. "It's nothing you need to worry about, all right?"

"Grammy's here with a snack tray," Macey said flatly, with no indication of what she was really feeling, of what she thought, of how much she'd overheard.

My mind slid back to the day my mother told me the harsh truth about my father. He wasn't the steadfast, loyal family man, the devoted, loving husband and father I'd believed him to be. In fact, he didn't love us at all. He was trading us in, moving on. She was foolish to have trusted him in the first place. . . .

"I better go." Macey's voice seemed far away.

"I love you, Mace," I said quietly.

"Love you, too, Mom."

Closing the phone, I lay down on the bed, let my head sink against the pillow as the sun crossed the ceiling and the dragonflies sailed around the room. There was no magic in it, only the painful memory of having left this place behind all those years ago.

Because of Hanna Beth.

Because of Teddy. Teddy, who was in the backyard now, building yet another lopsided bench to hold plants that, like Teddy, were waiting for Hanna Beth to return to this house. As usual, everything was about Hanna Beth.

Even though I didn't want them, resentments crept from hidden places inside me, emerged from old wounds, never properly healed. Closing my eyes, shutting out the dragonflies, I thought, *I don't need this. I have problems of my own. I could find some kind of halfway house for Teddy, have Dr. Amadi send my father to the nursing center with Hanna Beth, close up this house, go home and try to salvage what's left of my life. Why should I stay here? Why should I put Macey's future, my future, the future of my marriage, if there was one, further at risk?*

For Hanna Beth?

I lay steeping in the bitterness, filling myself with the emotions it would take to leave, to close up the house and let it all go. The idea felt good. It felt like justice, like a made-for-TV legal case in which the evidence turns over at the last minute, and everyone gets what they deserve. It tasted sweet, tempting. I pictured myself getting in the car, driving away from Blue Sky Hill, leaving behind the stacks of old mail and newspapers still piled in the corners waiting to be sorted, abandoning Teddy's ridiculous collection of fast-food trash and plants, walking out on my father's senseless piles of old paperwork and files—leaving it all to rot with the house. When we were gone, *those people* could take over. They could invade every corner, sift through the convoluted history of our family, learn all our secrets, then burn the evidence.

I'd be gone, and none of it would matter.

Standing between me and my imaginary escape, there was Teddy, his arms full of smashed cups and used foam containers, his eyes filled with need, with desperation as he asked me to promise I wouldn't leave.

Swinging my legs off the bed, I sat up, gathered my clothes, showered, dressed, sipped Sprite and nibbled on toast in the kitchen until my stomach settled. Then I went into the yard and told Teddy to put on some clean clothes. We were going to the nursing center to see Hanna Beth.

We detoured on the way to check on my father. Dr. Amadi was coming out the door as I went in. I stopped to talk to him, and Teddy paused beside me, his attention wandering to a fish tank built into the wall at the end of the corridor. "You can go look up close, if you want to, Teddy," I said. "Don't go any farther, okay? I'll be right here."

Teddy measured the distance with an uncertain glance. "Ho-kay," he said finally, and started toward the fish tank.

I waited until he was out of earshot, then turned back to the doctor. "How's he doing today?"

Dr. Amadi blandly recounted my father's condition while writing on his clipboard. Imbalanced electrolytes, blah, blah, blah, uncertainty about the medications in his system, blah, blah, blah, they were keeping him sedated for now, and they would know more tomorrow, blah, blah, blah. "He's resting comfortably," he finished, and raised a self-satisfied brow, as if that solved everything. "We will assess his progress today, then most probably move to some tests, MRI and ultrasound. There is the possibility that his rapid decline is the result of a secondary condition—head injury, stroke, a series of small strokes. These things can go undiagnosed in the dementia patient. If he has been alone in the house, all of these are possibilities." He gave me a narrow look. "Has he fallen recently?"

"I don't know," I admitted, feeling as though I'd been accused of something and should defend myself. "Not that I'm aware of, but it could have happened."

"I see." The doctor stepped away from the door, holding the clipboard against his chest, the silent message being that he was finished jotting notes and therefore ready to move on. "We will know more in two or three days, when the erroneous medications have been cleansed from his system, and his electrolytes are once again within normal range."

"Forgive me for not understanding," I said. It was a typical legal maneuver—soften up the opposition by apologizing for your stupidity, then ask the tough questions. "But yesterday I had the impression that he would only be here for a day, possibly two. Can't we go ahead and run the tests today?"

Dr. Amadi tipped his chin upward, bristling. "We will, of course, care for him to the utmost of our ability. We will be in contact as things progress. There is very little you can do for him now."

Sidestepping me, he brushed by and disappeared down the hall.

I gaped after him as he turned the corner, then I stepped into the room and watched my father sleep for a few minutes. Teddy came in, and we stood there together, neither of us saying anything. It was impossible to know how to feel about my father, finally quiet, crumpled in a hospital bed with his mouth hanging open and his gown wet because he'd been drooling on himself. I moved the pillows and adjusted his head. As I turned to leave, Teddy went back and covered him with the blanket, then stood over the bed, gently stroking his hand.

My emotions did a wild swing, and I exited the room, then waited in the hall. When Teddy came out, he patted me on the head as if I were a child. "It all right, A-becca. Daddy Ed sleepin'." He pressed a finger to his lips. "Ssshhhh. He sleepin'."

"Yeah," I answered, and we started down the hall.

"We gone see Mama now?" Teddy's face lifted hopefully. "Mama here?"

"Down the street at the nursing center," I answered. "We'll have to go in the car."

"Kay-Kay here?" He scanned the corridor and peered into the rooms we passed, as if he expected to see Kay-Kay in one of them.

I thought about what he'd said the day before, that Kay-Kay had gone to the hospital and not come back. If Kay-Kay had suddenly become ill, all of this might make some sense. Perhaps the stress of taking care of Teddy and my father had been too much. "I'm not sure, Teddy. We'd have to know her full name to check."

"Oh," Teddy said, and that was the end of the conversation. We stepped into the elevator, and he was fascinated by the buttons and the lights above the door.

As we drove down the street, Teddy asked questions about how the elevators worked at the hospital, what stopped them from bumping into the roof, the floor, and each other. At the nursing center, Ouita Mae Barnhill was sitting outside the front door in her wheelchair, her purse clutched in her lap. It seemed strange to see her there after having run across her at the hospital the day before.

"We just seem to show up at all the same places," I commented as the automatic door on the wheelchair ramp opened, and a worker came out, pushing an empty laundry cart. Teddy left me and walked up the ramp, craning to observe the top of the door frame. Inside, he looped around, came back out the center door, and headed up the wheelchair ramp, one careful step at a time, waiting to see if the door would open on its own again.

"There it go!" He cheered, fanning his hands in the air.

Ouita Mae laughed. "It'd be good if we could all get that excited about an automatic door, now wouldn't it? He's sure enough a cheerful chap."

"He's Hanna Beth's son." I wasn't sure what else to say. "Teddy."

"Oh." Ouita nodded. "She's asked about him. This morning, she woke up fussing about Teddy. I reckon she'd had a dream or something. She'll be glad you came today."

At a loss for how to respond, I changed the subject. "Are you headed out to lunch?"

Tipping her chin up, she smiled and nodded. "My grandson's taking me. He ought to be along any minute." She checked her watch and glanced expectantly toward the door. "Lands, I'll tell you, I can't keep up with that boy—so many things to do and people to see, and every time I turn around, his beeper is going off, and he's rushing here and there. I just have to sit down and wait, sometimes."

"I guess it would be that way." In a sense, I could relate. The more successful the law practice became, the more it seemed as if I ended up catching Kyle on the fly. He was always on his way to somewhere, in a hurry, overbooked, late for a consultation, a meeting, a mediation, a court date, an opportunity to schmooze with corporate executives in charge of big real estate deals. I loved the fact that he was successful, confident, good at what he did, but there was always that part of me whispering in my mother's voice that I should be keeping up, preparing to take care of myself and Macey, that I shouldn't make the mistake of leaning too much on Kyle.

Perhaps he sensed that. Maybe that was why he was attracted to Susan Sewell. Maybe she made him feel needed. . . .

The door swished open, and both Ouita Mae and I looked up. A doctor stepped out, slipping off his lab coat.

Ouita Mae smiled. "Well, there he is, finally," she said loudly enough for him to hear. He'd turned to look over his shoulder, watching as Teddy raised and lowered his foot on the mat by the handicapped entrance, setting off the chime that warned of the door opening.

The doctor finally turned away, pulled his sunglasses from his pocket and put them on. "Ready?" he asked, then noticed me and paused.

"This is my grandson." Ouita Mae tried to move her chair forward to make introductions, but slid in the seat instead and ended up teetering on the edge.

Both the doctor and I stepped forward to help. He ended up with the chair and I with my hand under Ouita Mae's elbow.

The rush of assistance embarrassed her. "I'll be glad when this leg gets stronger," she complained, situating herself in the wheelchair. "It's time I got back to normal."

The doctor gave me a covert look, and I understood the meaning. He was afraid his grandmother wouldn't be getting back to normal anytime soon. Steadying the wheelchair with one hand, he extended the other to me. "Phillip Barnhill."

"Rebecca Macklin," I introduced myself and shook his hand. His grip was warm, strong, steady. A nice sort of hand for a doctor.

His grandmother smiled proudly up at him. "The nurses call him Dr. Phil."

Letting his head fall forward, he grinned sheepishly. "All right, I'm sure she doesn't need the whole history."

"I was just trying to make her laugh," Ouita Mae defended. "She's had a tough go the last few days. We had a chat about it last night at the hospital, didn't we, dear? The two of us almost wrecked on the plane together coming into Dallas."

Dr. Phil turned to me curiously, and I blushed. "It's a long story." No doubt Dr. Phil's life was filled with long stories of aging parents and caretaking dilemmas just like mine.

"There's room for three at lunch," Ouita Mae offered, then glanced toward Teddy. "Four, I mean. You're welcome to join us."

"We can't," I said. "But thanks. I'd better take Teddy in before he wears out the door." There was more weariness in the comment than I'd meant to convey.

Ouita Mae smiled indulgently in Teddy's direction. "Hanna Beth will be so tickled to see you both." Glancing over her shoulder at her grandson, she said, "Rebecca belongs to Mrs. Parker— Hanna Beth. She flew here all the way from California to see about things." She turned back to me. "Phillip is your mother's doctor, you know."

I blinked in surprise. A million questions ran through my mind, but by the door, Teddy's investigation was causing the chime to ring incessantly.

"We can talk later," Dr. Barnhill offered. "If your mother knew she had visitors out here and I was holding them up, she'd bust my chops."

"Phillip!" Ouita Mae scolded. "Mind your language!" As they started down the sidewalk, she stretched upward in the chair and snatched at his earlobe. He ducked away playfully, and they continued across the parking lot.

CHAPTER 14

Hanna Beth Parker

I fell asleep after another morning session with Gretchen, and when I woke up, Teddy was sitting by my bed. He'd bent forward over the rail and taken hold of my hand. His cheek was resting lightly on my fingers, and he was just watching me.

"Hi, Mama," he whispered, smiling, his sweet, soft eyes looking into mine.

Teddy, I thought, *oh, Teddy, if you're a dream, I don't want to wake up.* My heart filled with a rush of love. I couldn't have forced words past my lips if I'd wanted to, but I was afraid to speak anyway. Disturbing the air might cause my Teddy to vanish like a mirage, and once again I would be alone in the room. I lay there and held his hand. It felt real. It felt so real. . . .

"Don' cry, Mama," he whispered, then took a tissue from the box and clumsily dabbed my cheek. "Don' cry."

They're happy tears, I wanted to tell him. *These are the happiest tears.* I gazed at Teddy, taking in the look and feel and scent of him to make him real. He'd been in the sun too much without his hat. His forehead and cheeks and the back of his neck were burned, his skin dry and leathery. He smelled of wood and soil and growing things— the damp, earthy odors of the garden house. His hair needed washing and a trim, but his clothes were clean. I was glad, because it meant someone was taking care of him.

I looked around the room, expecting to see Kay-Kay, or Edward, perhaps Rebecca, but there was no one. My mind succumbed to the fact that Teddy probably wasn't there, either. He couldn't possibly have come alone. My fingers squeezed tighter around Teddy's, as if that could keep him from vanishing when someone came in and woke me up.

I heard voices in the corridor, but I couldn't make out the words. They came closer, and I caught fragments of conversation.

". . . really doing better. You'll be . . ." It was Mary's voice. Perhaps I wasn't dreaming after all.

I couldn't hear the answer or identify the other voice. It was a woman's. Rebecca's? She was speaking in hushed tones, trying to keep the conversation private.

"She'll be glad," Mary replied. ". . . missed him. But I wouldn't tell . . ." The word "her" and whatever came afterward were muffled.

Wouldn't tell her what? I thought. *What?*

The answer was shrouded in a grave tone. A few moments later, Mary was gone, and Rebecca entered the room wearing a cordial smile and offering a pleasant greeting. "You look like you're doing better. Your nurse and your therapist are giving good reports. They say you've come a long way in the past few days. That's good, because Teddy has seedlings potted everywhere. I think he's counting on you to come home and help plant the flower beds. Isn't that right, Teddy?"

"Tha's right." Letting go of my hand, Teddy sat back in his chair and started cataloging flowers on his fingers. "I got mar-gold, and batch-er butin, see-nas, got butin mum, divide the iris and the daffy-dill . . ."

I laughed when he said "daffy-dill." That was one of Edward's words. The trees in the front yard were surrounded by daffodils. Edward always made nonsensical jokes as we worked out there.

Hey, Teddy, do you know what the silliest flower in the garden is?

Huh-uh, Daddy Ed. I don' know. Even years after he'd memorized the punch line, Teddy always answered the same way, so as not to spoil Edward's joke. *What the silly f-ower?*

Why, the daffy-dill, of course.

Teddy always threw his head back and slapped the ground, as if the joke caught him by surprise every time. *Oh, that a good one, Daddy Ed! That a good one!* He laughed and snorted until both of us laughed with him. Teddy loved to make people laugh.

A smile tugged my lips as I savored the memory. I tried not to imagine how the smile looked from the outside, my mouth hanging slack, my cheeks hollow. It felt like a smile on the inside, which was all that mattered.

"We gone go Wal-Mart," Teddy offered, his eyes widening with anticipation. Teddy enjoyed Wal-Mart, especially the gardening center with its rows and rows of flowers. Sometimes he would wander among the plants for an hour while I did my shopping. He talked to the employees, helped them with watering, pruned dead leaves, picked up spilled grains of fertilizer and fed them to the plants. "Gone go Wal-Mart, get some Mir-cal Go." He glanced at Rebecca for approval, and she nodded. "And some pizza. I like pizza. Got the flat meat." He held up his fingers with about an inch of space in between. "Little flat meat. Tha's good."

"Pepperoni." Rebecca shook a finger at him. "Last night, you stole all the pepperoni."

Ducking his head, Teddy honked and laughed. "No, I did," he said finally, his head and shoulders swaying back and forth as he smiled adoringly at Rebecca.

A pang of jealousy sliced through me, sharp and unexpected. I wasn't accustomed to having to share Teddy with anyone. Even though he and Edward loved each other, they were never close in the way Teddy and I had always been. Kay-Kay was pleasant with him, but generally she stayed about her business. Keeping the house and taking care of Edward occupied most of her time.

"Tonight, I'm guarding the pepperoni," Rebecca went on, and Teddy laughed again. I wondered if she was mocking him, if all of this was a performance for my benefit. Was it really possible that Rebecca, who'd resented Teddy all her life, could have developed an affection for him?

I reminded myself that to believe anything less was selfish and petty, not in Teddy's or Edward's best interests. We were, after all, at Rebecca's mercy. There was little choice but to hope Teddy's magic could win even her.

The conversation ebbed, and Rebecca's gaze flitted nervously over me. I searched for the truth in her face. What did I see there—resentment, fear, pity? How did she feel about her father, now that they had spent some time together? Why hadn't she brought him with her today? Getting Edward out of the house was a challenge, but between Rebecca, Kay-Kay, and Teddy, they could have done it. What if something was wrong with Edward? Changes of any kind were difficult for him. He relied on his daily routine, the same people present, the same things to do. How had he reacted to Rebecca's presence? Did he know who she was?

Gathering my courage, I made up my mind to try the question. But the words were a jumble in my head. Nerves pulsed in my throat. What would they think when they heard me like this? What if Teddy was frightened by it? I formed the words very carefully in my mind. Edward. Where is Edward? "Derrr-d, ger-ble Derrr-d?" It was only nonsense sound. The muscles in my jaw tightened in frustration. *Where is Edward?* "Derrr-d?"

Sensing the rising tide of emotion in me, Teddy patted my hand. He hated to see anyone upset. "It okay, Mama. It okay."

Rebecca fiddled with the strap on her purse, and she glanced toward the door, as if she were considering leaving. "Don't try to talk, Hanna Beth. Teddy just wanted to see you. To make sure you were all right. We'd probably better let you rest." She checked the door, took a step away.

"Nnnooo! Derrr-ddd!" I sounded like the screaming woman down the hall, like a deranged old person spitting out gibberish. "Derrr-ddd!" Grinding my teeth, I closed my eyes, tried to be calm, to relax, picture the sounds, do the things the speech therapist had taught me. I'd named, with some clarity, twenty-one cards today— comb, brush, car, boy, dog, milk, and a host of others. Now I couldn't manage to ask after my own husband? Was there no point at which I would finally become functional again?

"We'd better go." Rebecca put her hands on Teddy's arms to guide him out of the chair.

"Nnnooo!" I hissed. "Nnnooo!"

Teddy pulled inward, kneaded his fingers against his chest, his eyes darting toward his lap. Swiveling away from Rebecca, he curled into the chair. She froze, uncertain of what to do, then grabbed the nurse's call button and pressed it.

Mary came in the door. "Is everything all right?"

"She's upset about something." Rebecca held up her palms in a gesture of helplessness. "I don't know what to . . ."

Mary glanced at Teddy, folded in the chair, worrying the front of his T-shirt, then she leaned over the bed. "What's the matter, Mrs. Parker?"

"Derrr-ddd," I said again. Even with imagination, no one would ever decipher *Edward* from that.

Mary smoothed sweat-matted strands of hair away from my face. She took a washcloth from the nightstand, dampened it, and wiped my forehead. "All right now, Mrs. Parker. Stress only makes things worse. If you want us to know what you need, you have to calm down." The cloth felt cool and calming against my skin, soothing the heat in my cheeks. "Take some deep breaths, and really think about each sound, all right? You can do it. There's no hurry. We'll all wait until you're ready."

I closed my eyes, relaxed against the pillow, nodded, breathed in, breathed out, tried to clear my mind, then looked at Mary again. "Airrr? Wh . . . wh . . . airrr?"

Her head inclined to one side, her thin brown eyebrows arching together. "Where . . . all right. Where's what?"

"Derrr-ddd." Edward's name was no clearer than before. "Derrr-ddd."

Mary frowned. "I'm sorry, Mrs. Parker. I didn't understand that part. Do you want me to go see if the speech therapist is still around? You might be able to point it out on her cards."

I shook my head. There was no card for *Edward* in the speech therapist's bag of tricks. I took another breath, tried to think things through. "Howww-t," I said finally. It was a word I knew I could make. One Mary would understand. We'd been through this conversation before. "Wh-errr . . . howt?"

Mary considered the question for a moment. "Where's your house? Are you asking if you can go home now?"

I shook my head. Even I wasn't addled enough to believe I would be going home today.

Mary contemplated again. "Are you asking about your house? How things are there?"

"Yesh!" I exploded, my hands shooting off the bed in a moment of Herculean triumph. "Yesh, yesh, yesh! Howt?"

A buzzer going off in the hallway snagged Mary's attention. Someone else needed her. "Well, I imagine Rebecca and Teddy can tell you all about that. I'll leave you three alone to talk, all right?"

Rebecca gave Mary a grateful look. "Thank you for helping, Mary."

"Oh, sure." Mary pulled the front of her button-up sweater together, seeming embarrassed by the compliment. With her slim figure and no makeup, she looked like a shy teenager in a woman's clothes.

"Tanks, Mar-eee." Teddy crossed the room, grabbed Mary's hand, and shook it. As he'd grown into a man, we'd tried to teach him that hugging people wasn't usually an appropriate way of showing gratitude. Even his exuberant handshakes sometimes put people off.

Mary didn't seem to be bothered. She closed her free hand over their intertwined ones, smiled at Teddy, and said, "You're welcome, Teddy."

"Mama don' talk good," he observed.

Rebecca blanched.

Mary's gaze flicked in my direction, then back to Teddy. "Your mom's getting better. Sometimes after a stroke people have to work really hard for a while."

Teddy shrugged, blissfully unaware of the emotion in the room. "It okay, some-time I don' talk good, too."

The four of us laughed, and Teddy came back to the bed and sat down, smiling. He had a way of easing the most difficult situations. He responded with humility and love when other people were afraid to act.

"I'll leave you all alone," Mary said, and left the room.

"By-eee, Mar-eee!" Teddy called after her.

Teddy began telling me about the plants in the backyard, and how he'd gathered pots in which to start the seeds we'd saved from last year, and how he'd found some good dirt and carried it home in a bucket.

"Ere?" I asked. Teddy turned his head aside and ducked his chin the way he always did when he wanted to avoid answering a question. He knew I was wondering where he'd found pots and dirt. We hadn't been to the garden center to buy those things yet this spring, and last year, Edward had thrown away the box of seedling pots by mistake.

I was beginning to suspect that Teddy had been out of the yard. His look of avoidance confirmed it.

"I findin' dirt," he muttered, twisting his fingers in his lap, then checking to make sure the zipper on his pants was up. "Good dirt." He didn't look at me. He'd always been very good about not leaving the yard. Even when he saw neighbors pass by with bicycles and baby strollers and other things that fascinated him, he only went as far as the sidewalk, never past it. Why would he do such a thing now? Why would Kay-Kay let him? Why would Edward? Even on his bad days, Edward still knew that Teddy wasn't to wander alone.

"Daaa?" I asked, because I'd already failed at trying to make Edward's name understood. "Daaa-duh?"

"Daddy Ed gone hop-sital." Teddy watched my reaction closely, clearly wondering whether I thought it was all right. "Daddy Ed gone hop-sital, but he comin' back, Mama. A-becca say, Daddy Ed comin' back."

Rebecca's face went pale. She rubbed her thumb and forefinger over her eyebrows. Her hand was trembling.

A tidal wave of panic collided with my more mundane thoughts, sweeping them away, stirring everything into an impossible mix. Edward in the hospital? What was wrong? How could Kay-Kay let that happen without coming and telling me?

"Right, A-becca?" Teddy sought assurance from Rebecca when there was none from me. "Daddy Ed comin' back."

"Yes, Teddy, Daddy Ed's coming back home in a day or two." Rebecca looked as if she wanted to be anywhere but here.

"Not like Kay-Kay." Teddy combed his fingers over his hair, pulled slightly, then combed, then pulled. The motion was rough enough that it should have hurt, but he didn't seem to notice. He was focused on Rebecca, waiting for confirmation.

She paled another shade, nervously chewing the side of her lip. "No, Teddy, not like Kay-Kay."

I searched Rebecca's face, trying to make sense of the sudden riptide of information. Where was Kay-Kay? Had Rebecca dismissed her from her position? Kay-Kay would never just leave. She'd been completely devoted to Edward and Teddy for over a year now. Night and day, through all the trials of Edward's illness, through different medications, setbacks, progress, uncertainty, Kay-Kay had been there. Having worked with Alzheimer's patients in the past, she understood what we were going through. At a time when I didn't think I could carry one more burden, we'd found Kay-Kay . . . or Kay-Kay had found us. My brain was muddled this morning, but I knew that Kay-Kay was our salvation, our godsend. She'd taken up our burdens as if they were her own. Few people not compelled by the conscriptions of family would have done as much.

I reached toward Rebecca, aching for an explanation. "Pleee . . . Pleees."

She took a breath, pressed her lips into a straight, tight line, carefully planning her words.

"Pleees," I said again. "Trrr-ooo-th." *Tell me the truth.*

The moments ticked by on the wall clock, each movement of the second hand filling my mind with terrible possibilities.

"Edward is in the hospital," Rebecca confessed finally. It bothered me to hear her call her father *Edward.* "Dr. Amadi felt the need to put him in for a few days to run some tests, straighten out his electrolytes and his medications. He wasn't . . ." Whatever she'd been about to say, she reconsidered and finished with, "He was having some trouble, but Dr. Amadi seems . . ." Her gaze darted off again, searching for a word that might fit softly into the gap. ". . . confident." She sighed, rubbed the space between her eyebrows with her index finger. Her lashes fell closed. She had Edward's bright hazel eyes, but other than that, she looked like her mother. She was beautiful, like her mother. Beautiful, aloof, an island of guarded places no one else could touch.

"Kaaayeee-Kaaayeee?" The name seemed to take forever to produce.

Her gaze met mine very directly. "I'm trying to get in touch with Kay-Kay. Can you tell me her last name, where she lives, how I might contact her?"

Trying to get in touch with Kay-Kay. What did that mean? Had Rebecca run Kay-Kay out of the house and now she was sorry? Was Rebecca the reason Edward's condition had declined to the point that he was in the hospital? *He was having some trouble,* she'd said. What kind of trouble? What caused it? Was Rebecca's mere presence, or Kay-Kay's leaving, enough to tip Edward from the fragile precipice on which he'd balanced these past months?

I felt my jaw tense, my mind begin to spin into an impossible whirl of fear and supposition until everything was an unintelligible blur. A pulse pounded in my ears, made my face grow flush. Kay-Kay lived upstairs. For the past few months, she'd been staying in the garage apartment at night, so as to help with Edward. Hadn't she? Or were those only plans we'd made for the future, if and when Edward declined? My mind was tangled, the facts unclear. The more I tried to concentrate, the blurrier the details became, the faster they swirled, blending together, becoming impossible to decipher. To us, she was always just Kay-Kay, practically a member of the family, but she had a last name. She was a single girl and lived in an apartment off Greenville . . . didn't she? Or was I confusing her with someone else? How could I forget such a basic thing as Kay-Kay's last name?

Morris? No, Morris was the boy who worked at the convenience store down the road. Carson, Smith, Kenwood, Euless. . . .

My face grew feverish, my jaw more tight, the pounding in my ears louder and louder until my entire body burned and the charley horses in my legs ran wild.

"You shouldn't worry about this, Hanna Beth. It isn't . . . good for you," Rebecca soothed, sounding close to panic herself. No doubt she was worried that I'd have another stroke. "Everything's fine."

It was strange to hear Rebecca fussing over my health. The only impression she'd ever given was that she wished I would magically cease to exist.

"Kaaayeee-Kaaayeee?" Blood thundered in my ears and my fists clenched the bedsheets with more strength than I'd thought remained. "Howt? Myeee howt?" *I want to know what's happening at my house.*

Teddy retreated to the back of his chair, folding into himself.

Rebecca took a deep breath, swallowed hard. "I'm taking care of things at the house." Her voice held the forced softness of a mother trying to pacify a child. "It's all right. Just give me a little time to—"

"Myeee howt!" I heard myself shriek. My fists pounded the bed. I braced my hand, pulled my head and shoulders off the pillow, attempted to rise up, to be taken seriously. "My howt! Whyeee Kaaayeee-Kay ugg-go?" The string of words, the ability to partially sit up, surprised me. In any other circumstances, I would have been filled with elation.

Rebecca's cool demeanor snapped. "You know what, Hanna Beth? It's not your house. It's *my father's* house. My grandparents' house. I think I can be trusted to take care of it, but if you'd like to take over, please be my guest." Her hand flailed toward the hallway, inviting me to get up, walk out the door, and see to my own affairs. "I didn't ask for any of this. My daughter is sitting at home in California right now with a broken leg. I've got work piling up at the office, and my . . ." She clamped her lips shut, her nostrils flaring with a breath. "Look, I don't want to be here, all right? But I'm doing the best I can. I don't know where Kay-Kay is. I'm trying to figure that out. If I can't get her, I'll find somebody else to live at the house and take care of things." Her eyes narrowed, turned bitter and cool. "Then I can fly home, and all of you can just . . . just . . . go back to normal." Collapsing into the extra chair, she let her head fall into her hand. Her lips pressed into a tight, trembling line.

I sank against the pillow, the fire spent, my spirits sinking. How could this be happening? How could this possibly work, when I couldn't produce the most basic information about the affairs of our house, when Rebecca and I couldn't be in the same room for five minutes without descending into a confrontation?

In his chair, Teddy whimpered, as if he, too, were overwhelmed by the hopelessness of the situation. Weaving back and forth, he watched the reflections shift on the floor tiles. He was self-stimulating, trying to block things out like he used to when he was young. He hadn't done that in years.

Something metal rang against the door frame. Rebecca and I jerked toward the hallway. Teddy slowed his weaving, started to come back.

"Sorry about that." Claude's voice broke the silence as he struggled to get through the door. "Didn't mean to startle ya, Birdie. I just come to show my picture book. My little neighbor girl brung it to me from my house. Reckon she thought I'd enjoy seeing it, and . . . Well, hey there. I thought I heard someone in here."

A flush of embarrassment crept into my cheeks. Claude had probably heard every word of our argument through the air vent. Undoubtedly he'd come on purpose.

Pedaling past the bed, he headed for Rebecca. "How-do there. Good to see ya again. How are you, young man?" He held a hand out to Teddy, but received no response.

Normally, I would have tried to entice Teddy into reengaging, but it seemed pointless right now.

"Teddy, this is Mr. . . . . I'm sorry. I can't remember your name," Rebecca said.

"Claude Fisher." Claude nodded over his shoulder toward his room. "Next door. I just come by to show Birdie this old picture of my daddy's mules." I heard the faint sound of pages rattling, smelled the scent of aging parchment, as Claude opened his book and twisted it around so Teddy and Rebecca could see. Teddy stopped weaving and focused, the light returning to his eyes.

Claude smiled at him. "Look at this one. That strappin' young feller behind the mule team there is me, if you can believe it. That pair of white mules was brothers, both albinos. My daddy got them from an old black fella that couldn't farm no more. My daddy won many a pullin' contest with old Jes and Tab." He laughed in his throat, and Rebecca politely said the mules were beautiful. Teddy crooked a finger and rubbed it over the photograph.

Mr. Fisher laughed again. "That lanky lad in the picture underneath is me, too. I liked to sit that big yella horse a lot better than I liked starin' at the rear ends of them mules, I'll tell ya. I got that horse when I was seventeen—rode him all over Tom Green County. I'd made up my mind, I was gonna be a cowboy, not a farmer. Them mules was the talk of the county, though. Jes was blind and Tab was deaf—them things happen with albinos, sometimes. When you put them in harness together, Tab could see where they was goin, and Jes could hear my daddy give 'em *ge* and *haw* and *giddup* and *woah*. He'd call out, and Jes would move forward, and then Tab would take over and lead 'em straight down the row. When Daddy turned them two out to pasture, he'd put a cowbell on old Tab. Tab would walk a little way, and then he'd shake his head up and down like he was waitin' for Jes to catch up. Jes could follow that bell sound all around the pasture, uphill and downhill. He could tell that terrain just by how the bell sounded. He was a smart mule to figure that out." Pausing, he smiled at the picture, shook his head and pointed to Jes, the blind mule. "But the thing I always wondered was how'd the deaf mule know to keep shakin' his head after he stopped walking, since he couldn't hear the bell?" Claude paused, regarding Rebecca with a look of consternation. "It was the durndest conundrum the way neither one of them mules could get by on its own, but the two of them was just perfect as a pair. My daddy used to say there was a good lesson in it for people. Most of the time when we got a tough row to plow, the Good Lord makes us fall a little short and puts another mule in the pasture. You don't never know whether you're the blind mule or the deaf mule, but you're always one or the other."

"Fisher!" Gretchen's call echoed along the corridor. "I hear your squeaky voice around here somewhere. I'm gonna find you if I have to tear up every square inch of this place. We got a date in the therapy center."

Claude looked for a corner to climb into. "Oh, hang!" He turned his wheelchair around and started toward the door. "Maybe I can find Mary and get her to hide me. Y'all can hang on to my book and look at it for a while." He scooted out the door like an inmate on the lam.

Teddy pointed to the book. "How that mule know the bell?"

"I'm not sure, Teddy." Rebecca's voice trembled with emotion. I wondered if she was thinking about the mules, considering the idea, as I was, that there was a lesson in the story for us.

Teddy began leafing through the pages.

"I'll be back in a minute," Rebecca whispered as she got up and left the room.

Teddy smiled after her, then moved his chair so that he could share the pictures with me. "Look at him cowboy, Mama," he said, and pointed to a sepia photo of Claude, smiling atop a beautiful palomino horse. "And there the mule and the other mule. . . ."

We'd almost finished the book when Mary stopped by.

"I wanted to check on you before I left," she said, then noticed me looking at the clock and added, "I have to leave early. Brandon had an asthma attack at school and they gave him his inhaler, but it's empty now. I need to go pick him up." Tucking stray strands of hair behind her ear, she squinted toward the parking lot. I laid my hand on hers, and she turned back to me, forcing a wavering smile. "We slept with the windows open last night at home. We just shouldn't of, that's all." She turned to gaze at the book with Teddy. "Oh, Mr. Fisher brought you his book. Did he tell you about the mules?"

"Yeah," Teddy said, and smiled at Mary.

"That's a good story." She slipped her hand from mine and she headed for the door. I heard her meet up with Rebecca in the hall, but I couldn't make out their conversation. Undoubtedly they were talking about me.

CHAPTER 15

Rebecca Macklin

After a traumatic exit from the nursing center, during which Teddy temporarily melted down about having to leave Hanna Beth, we stopped by the hospital to check on my father again. He was awake, calmly watching a rerun of *Big Valley* and consuming the food on his supper tray. Dr. Amadi wasn't available, and the nurse had little information, other than the current regimen of medications and what they were for. When we entered the room, my father greeted us warmly and gave us details about the oil field accident that had caused his broken ribs. I played Marilyn, and Teddy hung out by the door, looking uncertain. My father wanted me to call his office, let his boss know he'd be out for a few days, but he would be phoning in for updates on the core samples from the exploratory drilling in the Garner-North field. He didn't intend to let this little medical emergency sideline him.

As I turned to leave, he reached for my hand, awkwardly catching my wrist first, then sliding to my fingers. Lifting his face, he met my gaze. His eyes narrowed upward, a contemplative network of wrinkles forming around the corners. For an instant, I thought he saw me—not Marilyn, but me.

"Tell Rebecca not to be scared," he said, and an unwanted tenderness gathered in my throat. I swallowed hard. He searched my face, looking for something. Bringing my hand to his lips, he kissed it, then cupped my fingers between his and held them against his chest. I felt his heartbeat, a slow, steady rhythm that drew me back to a day when we'd lain on a beach beneath a towering palm in Moorea. I'd rested my head on his arm, gazed into the swaying branches overhead, felt a steady pulse against my ear. My eyes drifted closed, and he stayed there while I slept.

I'd let go of moments like that one. It was easier to believe they'd never existed. But now, watching him in the bed, I saw the eyes of the father who waited patiently while I dreamed away the afternoon on the beach.

"Tell Rebecca her old dad's gonna be fine," he whispered, his lashes drifting closed.

Emotion overcame me. Pressing a hand over my mouth, I pulled away from him, turned and ran from the room.

Teddy followed me. In the elevator, I tried to rein in my feelings, gather them up, put them in a box and clamp the lid down tight.

Teddy patted my shoulder awkwardly, which seemed an odd turnabout, considering that a short time before I'd been the one trying to calm him as we prepared to leave the nursing home. "It okay, A-becca. It soo-kay. Don' cry, A-becca." The wall between me and the tears burst, and they tumbled forth, raw and pure. I stood sobbing in the elevator as we reached the ground floor. I wasn't even sure why. Amid the crushing tide of anxiety, some logical part of me was echoing Teddy. *It's okay. He's resting comfortably. Hanna Beth's doing better. Things are functional at the house. And Mary just made an offer that I can consider. Mary's suggestion could solve everything. . . .*

Sniffling and hiccuping, I wiped my eyes, aware of Teddy's heavy arm resting over my shoulders. "It so-kaaay, A-becca. It so-kaaay." He squeezed and patted, pulling me off balance. "We gone get pizza now. I like pizza. Egg-tra cheese."

I nodded, taking a tissue from my purse and wiping my cheeks.

"I don' steal no pep-poni today." Teddy pointed a finger and waved it sternly at me. "You don' steal no pep-poni, too, A-becca. You don' steal no pep-poni." He snort-chuckled, and I realized he was making a joke.

I hiccuped and giggled, and Teddy laughed along with me as the elevator opened, and we stepped into the parking garage. "I won't steal the pepperoni, Teddy."

He patted me on the top of the head as if I were a puppy. "You get all the pep-poni, A-becca. It soo-kay."

I felt an overwhelming sense of tenderness toward Teddy, followed by a measure of guilt. When he looked at me, there was only acceptance, blind faith that believed the best in me, that could love me, in spite of everything.

There were a million things I wanted to say, thoughts I didn't know how to express, especially to Teddy, so I settled for, "We'll order extra pepperoni."

He clapped, then jerked upright as the sound echoed through the hospital parking garage. Clapping again, he cocked an ear toward the reverberation.

"There's an echo," I pointed out. "The sound bounces off the walls and comes back. Like this, see?" Cupping my hands around my mouth, I hollered, "Hello!" and the sound came back, "Ello-ello-ello-o-o-o."

Teddy's eyes twinkled and his lips spread into a grin. "Pep-poni!" he hollered, and the sound came back, "Poni-oni-oni-oni."

I felt light, buoyant like the echoes themselves. I remembered standing with Macey on the rim of the Grand Canyon, shouting into the abyss and hearing our voices come back. "Extra pepperoni!" I hollered. The sound bounced through the parking garage before escaping onto the street.

"Egg-tra pep-poni!" Teddy repeated, then clapped his hands as his words Ping-Ponged around us. A family on their way to the elevator stopped to stare, the parents allowing only polite glances, while two young kids gawked openly, and a preteen girl rolled her eyes, whispering something behind her hand. I knew what she was saying—not the exact words, but I knew. I recognized the look. I could see myself at twelve, the day Teddy ran across the lawn to greet me and I slammed the door in his face.

If it were Macey standing there, what would she do? In the midst of all the Gifted and Talented classes in school, the gymnastics lessons, the dance lessons, the glitzy birthday parties filled with beautiful, brilliant little girls, had I ever tried to teach her the lessons that mattered most? Had I tried to show her what Teddy so naturally understood—that life is beautiful, awe-inspiring in all its forms? Had I ever attempted to combat the perfection-centered culture Macey saw on television, that she lived in every day—the culture that believed people like Teddy should be kept out of the way.

"Hieee!" Teddy waved at the family as they passed. They didn't answer, just walked on. The woman gave me a sympathetic look. I didn't want to respond, but my cheeks went red, and I quickened my step toward the car.

Teddy patted me on the head again as I pressed the remote and the doors unlocked. "You a good girl, A-becca," he said, then threw his head back and hollered, "Egg-tra pep-poni!" He listened for the reverb.

"Extra pepperoni!" I cheered with him, and our voices rang through the maze of concrete and steel. I didn't care who heard.

After Wal-Mart, we ended up at Chuck E. Cheese's with two sodas, breadsticks, and a double pepperoni pizza. Teddy ate like he'd never seen food before, then went to the game area to play ski-ball. Before long, he'd made friends with the little boy next to him and was sharing his game, letting the little boy make every other toss. They were cheering each other's accomplishments when the child's parents came and snatched him away, and Teddy was alone again. He went back to playing his own game, pausing to cheer when players nearby hit the 100,000-point hole.

Watching him, I had a sense of what his childhood must have been like for Hanna Beth, what it must still be like. Life outside the yard on Blue Sky Hill was a minefield for Teddy, a difficult place filled with nuances he didn't understand, unspoken rules he couldn't comprehend. Don't talk to strangers, don't be too friendly, don't yell in the parking garage. . . .

How would I feel if this were Macey's life? I knew the dreams I had for my daughter, the enormous place she filled inside me, the satisfaction of watching her learn to walk and talk, master each new stage of development ahead of schedule. I knew the joy of taking her to her first day of school, of good report cards, and year-end awards for excellence at school. I knew the hope of watching her grow, of considering the idea of more children, imagining them being as beautiful, and accomplished, and perfect as Macey. How would I have felt if those illusions, that imagined reality, had been taken away from me by something completely beyond my control?

Perhaps the way I felt when I turned my head, sitting idle at the stoplight, and saw my husband holding hands with a client, leaning across the table toward her, gazing into her eyes. One minute my life was normal, fulfilling all my expectations. The next minute the pieces were everywhere, and I was looking at the wreckage, realizing my idea of a made-to-order life was no more than a game of let's pretend.

Control is an illusion, I heard Bree telling me in the car as she dropped me off at the airport. *You have to relinquish control of the universe. . . .*

To whom? To the God we visited on Christmas and Easter when we were children? The God who promised atop the hospital chaplain's newsletter as my mother lay dying, *I will never leave you nor forsake you,* but then remained conspicuously absent? Who wasn't there when she suffered renal failure, when treatments were unsuccessful, when report after report delivered the worst possible prognosis? To the God who let my father's mind degenerate, who filled Teddy with kindness so that other people could shun it? Who allowed Hanna Beth, the one person both my father and Teddy needed most, to be sidelined by a stroke, rendered useless and dependent herself?

If this was all some sort of plan, it was a bad plan. A stupid, stinking, rotten plan. So far, we were up to our necks in floodwater and the tide was rising. . . .

My stomach started churning, and I pushed away the pizza tray, the combination of tomato sauce, cheese, and greasy pepperoni burning in my chest. I sat back in the stiff, uncomfortable booth, the red vinyl squealing as I pulled my legs up underneath me, let my head fall back and closed my eyes, trying to decide what to do next. I felt as if my mind were in a million tiny pieces.

There was no good end to this problem, no neat little package into which my father, Teddy, and Hanna Beth could be placed for safekeeping, yet I had to figure out something, and I had to figure it out now. In a few days, my father would be released from the hospital. In a few weeks, according to Mary, Hanna Beth could recover to the point of coming home, provided there were some modifications to the house and special assistance was arranged. I couldn't stay here forever. . . .

My mind drifted to my conversation with Mary in the hall outside Hanna Beth's room. She'd asked if I'd made any progress in finding a caretaker.

I told her about the visit to Dr. Amadi, about putting my father in the hospital. I admitted that I didn't know what to do next, or how to find someone to look after things at the house.

"I could do it," Mary rushed out. The offer seemed spur-of-the-moment, careless and ill-considered.

I stood silent, taken aback. Did she feel obligated because I'd discussed the problem with her, or perhaps because she was Hanna Beth's caretaker at the nursing home? "I didn't mean to . . . ," I said.

She focused on the rolled-up towel in her hands, clutched and unclutched it, her long, slim fingers disappearing into the white terry cloth. She continued on quickly, as if she'd anticipated my reaction and prepared herself for it. "I could start right away. My apartment lease is up this week, and I'm not . . . it's . . . I know you probably didn't want someone with kids, but the boys aren't any trouble. They're good kids. They mostly just play on their own, and they go to day care during the day, and I could . . . well, if you wanted someone to be there when I'm at work, I could share the apartment over your garage with Ifeoma. We work opposite shifts here, so we were thinking about getting a place together . . . to help with expenses. She's got a little boy back home in Ghana, and she's saving up to go and get him. She's been living at the women's shelter since she started work here, but her time there is up, so she has to go somewhere else." She stopped finally, glanced up at me, then dropped her chin again as she waited.

I wasn't sure what to say. On the one hand, there was the incredible temptation of quickly solving our problems by hiring someone who already understood Hanna Beth's medical needs, who was apprised of my father's situation and had experience working with Alzheimer's patients, who had already seen the house and met Teddy. On the other hand, I couldn't imagine bringing someone so young, so small and soft-spoken, with two little children, into the house. I had no idea how my father and Teddy would react to children living there full-time, or if the place was safe for them. Certainly, the way things had been these past few days bordered on insanity. Mary had no idea what she'd be getting into.

"It's probably not a good—"

"You can think about it." She cut me off before I could finish. "There's no rush or anything. I just wanted to go ahead and bring it up, because I have to leave early today." She paused to check her watch, and her hand slid into the pocket of her sweater, fingered a piece of paper there. "If you decide you're interested, you can just let me know, and I'll talk to Ifeoma. Like I said, she's really trying to keep her expenses down."

It crossed my mind that maybe this night-shift nurse, Ifoema, might be a possibility. "The apartment's not very big—just a bedroom, a bathroom, a little storage room, a kitchen and the living room area," I said, looking for excuses. "I don't think it would be big enough. It wouldn't be what you'd want."

"We don't need much space." Mary was surprisingly forthright. She seemed almost desperate for me to agree. Something in her expression caused me not to turn her down out of hand.

"Let me take a few days to consider it and see how my father's doing when he comes out of the hospital," I said finally.

Chewing a fingernail that was already down to the quick, Mary nodded, fidgeting from one foot to the other. "It'd probably be better if you didn't say anything to the administrator here. I mean . . . I can give you references and stuff, if you're interested, but I don't want my boss to think I'm quitting my job."

"Sure," I said, then she turned and headed off down the hall, leaving me to wonder about the motivation behind her offer. If she'd been a client in my law office for an initial interview, I would have hesitated to take her. Clearly, there was more going on than she was willing to reveal. . . .

Watching Teddy interact with the kids at the ski-ball games, I weighed the pros and cons again. Teddy would love having Mary's little boys in the house. He could show them bird nests, hunt lizards with them, help build twig forts in the corners of the yard the way they had yesterday. Having something to occupy his time might help curb his obsession with benches and pots.

Teddy loved children. Playing ski-ball, he was in a state of pure joy, alternately making tosses, then stopping to clap and cheer for the kids around him. It was a far cry from the scene when we left the nursing home this afternoon. He'd clung to Hanna Beth, sobbing inconsolably for almost an hour.

I'd finally convinced him we had to go because the plants needed to be watered at home. Hanna Beth started to weep, and I could feel everything descending into an impossible chaos. Mr. Fisher passed in the hall and I asked him if he would sit with her for a while.

"I'd enjoy the chance," he said, patting my hand and giving me a sympathetic smile, as if he were immune to the turmoil. Wheeling himself around the bed, he scooted between Teddy and Hanna Beth. "There, now, young fella. I'll take over for a while. Your mama's all right—she just wants to go home, but it ain't time yet, and these doctors flat don't let you out of here until they think it's time. I been trying to convince them to let me go home, but they said I've got to wait a little longer and make sure this pacemaker's gonna keep my ticker from gettin' the hiccups, so here I am. I sure do miss my cats. I hope that little girl's been feeding them. I wouldn't want my cats to go hungry." He tapped Hanna Beth's arm with a forefinger. "There now, Birdie. You stop that cryin', all right? You'll get that woman in four-B started, and she'll moan all night." He took a tissue from the box, and wiped Hanna Beth's cheeks. "Say, did I ever tell you about my trains?"

Hanna Beth started to laugh softly. Teddy tuned in to Mr. Fisher's story about the trains. By the time it was finished, Teddy's mood had changed. I took advantage of the opportunity to gather him up and leave for our trip to Wal-Mart and the pizza place. I promised to bring him back to see his mother tomorrow. As soon as I made the promise, I was filled with dread at the thought of keeping it. There was still so much to do.

Somehow, I had to stabilize the situation at the house and begin making plans for Hanna Beth to come home, but Mary wasn't the answer. Teddy and my father, and eventually Hanna Beth, needed someone older, capable, firm, and no-nonsense. As good as Mary was with Hanna Beth, as much as she seemed to want and need the job, she wasn't the right person. I couldn't risk inviting any more problems in the door.

I convinced myself of the wisdom of saying no to Mary's offer as Teddy and I drove home from the pizza parlor. Teddy happily investigated a marble maze he'd purchased with his ski-ball tickets. He was talking to the marble. My mind had drifted a million miles away.

"There go the turn, A-becca. There go the turn," Teddy commented, his pointed finger moving slowly from the front to the back of the car as we passed the corner where the blue gingerbread house used to be.

"Shoot!" I muttered. All the way home, we'd been bumper to bumper in Friday evening traffic headed to the party spots on Lower Greenville, and now I'd missed the turn. The back of my neck tightened as I glanced in the rearview mirror, looking for a chance to move into the left lane. I was ready for this day to be—

A city bus pulled out in front of me without warning, Teddy screamed, and I hit the brakes. Gasping, I swerved to the side, narrowly missing the bumper. I ended up on the shoulder by a bus kiosk, the car vibrating to a stop, a wild pulse racing in my ears.

"Bad driver!" Teddy hollered, and shook a fist at the bus. I had a feeling he'd learned that from my father, only my father would have used more colorful language.

Swallowing a rush of adrenaline, I let the car drift into a parking lot and caught my breath. I was ready for this day to be over. I just wanted all of this to be over. I wanted to sleep in my own bed, get up, take Macey to school, go to work, come home, do all the normal things.

"Bad driver!" Teddy hollered again as he tried to roll down the window, which my father would have done in order to add an obscene hand gesture.

"It's okay, Teddy," I said. "It's all right."

"Hey, there Mama church!" Teddy pointed ahead to where a man in a green fishing hat was watching us from across the parking lot. In one hand he held a tall pole, and in the other he carried a cardboard box with SIGNS printed on the outside in large block letters. Lifting the pole in greeting, he waved toward the marquee, then started in the direction of an old white clapboard church that seemed out of keeping with the urban neighborhood.

"There Past-er Al!" Teddy tried to roll down the window again, waving and hollering, "Hi-eee, Past-er Al! Hi-eee, Past-er Al!"

Pastor Al disappeared around the corner, and I turned back to the sign, taking in the large lighted header that read, "Harmony Lane Chapel, Est 1906, Visitors Welcome." Beneath that, the marquee added, "I will not leave you comfortless. I will come to you. John 14:18."

I let out a long breath and read the words over.

I will not leave you comfortless . . .
I will come . . .
I will not leave you . . .
I will come . . .
John . . . John . . . John . . .

I closed my eyes and fell awkwardly into a prayer. *Please send me a sign. Please send someone who can help. Please take away this burden. . . .*

Teddy's attempts to open the car door pulled my attention away. "Teddy, don't. Stay in the car."

"I gone see Past-er Al!" Teddy said, struggling to unhook his seat belt. "I gone see Past-er Al!"

"We're going home. Leave your belt on." I put the car in Drive and turned toward the road again. I read the other side of the church marquee while waiting to pull into traffic.

"Happiness doesn't grow where impatience grazes."

There was no Bible verse cited, just "Pastor Al."

I wish I could say that as we left the church behind I felt a sense of patience, of peace that was beyond understanding, but I didn't. Peace, my spiritually seeking law clerk had pointed out, required faith.

CHAPTER 16
Hanna Beth Parker

I woke in the morning with a sense of anticipation and began listening for Teddy's footsteps coming up the hallway. Before leaving last evening, Rebecca had promised to bring him. She'd offered the commitment in desperation, to convince Teddy to cease causing an uproar and depart from the nursing center. She didn't know that *tomorrow* didn't mean much to him. Teddy lived in the moment.

Finally, it was Claude's storytelling that had changed Teddy's mood, brought peace to the room. The beauty of a world like Teddy's was that sadness couldn't stay long in it. He didn't cling to pain, nurture and feed it the way most people do. It was natural for him to be happy, and so any little distraction could bring him back to joy. He left in a good mood after Claude's visit. Now I struggled to console myself with the promise that Rebecca would bring him back today.

Another temperate night had left the air-conditioning system inactive. I heard Mary sneak the boys in the back door and take them to Claude's bathroom to get them ready for school. Brandon wheezed and coughed, and she tried to quiet him. Despite Mary's efforts, the boys made such a racket I was afraid they'd be discovered. If I heard anyone coming, I decided I would scream, or pretend to have a seizure, to cause a diversion.

Brandon started crying, and Mr. Fisher came into the bathroom.

"What've we got here?" he soothed. "Got a little paint in those cheeks today, huh?"

"His asthma's still acting up," Mary said wearily. "He was awake all night, coughing. I shouldn't have tried using the old inhalers I had in the car. There's nothing left. I should have bought a new one yesterday."

"You got the money for that?"

"Oh, sure." Mary's answer was too quick, light and false. "I just hope he'll make it through school until I can go get his medicine. I have to work today."

"Miss Mary, you ain't never gonna have a career in poker," Claude scolded tenderly. "I got a little money the girl next door brung me with my picture book yesterday. Pharmacy's right down on the corner. You go on and get this boy's medicine before you put him on that bus."

I couldn't make out Mary's response, but after she spoke, Claude insisted she accept the money. "It ain't gonna do any good if he gets sick and you have to take off work again, now is it?" he pointed out. "You take my money, and no more fussin', you hear? All the good you done for me, it don't seem like much to give in return. Besides, if them circles under his eyes get any bigger, they're gonna hang plumb down to his feet."

Mary must have finally agreed, because she gathered up the boys and left in a hurry. Later on, I saw the three of them waiting for the day-care van. She had the pharmacy bag in her hand.

I went back to listening for Teddy and contemplating ways of attempting to communicate to Rebecca that, if Mary was in such need of money, I would like to help. Certainly, Edward and I could afford it. With our investments, and Edward's pension, we'd never suffered for money.

I pondered the question, trying to conjure a way to make Rebecca understand.

Betty breezed through the door in a hurry to finish her work in the B hall and clock out. I closed my eyes and tried to be somewhere else as she changed my disposable undergarment and the bedding. The odd thing this morning was that I felt it. I felt her skin touch mine, not because I saw it with my eyes and knew how it should feel. My eyes were closed, but I experienced the sensation of touch. I knew that I was hot underneath my back and cold on top. I could feel my toes touching the metal railing. It was cold, round. . . .

I'd been so busy thinking about Mary, I hadn't considered that something was different this morning.

"I fe-lll," I said, looking at my foot pressed against the bar. "I fee-ul . . . fooo . . . foo-ttt." A spray of spit went out with the word, and Betty curled her lip.

She glanced at my hand, at my finger lifting off the bed, pointing to my foot. "Comin' back, huh?" she muttered. It was a poor congratulation.

"Ye-sh." I felt the need to share my moment of discovery with someone, even Betty.

"Tell the OT to get you busy with a spoon. Then you can feed yourself," she grumbled, then gathered her things and headed out the door.

Claude came by on his way to the cafeteria. He said he was checking to be sure Betty hadn't lowered my window blind, but I suspected he wanted to watch Mary put the kids on the van, and from his room, the hydrangea bush probably obscured the bus stop. Perhaps he was looking to see how Brandon was doing.

"Mornin', Birdie," he said. "It's a pretty sky outside today. Mares' tails pointed up last night. Good farmin' weather ahead." I thought he was leading into the story about the mules again, but instead he sat staring out the window, as if his mind were elsewhere.

Finally he sighed, kneading his hands in his lap and watching his fingers. His lips moved back and forth in a pleated downward line. I'd never seen him seem so dejected. Was he concerned about Mary, or just not feeling well?

Drumming absently on the wheelchair arm, he sighed. "I thought I about had Doc Barnhill convinced to cut me loose from this place. After they put in this new pacemaker, Doc said if I could go a month without my heart giving a bad spell, it might be I could move on back home. I miss being home with my own things, you know? The little girl next door says she's keeping my cat dish full. They're just stray cats, but they've got used to coming to my place to eat. I got twenty-two now. I give 'em all names. Every critter deserves a name, and a full belly, and a little love, don't you think, Birdie?" He paused as if he were waiting for me to answer, then finally went on. "Neighbor kids call me the cat man, like that comic book character, you know? Cat woman? I miss sittin' out on the patio, taking my mornin' coffee and conversatin' with my cats. I got a big backyard on account of the creek runs behind my place and there's a flood plain back there. The kids come play baseball sometimes. I help 'em with their swing, or teach 'em how to make a good slide. Lots of kids don't have daddies to do that these days. It's comin' up on the end of school soon, and the kids'll all be home for summer. Time to get the back lot mowed and pull the bases out of the shed, keep those kids busy so they don't get in trouble. Time to be back in my own place."

A hollowness spread through me at the thought of his leaving. I couldn't bear the idea of passing the days without him stopping by, telling stories, opening the blind and saying, *Just look at that sky, Birdie. Ain't that a beauty?* I wanted to tell him, *You're needed here. I need you. You can't go.*

He sighed, shrinking into the chair so that his back was bowed, his hands hanging limp in his lap. "I had a spell last night. It was just a little one, but it showed right up on the heart monitor. Doc says I'm just to the point where livin' alone ain't gonna be practical for me anymore. I got to have somebody with me, in case I have a spell and need my heart started up again. He wanted to know, did I have any family I might want to move in with? I told him I got a niece I'm close to—Kathy. She used to come stay summers with my wife and me. We always hoped she'd have some babies and live nearby in our old age. She's got her a big-deal job with the Oceanographic Institution out in Seattle, though. She ain't much interested in the production of grandchildren. It ain't in her life plan yet—that's what she says." He chuckled. "Back in the day, we didn't think about a life plan. Folks just got married, set up housekeeping, and if you were lucky, the babies come along, natural-like. Life unfolded like a paper wad, and you made the best of it. Good job, little house, family. Heck, if we could afford a car that'd start regular, we was livin' high." He leaned over to watch something outside the window, his gaze drifting far away. "It was an easier time, Birdie."

"Yes," I whispered.

Claude lifted a hand and rubbed his chin, stretched the loose, gray-stubbled skin and let it fall into place again. "If I'd of planned my life, I'd of done some things different, Birdie. I would've stayed there when you got sick. I'd of lifted you out of bed and took you to the porch and set you in a chair in the sun, so it could get deep down inside. I'd of hooked up the team and took you all over the farm, and let you look out over the canyon and sit at the waterfall down by the creek." Shoulders quaking, he let his head fall forward. Tears traced the network of wrinkles on his cheek, fell and shattered against the arms of his wheelchair. "I shouldn't of let Daddy send me away and bring you here, Birdie. I shouldn't of run off to the army. I should of gone and brung you back home, but, truth is, I was weak. I couldn't stand to see you layin' in bed like that, so I left."

Silence enveloped the room as he surrendered to tears. I wanted to stand up, cross the distance between us, kneel by his chair and comfort him, tell him no matter what had happened in the past, he was one of the kindest souls I'd ever known. He might not have been there to save Birdie, but he had saved me. "Noooo," I whispered, reaching toward him. "Nooo, ssshhh, ssshhh."

He lifted his head finally, took his hankie from his pocket, and turned to me. Looking around the room, he seemed to realize where he was. "I'm sorry. I ain't sure where my mind goes sometimes. I know you ain't Birdie."

"All-rye-t," I whispered, clasping and unclasping my fingers to beckon him closer. He came to the bed, put his hand on the rail, and I laid mine over it. "All-rye-t. Ssshhh . . . ssshhh."

We sat that way, joined in a bond of shared need—to love, to be loved, to be understood and to understand. I wanted to tell him about Teddy, about all the times I'd wondered—if I'd done things differently, would Teddy be different?

There was a day, the lowest of my life, when Teddy was almost kindergarten age, and I finally accepted the grim prognosis the doctors had given. I packed Teddy's things, took him to a special school, and left him there. I prepared to sign over his custody to the state because I couldn't afford the sort of care and schooling he would need, because my parents thought it would be best, because I was young and it was time for me to get on with my life, because I couldn't manage on my own, because I couldn't bear to look at him and wonder if it was my fault.

I wanted to tell Claude about that day, about the weeks that followed, when I moved back to my parents' house, enrolled in city college, went out with girlfriends, breathed fresh air that didn't smell of strained food and soiled diapers on a child who should have been fully potty trained long ago. I never told anyone about that time, and Teddy couldn't remember it. He didn't know that I left him at the school for six weeks, or that I came back and told the director I was studying to be a teacher. I begged him to give me a position at the school, where I could be close to my son, learn how to teach him and help him. The director took pity on me, life went on, and I never left Teddy again.

I knew how it was to come to the breaking point, to struggle between self-preservation and selfless love. We were, all of us, only human, trying to be less imperfect creations and become more like our creator.

"Ssshhh," I soothed again, the way I might have calmed Teddy when he had an upset. "Ssshhh."

Claude wasn't of a mind to be comforted. Men so often choose to wear the hair shirt rather than to examine the causes of the pain. How many years had I pleaded with Edward to fly to California, to go to his daughter and explain everything to her? He felt that it was better to let her move on and lead her own life—that it was only fair, since he'd been the one to leave Marilyn, that Marilyn should have their child. All these years, he'd suffered in silence rather than confronting the mistakes and betrayals of the past.

"I'm sorry to bring up them old things," Claude said finally, then released the railing and pulled his hand away. "I don't know why that all come back, except it bein' my birthday, and my sister's, and I wanted to be home by now, back with all my old things, back with the old pictures of Birdie and me. There was gonna be a birthday party the year the two of us turned seventeen. My auntie had it all planned out. She come up from south Texas to help my daddy with all the preparations, but then Birdie got sick. We didn't know what it was at first. My daddy canceled the party and sent for the doctor. A part of me was mad at Birdie because she'd messed up the birthday fun. Birdie was always sick a lot. When the doctors told us she'd come down with the polio, all I could think was it was my fault, that I'd brung it on by bein' so selfish. No matter what we did, Birdie just lay there and got sicker and sicker.

"Finally, my daddy made plans to take her to a specialist. He give me the white mules to take to a sale and sent me off to my uncle's place in Tom Green County. It darn near killed me to saddle my horse and ride off pulling Jes and Tab behind me, but I understood it had to be done. We needed the money for Birdie. Right after the mules was sold, Birdie took a turn for the worse. When I heard about it, I packed my stuff and left my uncle's house, and I didn't look back." Moving away from the bed, he turned his chair around. "It's strange the way a young man's mind works. I told myself if I joined the army and did somethin' good, somethin' to earn a favor, God would heal Birdie's body, and she'd get stronger. But the truth is, bein' here in this place, I know the best thing I could of done for her was to sit at her bedside and hold her hand. Maybe that would of made the difference."

He rolled back to the window, and we sat together in silence. I couldn't offer the comfort he needed, any more than I could become the twin sister he'd left behind all those years ago.

Watching him, I thought about the young man in the picture with the mules, a sandy-haired farm boy greeting the world with a haphazard grin, alive with the follies of youth. I imagined him behind the team of white mules, breaking dry ground, changing the soil, patiently turning it over again, and again, looking forward to becoming seventeen, looking forward to a birthday party, making plans for a life that would soon take a path he hadn't expected, that would steal away his sister, lead him far from the farm, first to Tom Green County, and then to the killing fields of Europe. . . .

Tom Green County. . . .

I remembered the days of the polio scare, when parents, families, entire communities feared the ravages of that disease.

We'd been talking about it just the other day. Polio. Those frightening times when children you knew were healthy, then later they came back to school with twisted bodies and crippled legs. Claude's sister had a special saddle, and she liked to wear pants when she rode, so no one could see the braces. . . .

Was that Claude's sister? Had she been telling me about the livestock auction a few days ago?

But Claude's sister, Birdie, had died. She couldn't have told me her story. Where had I heard that story? Who was the girl riding her horse at the livestock auction? Had I only dreamed that? Read it in a book or seen it in a movie?

She flirted with a boy, shared a first kiss with him behind the barns, hid her legs in the creek when he passed by.

Later, she heard that his sister was stricken with polio. . . .

He ran away and joined the army. She never saw the boy again, but she'd always wondered what became of him, how things might have been different if she hadn't hidden her legs in the pool. . . .

My mind spun through the connections, nimble like a spider pulling together bits of a broken web, quickly weaving silken ties until everything was connected. The boy had blue eyes . . . the bluest eyes. Blue eyes like Claude's.

"Wee-da," I whispered. Ouita Mae was the girl with the braces on her legs. She'd been injured in a horse riding accident when she was young. . . .

Claude looked up from his musings.

"Wee-da," I said again, knowing there was no way I could possibly communicate to him that his story and Ouita Mae's melded together like puzzle pieces, creating a picture that seemed so clear now. She was the girl at the pool and he was the boy on the tall yellow horse. They'd passed by each other all those years ago, and now their paths had intersected again. "Wee-da Maaae."

"Ouita Mae?" Claude interpreted, glancing toward the door. "I imagine she'll be by to read to you after a while. She usually has breakfast with the doc down in the cafeteria first thing, before he starts to work. Never seen a man work as much as that fella does. I'm thinkin' I ought to introduce him to my niece. They could make a life plan together." Where he normally would have finished the joke with a grin, he managed only a little smile. "I'm sorry, Birdie. I ain't much company today." He turned his wheelchair around and started toward the door.

"Wee-da, pu-ll." "Pull" wasn't the word . . . *pool* . . . *pool. Ouita was the girl at the pool.* Even though I knew it was impossible, I tried again. "Wee-da, pu-ll."

"Yeah." Claude stopped in the alcove. "I imagine she'll be along to read the book in a while, but I'll tell her you're lookin' for her." Then he was gone. I fell back against the pillow, rigid with frustration. Somehow, I had to find a way to make Claude, or Ouita Mae, understand . . .but how? In spite of the frustration, I was filled with a new sense of purpose, the idea that, even lying here crippled in this bed, I had been given something important to do.

I drifted into my thoughts, listening for Teddy, imagining that, after all these years, Ouita Mae and Claude were meant to meet again. Gazing out the window, I lost myself in a daydream of the girl by the pool and the young farm boy on his golden horse, connected by a chance encounter, separated all these years, now brought back together. How strange a plan, but how miraculous.

Sometime later, I was pulled back to the present by the sound of a visitor coming. I hoped at first that it was Teddy, but I heard the *click-swish* of a wheelchair. When I looked up, Ouita Mae was appearing from the alcove.

"I hear you had a good chat with your family yesterday," Ouita Mae said, and smiled. "I'm glad. Thought I'd get on in here and read us some more in this book before your people come again." She picked up the book and leafed through the pages. "Let's see . . . where'd we quit?"

I tried to tell her Claude was the boy on the yellow horse. She only smiled indulgently and said, "Oh, he's fine, sweetie. I seen Gretchen come get him after breakfast and head for the therapy room. If he survives it, I imagine he'll come by and say how-do in a while." Finding our page in the book, she pressed it open against her leg, then held it up and squinted through her glasses. "I won't miss therapy when I go home, that's for darned sure."

"Ugg-go?" I asked.

Ouita Mae assumed I was worried about finishing the book. "Well, I'm not headed back home for a week or so," she promised, and started to read.

I hoped that reading about Gavin and Marcella would remind her of the boy at the pool, and she would bring it up again, but she didn't. When she put the book away, I tried to tell her about Claude, but it was impossible to communicate the thought, out of the blue.

Ouita Mae left, and I went back to listening for Teddy. He and Rebecca came just as the aide was bringing my lunch tray of mushy delights. Rebecca exited quickly to take a call on her cell phone. The occupational therapist popped in and showed Teddy how to help me put the special spoon in my hand and move it from the tray to my mouth. It was a messy process, and the motion was mostly on the part of my helper, but the therapist insisted that I must do as much as I could, so as to redevelop the muscular control required for independence.

Independence. Such a beautiful word to which we so seldom attach the proper weight. Teddy worked patiently, cheering me toward it. "Come on, Mama. You do it, now. Good job, good job! 'Nother bite, come on, Mama. . . ."

I couldn't help thinking of all the milestones I'd coaxed, prodded, dragged Teddy through over the years. Now we were operating in reverse. He was the teacher and I the student, my own words of encouragement being delivered back to me. His mouth hung partially open as he concentrated, trying to make his hands travel smoothly from plate to mouth and back, guiding mine. He helped me more than he should have. I wondered if, over the years, I'd done the same for him—if by helping and protecting, seeing that he took life in small bites, I'd thwarted his independence more than was necessary.

Rebecca came in to check on us after lunch. She spoke to me pleasantly enough, told me she was still waiting to talk with Dr.

Amadi about Edward's condition, but the nurse said he was improving. Rebecca warned that she and Teddy might not be able to come to the nursing center tomorrow, because they hoped to be making arrangements for bringing Edward home.

When they left, Teddy didn't cry. He was looking forward to eating supper and playing ski-ball at Chuck E. Cheese. He joked with Rebecca, made her promise to order extra pepperoni. She laughed and said she would.

Jealousy sent a sharp, painful stab through me that I tried to suppress.

The day passed by, and then another, and another. Betty and Ifeoma came and went, Ouita Mae read the book, therapists performed therapy. My focus was less than ideal. I was worried about Teddy, and Edward, and things at home. I would have asked Mary to go by and see about them, but Mary was absent for two days because her son was too sick to attend school. Ifeoma, Betty, and a nurse's aide from a temp agency covered her shifts.

I wondered where Mary was staying, because I didn't hear her in Claude's bathroom in the mornings. By the time she came back on the third day, I'd begun to worry that she wouldn't return at all. She entered my room looking exhausted and thinner than usual. "Sorry I've been gone," she said. Rubbing the back of her wrist across her forehead, she sighed. "Gretchen says you haven't been cooperating with your therapy as well as you could."

"Ffff! Grrr-chn," I grumbled.

Mary gave me a sad look. "She wants you to get better. It takes a hard person to do a hard job sometimes."

"Ffff!" As soon as the sound came out, I was sorry for it. I wanted to tell Mary I was glad she was back, and ask her if she knew why Teddy and Rebecca hadn't come. There was momentary confusion between my mouth and my brain, like a light switch flipping on and off. I threw my head back against the pillow, impatient to clear the fog.

"You have to try to . . ." Mary's urging lacked the usual enthusiasm. Pinching the bridge of her nose, she leaned away, her fingers trembling.

"Maryyy." I reached out and touched her arm.

"I'm sorry," she sniffled, covering her eyes. Her lips parted as breath trembled in and out of her. "I'm just . . . tired. I'm sorry."

"Maryyy," I whispered again. "Whyeee?"

She shook her head.

"Sss-it," I said.

She managed a wan smile, wiping her cheeks. "I can't. I'm so far behind today. If I don't get busy, I'll get fi— I'm sorry, Mrs. Parker. Just ignore me."

I caught her hand before she could leave. My fingers closed around it, strong and determined. Independent. "Maryyy . . . ssshhh . . . All-rye-t? Whyeee?"

Sighing, she sank to the edge of the chair. Her shoulders rounded forward into a weary arc. "Do you ever just . . . not know what to ask for anymore? Do you ever just feel like . . . like things will never be all right again?"

"Yes," I whispered, filled with a shared feeling of desperation, of loss and unanswered prayers. Even though I'd always had faith, always believed, I couldn't imagine where we would all go from here.

CHAPTER 17

Rebecca Macklin

After three days of calling home health care agencies, conducting interviews, dealing with my father's hospitalization, and trying to make arrangements for a power of attorney over my father's bank accounts, I was close to the breaking point. To make matters worse, back at the office, two important visa applications had been sent in without the proper supporting documentation, and I'd been spending hours on the phone with Bree, trying to clear things up before the potential employer, my client, decided to find another law firm. Kyle hit the end of his rope and wanted me to come home.

"Just hire someone to take care of it and get on a plane, Rebecca," he snapped. "It can't be that hard." As usual, there was the insinuation that he could handily take care of what I could not—that this situation in Dallas was dragging on because I was soft, unwilling to do what needed to be done. There was always, between us, this silent competition, one winner, one loser. He was the better lawyer, the more successful income producer, the one with the Pepperdine education, the one willing to put in the over-and-above time, the superhero who could tie things up in profitable little packages so everyone could be happy. No allowances were made for the fact that, while he was burning the midnight oil, I was raising our daughter and trying to create a home that was more than just a place where we kept our stuff.

"You know what, Kyle, it's not as easy as that. You can't just look in the want ads and hire a . . . a responsible family member to look after things." I didn't want to fight with him. I wanted to lean on him, to purge myself of all the details, to have him shore me up. I wanted to admit that I wasn't sure what to do next, or how to handle things, or whether I could. Instead of being honest, admitting weakness, I felt the need to defend my position.

"You're in Dallas, for heaven's sake," he pointed out. "There must be any number of agencies."

"And I've called them all." I could feel the discussion taking on a life of its own, spiraling into an argument. "I've either interviewed or talked to at least a dozen people the past few days, Kyle. That's all I've done, other than search my father's files and wade through the runaround at the bank. I was hoping to get my father out of the hospital two days ago, but instead he's still there and it's been two days since we've even made it by to visit, and a day longer than that since I took Teddy to the nursing center. He's about to have a breakdown, the hospital is *finally* discharging my father today, and I have no idea what shape he's in, because I haven't seen him. On top of all that, I talked to the nursing center administrator yesterday, and they'd like to brief me on the kinds of renovations needed to bring Hanna Beth home. Whatever personnel I hire here will eventually be dealing with that, on top of Hanna Beth's care, scheduling her physical therapy, taking her for medical visits. The list goes on and on. Meanwhile, I can't get into my father's bank accounts, but I do know that the water, phone, electric, and trash services were behind in payment due to lack of funds for the automatic drafts. There should be plenty of money in my father's accounts, but given his mental state when I got here, anything's possible. He may have cashed in all his CDs and buried the money in the backyard to keep it away from *those people*. I'm going flipping crazy here, Kyle. Instead of a butt-chewing about things at the office, a little *support* from my *husband* would be nice." To my complete irritation, a lump of tears blocked my throat—a reaction completely unlike me. In the throes of a negotiation, which this was, I never succumbed to emotion. Female lawyers couldn't afford that luxury.

"Macey needs . . ." Kyle stopped mid-sentence, puzzled. "Rebecca?"

"I'm sorry," I sniffed, trying to gain control. What was wrong with me lately? "I'm just so . . . wiped out. I think I'm allergic to something in this house. I haven't been sleeping well."

"You've been under quite a bit of stress, Beck." It felt good to have him recognize the fact, to hear a note of tenderness in the pet name he so seldom used anymore. I wanted to fall into him, have him wrap his arms around me long-distance and hold me up.

"A little." My voice was raw and hoarse. "Did Mace get her cast on yesterday?" One more thing that had been on and off my mind. The swelling in Macey's ankle hadn't subsided as quickly as the doctors expected.

"Yes. Pink." There was a smile in Kyle's voice. I pictured that smile, knew just how it would look if I were there in the room with him. I would smile back at him, feel warm and connected for a moment before we moved on to other topics. "My mother helped her glue rhinestones on the toe, and she took a Sharpie to school today to have everyone sign it. She wanted you to know she's saving a spot for you, though. She put a sticker over it so no one would encroach on your space."

I sniffle-laughed and felt homesick all at once. I wanted to be the first one to sign Macey's cast. I wanted to be there to help her glue rhinestones on it. "Did you go with her to the doctor?"

Kyle sighed. "Yes, I went with her. I sat outside the MRI machine, and I voted on the cast colors, and she overruled me. I voted for rainbow, and she picked pink because she thought you would like it."

"I'm surprised. Usually whatever Dad says is golden." A tenderness blossomed in my chest. My daughter picked pink for me. Macey was always seeking evidence of her father's approval—pulling out school assignments, gymnastics medals, performing new tricks on the living room floor in an effort to garner a bit of his attention.

"She misses her mom," Kyle said, and I felt the words cuddle me tightly.

"Thanks," I said. "Kyle, I . . ." For just an instant I was tempted to apologize for the fight, to say *I love you*. Then I remembered Susan Sewell, and it seemed ludicrous. The tenderness in my mouth turned bitter. "I *am* trying to wrap things up here and get back to the office. If Bree needs me, she can always call me on my cell."

"Mmm-hmmm," Kyle muttered absently, the tone delivering a sting of disappointment. He was already getting back to business.

Why should that surprise me? Why did I keep setting myself up for this—opening the door, fostering hope just so he could rip it out from under me? "I'd better go. I have a woman coming for an interview at ten, and I'm hoping she'll be the one. They're supposed to discharge my father at three o'clock, and I have to take Teddy by the nursing center to see Hanna Beth before then. He's been upset for days because he told Hanna Beth he would come feed her lunch again, and we couldn't. I called the nurse and told her to explain, but that isn't enough for Teddy. He's worried about breaking a promise." The profoundness of those words, of my saying them to Kyle, struck me hard. My father's mentally challenged stepson understood the importance of keeping a promise, but my husband had no problem holding another woman's hand in broad daylight.

Kyle hesitated on the other end. "Rebecca?" he said finally, his tone tentative, as if he were about to broach a subject I wouldn't like.

I swallowed hard. *He's going to tell me he's leaving. He's going to say it's over.*

"Yes?" The word was barely a whisper.

"Have you considered the idea that this caretaker who was working for your father and Hanna Beth—what did you say her name was? Kay something?" I didn't answer right away. I was still catching my breath, reeling to a stop after having hydroplaned into dangerous territory.

Kyle went on, completely unaware of my tempest of thought. "It's possible that this caretaker might have gained access to your father's bank accounts—that her sudden departure after Hanna Beth's stroke might not be entirely coincidental. Maybe she was afraid family members would be coming in, asking questions, and she got out of there. Maybe that's the reason there's no money, and you can't find any bank statements around the house, or any contact information for the caretaker. You remember we did the title work on that case up by Tahoe last year, the one where the hot little blonde bilked the old car dealer out of all his money, his businesses, everything. Remember that?"

My mind took a moment to adjust to the conversational switch. I was stuck on *hot little blonde*. Rage flamed in a tinder-dry place inside me. "I'm not stupid, Kyle." *I know all about hot little blondes and the men who fall for them.*

"It was just a thought." His words were impatiently clipped, the *Well, bite my head off* tone.

Stop, I told myself. *Get control of yourself. Now isn't the time for this.* "I've looked into it, all right. The bank won't tell me much, but the guy did take pity on me and tell me there's no indication that anyone other than my father and Hanna Beth had access to the accounts. My father has been doing most of his banking via automatic drafts and over the Internet. If I can find his passwords, I can log on to his accounts and see where the money's going. It's anybody's guess where he's hidden that information or what happened to his computer. He has things stashed all over the house. I find mail in the freezer, food under the bed. The file cabinet is full of washed clothes.

He hides things, and then he goes on tirades saying somebody stole them. Clearly, he's had a very limited grasp on reality lately."

"Hence my question about the disappearing caretaker." The comment was falsely light, intended to sound like a joke while backhandedly making the point that he thought I was being naive. "If this were one of my clients, the first thing I'd do would be—"

"This isn't one of your clients, Kyle."

"You're too close to this thing." His tone was flat, pacifying, the one he used with hysterical women involved in disputes over estate property.

"This is my *family*, Kyle! How could I not be close to it?" I exploded, then was immediately struck that I'd used the word "family" at all.

"You don't owe those people, Rebecca." How many times had I said that to Kyle over the past few years? I'd reiterated it right before I left for the airport. *I don't know why I'm doing this. It's not like I owe these people anything.* "You're just reacting to losing your mother—looking for a replacement. A year ago, if this had happened, you wouldn't have dropped everything here and gotten on a plane."

I sat down on the bed, feeling wounded. "That's not true." Was it? Was Kyle right? All this time in Dallas my one underpinning, my salvation, had been the belief that I was doing the right thing, a magnanimous thing, one that proved I was all grown up, bigger than what had happened in the past, no longer the little girl locked in the back of the car steeped in righteous anger. I was mature enough now to do the right thing just because it was the right thing. "I'm not . . ." Something on the other end of the line made me stop. I heard a voice, a laugh, Bree's laugh. "Is Bree in there?"

"Yeah. We're setting up for a deposition."

"You're in the meeting room?" My cheeks instantly burned with humiliation. He was in the meeting room with Bree, letting her hear everything we'd been talking about? Letting her listen in on our private conversation?

"We've got people coming in ten minutes," he said blandly.

I felt betrayed, wounded, embarrassed, both personally and professionally. How was I supposed to return to the office, command respect, after the staff heard my husband lecturing me over the phone? "I have to go. My interview should be here soon."

"All right. Talk to you later," Kyle answered, seemingly oblivious.

I hung up without giving a reply. Perhaps Bree would be pleased that the conversation ended with a simple *Talk to you later.* No *I love you*s to complicate things.

I tried to put it out of my mind as I waited for my interviewee to arrive. On paper, she looked like a perfect fit—fifty-seven, single, a woman who had stayed home and raised a family, then returned to home health care work. A nurturer. Exactly what my father, Hanna Beth, and Teddy needed. She was available now because her last client had moved into a nursing center.

I hoped she would be the one. She had to be. I was running out of time and options. Even though Dr. Amadi had reported that my father was doing well, behaving much more calmly and rationally now that his electrolytes were in balance and the mixed-up concoction of medications was working its way out of his system, I didn't think I could handle the house on my own again. If today's interview went well, I would hire my father's new employee, effective immediately. I'd pay for it from our account for now, and settle with my father's accounts as soon as I gained access. If, by some miracle, my father became capable of giving a satisfactory approval by authorizing a bank signature card, all of that would happen much faster.

The apartment and the rest of the house weren't ready for a new employee, but I'd tidied up as much as I could. I could only hope that, when my father met his new caretaker, he would react well to

her, that he wouldn't relapse or decide she was one of *those people*. I
hoped Teddy would like her. Looking out the window, I watched him
moving among his benches, watering his plants, talking to them and
tenderly petting the leaves. He'd been out there all morning, patiently
passing time while he waited for me to conduct the interview before
we went to see Hanna Beth and pick up Daddy Ed.

I straightened the living room while I waited for my interviewee
to arrive. By eleven o'clock, it was becoming clear that either she had
a severe problem with promptness or she wasn't coming. I called the
home health agency, and they confirmed it. The recruiter apologetically informed me that the woman who was going to solve all my
problems had taken a job yesterday. The agency had called earlier that
morning and left a voice mail canceling the interview. They'd probably called while I was in the shower.

"Don't you have anyone else you can send?" I asked, even though
I knew the answer.

"No, ma'am." The recruiter, Amanda, sounded sympathetic.
"But we have you on the list. We have people coming into the system
all the time, but it takes a few days to process the paperwork and
the background checks. I'm scanning our listings every day." Amanda
sounded about twenty-three, years away from understanding the
monumental task of caring for aging parents. She added, "I'm sorry,
Rebecca." After so many phone calls back and forth, we were on a
first-name basis.

"Thanks," I said glumly. Hanging up the phone, I sank into my
father's recliner and tried to think. What now? There was no more
time for searching this morning. If Teddy and I didn't head out, we
wouldn't be able to go by the nursing center before we were due at
the hospital. I had to be in my father's room when Dr. Amadi made
his rounds this afternoon, if I wanted to talk about medications and
discharge instructions with the doctor rather than a nurse.

I stepped out the back door and called to Teddy. He emerged

from the garden house, waving and smiling, enthusiastic about our day.

"Comin'," he said, then began the painfully slow effort of removing his Home Depot apron and placing his tools on the potting bench by the garden house door. He carefully lined them up in a pattern only he understood.

I checked my watch, took in and exhaled what my relaxation tape referred to as a patience breath, and went back inside. I'd learned not to interrupt Teddy's routines, no matter how time-consuming they were. It was as if his programming allowed only one rigidly defined way of doing things. Any deviation caused a system failure.

As usual, he'd left a peanut butter and jelly sandwich and milk for me in the kitchen when he made breakfast. For a change, my stomach reacted positively to the idea, so I ate the sandwich, then poured out the milk before Teddy came in. I explained our plan for the day while he meticulously washed his fingers, staring in fascination as the water ran over his hands. He loved the play of light on water. Finally, I turned off the faucet, and when all the water was gone, he was ready to dry his hands.

"Are you hungry?" I asked. It was almost noon, and he'd probably eaten his usual breakfast early that morning, two peanut butter and jelly sandwiches and about eight bowls of cereal.

"Not lunchtime yet. Not lunchtime," he said cheerfully, checking the clock over the mantel. I hadn't established whether Teddy could really tell time, but he knew where the clock hands should be to signal breakfast, lunch, and supper. At home, he adhered meticulously to the schedule. Lunch was at twelve thirty.

"All right," I said. "We can get a hamburger on the way to see your mom." Away from the house, Teddy would eat anytime, anywhere. The mealtime rule only applied at home.

"I like a hamburger." Grinning, he licked his top lip enthusiastically. "And I like ike cream. Chocolate wit' Oreo."

"We can get ice cream," I agreed.

Teddy snort-laughed with pure joy. After the fact, I realized I'd known he would do this, and I was looking forward to it. Patting me tenderly on the head, he added, "You a good girl, A-becca."

I felt a flutter of Teddy's happiness inside me. "You're a good boy, Teddy."

As we walked out the front door, he snorted again, threw his head back and shouted, "I like ike cream!" at the sky, then listened for an echo.

While watching Teddy eat a burger and ice cream at Sonic, I almost forgot to brood over my troubles. Teddy, I'd noticed, often had that effect on people. In the hospital, at the pizza place, in the grocery store, wherever he went, his smile, his awkward, honking laugh were always close to the surface, always contagious. Small things brought him overwhelming joy, and he radiated it, shared it, lived most of the time within it.

On the way into the nursing center, he paused to again experiment with the automatic door. I stood in the lobby and waited, thinking that no matter how hard it was, how long it took, I had to find the right person to assume the caretaking at Blue Sky Hill—someone who would allow Teddy to be who he was, rather than trying to manage or fix him.

There was nothing in Teddy that was broken. The more time I spent with him, the more I understood how much the rest of us were slaves to schedules, ambitions, resentments, appointments, expectations, reservations, preconceived notions of what life should be. I'd created a rigid existence in which there was no room for detours off the path, no time to walk in and out of the automatic door more than once just to see how it worked, no space for someone like Teddy.

Yet here he was. Here we all were.

A potent regret grabbed my chest. It shouldn't have taken thirty-three years and a call from the police to bring me home. I shouldn't have waited until my father's mind was gone, and the house was falling apart, and Teddy was spending his days hiding in the backyard. This was my family, and no matter how much I wanted to deny it, to root it out and throw it away, a part of me would always feel the need for a connection, the yearning for an understanding. It was as natural as drawing breath, and in trying to suffocate it, I'd suffocated a part of myself.

"I do that, too, sometimes." A voice startled me, and I turned to find Dr. Barnhill behind me, watching Teddy experiment with the door. His face was familiar, pleasant and friendly beneath tousled brown hair that looked like he hadn't taken time to comb it.

"Dr. Barnhill," he reintroduced himself.

I nodded, remembering his face. "Good to see you again. How's Hanna Beth doing?"

His pager beeped, and he paused to glance at it, then pressed the button and hooked it on the pocket of his lab coat. "Not as well the last few days, I'm sorry to report. Miss Hanna Beth hasn't been in the mood to cooperate with her therapy. She's been refusing to try the wheelchair, for one thing." His lips quirked to one side, his brows rising over dark eyes with thick lashes. "I have a feeling, though, that you two will be just what the doctor ordered. She's been worried about you."

"I'm sorry. I called and asked the nurse to make sure she knew we might not be able to come for a few days."

He nodded in understanding. "Well, some of the nursing staff has been out this past week, so it's possible your message got lost in transit. Anyway, I'm sure Hanna Beth will be relieved you're here. I think she's ready for a little company, other than my grandmother and the romance novel." He gave me a friendly, reassuring smile, Ouita Mae's smile.

"How's your grandmother doing? She told me she had some surgery while she was here."

"Well, they weren't able to do as much arthroscopically as they'd hoped. I'm not sure she's ready to face that fact yet." Shaking his head, he laughed softly. "She checked with me this morning to make sure I'd booked her plane ticket back to Houston, but the truth is it's not going to be feasible for her to go back home again. She's unstable doing a lot of things, and living alone in an old house that requires a lot of care is just not possible."

I groaned under my breath. "That sounds familiar." It was comforting to talk to someone who could understand what I was dealing with. "I've been going crazy this week, doing interviews, talking to home health agencies, trying to find a live-in caretaker for my father and Teddy, and eventually Hanna Beth. It's just . . . incredibly difficult."

"You might check with the administrator here and see if she has any ideas."

"I already did," I admitted. "She gave me the agency lists I've been using."

He nodded solemnly. "I know it's not much comfort, but it's good that they have you looking to their interests. So many of our elderly patients aren't so fortunate."

It was hard to think of my father and Hanna Beth as fortunate. "I should have come back sooner." Guilt welled up inside me and spilled over. The next thing I knew, I was telling him our family story—mine, my father's, Hanna Beth's. *He doesn't need to hear all of this,* I thought. *He's not interested in more problems. The man deals with tragedies every day.*

His pager went off again. He checked it and glanced toward the reception desk. I knew he needed to leave. "I'm sorry. I didn't mean to unload on you. That was completely . . ." *Unlike me. Unacceptable. Abnormal.* "I really apologize."

"I don't mind." He met my gaze in a way that acknowledged a connection, a shared battle between us.

"I'm sorry," I said again, and looked away. "Thanks for listening."

"Anytime." Tucking his pager back in his pocket, he glanced up as Teddy came in the door again. "Hey there, Teddy. You get that door working like it's supposed to yet?"

Teddy laughed, waving as Dr. Barnhill turned and headed toward the hallway opposite Hanna Beth's. Just before Dr. Barnhill disappeared around the corner, Teddy went out the door again.

I caught Teddy on his next trip through, and we proceeded to Hanna Beth's room. Hurrying ahead of me, he checked the names on the doors, peeked into the rooms, then went into Hanna Beth's.

"Hi-eee, Mama!" His voice echoed down the hall.

Hanna Beth's response was an outcry of pure elation.

Mary came out of a room across the hall to see what was going on. She hesitated as I approached. I suspected that she was waiting for me, giving me the opportunity to respond to her offer to move into the apartment over my father's garage.

"Hello, Mary," I said. "How's Hanna Beth doing?"

"She'll be better now that y'all are here." She peeked in Hanna Beth's doorway, her face filled with a tender concern. "She was really worried."

"I know. The last few days have been busy . . ." I paused before blurting out that I'd been interviewing prospective caretakers for my father. "I called and explained the situation to someone . . . Betty, I think? She promised she would tell Hanna Beth."

"Oh," Mary replied, her eyes narrowing with something as close to disgust as I'd ever seen her fashion. "She probably forgot." There was more to that, but Mary didn't elaborate. Smoothing the front of her scrub top, she stood waiting for me to say something.

"I'm sorry Hanna Beth was worried."

Mary nodded. "How's your dad doing?"

I was surprised she remembered that my father was in the hospital. "Better. His reports are good, and they're discharging him today. I wanted to come by here first. Once he's home, I don't know how things will . . . be." I realized too late that I'd just opened the door to a conversation about the caretaking job.

Her cheeks tightened and she swallowed hard, scanning the floor as if the right words might be scattered there. Her chin came up and her speech rushed out. "You know, if you need someone just temporary, I could do that. I mean, until you find someone permanent. . . . Not that I'm not still interested in permanent . . . me and Ifeoma, I mean. I talked to her about it, and she thought it would work out good. She gets off at two in the mornings, and she can't sleep past daylight. I could look after things at night while she's sleeping and gone to work. The boy's don't . . ." She focused on the floor again, twisted her hands together tightly. ". . . wake up much at night."

I stood silent, afraid to say yes, afraid to say no, afraid I would be inviting more problems into the house, afraid I couldn't handle things on my own any longer.

"Sorry," Mary muttered. "I didn't mean to be pushy. My apartment lease is up, that's all."

Somewhere amid all my own concerns, I was reminded that Mary had concerns of her own. Her hair was unwashed, her clothes wrinkled as if she'd slept in them, her normally clear skin red and broken out. She looked tired and stressed.

Whatever the reasons, whatever she wasn't saying, she needed me, she needed this job.

"I think something temporary would be good," I said. My heart fluttered upward, did an uncertain flip-flop. I hoped this was right. *Please, let this be the right thing.* "Let's start that way, and then we'll see how it works out."

CHAPTER 18

Hanna Beth Parker

In our little white church some years ago, Pastor Al preached a sermon about counting all things joy. We must believe, he asserted, that all things, even the ones we do not choose, work together for our good. Pastor Al was scheduled for cancer surgery the next week. He was facing a stiff regimen of chemotherapy and even odds for survival, and I suppose, as I sat there in the pew, I thought he was largely trying to convince himself.

I was steeped in my own worries, having for the first time left Edward home rather than bringing him out to church. Kay-Kay had insisted that the travel and all the people he had difficulty recognizing now were too upsetting for him, and she was probably right. I knew she would watch after Edward while I was gone, but it broke my heart to walk out the door and leave him sitting there. I found it impossible to count it as joy that he would wait at home while I went to service. It was impossible to see how this situation could be for anyone's good. It was impossible to understand how Teddy, sitting beside me rather than helping entertain children in the preschool room, was good. Teddy's banishment from the nursery was merely the work of a few closed-minded parents who judged Teddy at first sight and protested his presence with the children. Being new to the area, they didn't know Teddy at all and didn't care to.

The following Sunday, Teddy and I stayed home with Edward. There seemed to be no point in our attending a place where we were not wanted. At first, Teddy had a difficult time with the alteration in our Sunday routine. He was afraid God would be angry with us.

When I lay on the floor in the laundry room, fading out, unable to move, it crossed my mind that perhaps he'd been right all these months. I began attempting to strike a bargain. I promised that if God brought me through this, allowed me to return to Teddy and Edward, I would never question again.

All the same, lying for hours on end in the nursing center, with Edward now in the hospital and Rebecca taking charge of my house, I began to question again. But the day Teddy came back to my room, as he hugged me, and I heard Mary and Rebecca talking in the hall, a light shined down the well, and I wasn't looking through the glass darkly anymore. The plan was as clear to me as the ceiling overhead or the clock on the wall.

This illness, this time in the care center, was meant to bring all of us together. We needed one another, Mary, Rebecca, Teddy and Edward, me.

. . . *when we got a tough row to plow, the Good Lord makes us fall a little short and puts another mule in the pasture. You don't never know whether you're the blind mule or the deaf mule, but you're always one or the other.*

We were Jes and Tab in Claude's story, drawn together by needs we couldn't fully understand, but also couldn't deny. The empty places in each of us fit together like pieces of a whole.

Like members of a family.

The idea was at once wondrous and startling.

When Rebecca and Mary came in the door, I held out my hands, took both of theirs, felt a smile come. I was unashamed of its lopsidedness. "Gu-ood!" I said, my voice trembling with jubilant emotion. "Good! Good!" I felt as if I could throw off the covers, spring from the bed and scamper around the room. The next time Gretchen brought in the wheelchair, I'd show her a thing or two.

Mary laughed. "I guess you heard what we were talking about."

"Yesh!" I cheered. "Myeee how-t. Good! Shhhow . . ." *No, not show . . . so.* The letters were flying through my mind. "So go-od!"

The clarity of the words surprised Rebecca, pleasantly so. "I guess she approves." Rebecca turned to Teddy, who'd moved away a step, startled by all the activity. "Teddy," she said very carefully, "Mary's going to move into the apartment over the garage and help take care of Daddy Ed—like Kay-Kay used to."

Teddy reacted cautiously, trying to process the idea of a change. I held my breath, hoping Mary and Rebecca wouldn't mistake his response for a negative reaction. It was just Teddy struggling to make an adjustment. "No . . . ," he said finally, shaking his head. "No. Mary workin' here. She work here. Take care Mama."

I waited apprehensively. I wanted to be able to explain, to help all of them see that Teddy wasn't being difficult, just struggling to understand. For years, his doctors, his educational therapists, and schoolteachers had been trying to teach him to react more benignly to unfamiliar stimuli. The doctor described Teddy's routines as being hardwired into his body, reflexes like blinking, or swallowing, or breathing. When those things were interrupted, it was akin to being deprived of oxygen, held underwater. Panic was only natural.

To my surprise, Rebecca reached out, stopped his frenzied movement. "Mary's still going to work here during the days and take care of your mom. Then in the evenings and at night, she'll be with us. In the daytime, we might have another nurse there, named Ifeoma."

Teddy pushed his lips upward, his regard traveling back and forth between Mary and Rebecca. I heard the faint tapping of his teeth. He'd always done that when he was trying very hard to assimilate new information, to connect to events that lay far outside his practiced spheres of thought. His focus moved slowly away from Rebecca, drifted to the lights overhead. It was a bad sign, a signal that he was pulling into himself, drawing back to comfortable stimulations.

The silence in the room seemed deafening. I reached for Teddy, but he didn't react.

Rebecca rubbed his shoulder like she was trying to increase blood flow. "What do you think about that, Teddy?"

Teddy drew away, stared up at the light.

Mary tucked stray strands of hair behind her ear, then folded her arms over her stomach. "It's okay if he needs some time to think about it." Her gaze darted toward the parking lot—toward her car, perhaps? Was she wondering whether she and her boys would be sleeping there tonight?

Teddy stood unblinking by the wall, watching the lights, his face relaxed, his mouth hanging open slightly, his expression vacant.

"Teddy?" Rebecca ventured again. She touched his hands, and he jerked away, as if the contact were surprising, or painful.

Swallowing hard, taking a breath, I tried to remember the voice we'd used in therapy at the institutional school, the low, guttural tone in which we said students' names when they were distracted, almost more of an animal sound than a word.

"Tad-eee!" The utterance bounced around the room like the bark of a dog. Both Mary and Rebecca drew back, their eyes widening, but Teddy didn't respond. "Tad-eee!" I said again. "Tad-eee!"

A buzzer beckoned from the hallway, and Mary took a step toward the door. "It's okay. I don't need an answer right now."

"No. Mary, it's fine." Rebecca chewed a fingernail, then pressed the pads of her fingers together, looking tired and worried. "It'll be fine. Just plan on it, all right? By the time you get off work, we should be home from the hospital with my father."

Mary's response was a tentative nod. "I'll talk to Ifeoma about everything when she comes in, if you want. I can let her know it's just temporary and stuff."

"That'll be fine." Rebecca pulled her lip between her teeth, look-ing at Teddy, no doubt wondering what to do next, how she would manage to get him out of here, and whether the afternoon would come off as planned.

"Okay," Mary said. "I'm sorry if I made Teddy upset."

"It isn't you," Rebecca answered, her helplessness, frustration, and uncertainty unmasked. I understood all of them.

I reached for her, pulling her hand into mine. She pushed her lips into a reassuring smile. "Don't worry. We'll . . ."

"Where she gone put the boy and the udder boy?" Teddy's ques-tion came out of the blue. All three of us turned to look at him. "Where she gone put the two boy?"

I felt like laughing and weeping all at once. I wasn't sure Rebecca understood the question, but I did.

"Rrrr howt," I said. "Arrr how-se." Mary gave the words a pleased smile.

"Where's she going to put the boys?" Rebecca was a bit slower in deciphering Teddy's question.

"My room?" Teddy's eyes widened, and he patted his chest enthu-siastically, indicating that he thought keeping Mary's boys in his room would be a grand idea. Back when Teddy helped with the children at church, he always wanted to bring them home with him, show them all of his treasures in the backyard and the collection of model cars and airplanes in his room. As a youngster, Teddy didn't play with the toys as they were meant to be played with. He liked to turn them upside down and watch the wheels spin. Even so, Edward never came home from a business trip without bringing Teddy something with wheels on it.

Mary and Rebecca exchanged bemused glances. Not knowing Teddy very well, they didn't really understand what he was asking.

Rebecca shook her head. "You don't have to give up your room, Teddy. The boys will sleep in the apartment with their mom."

Teddy let his smile fade. By now, he should have been accustomed to parents telling him he couldn't play with their children, but it was always hard for him to accept.

Mary came a step closer, her lips pursing sympathetically. "You wouldn't want the boys in your room at night, Teddy." Leaning across the bed, she put a hand beside her mouth like she was going to tell him a secret, and whispered, "Brandon snores."

Teddy laughed, his voice echoing down the hall, a strangely happy sound in such a solemn place.

Mary smiled, and Rebecca pressed her index finger against her nose, holding back a chuckle. I laughed with Teddy, abandoning myself to happiness until I was breathless with it. By the time I was finished, both Rebecca and Mary were watching me with consternation. I suppose they thought I'd lost my mind.

"Good!" I gasped, and waved an arm around the room. "Allll good!" If I'd had a thousand words, I couldn't have come up with better ones. It was as if I'd been cold for weeks, and had suddenly been wrapped in a comfortable old quilt. The warmth went deep inside.

"They gone my room som-time?" Teddy was still concerned as to how the new living arrangements would work out, in terms of playtime.

"Sure, if you want them to," Mary said. The hall buzzer sounded again, and she excused herself from the room.

Teddy moved his chair near the head of my bed and sat down. "I gone show my car the boy and the other boy, Mama. All my car. My hun-erd fit-ty-two car." Teddy knew exactly how many cars were in his collection. He and Edward had counted each time Edward brought home a new one.

"Good," I said. "Ffff-fun." *That'll be fun.* I wished I could be there to watch Teddy show the boys his cars. It was disappointing to think of everything happening at home without me. For the first time since my arrival in nursing care, I was ready for Gretchen to come, so I could get on with my therapy.

"Mary a good girl," Teddy observed.

"Yesh," I agreed.

Teddy snorted and chortled, turning his head aside and ducking his chin. "Ban-don snore," he said, as if he were telling a secret.

"Yes," I agreed, and chuckled with him.

Teddy's head swiveled as he looked around us, scanning for something interesting to hold his attention. "A-becca a good girl," he said, bending backward in his chair so that he was gazing at her upside down.

"Yes," I whispered, my gaze meeting Rebecca's. "Yes." It was impossible to explain what I was feeling, to share the depth of my gratitude, the magnitude of my amazement that, after all these years, after all that had happened and the things Marilyn had undoubtedly told her, she would be the one to save us. Who could have predicted we would ever be together like this?

"You a good girl, Mama," Teddy added, then focused on the overhead lights and didn't say anything more.

Rebecca moved to the other chair, searching for a new topic of conversation. In a hospital, there isn't much. "I see you've got another book," she said finally, and reached for the volume of Texas history that Ouita Mae had selected from the library cart when we'd finished *Pirate's Promise.*

"Yes," I agreed, sinking back against the pillow. After the morning's wild emotional swings, I felt tired and limp.

"Want me to read to you for a while?" Rebecca leafed through the pages to the marker.

"Ohhh-kay." Closing my eyes, I let out a long, slow breath. Reading for a while would be good. Communication was hard work, and I needed to rest up for today's therapy session. "Hhhhank-ooo."

"You're welcome," Rebecca said, then began reading about the results of an archaeological dig outside San Antonio.

I let my mind drift in and out.

"This is kind of dry," she said after a while.

"Yes," I agreed.

"I'll pick up something new for you at the hospital gift shop today."

"Hhhhank-ooo!" I said enthusiastically. Even with Ouita Mae's colorful reading, this book made me feel like I had one foot in the grave already. I missed the excitement and romance of *Pirate's Promise*, and, aside from that, our new study of Texas history left little possibility of Ouita Mae, once again, being reminded of the boy on the yellow horse and her first kiss. Without the aid of context, I'd never be able to communicate to her the truth about Claude.

"Anything particular you'd like?"

"Righ-per . . ." The word arrived on my lips as a jumble of sound. *Pirates. Pirates.* I could see in my mind. "Righ-pits."

"How about another pirate novel?" Rebecca suggested.

"Alll-rye-t. Good."

"Maybe there's a sequel to *Pirate's Promise*," she said, and we laughed together. In spite of the stern exterior, she had a sweet laugh. Edward's laugh. I wondered if, having spent some time with her now, he'd recognized that—in spite of her resemblance to her mother—she was very much like him.

With his being in the hospital, perhaps they hadn't had time to make those connections yet. I hoped they would now. Perhaps she would learn how very proud her father was of her, that he never stopped thinking of her or wanting her to have a good life. So many times, I'd walked by his office door, glanced in and found him sitting at his desk, staring out the window with the Web site for her legal firm on his computer screen. I knew he was thinking of her, searching the Internet for postings with her name or Macey's attached, wishing, even though he was too proud to admit it to anyone, that circumstances were different.

Leafing through the book, Rebecca came upon a section about Native American tribes in Texas. Her phone rang before she could start reading. Teddy tuned in as she fished the phone from her purse and answered it. "Hi, Macey. What are you doing calling so early?" Checking the wall clock, she added, "You should be in school for another hour and a half yet."

Teddy waved at the phone. "Hi-eee, Ma-shee!"

Rebecca smiled indulgently. "Teddy says hi." Macey's high-pitched voice echoed through the receiver, then Rebecca translated, "Macey says hello."

"Hi-eee!" Teddy repeated.

"So, why aren't you in school?" Macey's reply came in a rapid rush of words. "Slow down," her mother told her. "A gas leak? Is everyone all right?" Teddy and I waited for the answer as the echoes of Macey's girlish chatter flitted about the room. Finally Rebecca broke into the conversational stream. "Well, that does sound exciting. Hang on. Put your phone on video. You can tell us all about it. We're starved for entertainment here." Winking at me, Rebecca switched a few buttons on her phone, then held it out toward Teddy and me. There on the screen was a precious little blue-eyed girl whose name I knew, whose face I'd seen once, when Edward found an article about her gymnastics team on the Internet. Edward's granddaughter. Her wheat-colored hair was up in ponytails, her suntanned face alight with enthusiasm.

"Say hello to Teddy," Rebecca instructed.

Macey put her face playfully close to the camera. "Hi, Teddy!"

Teddy craned toward the hallway, as if Macey might be out there. "Hi, Ma-shee!" He gave the phone a once-over, then leaned toward the screen until he was eyeball to eyeball with her image.

"Whoa!" Giggling, Macey retreated from her own phone, holding it at arm's length. "Cool hat, dude."

Pulling his Dallas Cowboys cap over his face, Teddy snorted and laughed.

"So what, exactly, happened at school today, Mace?" Rebecca scooted close to Teddy and leaned over the arm of his chair so that all three of us could watch the tiny screen at once.

Macey's eyes opened wide. "Oh, my gosh, you totally won't believe it. We were sitting in reading class, and then we heard this big boom outside—like, we thought the windows were going to fall out, and then . . ." Macey went on with a story about a city road crew having hit a gas line, causing an emergency evacuation of her elementary school. Macey, on crutches apparently, had to be carried down two flights of stairs piggyback by one of the other students—as it turned out, a boy with whom she shared a crush. Once they got to the safety zone, the boy stayed with Macey, even after most of the kids had been picked up by their parents. "He could've called his mom, but he hung out with me instead, because I was, like, stuck there. Isn't that so cool?" Macey finished.

Rebecca looked mildly shell-shocked. "Macey, why didn't you call Dad or Grandma to come get you?"

"Grandma had to go back down to Encinitas for the day, and Dad didn't answer his phone for a while," Macey reported, and Rebecca's face got tighter and tighter, her body stiffening. "Then Bree came and got me and took me home. She's cool."

A muscle ticked in Rebecca's cheek. "Where's your dad?"

"He's busy at work," Macey replied, as if that were perfectly natural. "Grandma's almost back, though. She got stuck in traffic."

"You're home alone?"

"Mom, I'm fine."

"Macey . . ." Glancing self-consciously at Teddy and me, Rebecca sat back in her chair. "All right. Call if Grandma's not there in a half hour, okay?"

" 'Kay."

"Love you." Rebecca's lips trembled, and she swallowed hard, her mouth framed by strained, angular lines.

"Love you, too, Mom."

"Call me if Grandma doesn't show up soon."

"Okay, Mom." Macey rolled her eyes, then waved at the screen. "Bye, Teddy. Bye . . . ummm, Hanna Beth."

Teddy and I said good-bye, and when Rebecca hung up, the festive mood in the room was gone. She stood up and started toward the door, her movements stiff, tightly controlled. "I'm going down to get a soda. Teddy, do you want anything?"

"I like soda," Teddy answered.

Rebecca nodded and disappeared out the door. By the time she came back, Gretchen had arrived to begin my therapy session. She'd shooed Teddy from his chair, and he was waiting in the corner by the window, trying to stay out of Gretchen's way. Fortunately, Rebecca was able to convince him to leave quietly by telling him he could open his soda when he got to the car.

Gretchen cracked her knuckles, then pushed a wheelchair close to the bed. "So, you gonna be stubborn with me again?"

"Noooo," I answered. "Eg-go. Rrr-eddy." *Let's go. I'm ready.*

CHAPTER 19

Rebecca Macklin

My father's homecoming was quiet. He left the hospital after having been given a mild sedative to aid in making the trip. Teddy helped me transfer him into the passenger seat, and on the drive, he sat gazing out the window with drowsy disinterest. Teddy watched warily from the backseat, unsure, as usual lately, of what to expect from Daddy Ed.

"It sooh-kay, Daddy Ed," he said when a traffic jam trapped us on Lower Greenville. "We gone home."

My father let his eyes fall closed, his head nodding forward.

"We gone home," Teddy repeated, as if he were trying to push the words around my father like a comforting arm.

The traffic sat unmoving, and finally I turned around and went the long way, winding through the old brick warehouses and trendy remodeled restaurants. Beyond the business district, we passed neighborhoods much like the ones around Blue Sky Hill, where Prairie- and Craftsman-style homes languished in various states of disrepair and renovation. Here and there, entire blocks waited, largely empty, their peeling paint and boarded windows testifying to the fact that property owners had sold out, moved out, passed away, allowing land speculators to accumulate the spans of real estate necessary for future shopping areas and condominium complexes as the neighborhoods made the change from out of fashion to trendy and hip.

As we drove, Teddy observed the construction equipment with interest, pointing out the window. "There a dump tuck. Oh, oh, crane, crane! Tha's a big one!" Pressing his cheek against the glass, he watched as we turned a corner, finally coming to a road that wasn't packed with traffic and would lead us back to Greenville. "There the school." We pulled into the right lane, and he pointed to a middle and elementary school complex. The deco-era red brick buildings had been nicely remodeled, in keeping with the area's improving tax base, though the tall chain-link fence and locked gates confirmed that the neighborhood didn't yet qualify as rehabilitated. "Oh, there some pots." Teddy pointed to the potpourri of food trash lying in the ditch and stuck in the fence, where kids, lolling on the grounds after lunch, had chosen to forgo the trash can and, instead, poke their cups through the chain link.

As we drifted by, Teddy reached for the door handle.

"We don't need any pots today, Teddy," I said, relieved that the rear doors locked automatically, a child safety feature. "We bought some at the grocery store, remember?" I glanced in the rearview mirror.

Still watching the treasure trove of discards as we passed by, Teddy nodded. "We got red one, and blue one, and green one. . . ." He stretched the words out, conveying his high regard for the new package of multicolored plastic cups. "I like green."

"Me, too," I agreed, glancing at my father. He'd shifted slightly in the seat, straightened a bit to look out the window, but he seemed calm enough.

"The lady got bread and pea-nit butter." Trying to roll down the window, Teddy waved as we went by a loading dock where a service truck was delivering pallets of mystery food, while a cafeteria worker in white work clothes and a hairnet poured a bucket of water off the back steps. "She a nice lady," Teddy added, disappointed that the window wouldn't go down.

A sad, uneasy feeling settled in my chest as we passed by the school Dumpsters, where a homeless man was investigating the day's leftovers. "Teddy, is this where you got the food that was in the house when I came?" Was it possible? The school was at least four miles from my father's house, past active construction sites, through less-than-stellar neighborhoods, under a highway interchange where homeless people slept, past a shopping center, across two busy streets. Had Teddy come this far? Could he navigate through the obstacles?

I pictured Teddy at the school, wandering around the Dumpsters in the dirty clothes I'd found him wearing my first day at Blue Sky Hill. He would have appeared to be a homeless man, picking up old cups and foam containers, begging for food at the cafeteria door. How hungry had he and my father gotten before Teddy went looking? How long had they been out of food before I arrived?

A painful guilt welled in my chest.

"She my friend," Teddy remarked.

"You know you can't come up here again," I said. "You have to stay in the yard, all right?"

Teddy ducked his head. He knew I was still upset about his wandering off. Nodding earnestly, he turned to watch the cafeteria and the trash-decorated fence disappear from view. "Ho-kay, A-becca."

I felt like an ogre, his prison matron, the mean, overly controlling mommy Macey so often rolled her eyes at. Except that Teddy wasn't a child. He was an adult. My stepbrother. He was a forty-seven-year-old man, yet he wasn't competent to leave his own yard.

The sadness of that idea was monumental. How many times had Hanna Beth looked at Teddy and wondered what the rest of his life would be like, who would take care of him when she and my father were gone?

If the restrictions gave Teddy even a moment's concern, he didn't show it. As the school disappeared around the corner, we passed the little pink house with the estate sale in progress, and Teddy waved at the women running the cash table. A few blocks farther, near what used to be the park, a sidewalk snow cone stand was playing tinny music, and he turned his attention to that. My father smiled at the tune and began singing along to "You Are My Sunshine."

I drew back, startled as much by a heavy sense of déjà vu as by his voice. I remembered him singing that song when I was little. I hadn't unearthed the memory in years, hadn't allowed myself to think of it. Now it came back, clear and pure, and it seemed as if I were with my father, *really* with my father, for the first time since I was twelve. The empty place created by his absence lay like the cool, still mountain craters Kyle and I had visited on our fifth-anniversary trip to Hawaii. Standing on the rim, I had the eerie sense that the peaceful appearance was a façade, a thin covering of surface matter and vegetation with something powerful churning beneath.

My father's song, his deep baritone voice so like it had always been, cracked the surface. Warmth bubbled up. Affection, need, yearning. In spite of the passage of years, and the water under the bridge that had built an ocean between us, I still wanted to know that he loved me. I wanted to believe he was singing that song because, somewhere within the heart that had turned cold to me, within the withering body and the decaying mind, he remembered singing it as he carried me high on his shoulders, off to bed.

"Daddy . . ." The word was so soft no one could have heard it but me.

In the backseat, Teddy started humming along, occasionally chiming in on "sunshine," "gray," and "away."

Clearly, he knew the words. My father wasn't singing that song to me, remembering the special, private moments of my childhood we'd shared. He was merely replaying a tune locked somewhere in the neurological tangle of his memories. Teddy knew the song because they'd sung it together.

The tenderness inside me whiplashed into jealousy, and even

though I didn't want the sensation, I felt it burn hot and bitter in the back of my throat. *Even that one little thing—that one song—he couldn't have saved for me?*

Teddy and Hanna Beth got everything—even "My Sunshine."

Leaning down to look in the side-view mirror, my father stopped singing. "Let's stop off for a snow cone, like we used to." His voice was clear, no sign of the tremors that had slurred his speech before he went to the hospital. Dr. Amadi had been pleased with his progress. The doctor was hopeful that, when today's sedative wore off, and with some time for the new medication to work, at home among familiar surroundings, my father would continue to regain his grasp on reality.

His clarity of speech was an improvement, but it didn't feel like a victory. There was no snow cone stand on the corner when I was a child here. My father and I had never stopped on this corner to listen to the Good Humor tune and buy a treat.

He was talking to Teddy.

"Okay, Daddy Ed," Teddy said, licking his lips and swallowing. "I like red."

"Maybe tomorrow," I said, and drove on, frustrated with the situation and with myself. Would there ever come a day when my thoughts, my emotions toward my father, toward Hanna Beth and Teddy, weren't bound in a sticky web of past transgressions and remembered pain? The memories were slick and black, agile and bloodthirsty, operating with the deftness of a black widow. They quickly grabbed anything new that fluttered by, wrapped it in sticky silk, and drained it of life.

How could I make it stop? How could I leave behind this childishness and let the future be . . . whatever it was meant to be? I wanted to heal. I wanted to stop dredging up the anger, the guilt, the pain. My stomach had been clenched in a churning knot for days. At night, it burned into my throat, waking me from a fitful sleep that was filled with strange dreams and half-conscious thoughts.

In the seat beside me, my father sighed, sank against the armrest, and sat looking out the window. We traversed the remainder of the streets in silence, then pulled into the left lane waiting to turn onto Vista.

Rubbing his knuckles across the glass as if he were trying to clear away condensation, my father craned close to the window. "They've torn down your old blue house." His voice was almost too faint to be audible. In the back, Teddy gave no indication that he'd heard.

A softness bloomed inside me again, like an early daffodil probing the winter chill. The absence of the blue gingerbread-encrusted house with its wraparound porches was the first thing I'd noticed, arriving back on Blue Sky Hill. I'd never imagined the place would be gone. "I always loved that house," I heard myself say.

My father turned to look at me then, the movement coming slowly, purposefully, as if he had something fragile in his head and was being careful not to shake it. He studied me for a long time, his lashes slightly lowered, his hazel eyes curled upward at the corners, mirroring a smile that was in his mind but hadn't found his lips. "It always let you know where the turn was." Chuckling softly in his throat, he extended a hand across the space between us, patted my arm. The haze lifted from him, so that I felt as if he were seeing me, really seeing me. Rebecca, a grown-up version of the little girl whose Cinderella castle was the towering blue gingerbread house on the corner. "You always wanted to know where we were going," he added, then turned back to the window, his lips trembling with some sentiment I could only guess at. He drifted away, seeming to fade slowly from himself, until he was just a shadow, sitting there. Head nodding forward, he gave in to the sedative again and let his eyes close.

"Don't fall asleep, all right? We'll be home in a minute," I said, then shook his shoulder. A gap in traffic presented itself, and I gunned the engine. The tires squealed as we rocketed through.

"Good Lord!" My father snapped upright, coming back to life as we whipped onto Vista Street.

"Wooh-weee!" Teddy made motor sounds, then imitated the squeal of the tires. As we passed the construction sites, he described the heavy equipment while waving at the workers. "There my friend," he observed as one of the men returned his greeting. "There my friend, Daddy Ed."

Daddy Ed didn't answer. He was fading again. I hurried through the neighborhood, past the remainder of new construction, around the corner onto Blue Sky Hill Court, where the old houses with their iron fences and stately yards sat drowsy and faded beneath the graceful patinas of time. The man with the art portfolio was just arriving home again. Teddy waved, but the man pretended not to notice.

My father was oblivious to his presence. His head nodded forward as we reached the end of the street and pulled into our driveway. By the time the garage door closed behind us, he was almost completely asleep. Teddy led him into the house, carefully, up one step at a time to the cloakroom.

Setting down my purse and briefcase, I watched as my father stood there, seeming lost, like a guest in his own home. "I have some roast beef sandwiches for supper. It'll only take a minute. Why don't you go on in and sit down in your chair? It's been a long day."

He cocked his head, momentarily perplexed by the statement, then turned and shuffled across the coatroom, disappearing through the door without a word. Teddy's brows formed a worry knot.

"It's all right," I said. "Just let him go sit down and rest a while. He'll feel better when the medicine Dr. Amadi gave him starts to wear off."

"Ho-kay." Teddy's reply conveyed complete faith in my ability to have all the answers. "I gone go my plants." As usual, he waited for permission.

"That sounds fine. We'll have supper in a little while."

"Mary gone come eat supper?" He scanned the front window.

Apprehension kinked the muscles in the back of my neck, squeezed like a fisherman's knot, causing me to wonder if a migraine might not be far behind. I realized, dimly, that I hadn't had one since the evening I arrived in Dallas. Perhaps my body knew there just wasn't time for it.

I hoped this arrangement with Mary worked out. Right now, it felt as if I'd invited overnight houseguests at the worst possible time. The apartment needed cleaning. There was the issue of buying more groceries—we hadn't even talked about who would pay for what, or which responsibilities Mary would assume, or when and how Ifeoma would come and go.

The plan suddenly seemed ill-advised and likely to end in disaster. "I don't know exactly when she'll be here. In a little while, I think. I don't know how much packing she has to do at her old apartment."

"She gone bring the boy and the udder boy?" Teddy's level of enthusiasm far surpassed mine.

"I imagine so."

Teddy clapped his palms together, fingers stiff and outstretched.

I felt the need to rein him in, to make sure he understood the parameters of the situation. "It's only a little while. You remember, I told you that at the nursing center? Mary's just doing this until we can find someone to live here all the time."

"Uh-huh." Teddy nodded, while looking over his shoulder toward the door. The practicalities of the situation didn't interest him. "I gone my plants."

"All right."

Teddy hurried off, and I proceeded into the house. My father wasn't in the living room. A mild note of panic struck me as I checked the kitchen, the maid's pantry, the bathroom, his office.

I found him in his bedroom, curled up atop the covers in nothing but his underwear. The clothes he'd left the hospital in were hung neatly on the dressing rack that had held his daily business suit for as long as I could remember. He'd tucked his slippers underneath, where his black wingtips had always been.

Watching from the doorway, I vacillated between waking him up, insisting he eat supper, or leaving him to sleep until the sedatives wore off. Finally I covered him with an extra blanket. Supper could wait. I needed to check the supply of groceries, maybe transfer a few starter items to the apartment kitchen, scan the e-mail from my office, let Kyle know that if my father continued improving, and Mary worked out, I could fly back to California for a few days, do a little firefighting at the office, then return here when Hanna Beth was closer to coming home. By then, perhaps, through some phone interviews, I could have a permanent caretaker lined up.

I carried my father's new prescriptions in from the car and arranged them carefully in the back of an unused silverware drawer, where I was fairly certain he wouldn't find them if he went looking. I left the bags and slips on the counter with his discharge papers so I could apprise Mary of all the instructions. I hoped that when she realized what she was getting into, when she actually *saw* the apartment over the garage, she wouldn't run away screaming. Teddy and I had picked things up and moved out various stored boxes, so the apartment could be shown to prospective employees, but, like most of my plans, finding a housekeeping service to give the place a wall-to-wall cleaning remained on the to-do list.

Glancing at the clock, I realized it was later than I'd thought. Mary could arrive anytime. The sink was full of dishes, the counter cluttered, so I hurried through a cursory cleanup, stuffing the dirties in the dishwasher. My cell phone rang as I was putting soap in the dispenser. Bree was on the other end with some questions about a meeting for an upcoming Immigration Court hearing. I'd checked the client's application for asylum that morning and e-mailed it to the office. Bree sounded frustrated. She was quick to divulge that

Kyle was on a rampage because he and my paralegal would have to cover the meeting at four o'clock. My clients had already phoned in with questions he couldn't answer, immigration not being his area of expertise.

"I'm sorry," I told Bree. "Let him know it's my fault. I didn't see his e-mail until this morning. I should have checked last night." Somewhere between the shower and computer the night before, I'd made the irrational decision to lie down for just a minute before logging on to take care of my in-box. I was out like a light the minute my head hit the pillow. When I awoke, it was after midnight, the house was dark, and Teddy had covered me with a blanket, then gone to sleep.

"It's all right." Bree emitted a frustrated sigh, as if she were considering giving up legal work altogether. "The file didn't download right, though. The last half is some kind of encrypted garbage. Can you send it again, real quick?"

"It'll take a few minutes."

Bree sighed again. "All right. Sorry, Mrs. Macklin."

"Don't worry about it. It's not your fault." It seemed strange to be comforting Bree, considering that not so long ago I'd been upset about Kyle letting her listen in on our private conversations. "Things happen."

"It's not easy filling your shoes," she lamented, then seemed to think better of the comment. "Sorry."

"I'll have the file to you in a minute," I promised, taking the phone with me on the way upstairs. I balanced it between my chin and shoulder as I unpacked my laptop on the bed and turned it on. "Thank you for going after Macey earlier, by the way. She called and told me all about the big adventure at school."

"Sure," Bree answered. "I don't mind picking her up. She's always real sweet."

I was focused on the computer, trying to hurry the Windows

screen along by watching it. The word "always" took a moment to cause a ripple in my thoughts. *Always?* "I didn't realize you'd picked her up before."

"Just once when the kid she was supposed to ride with got sick at school, and another day, when her ankle was hurting, and the nurse couldn't reach her grandma, and her dad was . . ." Bree hesitated, a tiny pause in the stream of singsong communication, during which I imagined all sorts of things. Finally, she finished with, "Out of the office."

The computer logged on, but all I could think was, *Out of the office. . . . Out? Out where?* If he was in court or had gone to a meeting with a client, why wouldn't Bree just say that? Why the careful, cagey response? Was she protecting him? Did she know things she didn't want to divulge? "Hang on a minute," I said, then focused on the computer long enough to attach the file to an e-mail and let it upload into cyberspace. "All right, the file should be on its way."

"Thanks, Mrs. Macklin. I'd better go."

"Bree?" I said, even though I knew she had work to do.

"Yes, Mrs. Macklin?"

"Do you know *why* Kyle was out of the office when the nurse called about Macey?"

"No, ma'am. I don't." Her response was quick, almost an apology, as if she'd considered it ahead of time. "He just called and asked me to pick up Macey. That's all I know."

"He didn't say where he was?" *Stop it, Rebecca. Stop. This is inappropriate. It's pathetic. It's unprofessional.*

"I didn't ask. Listen, Mrs. Macklin, I know—"

"It's all right," I cut her off before she could say anything more. Downstairs, the doorbell was ringing. "Call me back if the file doesn't come through."

"All right, Mrs. Macklin. Thanks."

"Good-bye, Bree."

I hung up the phone and hurried downstairs. Mary was on the porch. Brandon stood shyly holding her hand, and Brady was asleep on her shoulder. "Sorry," she said, cuddling his head with her chin. "I tried to wake him up, but he's out." Brady's lips pursed, his shoulders rising and lowering as he exhaled the long, slow breaths of childhood.

"He looks tired," I agreed, remembering the days when I would get Macey out of the safety seat, carry her through a shopping mall, put her back in the car, and drive home without waking her up. "My daughter always slept like that when she was little."

Mary fluttered a slight smile, as if she sensed the invisible language of motherhood between us. "They didn't get much sleep the last couple nights. Normally, he's pretty independent." She glanced pointedly at me, indicating that she wouldn't have a preschooler attached to her hip all the time.

We stood in awkward silence. "I guess you all would probably like to see the apartment, maybe get settled in, huh?" I offered finally.

"Whatever you want to do first." In one practiced motion, Mary hiked Brady higher onto her hip.

I pointed toward the side of the house, pulling the door closed behind me as we started in that direction. "There's an inside door to the apartment in the upstairs hallway, but it's probably easier to just go up the stairway by the backyard gate."

Brandon shot a glance upward when I said *backyard.* "Is Teddy there?"

"Brandon," Mary scolded, giving him a reminder look that told me she'd instructed him to be seen and not heard.

"I think so." I crossed the driveway and started around the side of the house. "Let's go upstairs for a minute, and then we'll find Teddy, and he can help you bring in your things." I flinched apologetically as we walked through the gate and started up the wooden stairs to the garage apartment. "I really have to apologize for the condition of things up here. I wanted to have it cleaned before anybody . . ." I was about to say "moved in," but that seemed too much an indication of permanence. "Stayed here."

"It'll be fine," Mary answered, almost too quickly. "The boys and I can clean it up. They're good helpers, aren't you, Brandon?"

Her son shrugged, trudging unenthusiastically up the stairs, with an eye toward the backyard. I wondered where Teddy was.

Opening the apartment door with Mary and Brandon next to me on the tiny landing, I felt the need to apologize again. Compared to the grandeur of the house, the apartment was terribly Spartan. "I checked to make sure everything was working out here, but I have to warn you that it's very bas—" The last syllable, "ic," slipped from my lips and disappeared as the door fell open.

The upstairs apartment was anything but basic. In fact, it was a sea of color, a bouquet of scent, and light, and texture, a masterpiece of living treasures. Brightly blooming moss roses and vincas trailed along the tabletops and the arms of the sofa and chairs. On the empty bookshelf, tiny seedlings stretched upward in a carefully arranged rainbow of plastic cups, and along the windowsills, iris and daylilies waited in colored glass bottles that caught the evening sun and showered the room with tiny prisms of painted light.

In the time I'd been downstairs fretting over the dishes, Teddy had filled Mary's room with growing things, creating a welcome card of life, and hope, and possibility. Where there had been only a silent, dusty space, suddenly there was a home.

CHAPTER 20

Hanna Beth Parker

There are times when you awake, and sense the coming day hovering just beyond the edge of the world. Your heartbeat quickens, anticipating the blinding brightness of it, grasping its awesome possibility. You await the first rays of dawn, feeling that God must have whispered something in your ear just before you roused from sleep. You can hear the voice, not quite the words, but you feel, you know with everything in you, that a promise has been made. The dark night of your soul is fading and dawn will soon arrive.

Claude, already moving around in his room, must have felt it, too, or perhaps he was just restless, a bit lonesome with Mary and the boys not coming to wash up for several mornings now. He was happy that they were settling in so well at my house, but still he missed them. Mary promised that on the weekend when she was off work, she would bring the boys to see him. Claude said she didn't need to bother with him on her day off, but it was clear that he wanted the visit. I felt sorry for him, having no one to come see him in his old age.

He wheeled himself to my door, hesitated there. "Pssst. You awake in there, Birdie?" He kept his voice low, because if Betty heard him prowling around this early, she'd put him back to bed.

"Yes," I answered. The word, like my mind, was clear this morning. I felt as if I were my old self, as if I could sit up, swing my legs around, get up and raise the window blind to greet the day. If they'd left the wheelchair yesterday, I would have been tempted to try it. Perhaps Gretchen was afraid I might, and that was why she'd taken the wheelchair away, after letting me sit up for quite a few hours the last few days. Being upright again felt glorious.

Gretchen warned that I shouldn't do too much at once, as she hefted me back into bed. It was strange to have Gretchen telling me to slow down. Mary's moving in at my house and the news that Edward was doing well after coming home from the hospital had filled me with vigor. I couldn't wait to get better, go home, and see him again. The sooner I became operational in the wheelchair, the sooner that would happen.

Claude came in my door and moved straight to the window. "Morning, Birdie," he said. He was cheerful, but not so much as in the past. The idea that he couldn't go back to live alone in his house weighed heavily on him. The rates for the supplemental insurance that was helping to pay for his stay in the nursing center had been raised, and he knew that, in the long run, he wouldn't be able to keep up his home and pay the added insurance costs. He'd had some discussions with his niece about moving to Seattle to live with her, but the idea of giving up his home was impossible for him to face. He talked often about his place, and all the memories he had of it.

"Looks like Betty's closed the blind again," he said as he entered my room. He pulled the cord and fished the pushpins from the windowsill. Even Betty had finally given up and begun leaving them to keep Claude from sneaking down the hall and stealing more. "She ought not do that. The view from this window's too pretty to miss. All I got's a durned flower bush."

We sat and enjoyed the sunrise together, partaking of it in shared silence until the last shades of amber and crimson faded, and the clouds lost their silver linings. After that, Claude gave the play-by-play of the morning workers coming in. "There's our Mary," he said. "Good to see her looking better rested. I sure keep thinking that young husband of hers'll come back. I never would've guessed him for the kind of man who'd run off and leave his family. Sad thing."

"Yes," I agreed.

Claude went on talking, his habit as our conversations were mostly one-sided. "Why, there's Dr. Barnhill and Ouita Mae. Guess she couldn't resist comin' in for breakfast. Can't blame her. Now that she's officially checked outa this place, she's probably bored, sittin' around the doc's apartment alone." Swiveling in the chair, he glanced at the wall clock. "Guess I'll head on down to breakfast myself." With sudden enthusiasm, he backed up the chair and turned it around. Over the past few days, I'd begun to suspect that Claude had taken a shine to Ouita Mae, but as far as I could tell from watching her, he might as well have been a toad under a bucket. She couldn't see him at all. The times I'd tried to bring up his name, she'd made it clear that, having had a long marriage that was pleasant enough, but never really a love match, she had no interest in old men coming around. She was content to be a widow and someday, if her grandson would cooperate, a great-grandmother.

If she knew who Claude was, would she feel differently? Would she look at him and see the blue-eyed boy with whom she'd shared her first kiss, the boy she still remembered after all these years?

As the nursing center came to life around me, I considered the possibility.

Gretchen, to my delight, had me first on her list after breakfast. When she was finished, she put me in my chair and gave me what seemed like a tender comment. "You're just a fireball this morning, aren't ya?"

"Yes," I said, and she pointed a finger at me as she turned to leave.

"You keep that up, we're gonna have to send you home."

"Yes." I thought she might have been smiling, but she remained bent over her cart, so I couldn't see.

"Just behave yourself there," she said before disappearing out the door. Passing Claude in the hallway, she told him he'd better save up his energy, because she had some things in store for him today, then she moved on down the way.

Claude came in my door seeming as pleased as I'd seen him in a while. "Why, look at you, up and around, chipper as a chipmunk. How about we go for a stroll in the garden? We can pull ourselves to the top of the hill, then put our feet up and see who rolls down the fastest."

I laughed. "Mmm-beee lay-der."

"I think I done found someone to rent out my house for a while," he said, clapping his hands briskly together. "I knew I was gonna have to do somethin'. I can't afford to keep it settin' there and pay the home owner's and taxes and lawn care, and also my Medicare supplement and such. But I think I got my problem solved just now."

"Oh?" I was surprised to see Claude so enthusiastic about someone else living in his house.

"Sure enough. Funny thing turned up at breakfast. Just happened that I was goin' in as the doc and Ouita Mae was headed through the line. So, I says, 'Hey there, Doc, how's about we share a table?' He thought that'd be fine, of course. Anyhow, he had the want ads with him, and turns out he's lookin' for a bigger place to rent, on account of Ouita Mae not moving back to Houston. So I says, 'Doc, why don't you rent my house from me? I can't go back and live there alone with my ticker havin' spells. I can't afford to hire help, the place needs to be took care of, and I need the money to pay expenses.' He said, sure, he'd go by and look at it, so we called my little neighbor girl and set it up." Claude gave the biggest smile I'd seen from him since his birthday. "Now, how's that for a stroke of divine providence?"

"Good," I said, and it did seem like divine providence. Perhaps the connection between Claude and Ouita Mae would yet be made, even if I couldn't bring it about myself.

"I'll have to get my niece to come help me pack up some stuff." Claude gazed out the window, seeming a little more melancholy. "Might be, Doc Barnhill'd be all right with me leaving the things from my trains out in the work shed. He probably ain't much of a gardener, anyhow. I got my bell and engine number out there, my hat and coat, an A & NR Railroad plate, and a sign from the old station at Lufkin. They let me go get them treasures when they retired my engine. The neighbor kids like to come and look at it sometimes. Say, Birdie, did I ever tell you about my trains?"

"Yes," I said, in the kindest way I could.

"I tell you the story about them white mules?"

"Yes."

Claude laughed. "Well, hang. You done heard all my tales. I guess we been spendin' too much time together."

I laughed along with him. "No."

We sat silent for a few minutes until Dr. Barnhill came in the door. "Heard you were up and around this morning, Miss Hanna Beth," he said.

"Yes."

"Hi-a, Doc." Claude about-faced his wheelchair and started toward the door. "I'll get out of your way. I want to put a call in to my niece and tell her about maybe rentin' out the house. Now, don't worry about it, though. Anything I want to do will be fine with her. She knows I can still decide for myself."

As usual, Dr. Barnhill seemed in a hurry to accomplish one task and move on to the next. Claude had probably bent his ear about the house enough at breakfast. "We can talk more about it this evening, after we've seen the place. If things work out, there's no big rush. My grandmother is still adjusting to the idea of not moving back to her own place." He winced, giving an apologetic smile. "Don't tell her I said that, though."

Claude locked his lips and threw away the key, then disappeared into the hallway.

Dr. Barnhill proceeded to ask me a series of questions about how I was feeling, whether I had any dizziness, how the chair was working out. He complimented my recent performance in therapy. "If I didn't know better, I'd say you were in a hurry to leave us," he joked.

"Yes. A lit . . . a lit-ul."

Tapping his fingers on the bed railing, he frowned. "Well, let's see what we can do about that. I'm going to recommend you be scheduled for a few tests, and an ADL—Activities of Daily Living—study. Then we'll see where we're at. If things look good, and provided there's adequate home and outpatient care arranged, we may be able to set up a Care Plan Meeting and begin working toward transitioning you to an outpatient regimen."

Gratitude welled in my throat, and I swallowed hard. I didn't want Dr. Barnhill to think I was the least bit fragile. I nodded, because I didn't trust myself to speak.

He probably thought I couldn't form the words. "Be patient, now. We're not talking about tomorrow or the next day. It's a lengthy process. We'll start with a home study visit to look at alterations that would be needed in your house. Then, when the physical things are in place, we'll arrange your first home visit, and see how things go."

I nodded a second time.

"All right, then." Dr. Barnhill moved toward the exit. "We'll talk again." He stopped in the alcove, focusing on someone in the hall. "Well, hello there." Leaning against the doorway, he indicated that his rush to be on about his work had suddenly dissipated. I craned against my chair, trying to see who was outside.

"Is she awake?" The voice was Rebecca's. She must have come alone, because there was no sign of Teddy bolting through the door.

"Absolutely," Dr. Barnhill answered. "She's not only awake, she's up in the chair and looking for clearance to go home."

"Really?" Rebecca's uncertainty was obvious. "I mean . . . I didn't think . . . today?"

"No, no. But we're working toward it. We're scheduling some studies, and we'll know more in a few days. The staff here will need to talk with you about a home study visit and her eventual care plan."

"Oh." Rebecca was clearly relieved that I wasn't on my way back to Blue Sky Hill right now. "Well . . . we've brought her a surprise."

Outside, I heard Teddy say, "Ssshhhh."

Dr. Barnhill nodded and stepped aside. "It looks like I'd better move before she falls out of that chair trying to see what's happening." Ushering a hand in my direction, he winked at me, then left.

As I watched, a shadow fell over the doorway, curled and stretched into the room, and then I saw Teddy, his sneaker first as he moved sideways into the opening. Another step, and I could see all of him. Pressing a finger to his lips, he whispered, "Ssshhh," as if he'd momentarily forgotten I was the one the surprise was for. A raspy giggle convulsed from his throat, and he put a hand over his mouth, but his happiness, as always, was not to be contained. Taking another step, he moved to the right side of the doorway, and there on his arm, standing at the threshold, was Edward. The vision of him was like something from a midday dream when the sleep is not quite deep enough to sustain an illusion. I held my breath, afraid that if I moved this reality would shift like a cloud shadow, skitter across the floor and be gone.

"Edward?" My voice trembled into the air, stretching forward like a hand in the darkness. Could it really be him? He didn't look well. He'd lost so much weight. He hung stooped over Teddy's arm like a scarecrow that needed more stuffing.

Yet, the presence in the doorway couldn't be anyone but my Edward, the man I'd loved all my life, finally here.

Tears filled my eyes, and I lifted my hand, beckoned him with a twisted wrist and thin, curled fingers I had no time to be ashamed of now. I only wanted Edward to close the space between us, to touch me, to be beside me as we had always been, as we were meant to be.

"Bethie?" he whispered, and my heart sang. Edward had always called me Bethie, a pet name the children at school teased me with when he was a strapping teenager and I just a knobby-legged tomboy who adored him from an impossible distance.

"Yes." Tears welled in my eyes, spilled over, blurred the vision of him, and I wiped them impatiently, beckoning him with my hand again. "Yes."

Pulling away from Teddy's arm, he stepped over the threshold and moved across the room in a slow shuffle, the careful steps of an old man, but in my eyes the confident strides of youth. In my mind, he was always that boy whose every move I worshipped. The reflection of that beautiful young man would be forever cast over him.

How can it take an eternity to cross such a small room? Finally Edward was there, his hand first, slipping into my hand, his fingers closing, glorious and warm and strong. He moved around the chair, touched my face, gazed into my eyes with uncertainty. Perhaps he didn't know me at first, perhaps he was searching the scattered strands of his memory, trying to gather the bits and pieces that formed the tapestry of our lives.

"All-rye-t," I whispered, taking his other hand, laying my cheek against it. "Ssshhh."

His gaze met mine, his face filled with love, filled with all that we had shared over a lifetime together, memories he couldn't always put in order—shared years, weeks, days, moments, moving past his mind's eye like scenes on the opposite side of a window, misted with the dew of a winter night.

Softly, he began to sing the first lines of "Let Me Call You Sweetheart."

From somewhere that seemed far away, Teddy hummed along, occasionally echoing the words. Rebecca sniffled, and dimly, I heard Teddy move forward, and Rebecca gasp as Edward began to sink, collapsing toward the floor like a blow-up decoration slowly losing air, until he was folded beside my chair, his head resting in my lap, our joined hands beneath his cheek as he sang.

"Ssshhh," I said, stroking his hair as his tears soaked my dressing gown. I felt his joy, his relief, warm and damp against my skin. Where only weeks ago there had been no life, no sensation, now I could feel him.

I wasn't certain how long we sat that way. Rebecca gathered Teddy and left us alone together. Mary came in the door, making her rounds, then stopped abruptly in the alcove, her shoes squeaking on the tile.

"Oh," she whispered, studying us for a moment, perhaps wondering if Edward needed help. Finally, she turned and quietly left the room.

By the time Rebecca came back with Teddy and Mary, I knew Edward was drifting to sleep, exhausted by so much activity, by the rise and fall of emotion. Still, I didn't want him to leave. I wasn't ready to let go.

"We need to take him home now, Hanna Beth." Rebecca was apologetic, kind. "It's been a long morning."

I nodded, determined that I wouldn't cry or cause a scene.

"We'll try to bring him back tomorrow, if he's having a good day," Rebecca promised as Mary roused Edward and Teddy moved into position to help him up. Teddy, being the big, strong boy that he was, lifted his father with no trouble, then dusted him off tenderly. "There go, Daddy Ed," he said, and Edward smiled at him.

Rebecca reached into her purse and fished out some money, then put it in Teddy's hand. "Teddy, do you think you could take Daddy Ed down and get a soda in the cafeteria? Just put your dollar in the machine like I showed you, remember? If it spits your money out, turn it around and try again."

"Ho-kay." Teddy brightened at the idea of a sugary treat, or using the soda machine, or both.

"I'll go with them," Mary offered, taking Edward's other arm. "I'm on break for a few more minutes."

"Thanks, Mary." Rebecca gave her a private look of gratitude.

After it was just the two of us, Rebecca couldn't seem to decide what to say.

"Uhhht?" I asked finally, then tried again. I'd practiced question words and *W* sounds with the speech therapist yesterday. "Whhh-at's rrrr-ong?"

Rebecca pushed a ribbon of dark hair away from her face, seeming to carefully decide what to say. "We went to the bank this morning to sign some signature cards to add my name to the account," she revealed finally. "He was having a really good day, and I thought we should do it while we could. I need access to the accounts to . . ." She paused, chose her next words carefully. ". . . set up some autopayments for the bills and so forth. Do you know anything about some kind of an investment with a company called LMK Limited?"

"No," I admitted. The truth was that, beyond the normal day-to-day operations of the household funds, I knew far less than I probably should have. Edward had always been good with money, spending hours on the computer, carefully managing investments. When he became aware that his memory was slipping, he had moved the money to some safe investments, arranged for everything to be taken care of automatically. He'd documented the changes in his files, in case there came a day when I needed the information.

"Hizzz files," I said.

Frowning, Rebecca sat on the edge of the bed, folded her hands in her lap. "His files are all over the house. He has them hidden everywhere."

"P-leater." *Computer, computer.* I tried to think the word to my lips. "Com-peater. Com-poot . . . terrr."

Rebecca shook her head. "There's no computer in the house, Hanna Beth."

"Izzz," I insisted. Of course there was a computer in the house. Edward would never have allowed anything to happen to his computer. Even after he couldn't remember how to do much with it, he still took comfort in watching the slideshows on his screen saver.

Rebecca shook her head. "There's no computer. I've been all through the house."

I searched my mind. Perhaps I was wrong. Perhaps, because of the stroke, I wasn't remembering correctly. Had Edward gotten rid of the computer, after all? Why couldn't I be sure? My heart raced, and blood burned hot in my cheeks, making my head pound and my body tense up until it was painful. I felt myself floating in the chair, reeling sideways.

"Hanna Beth . . ." Rebecca's voice seemed far away. "Hanna Beth?" Through the haze, I saw her press the nurse's call button, felt her patting my hand as the dizzy spell slowly passed.

"No," I said, because I didn't want them to come in and put me back to bed. "I donnn't . . ."

Rebecca rubbed my hand between hers. "Don't worry," she said, then assured me that everything would be all right.

But her face said otherwise, making the promise feel hollow.

CHAPTER 21

Rebecca Macklin

It seemed strange to be making plans for Hanna Beth's eventual homecoming. Considering how I'd always felt about her presence in the house, I'd never imagined calmly meeting with nursing center committees, arranging for a special bed, a bathing chair, grab bars, and wheelchair ramps. I'd never guessed that I would watch delivery trucks and workmen move in and out, and be filled with a sense of anticipation. At some point during my time on Blue Sky Hill, I had ceased to see my own mother, my own childhood, here. I no longer rounded corners and caught shreds of memory floating like dust motes in the air.

The house had become Hanna Beth's house, Teddy's house, my father's house. It took on a new life, a life of its own, with my father in a more stable mental state, Teddy coming and going from his flowers, Mary and her boys spending evenings in the yard or the living room, and Ifeoma sitting with my father during the day, telling stories about Ghana. Ifeoma's strong, confident presence captured my father's attention, helped him pass the long afternoons peacefully. Now that he no longer saw *those people*, he was tolerant even of the construction work and deliverymen passing through.

With new help in the house, I was able to develop a daily routine that included minimal direct contact with my father. Despite long medical dialogues with Dr. Amadi, information from Internet pages on Alzheimer's disease, and input from Mary and Ifeoma—despite the fact that my father's behavior and lapses were typical of an Alzheimer's patient, particularly considering his recent medical trauma—it hurt that, so often, I was one of his lapses. Much of the time, I was still Marilyn. On good mornings he knew me, at least after some prompting. "Oh, yes, Rebecca," he'd say, blinking slowly, his eyes turning upward and to the left, as if he were trying to draw the tattered information from his memory banks. "Have you been away?"

"A while," I'd tell him. It comforted him to believe he didn't recognize me at first because I'd been gone on some sort of vacation.

"I thought so," he'd answer. "Did you have a good trip?"

"Yes, I did."

"Wonderful. Have you seen Hanna Beth today? I was looking for her this morning."

At that point, in spite of all sense of reason, the choking rejection would coil around me. I'd feel myself grasping at bitterness like an addict reaching for a fix. "She's in the nursing center, remember? That's why the workmen are building the ramps, so she'll be able to come home."

"Oh, of course." He'd look benignly around the house, observing the changes. "Teddy could help them. He loves to build things."

It hurt that he always remembered Teddy. A small, vindictive part of me liked things better when Teddy was one of *those people*, less welcome in the house than even I was. I hated that part of me. If I was finding it easier than I'd thought to give over the house to Hanna Beth and Teddy, giving my father to them was turning out to be more difficult.

I couldn't imagine why. Thirty-three years ago, I'd done everything I could to wipe the need for him from my heart. So why was I still clinging to his words, his actions, waiting for something I would probably never receive?

It was a question I couldn't answer, so I concentrated on the bank accounts instead. Solving the riddle of my father's convoluted financial system became paramount, as the bills for medical equipment and remodeling mounted and the need for paychecks to Mary and Ifeoma arose. I couldn't keep covering his bills from my checking account. Kyle had already mentioned, somewhat offhandedly, that he would have to transfer some money from our 401(k) to fund the unexpected expenditures. He was understanding about it, supportive even. We talked one night as he was leaving the office. He'd hired a new nanny for Macey, which freed him up to stay late in the evenings again. While his mother was staying with Macey, he'd been trying to make it home for supper.

"If you need me to move more money over, just let me know," he said. He was in a good mood. He'd just settled a potentially costly property dispute for a corporation out in Silicon Valley.

"I will," I said. "Thanks, Kyle."

"Sure." He sounded as if he couldn't imagine why I'd be thanking him. "Have a good night, hon."

It was comforting that he'd added the little endearment on the end. *I love you* was on the tip of my tongue. I said, "You, too," instead. *He probably doesn't want you in the 401(k),* my mother's voice whispered in my head. *That's why he took care of the transfer himself, rather than reading off the passwords to you.*

I brooded on the idea overnight, tried to decide whether I was just being paranoid and suspicious. Thinking the worst of everyone and every situation was one of my mother's characteristics that I'd tried hard not to inherit.

The next day, a CD came to maturity at my father's bank, was deposited into my father's checking account, and almost before I could stop it, the money was routed to a payee account listed under LMK Limited, Inc. I was online, arranging for autopayment of some bills, as it happened, and I was able to call the bank and stop the transfer before the wire went through.

I made certain there would be no more transfers, and no withdrawals could be issued, other than those I'd authorized. For several days, I'd been trying to dissect the complicated nature of my father's association with LMK Limited, Inc., and another entity called Blue Sky Real Estate Trust. Most of my father's money seemed to be one place or the other. In the past, only small amounts of money had been transferred to LMK Limited each month, but within the last few weeks, the transferred amounts had grown. Monthly deposits came into his checking account from Blue Sky Real Estate Trust, his retirement, annuity, and Social Security checks, and then were quickly routed to LMK Limited, leaving the checking account dry.

Even after searching through my father's stacks of paperwork and spending hours researching through the Internet, phone calls, and the county courthouse, I'd found no information about LMK Limited or Blue Sky Real Estate Trust. My father couldn't tell me anything about either one. The names, like so many other things, were a mystery to him. In the back of my mind was Kyle's nagging theory that my father was being duped out of his money. Without the financial files or his computer, it would be difficult to tell.

Once again, I enlisted Teddy in helping me to hunt for files. We dug through closets, crept under beds, searched the attic, uncovering file folders filled with everything from outdated drilling leases to pictures my father had torn from Wal-Mart ads.

"I don' got no more," Teddy said finally.

"Me, either." Sitting on the floor amid the pile of folders we'd amassed in the maid's pantry, I rested my elbows on my knees and buried my hands in my hair. I wanted to go somewhere quiet, curl up, and fall asleep. Lately, all I wanted to do was sleep, but at night when I slipped into bed, I lay awake for hours.

Teddy squatted down beside me. "Sorry, A-becca." He patted my shoulder so hard my head bounced. "Don' be mad. I gone look more."

Teddy was nothing if not helpful. All he wanted, all he ever wanted, was to do everything he could to make the rest of us happy.

It probably seemed to him that I was never happy. "I'm not mad, Teddy. I'm just . . . stressed." I was always stressed, going in a million directions at once. When I was home, could Macey feel the self-imposed tension around me?

"Ohhh-kay," Teddy said, leaning over to see my face. "Don' be stress, A-becca."

I chuckled, and Teddy smiled with me. I felt better, despite being surrounded by files that had to be searched and then put away, because we'd stacked them in the maid's pantry, which was slated for delivery of a hospital bed and wheelchair. "All right. I won't be stressed."

"Ho-kay," Teddy replied, then braced his hands on the floor and pushed to his feet. "I gone look some more."

"All right, Teddy," I said, even though we'd searched everywhere. "I'll finish checking through these, then maybe we can get some of those empty cartons from the garage and box them up, get them out of the way, at least for now."

"How come?" Teddy asked, even though he already knew the answer. He'd asked the question repeatedly as we were cleaning plants and old furniture out of the room the past few days.

"Because the men are going to put your mom's new bed in here so we can be all set for her first home visit."

Teddy's face opened into a broad smile, and he sucked in a hissing, conspiratorial laugh, unable to contain his excitement. "She comin' in here?" He pointed to the room as if the plans were a mystery to him. His eyes glittered with anticipation.

"Teddy . . . ," I admonished playfully. "You know she's coming in here. We've been cleaning this room for days."

"How come?"

"Because your mom's coming for her first home visit soon."

Teddy giggle-hissed again. "When Mama comin' home?"

I laughed, as much at the expression on his face as at the game of verbal volleyball. "Well . . . that depends on the doctors, but so far, her tests look good. Dr. Barnhill told us that, right?"

"He nice."

"Dr. Barnhill?"

Teddy nodded, then giggled again. "He gone send Mama home."

"Yes, he is, Teddy." I looked around at the stacks of files on the floor. Piling them in here probably wasn't the best idea, but I'd wanted to put them out of the way, where I could close the door so my father wouldn't see, in case finding us with his files might upset him. "We'd better get to work. If Dr. Barnhill sent your mom home right now, we'd have to put her on top of all these folders."

Teddy's honk-laugh reverberated through the empty room.

The dismal project ahead fell over me like a shadow as Teddy turned to leave. After going through all of these files, I probably wouldn't be any closer to resolving the banking situation. "If we could find Daddy Ed's computer, it'd sure make things a lot easier," I muttered.

Teddy didn't answer, just headed off to look for more files.

I started sorting through what I had. Two hours later, I'd netted a couple of bank statements from the previous year and the quarterly paperwork for some oil royalty payments that had, at least in the recent past, been deposited regularly into my father's account. I plugged in my laptop, set it on the floor beside me, and looked at his bank statements online. No royalty deposits had come in for several months now.

One thing was certain. The account activity from the previous year was a far cry from the account activity from the past few months. Tomorrow, I could start by calling the oil companies to see where the royalty checks were being sent.

I was writing down the phone number from a statement when

Ifeoma stuck her head in the doorway. Her usually calm countenance held a wrinkle of concern. "Is Teddy in here, missus?"

"No," I answered, realizing how much time had passed. My body was stiff, my legs numb from sitting on the hardwood floor. "He should be in the house somewhere. He went to look for more files. If we can get everything in one place, I'm hoping to . . ." Glancing at my watch, I realized there was no way Teddy could still be looking around the house. "Maybe he went outside to work with his plants."

Ifeoma shook her head. "I have searched for him, missus. He is not outside."

"He wouldn't leave the yard. He promised he wouldn't leave the . . ." I pushed the papers aside and stood up. My body yawned to life, uneasiness stirring my pulse. Teddy wouldn't wander off again. He'd promised never to leave without permission. "Are you sure he's not here? Did you check the garden house?"

"I have searched all places. He is not here." Ifeoma's rhythmic accent made the words sound pleasant, like poetry, completely out of keeping with her apprehensive expression.

"Let me check the attic. We were up there earlier. Maybe he . . . fell asleep there or something." It sounded like a ridiculous scenario, but part of me insisted, *Teddy wouldn't wander off again. He promised he wouldn't.*

Ifeoma followed me upstairs to the attic door and into the musty stillness beyond. Amid the bits of discarded furniture, boxes of old holiday decorations, dried-up paint cans, storage crates, metal sea chests filled with outdated oil field charts and topography maps, and plastic tubs of keepsakes from Teddy's childhood, it quickly became clear that Teddy wasn't there.

"I can't believe he would do this again." My heart sank, not only because I was wounded, in an irrational way, that Teddy would break a promise to me, but because if he couldn't be trusted to stay home when I was right here, there was no possible way I could go back to

California, leave him with hired help, and expect everything to turn out all right. If he wandered off when Mary was on duty, what was she supposed to do—load my father and two kids into the car and canvas the neighborhood?

I took in a breath, held it tightly in my chest, tried to think. "He did this once before. I found him near the construction sites on Vista Street. He'd been down to the school. And I'm not sure where else."

Ifeoma's eyes widened, and I knew what she was thinking. *The school? Four miles away and across two busy streets? Past the bridge where the homeless people live.* "I can go in search of him in my car." She shot a glance out the attic window, hoping, no doubt, that she'd see Teddy walking casually down the street.

"We'd both better go." I followed her back to the hall and closed the door. "You head down to the school. I'll ask around the construction sites and check the shopping center and the old park." My father's mention of the Good Humor wagon on the corner came to mind. Teddy had been asking about snow cones off and on for days now.

"What shall we do about Edward and the workmen?" Ifeoma asked as I grabbed my purse from the bedroom and we started down the stairs.

As always, the complications of managing the house were staggering. Take my father along? Send him with Ifeoma? Leave him here with the construction crew? Leave the workmen unsupervised in the house? "You go ahead. I'll take care of it."

I fished a business card from my purse as we reached the downstairs landing. "Here's my cell number. Give me your number, and we can call if either of us finds him."

Taking the card, Ifeoma frowned apologetically. "I do not have the benefit of a mobile phone, missus."

"Just check back here at the house every little while. Call me from here if you find him." If I hadn't been focused on the situation with Teddy, I would have been embarrassed. Of course Ifeoma didn't have a phone. She was working two jobs and living wherever she could to save money to bring her son over from Ghana. In the midst of my own issues, it was easy to forget that other people were struggling, too. "Do you need money for gas or anything?"

"No, missus." With a confused, sideways look, she moved past me, tucking the card into her pocket. "I will go ahead of you now. Perhaps I will find him even before you leave."

"I hope so," I said, but it didn't seem likely.

"Your father is sleeping by the television," she called back, then skirted a pile of construction supplies and disappeared out the door. I heard her car rumble to life outside as I tracked down Sy, the leader of the three-man remodeling crew I'd hired on the recommendation of the site foreman down the street. Sy did light construction during the day and played guitar in a fusion band at night. So far, I'd been pleased with his work, but I'd made a point of not leaving him and his crew in the house alone.

He paused to listen as I explained the situation.

"Yeah, Andy told me the Tedster headed out a couple hours ago," Sy answered, unconcerned. Sy and his crew had taken to calling Teddy *the Tedster* and *Tedman*, which Teddy loved. "I was gonna let him help bring some stuff in on the dolly, but Andy said he pushed it off down the street." Sy shrugged. "I figured he had somethin' to go get with it, or maybe he was just havin' some fun."

My jaw tightened in frustration. Why hadn't Sy said something to me? "He isn't supposed to leave the yard on his own."

"Oh, dude," Sy lamented. "Dang. I'm sorry. I didn't know."

"It's not your fault." I should have told them Teddy wasn't supposed to leave. "I just need to go find him, that's all. Why would he take your dolly?" There were many social nuances Teddy didn't understand, but he did know it was wrong to take things that didn't belong to him. Of course, he also knew he wasn't supposed to leave the yard.

Sy lifted his hands, palms up. "Don't know. Maybe he was headed down to get some more boards to build them benches he likes."

I hoped that was it, but the truth was that Teddy could have walked down to the construction sites and back four times by now. "I hope so," I muttered, digging my keys out of my purse. "I'm going to drive around the neighborhood and see if I can find him."

Sy wagged a thumb in the direction of the living room. "You want me to watch the old man?" I had made a point of telling the crew when they'd started that my father had Alzheimer's and under no circumstances was he to leave the house. So far, he had never tried.

My mind whizzed through a quick mental debate. Rousing my father and getting him into the car would take time, and he didn't always awaken in the most amiable mood. On the other hand, I would be leaving him in the care of Sy, who thought it was fine for a mentally handicapped man to wander off down the street with a dolly and not come back for hours.

"It's cool," Sy offered, as if I were telegraphing my conflicting emotions. "I got a grandpa like that. He can't remember stuff, I mean. I go by there in the evenings and sit and watch TV with him. If the old man wakes up, I'll find him somethin' to watch."

I felt myself bonding—with Sy, of all people. If he hadn't been covered with sweat, sawdust, and garish tattoos, I might have hugged him. "Thank you."

He stepped back, as if the expression of gratitude made him uncomfortable. "Oh, hey, it's cool. Go on and look for the Tedster. Tell him I need my dolly back." A lock of artificially blue-black hair fell over his eyes as he grinned impishly and headed off toward the living room. I hoped that, if my father woke up and found himself sitting with a rock-star-slash-construction-worker rather than Ifeoma, he wouldn't go into shock.

I hurried to my car and backed out of the driveway, then continued down the street to the corner, where the construction sites came into view. I searched among the trucks, cement mixers, welders, stacks of brick, rock, insulation, and supplies. No sign of Teddy. One of the workers passed by the front of the building as I pulled up to the curb. I recognized him from my last visit to the site. "Excuse me."

The worker—Boomer, I remembered now—stopped and looked over his shoulder, shrugging long dreadlocks off his chin. "Hey," he said, seeming friendlier than during my previous visit. "You lookin' for that guy that likes the paper cups?"

My heart skipped into my throat. "Yes." *Please let him be here. Please.* "Have you seen him?"

"Hang on a minute," he said, then he hollered into the building. "Rusty. His mama's here."

Rusty leaned out a second-story window, taking off his cowboy hat and swiping his forehead with the back of his arm. He waved, then disappeared and a moment later came out one of the doors. "He's out back."

Boomer motioned for me to follow as Rusty started around the corner of the building. Crossing the lawn and passing through the narrow alleyway between the condos, I tried to imagine why Teddy would have been here for hours, and why the crew would have allowed him to wander around the site. It was probably against company policy, and undoubtedly dangerous.

When we rounded the corner, my stomach dropped to my feet, and I instantly felt sick. In the shade beside one of the trucks, Teddy was curled up with his knees against his chest. His clothes and skin were covered with soil and stains, and his hair hung around his face in sticky, dirt-encrusted tangles. "Teddy?" I whispered, but he didn't answer, just pulled his knees tighter and shied away. "What happened? What's wrong?" My mind spun as I tried to imagine how Teddy could have ended up like this.

"Boomer got him a little upset, I think," Rusty answered.

I turned on Boomer, clenching my teeth to contain my rising fury. "What did you do to him?"

Boomer fanned his palms at me, his eyes wide against his dark skin. "Hey, lady, I was just tryin' to do my good deed for the day. I didn't know the dude was gonna go all Rainman on me. I was comin' back after break, and I seen him up by the school. He was pickin' up trash and stuff by the fence, and the kids was throwin' their Cokes over the wire, kind of like a game or somethin'. I guess it was a game. Dude was laughin', runnin' in and out from the street to see if he could get the cups before they hit him with stuff." Squinting at me, he gauged my reaction, then squatted down next to Teddy. "It just didn't seem right, okay? I didn't mean to scare him. I just wanted those little butt-heads to know if they didn't stop throwin' stuff, I was gonna kick me some tail." Shrugging the dreadlocks over his shoulder, he frowned. "I didn't know the dude was gonna freak out. When I got him in my truck, he kept talkin' on about Dolly bein' mad. You Dolly? Anyway, I told him not to worry about Dolly, and dude just started rockin' back and forth like this. He didn't want nobody to mess with him, or nothin'. I had to get back to work before the foreman marked me late, so I just brung him here and let him set. I figured sooner or later, he'd get over it and go home."

A baseball-sized lump rose into my throat as I squatted down next to Boomer. "I'm sorry," I whispered to him, or to Teddy, or both. The sense of order that I'd started to cultivate came crashing down around me. I didn't know what to do or say.

I sank down next to Teddy and covered my face with my hand, my hopes in freefall. I was fooling myself, thinking I had this situation under control, believing that I *ever* could. On any given day, despite the rules, despite the stacks of newly purchased plastic cups in the garden house, despite the hired help, despite the dangers, Teddy might decide to wander off in search of restaurant trash.

"Hey, lady, you all right?" Boomer asked, like he was wondering if he'd traded one emotional meltdown for two.

"We can help get him in your car, if you want," Rusty suggested. When I didn't answer, he leaned over my shoulder and said it louder. "You want us to help get him in your car?"

"Dude don't want nobody messin' with him," Boomer warned, standing up. "He's pretty strong."

I shook my head, wiping my eyes as I struggled to think. Try to put Teddy in the car by force? Try to reason with him? Sit here until he finally stopped rocking and agreed to leave? Meanwhile, Ifeoma was searching the area, and my father was home alone with Sy.

"Teddy?" I said finally. "We need to go, all right? Daddy Ed might wake up, and we need to be there." I reached toward him, but he pulled away. "Come on, Teddy, we have to go, so these men can get back to work. You can't stay here."

Teddy stopped rocking. From the building, someone hollered at Boomer, then spat out a string of expletives, asking where the nail gun was.

Throwing up his hands, Boomer paced a few steps away, then came back. "We gotta do somethin', man. Foreman's gonna come back any minute, and the dude can't still be here."

"Teddy." I tried to make my voice low and firm. "We have to go now. Nobody's mad at you, but we have to go." Slipping my fingers under his arm, I folded my legs under myself and lifted upward as if I could single-handedly bring him to his feet. My skin bonded to his in a sticky film of dried soda pop.

Teddy whispered something, but I couldn't make out the words.

I pulled on Teddy's arm again. "Come on, Teddy. We can talk in the car."

He didn't budge.

"Want us to get him up?" Rusty offered.

Someone shouted for Boomer again. "Listen, I gotta go," he said. "Holler at me if you need help."

Teddy repeated himself a little louder. I leaned close, but I still couldn't make out the words.

"Teddy, I can't hear you." I hovered somewhere between relief and frustration. At least Teddy was talking. "Come on. Let's get out of here, and we'll talk on the way home."

Teddy shook his head vehemently, slanted a glance up at Rusty, then tucked his chin and leaned close to me. "I don' got Sy dolly. Sy gone be mad." His voice was hoarse from crying, still little more than a whisper.

I rubbed a hand over my collarbone, feeling my pulse go back to normal. "Sy's not going to be mad. He'll understand. We'll buy him a new dolly."

"Sy gone be mad. He gone be real mad."

I tried a new tactic. "We'll go find the dolly. Do you know where you left it?"

Teddy's hands tightened against his chest, and he ducked away, as if he wanted to avoid the question altogether.

"I got a dolly you can borrow," Rusty offered. I'd completely forgotten he was there.

"I think we're okay, but thanks," I said. If Teddy hadn't been covered with dirt and dried soda pop, the conversation would have seemed almost laughable. "Where did you leave Sy's dolly, Teddy? Is it at the school?"

Teddy shook his head.

"Did you park it somewhere along the way?"

Another negative response.

"Did the kids take it from you?" The image of Teddy running around the fence while kids threw trash at him made my skin burn with anger.

A look of apprehension pressed Teddy's mouth into a frown, and he turned to me, his eyes wide, shifting nervously between Rusty and me. "The man get mad at the kids. He real mad." He sucked in a quick breath and his mouth began trembling. "I don' wan' get the kids trouble."

"Teddy." My body went limp, and I rested my cheek against his hair. It smelled sticky-sweet and earthy, a mixture of sugary syrup and catsup, dirt and sweat. "Teddy, you didn't get the kids in trouble. They got in trouble because what they did was wrong. It's wrong for people to do mean things to you, Teddy. It's not okay."

Teddy's body relaxed against mine, sagging over my shoulder, his weight pressing me into the ground until I felt as if I couldn't breathe.

"Boomer ain't mad at you, dude," Rusty reassured him. "Them little butt-heads just needed a lesson, that's all. Rich little brats move in here, and they think they own the neighborhood. They're lucky all Boomer did was yell at 'em."

"Let's just go home," I whispered, pushing Teddy off my shoulder. "Come on, Teddy."

He began gathering himself up. Rusty helped him to his feet as I stood waiting.

"Y'all be careful," Rusty said, then headed back to work.

"Thanks." The word was inadequate, but I didn't know what else to say.

My body felt weak and rubbery as I led Teddy through the alley, then across the uneven dirt at the front of the construction site. My head floated somewhere above the situation, as if I were watching it rather than living it, as if all of this couldn't possibly be real. I felt myself detaching from it as we climbed into the car.

"You mad, A-becca?" Teddy asked.

"No, I'm not mad," I answered numbly. I didn't want to talk anymore. I just wanted to drive home, lock myself in a room, and not think of anything. "I need to go home and sit down a minute. I don't feel too well right now."

"We gone get Sy dolly?"

I started the engine and pulled away from the curb. "Where's the dolly, Teddy?" Wherever it was, we were going to leave it and go back later.

"The church." Teddy swung his finger in a general westward direction. "Past-er Al church."

"The little white church?" I gasped. "You walked all the way to the little white church?" The church was even farther from the house than the school. "Teddy, why would you do that? Why would you walk all the way to the church?"

"I gone get com-pooter," Teddy replied simply. Now that the crisis was over, he'd returned to his normal, cheerful manner. As usual, we were talking in two completely different universes. I couldn't imagine how we'd moved from the dolly to the church to computers.

"What computer? If you wanted to go to the church, why didn't you tell me? I would have driven you there. Teddy, when you want to go places, you have to tell me. You can't just walk off."

Shaking his head, Teddy threw his hands in the air. "You say, Teddy, go get it."

"I told you to go get files, Teddy, in the house. What computer? What are you talking about?"

Teddy threw his hands up again. "Daddy Ed com-pooter. I gone get Daddy Ed com-pooter."

All right, let me get this straight. "You took the dolly to the church to look for Daddy Ed's computer?" How in the world did Teddy get such a crazy idea?

He nodded emphatically, relieved that he'd finally made himself understood. "You say, 'It be easy we got Daddy Ed com-pooter, Teddy.' I gone get Daddy Ed com-pooter."

"At the church?" A painful tenderness flowed through me, left me warm with the realization that, whether it made sense or not, Teddy had pushed the dolly all the way to the church trying to do something for me.

He nodded again. "Kay-Kay take Daddy Ed com-pooter to church."

My mind sharpened with the realization that Teddy's actions weren't as random as I'd thought. "Kay-Kay gave Daddy Ed's computer to the church? When?"

"The big sale. Past-er Al church."

My thoughts raced forward. "Big sale? Like a rummage sale? The church was having a rummage sale?"

"Yup," Teddy confirmed. "Big sale. Lotsa stuff."

"How long ago?" Could it be possible that the computer was still there, that I could get it back? "Did she take it before Hanna . . . your mom got sick, or after?"

"After Mama gone hop-sital."

Alarm bells rang in my head. Why would Kay-Kay be taking things to a church rummage sale while Hanna Beth was in the hospital? "Did your mom ask her to?"

Teddy shrugged.

"When you went to the church today, did they still have the computer there? Did you talk to anyone?"

Teddy shrugged again. "Nobody there. No Past-er Al today."

"No one was there?"

Teddy shook his head. I checked the clock on the dash as we pulled into our driveway. It was after five on a Thursday. Not much chance anyone would be there tonight, but tomorrow, I knew where I'd be first thing in the morning.

CHAPTER 22

Hanna Beth Parker

There was a new sense of urgency in me, a feeling that something wasn't right. It stirred me in the dark hours of the morning, whispered, *Get up, get out of bed, Hanna Beth Parker. You're needed.*

I struggled to decipher it, wondering if it was my imagination or a whiff of premonition. The sensation was uncomfortable, tight and tense like a muscle about to be knotted by a spasm. Had I dreamed something? Or perhaps there was a storm on the way, and I was only feeling the changes in barometric pressure.

Using the pull bar, I turned to the empty wheelchair, just a shadow in the dim hallway light. I wanted to rise up and wheel around in the darkness, check on things the way people do when startled from sleep by an unexpected sound—look in the corners, open the closets, make certain nothing was hiding there.

I felt as if I could do it. Yesterday had been a good day. After a session in the therapy room, Gretchen pushed me down to the commons area rather than returning me to my room.

"Might as well leave you here," she said gruffly, but the corners of her mouth twitched, cracking her salty mask. "No sense going all the way back down the hall."

It was wonderful to be out among people again, watching visitors and nurses come and go. Claude found me, and we played a one-sided game of chess in which Claude positioned most of my pieces for me, then we watched the *Oprah* show and the news. Mary came a bit later, and I took my supper with the ambulatory patients. My plate was liquid and mush, but I felt like a human being again, even though I still required help with the spoon. Mary's boys came in from the van, and they sat with us, little Brady watching with consternation the spectacle of an adult being spoon-fed like a little child. He couldn't understand that this felt like a triumph.

Mary chatted on about the construction at my house. Perhaps she was trying to explain why Rebecca hadn't come today, but I understood. Rebecca had her plate full, and now that I could see a day ahead when I would be going home, these long, slow hours weren't so unbearable.

"Teddy got car," Brady offered, crinkling a brow as he tracked the slow progress of the spoon from the tray to my mouth. "He got wotsa car. Got blue car, red car . . ."

"Hey, one car, two car, red car, blue car," Brandon observed. Mary laughed and ruffled his hair. It was good to see Brandon brightened up and feeling better, coming out of his shell a bit. He was still silent and sullen much of the time, like a little boy with too much on his mind, but the hollows were gone from beneath his eyes and his cheeks had a healthy glow. He laughed once in a while. Living on Blue Sky Hill with a yard to play in and a warm bed at night was good for him.

Mary looked better, too. Her hair was freshly washed, and she'd gained a little weight, not quite the sallow rag doll she'd been. Dr. Barnhill seemed to notice her when he passed our table. He smiled at Mary, and she fluttered her gaze away, folding her hands in her lap.

"Wee-da?" I asked, just to make conversation. I knew that Ouita Mae had left with a cousin two days ago to travel to Houston and make arrangements for having her things packed up and moved to Claude's house. I missed my daily visits with Ouita Mae. Claude tried reading my book to me, but everything reminded him of some old story, so it wasn't a very successful endeavor.

"She'll be back tomorrow," Dr. Barnhill answered. Then he and Claude began talking about preparations at Claude's house.

After a while, I asked Mary to take me to my room, and she obliged. She and the boys sat with me for a while, watching *Wheel of Fortune*. Little Brady even curled up in the bed with me, and I rested my chin on his head, drank in the little boy smells of sweat, and sand, and hand soap from the washroom.

It had been a good day yesterday, a good evening. Claude and I had watched the moon rise outside the window. He'd quoted an old poem I hadn't heard in years.

> *Moonbright, moonbright,*
> *Ah, so sweetly shines,*
> *She swings her hair,*
> *She swings her hair,*
> *A bonnie lass,*
> *A smile fair,*
> *A fallen star,*
> *She flies toward dawn.*
> *My heart falls earthward,*
> *Unaware.*

He'd laughed and said he hadn't remembered that verse since he was a boy, before he went off to the war.

I imagined that he was thinking of the pretty girl on her pinto horse. When he left, I fell asleep feeling boneless and weary, but content.

So why was I lying here in the darkness now, doom pressing down on me like the heavy lead cloak the dentists use? Why did I feel smothered, trapped, as if disaster were speeding around the corner and I was powerless to stop it?

I listened for Claude in his room next door, but there was no sound. I wished, for once, that the screaming woman would start into one of her tirades and wake him. I didn't want to be alone, but I wasn't sure why.

I pushed the nurse's call for Ifeoma. She came a few minutes later. "Why do you lie awake now, missus?" she asked, checking me over.

"My houwse?" I didn't have the words to express my vague unease. Even if I could have put together a full sentence, I couldn't have expressed it properly.

"The house is good, but you must rest." Ifeoma wasn't one for nonsense. She was always efficient, seldom indulgent. "You must sleep now, missus. Shall I bring a medication to help you rest?"

"No," I said. I didn't want to be groggy when Mary came in the morning. She always stopped by to give me the morning report on Edward, and the ongoing house renovations. Sometimes she brought tiny plants or pictures that Teddy and the boys had drawn for me. Teddy's were never anything you could make out, but he always labeled them with the letters and symbols he used to mark his flowerpots, so I knew he was thinking about the garden. When I imagined myself home, that was the place I always envisioned. When I was finally ready for an actual visit, I wanted to go there first, to sit and take in the scent and the feel and the sounds of the garden.

"Do you need to be aided to the bathroom, missus?" Ifeoma asked.

"No," I answered, though after weeks of protective undergarments and bedpans, going to the bathroom largely on cue was a particular thrill.

Ifeoma wagged a finger at me. "Then you should sleep."

"I wors . . . wor . . ." "Worry" was a word the speech therapist didn't help you practice. It wasn't on any of the neatly-printed cards. "Wor-ree."

Ifeoma's lips parted, her teeth glowing white as she made a

quiet *tsk-tsk-tsk*. "Ah, to worry is a useless thing, missus. The man who would worry is lacking confidence in his God. Sleep now," she said, and smoothed a hand over my hair. "Good things come in the morning."

"I'm nnnot . . ."

"Ssshhh," she said. "Quiet now. You will wake the old rooster, and then we will listen to him crow all night." Pressing her lips together, she cut a glance toward Claude's room.

I felt a bit better. If anything were really wrong, Ifeoma wouldn't be poking fun at Claude. Ifeoma was seldom so lighthearted.

"Sleep," she whispered. "Tomorrow is on God's hands."

She turned and left the room, pulling the door shut to keep out the night noises in the hallway. I closed my eyes, but the anxiety was still with me. Down the hall, the screaming woman began to moan as if she felt it, too. Her voice crept around the edges of the door like a faint red light, disturbing the darkness, pushing back the moon glow, leaving no peace.

In the morning, Claude was up early. I heard him moving around his room, getting into the wheelchair, and then his voice came through the vent. "You up in there, Birdie?"

"Yes," I answered.

A moment later, he was at my door. "You takin' visitors?" Now that I was capable of answering, he'd started asking permission to come in.

"Yes," I replied. "Com-minnn."

Claude wheeled himself into the room, yawning and rubbing his eyes. "Don't know how anyone could be sleepin'." He glanced toward the screaming woman. "She ain't quieted a bit for hours."

"No." I lifted my hands, moving them clumsily toward my ears, and Claude gave a guilty laugh. We both knew, at some level, that it could be either of us in the bed down the hall, moaning incoherently all hours of the day and night. "Ssstorm." I motioned to the window. Outside, a towering line of thunderheads had blotted out the sunrise. The moaning woman always became restless when the weather was changing.

"Hope it blows on over before tomorrow. Ouita Mae's supposed to come back, and we're all goin' out to my house to talk about what stuff to have the movers pack up and what to leave. Doc wants the old piano. I didn't know he played, but he does." Drawing a breath, Claude looked out the window, as if he could see his house there among the parked cars. "Lots of memories in that old piano. Emelda gave lessons on it for years." Claude seldom talked about his wife, an Italian woman he'd met and married while he was overseas in the army. She'd passed away from cancer some years ago, but that was about as much as I could gather. "It'll be good to pay a visit to the old place."

"Your ubbbook." For days, I'd been trying to prompt Claude to show Ouita Mae the memory book he kept in his room. If she saw the photo of the young man on the yellow horse, perhaps she would finally recognize him, and they would discover the secret I had been unable to make known.

Claude nodded. "Oh, I'm sure they'll want my books moved out of there. Doubt Doc's interested in reading about them old war planes, and tanks, and trains and such. You know, I half thought about askin' Doc, could I just move my stuff out to the woodshop out back, and maybe, if Doc and Ouita Mae get settled into the house and like it there . . ." His voice trailed off. "Oh, well, it's probably a silly idea. I just thought, maybe sometimes I could get my neighbor girl to take me out to home, and I could stay in my shop house for the day, read my books and help the kids play baseball and such. Probably Doc and Ouita Mae wouldn't want that, though. It's gonna be their place now."

I huffed, frustrated with the things I couldn't communicate to Claude. "Shhh-ow Ouita uuubbbook!"

Claude frowned over his shoulder. "Doubt if Ouita Mae's interested in them old war machine books, either. Say, did I ever tell you I drove them trains in Europe after the war?"

"Yes," I answered, but Claude didn't seem to hear me.

"My daddy was sure upset with me for goin' over there. Seemed like he got old in a hurry, after Birdie took sick and I ran off. He got down with pneumonia, and by the time I brung Emelda home to meet him, he was an old man. I never did try to make my daddy understand why I left for the army the way I did. I just thought, because he loved me, he should let it go, and if he couldn't, well then, he didn't love me like I thought. Young folks get love and understandin' backward, don't they? Love don't come galloping across fresh pastures like a fine white horse with understandin' riding soft and easy on its back. Understandin' plods in like an old plow mule, breaking sod. It shades the earth with its body, and waters it with sweat. Love grows up in the furrow that's left behind. It takes some patience. I was an impatient young man. I took Emelda, and we moved down to the Piney Woods, and I didn't look back.

"I didn't talk to my daddy for almost ten years after that. I reckon we were too much alike—stubborn, proud, bullheaded. I hated those things about him. But ain't it always the way, Birdie, that the easiest faults to find in other people are the ones you got yourself? I didn't see my daddy again until my mama called to tell me the doctor'd said my daddy's heart was bad, and I'd better come. I packed a suitcase and I drove all night until early mornin'. When I got to the house, I turned out the headlights and coasted up the lane real quiet, thinking I'd sleep in my truck 'til daybreak, but I'd no sooner rolled 'er to a stop than the door swung open wide, and there was my daddy. He didn't say a word, just lit the lamp and put on the coffee, and I knew I was welcome home."

Letting his eyes fall closed, Claude took a deep breath, as if he could smell the coffee and the damp morning air even now. "We had five good years after that. Turns out doctors don't know everythin'. I was with my daddy at the end of his life. He apologized for dyin' and leavin' me with a crop in the field, then he said, 'You been a dandy, Johnny Claude. I expect I been more trouble to you than you ever been to me.' After that, he died, and I sure wished I could of had them ten years back. Birdie, wouldn't it be nice if the eyes in the back of yer head weren't so much sharper than the ones in the front? Seems like most the important things in life come to me in hindsight."

Claude fell silent, and the two of us sat for a long time. Outside, the storm rolled in, and I felt a chill slip over me. The clouds blew over in a fury of wind and rain, then passed quickly, giving way to muted rays of morning sun that pressed through the window and lighted the shadowy corners of the room.

In his wheelchair, Claude dozed off, and outside the window, a cardinal began to sing among the last of the yellow blooms.

Despite the warm, dawning sun and the spectacle of color and sound, I couldn't shake the chill that hung in the air, or the sense that another storm was coming.

CHAPTER 23

Rebecca Macklin

A thunderstorm struck early Friday morning, putting on a lightning show and rumbling over the house. I watched jagged streaks of electrical current crackle across the line of thunderheads as I sat with my laptop and sorted e-mail. Bree would be surprised when she arrived at work and found that I'd already checked the files she'd e-mailed late yesterday evening. Poring over the applications and supporting documents, I temporarily forgot I wasn't back at the office.

Downstairs, the garage door rattled upward, and I came back to the present. I heard Teddy talking to Sy and the crew as they carried in their tools.

I stood up and hovered by the desk a minute, feeling lightheaded and strange. The sensation clung to me as I carried my clothes across the hall, showered, dressed, and went downstairs. Ifeoma was already on duty. As usual, she'd proceeded directly to my father's room to get him out of bed and dressed. She found it easier to begin the day with him while he was still groggy from the effects of a deep, medication-assisted sleep.

She met me in the kitchen after bringing him to the living room and turning on the TV. "Shall I prepare an omelet for your breakfast, missus?" Every morning, she treated my father to a five-star meal, and he fell in love with her anew.

Groaning, I laid a hand on my stomach. "No, thanks. I don't feel so well this morning."

"Again?" She cocked her head to one side. So far, I hadn't felt the desire to partake of her breakfast creations, even once. In the mornings, I woke with my stomach churning and a million things on my mind. Food hardly seemed a temptation.

"I think it's stress," I admitted, rolling my eyes to indicate that I recognized my type A personality, even if I couldn't control it. "The good news is I've lost five pounds."

"You do not have five pounds to spare." Shaking a finger at me, she smiled. Over time, Ifeoma's cool, detached demeanor was slowly warming up.

It was strange to have someone worrying about me. Typically, that was my job. "Well, thanks, but it's nice to lose a little."

Ifeoma tutted under her breath, then pulled out the eggs and started cracking them into a bowl.

My stomach rolled, and I angled my line of vision away from the egg whites oozing over her hands. Drawing a glass of tap water, I plopped in a couple Alka-Seltzers and waited for the tablets to stop fizzing.

"I have used all of the eggs," Ifeoma said, then took the cap off the milk. "Milk and bread will be needed soon as well."

"I'll pick some up." During yesterday's excitement over Teddy's absence, I'd completely forgotten to get groceries. "I want to go to the little white church down on Hayes this morning. Teddy thinks some of my parents' things may have been taken there for a yard sale after Hanna Beth had her stroke. I'm hoping they might know where my father's computer is." A glance at the clock told me it was almost eight forty. "Surely someone will be there by nine."

Ifeoma nodded, searching the drawers. "The building is opened at eight. Father is often down the road taking breakfast." Pausing, she pulled out the whisk and began whipping the eggs. "I stop there each morning to pray for my son. So he will be well."

It struck me again that Ifeoma's son was half a world away. What would that be like? Ifeoma seldom mentioned him, but she often stared out the window, rubbing a small, beaded cross that hung around her neck. The onyx stones were worn smooth and glossy. "How old is he?" I asked. "Your son."

"He is eight years old this month," she answered, staring into the bowl. "A small boy for his years, but a good worker."

I tried to imagine sending an eight-year-old child, a boy not even Macey's age, to work. "How long have you been away from Ghana?"

"It was one year and six months ago that I must take my son from his father's town. For some time I search for a good job elsewhere, but very soon I know I must do something," she answered, without looking up. "My son is a smart boy. I want him to go to school, but where he is living now, there is no school."

"I'm sorry," I said. How many times in my work had I sat across the table from people like Ifeoma, separated from family, caught in political limbo, waiting for consulate interviews, the lifting of annual visa caps, I-140 petitions to be approved and slowly processed so their relatives could follow?

Ifeoma held the whisk above the bowl, waiting while strings of raw egg oozed downward. "I hold dreams for my son. I tell him he must work very hard where he lives, and in return, the fisherman will provide food for him and give him a bed at night. Each day, I pray that God will keep my son until I am able to come for him. The work of the fishermen is dangerous."

My mind swirled with a mixture of dripping eggs, an electric drill squealing in the downstairs bathroom, and fishing boys, compelled to live alone, forced to take to the water to earn a living. My stomach rebelled as the first sip of Alka-Seltzer settled, and the next thing I knew, I was clutching the sink, writhing in a spasm of dry heaves.

Ifeoma wet her hand and rubbed cool water over the back of my neck, and the spasm ended as quickly as it had begun. Pushing away from the counter, I caught a long breath and shook off the last of the headrush.

"I'm all right." I wiped my face with a paper towel and caught my breath. Finally, I grabbed my purse. "I probably just need to get some fresh air. I'm going to take Teddy to the church with me. We'll be back in a half hour or so. If it takes longer, I'll call." I started toward the patio, where Teddy was carefully watering his plants. "Sorry for all the drama. I don't know what's wrong with me this morning."

The cutting board rattled as Ifeoma pulled it off the wall, then opened the refrigerator. There was no telling, on any given day, what she would choose to put in the omelets, but my father was always pleased.

"Might you be pregnant, missus?" Ifeoma's question caught me as I reached the doorway. Without seeing her face, I couldn't tell whether it was a serious inquiry.

My sardonic laughter was both an instantaneous reaction and an answer. "Not likely, thank goodness. We'll be back in a little while. Thanks for making breakfast, Ifeoma."

"It is my pleasure. I am hungry as well."

As I went out the door, I heard her singing a slow, rhythmic song that reminded me of some long-ago trip to Morocco with my parents. Early in the mornings, the fishermen sang outside our bungalow as they went to sea in their boats. I sat in bed sometimes and watched them prepare to go out, the men barking orders as young boys scampered about, porting crates, readying nets, mending broken ropes.

I never wondered about the children, their dreams interrupted, while I lay peacefully sleeping.

Thoughts of the fishermen followed me as Teddy and I drove to the little white church. In the passenger seat, Teddy was talking about the seeds he'd planted with Brandon and Brady. The boys were excited because tiny marigolds were coming up in the cups.

I couldn't focus on Teddy's intricate description of baby plants.

Baby plants . . .

Might you be pregnant, missus?

Might you be? Pregnant?

Baby plants. Baby . . .

Was it possible? Four years ago, when Macey started kindergarten, Kyle and I had agreed that one child was enough for us. With my mother suffering more frequently from lupus-related illnesses, me helping with the boutique, and Kyle working twelve-hour days, we were both at the breaking point, and there seemed to be no room for anything else. Kyle went in for a vasectomy, and our busy life moved into the next phase.

Vasectomies have been known to fail. Was it possible? Kyle, himself, was the product of a failed vasectomy, a late-in-life surprise to his parents. Six weeks ago, Kyle and I had been on our anniversary trip to San Diego. We'd stayed in the historic Hotel Del on Coronado Island, tried to recapture the magic of our honeymoon, but old issues crept between us.

We made love to silence the discussions, agreed to leave issues until later, just relax for the weekend. We laughed, flirted, walked on the beach, enjoyed a long, slow dinner together, made love again as a luminous, orange moon rose above the water. After so many years of being consumed by the obligations of life, I was certain that we were finally finding our way back to each other.

Was it possible that weekend had produced a baby? On the heels of the thought came Susan Sewell sitting in the café, cuddled intimately close to Kyle, going through yet another divorce.

I felt sick again. My breath came in short, quick gasps, and my chest burned until I couldn't get enough air. I wanted to pull over, throw open the door and run.

What if I was pregnant? What then? What if it wasn't just Macey and me, but Macey and me and a new baby to consider?

Don't, a voice whispered inside me. *Don't do this now.*

"There Mama church." Teddy broke into my thoughts. "A-becca, there Mama church."

My mind came back to the present as we passed the driveway. I took the next opportunity to make a U-turn, and went back.

"There Past-er Al." Teddy pointed to a man in a green fishing cap, who was pruning rosebushes in the small memorial garden beside the church. After stopping his work as we pulled into a parking space close by, he exited the garden, removed his gloves, and set his pruning sheers on a bench by the antique iron fence.

" 'Lo there," he called, pausing to wipe his eyeglasses on his knit shirt, then put them back on as Teddy and I climbed from the car.

"Hieee, Past-er Al!" Teddy called, moving up the path in a lumbering trot.

"Why, Teddy!" Pastor Al opened his arms as I hurried to catch up. "My word, son, did you grow another foot?"

"I been this foot." Teddy gave Pastor Al an exuberant hug. The pastor disappeared momentarily behind Teddy's body. His lightweight hat drifted to the ground, and he scooped it up as Teddy released him.

"Who you got with you there, young Ted?" Pastor Al squinted through thick lenses.

Grinning, Teddy brought me forth like a new toy. "This A-becca. This my sister."

Momentarily confused, Pastor Al rested a hand on Teddy's arm, cocking his head to study me. I could imagine what he was thinking. *What sister?*

"I'm Edward's daughter. Rebecca Macklin," I explained, and Pastor Al's lips parted in a breath of comprehension.

Shaking my hand, Pastor Al smiled warmly. "Well, good to meet you there, Rebecca, and good to see young Ted again. We've missed you around here, son. These flowers sure looked better when you watched after them. Afraid they're on their last legs right now. I thought if I cut them back, maybe it'd help."

Peering around Pastor Al, Teddy checked the flowers. "Uh-oh."

"Maybe you better go see what they need," Pastor Al prompted. "In all my years, Teddy, I've never seen anybody better with flowers than you."

Beaming, Teddy started toward the garden. "I gone see, Past-er Al." As he turned, he pointed toward a two-wheeled dolly propped against the side of the church. "There Sy dolly. I gone take Sy dolly home."

"I wondered who left that here," the pastor commented as the two of us watched Teddy move down the path. Pastor Al turned back to me, his jovial demeanor straightening into an expectant look.

I tried to decide where to begin. "I'm not sure how much you know about my father and Hanna Beth's situation lately."

Pastor Al sighed regretfully. "Not a lot, I'm sorry to admit. We haven't seen your family in close to a year. I have to apologize for that. I was out for cancer surgery and then treatments most of last year, and best I can gather, there was some brouhaha about Teddy helping keep the children in the nursery during service. I want you to know that should never have happened. Sometimes new people coming into the congregation can be quick to judge, but Teddy's never been anything but good with the little ones. He's as gentle with them as he is with the flowers." He glanced over his shoulder with an obvious fondness. Teddy was squatted down next to a rosebush, talking to it as he carefully pruned dead leaves. "I'm sorry your mother was upset."

"Hanna Beth isn't my mother." The words were a knee-jerk reflex, out of my mouth before I considered how they would sound.

"Of course." Pastor Al gave me an astute look, and we hovered in a moment of uncomfortable silence. "Will you tell her I'm sorry for the misunderstanding about Teddy? He's welcome here anytime. The truth is that if everyone else were as accepting as Teddy is, there'd never be any problems in the church. I tried to go by a few times to tell that to Hanna Beth, but their caretaker said your father wasn't doing well, and they weren't taking any visitors."

"My father hasn't been doing well," I agreed. "Hanna Beth had a stroke last month and has been in a nursing center care. We hadn't been . . . in touch, so I didn't know until some weeks after the fact. When I got here, Teddy and my father were living in the house alone. There was no caretaker, and from the looks of the house, there hadn't been anyone for some time."

Pastor Al frowned, rubbing his chin, the skin stretching back and forth between his fingers. "That's odd. I had the impression the care-taker was living there. I'm sorry to hear about Hanna Beth. How's she getting on?"

"She's better, but unfortunately her speech and memory were af-fected, so she hasn't been able to tell us much about what was hap-pening in the house before she was taken to the hospital. My father's memory is pretty fragile, and all Teddy knows is the caretaker's first name, Kay-Kay. I was hoping you might have some information about her—a last name, where they hired her, where I might find her?"

The pastor sighed. "Afraid I can't be much help. About all I could tell you is what she looked like. Brown hair, kind of heavyset, in her fifties, maybe. Dark skin, but I don't think she was Hispanic, more like Greek or Italian, maybe. Wore glasses. Real friendly. Seemed sorry to have to tell me I couldn't visit with your folks. She didn't give me a last name, not that I recall anyway. Just said she was helping Hanna Beth look after Edward and that it was too hard on him to have strange people in the house."

My hopes flagged. That wasn't much to go on. "Teddy said he and Kay-Kay brought some of my father's things here for a rummage sale several weeks ago—a computer? I was hoping it might still be here, or possibly you could tell me who bought it? I think my father's financial records were on it. I'm trying to straighten out his accounts."

Pastor Al frowned, as if he knew there was more to the story.

"Could be," he said. "No telling who brought what for the rummage sale. Proceeds go to benefit the recreation center down the road, give kids in the older neighborhoods something to do other than hang out on the streets. For a while, we had so much stuff piled around here, the trash men couldn't even get to the Dumpster to empty it."

"Do you know what happened to my father's computer?"

"Most likely it's still in the shed." Pastor Al shrugged toward a metal building out back. "The rummage sale was rained out after the first couple hours on Friday. That was the weekend of all the floods. Some of the stuff got wet, and with so many houses around here suffering water damage, we just haven't had a chance to sort out the shed and see what got ruined. You're welcome to look if you'd like. There was a whole table of computer equipment of various types. Don't know what shape all that stuff's in now. It's a mess back there."

Pastor Al called Teddy over as we walked to the shed. The musty scent of decaying paper and damp wood wafted outward as he and Teddy pulled open the doors.

I groaned without meaning to and turned my face away from the escaping cloud of fungus.

Pastor Al chuckled. "We dried it out the best we could without moving everything. You sure you want to do this?"

"Yes," I said, then asked Teddy if he recognized anything. Teddy started into the shed, pointing out magazines, books, some old plastic storage boxes he thought had come from my father's house.

"The computer," I reminded him. "We're trying to find Daddy Ed's computer, okay?"

"Ho-kay." Teddy proceeded farther into the building, weaving his way through stacks of furniture and disintegrating boxes. "I don' see Daddy Ed com-pooter."

"Keep looking," I urged as Pastor Al and I followed him into the slanted light cast by three dusty windows on the east wall.

"Sorry it's so dark," Pastor Al apologized. "Storm got the electric pole. Most of the computer equipment's back there in the corner. They moved that in out of the rain first."

"Oh," I muttered. "Good thing, I guess." Something rustled under a pile of boxes nearby, and I gasped.

"There a little rat," Teddy observed cheerfully. "Hellooo, little rat. Go way now."

A shiver crept over my skin. I imagined small, hairy things dashing from the piles of rummage and scampering over my sandals.

Ahead, Teddy stopped, braced his hands on his knees, and leaned forward to peer over a pile of clothing.

"Teddy, do you see something?" I slipped around a daybed frame to move closer.

"Got little baby rats," Teddy reported. "Little pink one, two, three . . ."

"Uhhh-uhhh-uhhh-uh," a guttural heebie-jeebie escaped my throat, and I moved back around the daybed frame, unconsciously fanning my hands in front of me.

Pastor Al glanced over with a benevolent smile.

"Them don' got eyes yet," Teddy went on.

My stomach gurgled up my throat. I tasted something I must have eaten last night. "Teddy, we're looking for the computer. Do you see the computer?"

Pastor Al squeezed past him. "Come look on this table back here, Teddy." He moved to the corner of the room, then pulled away a blue tarp and sent a cloud of musty-smelling dust dancing into the window light.

Teddy proceeded to the table and began surveying the jumble of cast-off computers and printers. Craning up and down, Teddy checked each piece of equipment. "No . . . no . . . nope," he muttered, then lifted his hands palms up, shaking his head.

Pastor Al finally pulled the tarp back over the table. "Well, I'm afraid there's no telling." Dusting off his hands, he frowned apologetically. "Could be it was sold before we closed up on Friday." He returned to the center of the room, where my hopes were crashing around me.

Sighing, I pushed my hair off my face. Despite the smell and the rats, I wasn't ready to accept another dead end.

Pastor Al laid a hand on my shoulder, guiding me toward the door. "Why don't we go on inside and get something to drink, see what other ideas we can come up with?"

Reluctantly, I followed him. Behind us, Teddy wandered among the junk piles, searching for more baby rats.

"Come on, Teddy," I said as he turned sideways to slip between an old refrigerator and a mattress. "Teddy, come on. We need to go."

He didn't answer. The pastor and I stopped near the door.

"There, that one!" Teddy announced, having discovered something new behind the refrigerator. I didn't want to think about what it was. "There Daddy Ed com-pooter!"

Pastor Al hurried back into the building, and I followed. A moment later, the mattress shifted. Teddy was standing behind it, pointing to a monitor, speakers, keyboard, and CPU resting in a jumble atop a small, gray metal worktable.

"Ahhh . . . that's the one," Pastor Al observed. "That stuff was left by the Dumpster the night before the sale. Nobody seemed to know who put it there, but we figured it was for the rummage."

"Me 'n Kay-Kay bring it," Teddy offered.

Coming closer, I peered between the mattress and Teddy's body. The computer's plastic cases were yellowed and pockmarked with mildew spots, but all the pieces seemed to be there. The front of the CPU was labeled with my father's name. He'd always labeled everything.

As Teddy cleared the debris from the table, I was struck by a tender memory of my father commandeering the small two-drawer metal typing stand from a field office in Saudi. He hated the ornately carved wooden desk in our living room there, so he brought home something practical. My mother despised the gray metal secretary stand. She said it spoiled the decor, but my father insisted on keeping it. I sat on his knee as he worked there. When I set my water glass on the tabletop, no one fussed or told me to use a coaster. I liked the gray metal desk because it was like my father—strong, pragmatic, practical, indestructible. Each time he was away in the oil fields, I sat at the desk to do homework. When I opened the drawers, I could smell the scent of him—dried ink, pipe tobacco, carbon paper, Old Spice. . . .

Teddy and Pastor Al began retrieving computer equipment from the tabletop, untangling hastily strewn cords and winding them up for travel. Pastor Al handed the speakers and the computer cord to me.

"Can we take the desk, too?" I said impulsively. "If I put the backseats down, it'll probably fit." I was glad I'd chosen the hatchback rental car instead of the coupe.

Pastor Al surveyed the surrounding junk stacks. "I think we can get it out."

As Pastor Al and Teddy began working to free the desk, I hurried outside, brought the car around, and put down the backseats. I carried out pieces of computer equipment while Teddy and Pastor Al hauled my recovered family treasure to the front of the building and prepared it for transport.

Loading the heavy metal typing stand turned out to be harder than I'd thought it would be, particularly because the CPU was either bolted or glued to the desk—perhaps the reason the computer had ended up beside the Dumpster rather than in it. We maneuvered as carefully as we could. Fortunately, Teddy was strong, and between the three of us we managed to wrestle the desk and Sy's dolly into the back of the car.

Pastor Al shook Teddy's hand as we prepared to leave. "Teddy, you come help me with those flowers, you hear?"

Teddy was noticeably pleased. "Ho-kay, Past-er Al."

I thanked Pastor Al, and he shook my hand, then kept it in his for a moment. "I'll be by to visit your folks. You let me know if there's anything else I can do."

"I will," I said. Then Teddy and I climbed into the car, Teddy folding his legs against the speakers and keyboard, and carrying the monitor in his lap, because there wasn't anywhere else to put it. When we got home, we spilled out of the car like clowns from a Volkswagen.

"Hey-eee, Sy, I gone get the dolly!" Teddy called into the house. Sy came out and helped us unload the typing stand and equipment. I cleared a space for the desk and computer beside the workbench in the garage, to avoid bringing the smell into the house.

"Man, where's this thing been?" Sy asked as he stacked the monitor atop the CPU.

"Waiting for a church yard sale," I answered, leaning over to connect the cables. A slip of paper protruding from one of the desk drawers caught my eye. Pinching it, I pulled, slowly bringing the paper out, discovering it bit by bit—a faded black-and-white photograph, a passionflower vine, a brick sidewalk, my feet in little Mary Janes, the black wingtips my father wore to the office. His pant legs, my knees, the hem of a lacy dress, pink, maybe lavender, an Easter basket, his hand holding mine, my white Peter Pan collar, his suit coat, our faces smiling as, behind us, kids lined up for an Easter egg hunt. I didn't know where the picture was taken, didn't remember the dress. I was six, maybe seven. I remembered how big his hand felt, clasping mine.

"Guess that ought to do it," Sy said, plugging the computer into the wall. "I better get back inside before Tony screws somethin' up."

I barely heard him. I'd lost myself in the photo, a picture my father had kept in his desk all these years. I reached down, pulled the drawer handle. The stop rattled in the lock. "Teddy, do you know if there's a key to this desk?" Perhaps the drawer had been locked all these years, the old photo trapped there along with dried-up pens and bills paid long ago.

Or perhaps the man I'd thought had forgotten me had kept in this one private place—his place—a picture of the two of us, father and daughter in another life.

"Daddy Ed got lotsa key," Teddy offered. Rummaging around the workbench, he came up with a small metal box filled with spare keys, most of which probably didn't fit anything anymore.

"Thanks," I said, pressing the power button on the computer and listening as it whirred into action, the cooling fan rattling but apparently operational.

"Hey, Tedman, bring that dolly in here," Sy called from the hall-way. Teddy gathered up the dolly and proceeded into the house.

The computer screen crackled to life with a warning that the system had been improperly shut down and loss of data could result. Windows clicked off, and the software began moving through a disk check.

Setting the Easter picture on the CPU, I spilled the box of keys onto the desktop and began trying anything that seemed the right size.

The computer continued its lazy attempt at resurrection. I sifted through the keys and tossed the rejects into the box one by one. The box was half full again by the time an ancient version of Windows materialized in the corner of my eye, and I turned my attention to the screen. I began searching for the financial records Hanna Beth had told me should be there—bank transactions, checks, deposits. There was a copy of Quicken with a history of regular use until nine months ago, but the data folders were missing. Almost all of the data folders were missing from the hard drive. My father, or someone, had stripped them away, perhaps in preparation for disposing of the computer, or perhaps to prevent anyone from gaining information later. Would my father, in his growing paranoia, have done such a thing? Would he have been capable of it? Or was this the work of Kay-Kay, the mystery woman?

I moved to the Favorites folder on the hard drive. The activity there was more recent, visits to various Web sites about Alzheimer's, an online banking page, a Las Vegas gaming site, online pharmacies, a MySpace page for Kenita Kendal. Kay-Kay? Had I finally found a link? I'd have to take the computer inside and connect the modem to a phone line to find out.

I paged through the remaining file tree, into a folder of stored photos and information from various Web sites. A year ago, my father had been researching experimental treatments for Alzheimer's. He'd also been doing family genealogy. Clicking on the folder marked FAMILYHISTORY, I scanned the contents, found a folder with my name on it. As it opened, the screen filled with a thumbnail sheet of tiny images. The pictures were familiar—Macey's gymnastics team posing for a newspaper article about the state meet; photos from the boutique Web site, me behind the counter, Macey and Kyle pretending to be shoppers; a photo of us participating in the Walk for a Cure in honor of my mother. The images scrolled on and on, my entire life history—Macey's birth announcement from the newspaper, a picture of my high school senior class someone had posted on the reunion site, me with my clarinet in the eighth grade, proudly holding up a state solo and ensemble medal.

Tears blurred my eyes, but I wiped them away impatiently. I wanted to see it all, to know, finally, that the father who I'd thought had forgotten me had known me all along.

I sat for a time just looking at the pictures, taking them in, my soul rising with joy, an empty place inside me filling, an incompleteness now complete, as if I'd been waiting for this moment for thirty-three years. The scents of oil and mildew, old grease and crumbling plaster faded away, leaving only my father and me. The tall, ramrod-straight man in the picture, and the little girl in the white Mary Janes, holding hands as if they would never let go.

I returned to the pile of loose keys, began trying them in the drawer, ruling out one, then another, another, another, until finally one fit, turned. The lock gave way, and I pulled the drawer open, took out the items stored there, savoring each individually. My baby book, a sloppy handmade Father's Day card that read "I Love You Daddy." I'd signed my name in clumsy letters with a backward *R*. Underneath the card was a faded Crayola flower made from a paper plate. I remembered drawing it on the long plane trip to Saudi. Picking it up, I traced my finger along the bleached lines, indulged myself in the memory, then looked into the drawer again. There was nothing left but a small manila envelope. It was addressed to me, but the stamp had never been postmarked. I picked it up, turned it over in my hand, read my father's handwriting on the flap, "For Rebecca from Dad." There was no further detail. No explanation of how the envelope had become hidden under the pictures, why it hadn't been sent, or how long it had remained locked in the drawer.

Slipping my finger under the flap, I split open the seam carefully, like a historian studying the fragile documents of some long-past civilization. Inside, there was a piece of paper—a single folded sheet of letterhead that seemed hardly worth all the drama. As I pulled it out, the envelope remained heavy in one corner, bulky, so that I knew something other than paper remained. I listened as the object scratched along the inside of the envelope. It landed in my palm, a single brass key, brown with the patina of time, slightly cool after its long stay in the darkness. There was no tag on the key, no explanation. I unfolded the paper.

The writing was my father's, the sheet crisp with age, slightly yellowed around the edges, an old piece of company stationery. The letter was dated two years ago. The handwriting was the hurried yet crisp penmanship I remembered, not the shaky, barely intelligible scrawl from various file folders and notes now hidden from *those people*.

The text was short and to the point, the beginning unsentimental.

Rebecca,

> *I hope this letter finds you well. It has never been my desire to prevail upon you or to interrupt your life in any way. These many years now, I have made a point of abiding by your wishes and your mother's, but the doctors have informed me that my time to attend to important affairs may be more limited than originally thought. Some days, I can feel my mind slipping, even now.*
>
> *While the past remains clear to me and the necessities of the future are still evident, I've gathered together what matters most and taken a safe-deposit box for you at the bank. It will wait until you are ready, if I cannot.*
>
> *There are things you must know.*
>
> *I think of you often—*
>
> *Dad*

At the bottom of the page, the bank address and the box number had been carefully written. I stood staring at them, my mind spinning ahead, imagining driving the few blocks, entering the vault, taking down the box, opening it, and discovering whatever my father had left for me. What would be inside? Simple financial details, legal information, bank account numbers? Or would I find something more, something deeper, something I'd been searching for? Was the safe-deposit box merely a way of attending to affairs, or was it an extension of the desk drawer—final proof that I had always been close to the mind and heart of my father?

Closing my fingers around the key, I went into the house for my purse, hoping that today would be the day when all the questions were finally answered.

CHAPTER 24

Hanna Beth Parker

Ouita Mae came to my room when she arrived from her trip back home. She'd taken a cab from the airport, because her grandson couldn't go after her. An unexpected crisis had slowed down his day and delayed their trip over to Claude's house. Ouita Mae didn't seem to mind. She picked up the book and started reading to me while she waited. I tried again to bring up the subject of Claude's photo album, but she thought I was talking about the things in Claude's house.

Down the hall, the screaming woman had been quiet for hours. I suspected that Dr. Barnhill's medical crisis was with her. I heard the chaplain pass by with family members, their voices mixing in the muted tones of grief and consolation. Shortly afterward, Dr. Barnhill came to collect his grandmother. He seemed in a fine mood. I wondered if this process of living and dying ever struck him as anything other than a day's work—if the young ever consider that time is not an endless river, but the stream pouring from a potting can, the interior a mystery, the flow dependent on the hand of the gardener and the amount of water inside. So often, the grooming of obligations and future plans causes us to miss what blooms wild and untended in the present. If I'd learned one thing from the progression of Edward's disease, it was that the people we love do not always stay with us as long as we'd like. I hoped that, in the midst of all his important com-

mitments, young Dr. Barnhill would find some quiet moments to
truly appreciate this time with his grandmother.

I heard Rebecca striding up the hall before she came in my door.
I'd learned to recognize the quick, curt sound of her footsteps. The
nurses didn't normally move in such a hurry, nor did they wear sandals with hard soles that echoed against the tile.

"I need . . . ," she said, then stopped, because Dr. Barnhill and
Ouita Mae were in the room.

Dr. Barnhill was talking about the plans for my first home visit,
perhaps as soon as next week. I expected Rebecca to be interested
in that, but instead she breezed in and stood with her arms crossed,
her body language conveying that she was impatient to be alone
with me.

Dr. Barnhill went on reviewing my care plan. Rebecca seemed
preoccupied, even though Dr. Barnhill was more attentive to her than
he was to most people. I suspected that most men were probably
that way with her. Rebecca was a pretty girl, but not in a fashion that
seemed as if she worked at it. Today, her cheeks were flushed. Wisps
of dark hair swirled around her face in wild disarray, as if she'd been
rushing around and hadn't had time to give thought to her appearance. She didn't ask any questions about my tests or aftercare, which
seemed odd. She merely listened until Dr. Barnhill was finished, and
Ouita Mae said they should go because by now Claude would be
waiting for them in the foyer. I suspected she could tell that Rebecca
wasn't in the mood for company.

"Cl-ood buk," I said, as she was leaving. *Claude's book.* "You tsssee
Cl-ood book, tic-cher." *Picture. Picture. The pictures in Claude's book.
See the boy on the yellow horse.* Frustration made my muscles tight, my
lips uncooperative. "Cl-ood book."

Ouita Mae smiled on her way out the door. "Oh, sure, sweetie.
We'll read some more tomorrow. Y'all have a good visit, now."

Rebecca began pacing back and forth by the window. A knot

formed in my chest as she braced her hands on her hips, let her head fall forward, drew a long breath. She waited until the squeal of Ouita Mae's walker had disappeared down the hall, then she turned to me. Unmasked now, her expression was an unsettling mix of anxiety and pain.

Perhaps my premonition that morning had been correct. Was something wrong with Edward? Was he back in the hospital? Perhaps the prognosis was worse this time. "Utt? Whh-at?" I concentrated on forming the words correctly. "What rrrr-ong?"

"Did you know my father left a safe-deposit box for me?" She moved to the side of the bed and stood over me. "I need to know, Hanna Beth." It wasn't a plea, or an order, but something in between. "I found a safe-deposit box key with my name on it. In his computer desk."

I shook my head. I knew he kept pictures of Rebecca and Marilyn, of his old life, in the top drawer of the metal desk. I never questioned him about it. He thought, perhaps, that I wasn't aware of his secret place. He kept the key to the drawer in the garage among a box of discards. I knew which key it was, but I never took it out. I never opened the drawer. To do so would have been a betrayal. If I walked by the office when he had the drawer open, I always moved past and let him keep his thoughts, his memories, to himself. "Nnno."

"Did you know what was in the box?"

I shook my head again, unsure how to feel. Edward had kept a safe-deposit box? Even when his memory began to fade, he hadn't bothered to tell me he had left something stored away to be unearthed . . . when, exactly? By whom? Rebecca's name was on the key.

I turned to Rebecca, reached for her, my hand hanging suspended in midair, the fingers still thin, but not so curled as before. "What boggs? What . . ." *What box? What did you find?* I wanted to scream it out. *What was he hiding there?*

Her eyes narrowed as she took in another breath, tightened the barricade of her crossed arms. "Is Teddy my half brother?"

The simple question hung in midair like a volatile cocktail of gunpowder and nitroglycerin. I lay unable to do anything but watch it fall. "Whhh . . . wh-at?"

Rebecca's eyes sparked with an unmistakable hint of Edward's temper, threatening to ignite the unanswered question into something neither of us would be able to control. She was her father's daughter—slow to grow angry, but now angry all the way. "You heard me, Hanna Beth. There was a letter in the box, dated two years ago, in my father's handwriting. It explains . . . things . . . the past. Is it true that Teddy's my father's biological son?"

I lay mute, stunned. All these years, Edward had insisted that Rebecca was better off not knowing, that no good could come from her being told what had happened so many years ago, from her learning of Marilyn's part in it. Had he left the key to the truth for her in the desk drawer, along with the old pictures and mementos from her childhood? Should I confirm it for her? What would happen if I did? What if she became angry, bitter with us all over again? What if this fractured the fragile bridge that had begun to bind us together as a family? We needed Rebecca now. We couldn't manage without her.

Part of me suspected that she needed us, too. But how would she feel, learning these facts so soon after the death of her mother? What if Rebecca rejected them altogether? She loved Marilyn. She wouldn't want to accept this version of history. It would be less painful to walk away, to leave us behind and preserve the picture of the mother she loved. The dead travel about our memories in a soft, white light. It's never easy to recall that, while living, they had flaws, committed wrongs, made mistakes for which they never sought atonement.

"I want the truth." There was no hint of Rebecca's emotions in the statement, no sign of which way she wanted these revelations to fall. How could I explain the past without the words to tell the story?

I rested against the pillow, tried to think. I wished I were in the wheelchair. It would have been easier to face her sitting up.

Rebecca studied my face, gauging my reaction. Her eyes slowly filled with tears. "Is it true?" she choked out. "Is Teddy my father's biological son?"

"Yes," I whispered.

Rebecca shivered, swallowed hard, pressed her lips together to stop them from trembling. "In the letter, he wrote . . . he said . . . Did my mother know you were pregnant before she married my father?" Her disbelief was evident, even now. Her expression begged me to revise the past, to render Edward's letter in the box merely the delusional ramblings of an old man whose memories were tangled like the string of a windblown kite.

I considered denying it. What good could possibly come of this now? Didn't Marilyn—even Marilyn—have the right to be forgiven the mistakes of her youth?

But why should she be forgiven? All these years, she'd done everything she could to poison Rebecca against her father. She'd taught Rebecca to hate him, to hate me, hate Teddy.

"Did my mother *know*?" Rebecca repeated insistently. "Did she know?"

I took a breath, closed my eyes so I wouldn't have to look at her. "Yes." It was barely audible, barely a word. That single utterance would change everything she understood about her life, the very soil in which she'd been grown.

I heard her stagger backward a step, sink into the chair Ouita Mae had pulled close while reading to me. "Before they married, was my father aware that you were pregnant?" I knew she was grasping, clinging to a last fervent hope, curling it protectively around the memory of her mother. She wanted to believe Edward and Marilyn had made the choice together—that they'd decided to marry despite my carrying Edward's child.

She grasped the rail, waiting for an answer.

Slipping my hand over hers, I circled her fingers with mine. "No."

A tiny sob escaped her, trembled against her lips. "Did she keep it from him? Is what he wrote in the letter true—did she and my grandmother have the lawyer tell you that my father denied all responsibility?" Motionless, she waited, her attention focused on me, unwavering, her face filled with dread.

"Yes," I whispered, and tightened my fingers around hers, holding on. This was the moment the secrets finally ended, allowing truth to save or to destroy. The choice was Rebecca's.

"Oh, dear God," she whispered. "My God, I can't . . ." The sentence dissolved into a sob that doubled her over, shook her to the core. Bending forward, she covered her face with her hand.

"Ssshhh," I whispered, squeezing her fingers. "Ssshhh, Rrr-becca. Hushhh, sss-weet. Ssshhh." *It's all right, I wanted to tell her. Don't cry. It's so long ago. It's so long ago.* How many years had I dreamed of this moment? How many times had I imagined the truth coming out? I'd pictured the way it would feel, how it would taste. Revenge is sweet to the imagination, yet so often bitter in reality.

I had only to look at Rebecca's face to know how deeply this wounded her. All these years, she'd been a pawn in this game of chess for which there seemed to be no good finish. A logical part of me had always known, just as Edward knew, that it would end this way. Giving her to one parent would mean destroying her love for the other.

"I was with her when she was dying," Rebecca sobbed. "I was holding her hand. Why didn't she tell me then? Why didn't she tell me I had a brother?"

Even if I'd been able to form the words, I wouldn't have known the right ones to deliver then. There were none. All I could do was stay there with her, hold on as she doubled forward, letting her forehead rest against our intertwined hands. I turned in the bed and stroked her hair, felt her tears on my skin, saw the wounded little girl who'd watched her belongings being moved from the house on Blue Sky Hill all those years ago. Edward's daughter. My daughter. Our daughter.

The thought slipped through my mind, painted something warm and new over me, until my heart took on the color, too. For so long, Rebecca had been a shadow in our lives, a regret, a casualty of war, a loss my husband felt but didn't speak of, a child to whom I felt obligated. An obligation. That's what Rebecca had always been to me. Now I had become an obligation to her, and that was as much as I'd dared envision. I'd hoped she would take care of Edward, of Teddy, even me, out of a sense of duty to family. But now I touched upon a startling possibility, an awakening of something I'd never imagined, never been bold enough to fully realize.

I felt a sense of love for Rebecca. It grew in the part of me that loved Teddy, that loved Edward. It was a small and tender thing, like a tiny seedling just stretching above the earth. I curled my body to the side and held her while she wept. When she was cried out, I stroked her hair and shushed her as if she were a child.

Finally, she grew embarrassed, sat up and apologized. I shushed her again and held her hand.

"It's been a . . . strange day." Her voice was hoarse, her face flushed and tear-streaked.

"Yes," I agreed.

She checked her watch, seemed surprised by the time. "I'd better head home before Ifeoma leaves for work."

"Okay." I caught her gaze and tried to smile, then nudged her fingers. Her face was a mask of sadness, as if she'd lost her mother all over again.

Her expression softened, became tender. "Thanks for telling me the truth. It . . . I needed to know."

New words came to my mind, something we'd practiced today in speech therapy. "Lovvv you."

Her eyes welled again, and she pushed them closed, her mouth trembling with emotion.

The cell phone rang in her purse. Rubbing her cheeks, she picked it up, checked to see who was calling, then put the phone away. "I can't talk to him right now," she murmured. I wasn't certain whether she was speaking to herself or to me. She wiped her eyes, then stepped away from the bed, crossed her arms and rubbed her hands up and down them. "I'm sorry. That summer I wouldn't come . . . when I was supposed to. I'm sorry I didn't come."

"No," I soothed. "No. No." *There's no place here for regret.*

Her phone rang again. She checked the caller, cleared her throat, and answered without putting it to her ear.

Ifeoma was on the other end. Her voice echoed through the speakerphone, deep and resonant. "Missus? It is time for me to depart to work, but—"

"I'm on my way home." Rebecca checked her watch again. "If you need to leave, go ahead. Is everything all right with my father and Teddy?"

"Yes . . ." Ifeoma's answer was tentative, unfinished. "Mr. Parker is asleep, and Teddy is about his work in the garden house, but . . . a man has arrived, and he has asked if I am the current resident of the home. He demands that I must sign a legal paper."

Rebecca regarded the phone with a puzzled expression. "What kind of paper? Did he say what it's about?"

"He says to me that the house has been sold by the owner, and we must vacate immediately."

"What!" Rebecca squinted at the screen. She turned off the speaker and pressed the phone to her ear. "Ifeoma, tell him that's not possible. He has the wrong address."

Straining toward her, I tried to hear the reply, but I could only make out the increasingly rapid cadence of Ifeoma's voice, and then Rebecca's replies. "Well, that's not possible, he . . . Let me talk to him. . . ."

Ifeoma replied again.

"All right, then tell him I'll be home in twenty minutes. Ifeoma? Ifeoma? Can you still hear me? Don't sign *anything*." Dropping the phone into her purse, Rebecca spun around and hurried toward the door. Before crossing the threshold, she held a pacifying hand palm out in my direction. "Don't worry. I'm sure it's all a mistake."

Then she was gone, and I was left behind, realizing that my grim premonition that morning might have been correct, after all.

CHAPTER 25

Rebecca Macklin

As I fought to make my way home through rush-hour traffic, the events of the day collided around me, flashing past like the bright white slashes of a meteor shower, rapid and random, temporarily blinding.

A man has arrived . . .

Legal paper . . .

The house has been sold by the owner . . .

Is Teddy my half brother?

Did my mother know? Did she keep it from him?

Might you be pregnant, missus . . . ?

The house . . . pregnant . . . I want the truth . . .

I felt myself floating in space, whirling through a vacuous place where there was nothing solid to grasp. *This can't be happening. All of this can't be happening at once.* A nervous sweat broke over my skin, made my heart race, and stole my breath as traffic backed up under a highway on-ramp.

Teddy's your brother. He's your brother.

I hadn't asked for this responsibility. I hadn't asked for an aging house, my father, Teddy, and Hanna Beth to care for. I hadn't asked for a potential pregnancy, years after we thought we were done having our family, when the future of my marriage was uncertain.

I began counting the weeks as the car inched forward. How long since my last period? How long? It was the week of Macey's regionals. A Saturday. I pulled out my DayMinder, flipped backward through time. Seven weeks ago, almost eight.

Reality struck me like a painful blow to the stomach. I was never three weeks late. I was never a week late. Give or take a day, two, maybe three, my body operated like clockwork.

It could be stress. . . . I knew better, of course. Our life was *always* stress-filled, in hyperdrive, all-out, all the time. The last few years of dealing with my mother's lupus had been nothing but stressful. Yet I'd never once skipped a cycle. I'd never even been significantly late.

Ahead, traffic ground to a halt as a train crawled by. Impulsively, I pulled off to the right, bumped along the shoulder to a Mom-and-Pop pharmacy, hurried in, grabbed a pregnancy test from the shelf, felt silly paying for it. Back in the car, I wrapped the sack around it so the label wouldn't show though. Traffic was moving again by the time I pulled out. Inching toward Vista Street, I tried to focus on the situation at the house.

When I finally pulled into the driveway, Ifeoma was pacing back and forth on the front walk, impatient to leave for work. There was no other car, no stranger with legal papers.

Ifeoma, normally unflappable, was rattled. She rushed to me as I stepped out. "Please, missus. I was afraid. I signed what he instructed me to. He said I must. He said to me, 'This is not your problem. You should not bring trouble upon yourself for the people who live in this big house. They do not own this big house. You should not lose your permit to work in order to defend these people. They would not do the same for you.' He said, 'You are a guest in this country. If you do not cooperate with the court, the court will send you back to your own country.' "

Anger boiled hot inside me. I wanted to get in my car, find the man who'd coerced Ifeoma into cooperating, and ram the papers down his throat. How many times had I defended clients who, because of their immigrant status, because of a lack of knowledge of the U.S. legal system, were forced into making dangerous decisions? Now, when the issue landed on my doorstep, I wasn't there to handle it. "He can't have you sent back, Ifeoma. Justice of the Peace Court and Immigration Court are two completely different things. He was just trying to force you to sign for delivery of the eviction notice." My body, tense and prepared for confrontation a moment ago, went limp and numb. There was nothing to do now but look at the papers, and try to make some sense of them. It was almost five on a Friday afternoon. No doubt, the J.P. Office wouldn't be answering phones until Monday. "Where are the papers?"

"On the table in the front entrance." Ifeoma's expression moved from fear to anger. Tightening her fists at her sides, she glared down the street. "Please accept my apologies for my foolishness, missus. I was in consideration of my son. There is no life for us in Ghana."

"I understand. It's not your fault. I'll take care of it. Are my father and Teddy all right?"

"Teddy and your father are watching a television program. They do not know of the man. I placed the papers inside, and I awaited your arrival."

"Okay." I felt the weight of the eviction notice, the pregnancy test, everything. I wanted to be alone, to think. "You can go on to work now. Thanks for waiting."

She apologized again, then hurried toward her car, already late. I went into the house quietly and took the envelope from the table, then tucked it under my arm with the pharmacy bag and the bank folder into which I'd hastily scooped the contents of my father's safe-deposit box before rushing out of the bank to confront Hanna Beth.

I walked silently up the stairs. Alone in my bedroom, I laid all three on the bed, stood staring at them, trying to decide which to open first.

None of them. None. . . .

Finally, I picked up the envelope, pulled the delivery slip off the front, sat on the edge of the bed and took out the papers. Leafing through the stack, I tried to make sense of the contents—notice of eviction, foreclosure paperwork, an official-looking document in which an LMK Limited, Inc., claimed to have legal ownership of my father's house. Who was behind LMK Limited? My father had been transferring money to the company regularly—making investments? He'd always been known to lightly invest in various speculative drilling projects. Had he made some sort of bad investment with LMK Limited? Surely he wouldn't have offered the house as collateral in some sort of business deal. The contents of the safe-deposit box made no mention of LMK Limited. There was a folder detailing some of his investments and a letter from a local law office—something to do with my father's interests in Blue Sky Real Estate Trust—but I'd only given it a cursory glance.

What if my father didn't know LMK Limited existed? What if he'd never arranged for money to be funneled from his checking account into LMK? What if someone else had made those arrangements without his knowledge? Kay-Kay, Kenita Kendal? If she could siphon money from my father's checking account, what else could she do? Convince him to sign over ownership of the house? Take everything he had?

It *was* possible. Of course, it was possible. In fact, my father, Hanna Beth, and Teddy were perfect targets. What would have happened if I hadn't come to town? Trapped in the nursing home, Hanna Beth would have no knowledge of events taking place at the house. My father and Teddy could be evicted, perhaps turned over to Social Services. No one would ever know the difference.

Kenita Kendal could walk away a wealthy woman. . . .

Over my dead body. No way would I allow this to happen to my family.

Family. The thought was surprisingly concrete, startlingly real. Since my mother's death, family had included only Kyle's relatives, myself, and Macey—a tiny group of kin with no biological ties remaining on my side of the genetic tree. Now, I belonged once again to the Parker family, whose history was rooted in this house on Blue Sky Hill.

If Kay-Kay was behind the eviction notice, she was about to find out that the Parkers didn't give up without a fight. We'd file charges, fight this thing in court all the way to the end, if we had to. The first order of business was to more closely examine the papers from the safe-deposit box—study every scrap, see what clues my father had left for me.

Standing up, I tossed the eviction notice onto the bed. The pharmacy bag slid off, spilled open. *Sixty-second result!* the package touted. In sixty seconds, I could know for certain, rule out the possibility and concentrate on the immediate threat of the eviction.

I picked up the pregnancy test, read the instructions as I walked to the bathroom. *Over ninety-nine percent accuracy in less than sixty seconds. One line, not pregnant. Two lines, pregnant. Easy-to-read results. . . .*

Why wait? the box said. I stared at the words as I closed the bathroom door, performed the test, set it atop the box and stared at the indicator, uncertain of what to hope for.

I'm overreacting. This is silly. I'm overreacting.

What would I do if it was positive? Would I tell Kyle? When? Before confronting him about Susan Sewell? After? What was the proper order?

There was nothing proper about a pregnancy in this situation. Nothing. I couldn't even wrap my mind around the idea, couldn't picture myself showing up at the kindergarten door, one of those perimenopausal moms the twenty-somethings looked to for advice. Macey would be in high school, a sophomore by the time this baby entered first grade. What in the world would Macey say if I told her there was a baby on board? For so long, she'd been the only one.

How could I bring a child into our life? Our crazy, mixed-up, disintegrating situation didn't even allow time for the three of us, and now included responsibility for the care of my father, Hanna Beth, and Teddy. . . .

I couldn't possibly be pregnant.

I couldn't be.

Pregnant.

My head swirled as the results took shape on the test strip. Faint, at first. One line, then two, the second wavy and pale, as if the test kit were toying with the idea.

I wished the second line away, closed my eyes. *No. No. No.*

I heard Mary and her boys come in downstairs. My hands jerked self-consciously toward the test, my heart raced, and I glanced toward the door like a teenager smoking in the bathroom.

Swallowing the acidic, pulsating lump in my throat, I turned back, met myself in the mirror—tired hazel eyes and sallow skin from so many nights of not sleeping. Worry lines around the corners, still faint, but in a few years I'd either have to resign myself to aging or to having those treated. In Southern California, plastic surgery is always on the leading edge, a socially acceptable topic of conversation.

I'll get a face-lift between diaper changes . . .

The idea pushed a painful, sardonic laugh past the lump in my throat.

Stop, just stop.

Bracing my hands on the counter, I turned my gaze downward, past the ornate gold mirror frame, past the black and white octagon tile backsplash, past the clamshell-shaped sink, to the right, to the right, to the right, until the test came into view. I stood staring at it, feeling the room, the house, the world spinning around me, whirling, whirling, until I couldn't keep my balance. An oozing blackness

closed in, tightened around the corners of my vision. I tried to blink
it away, dimly felt myself reeling backward, floating like the leaf in
the Japanese garden, twirling, falling. I heard myself crash against the
cabinets, felt the slight stab of pain as my head hit the counter, and
then, mercifully, everything was quiet. I let the breath go out of my
lungs, and sank into silence.

I awoke amid softness, lying on something tilted, so that my body
leaned in one direction. Blinking my eyes open, I took in the blurry
image of the dragonfly light, the bulb pushing a painful brightness
through the bits of colored glass. Outside the window, the sun had
descended behind the pecan trees. Teddy was sitting on the edge of
the bed, his weight pressing down the mattress on one side.

"Hieee, A-becca," he whispered, then called toward the door.
"She wakin' up!"

I heard Mary enter the room. Bending over the bed, she looked
into my eyes, first one, then the other. "Do you feel all right? I called
Dr. Barnhill. He said we should probably bring you to the emergency
room so they could check you out. You could have a concussion. You
hit the floor pretty hard."

The floor, I thought. *The floor . . . I hit the floor? What floor?* Blinking again, I tried to get my bearings.

"Bonked your head," Teddy offered. "Me and Brandon gone get
my hun-erd fit-ty-two cars, and boom!" Wheeling his hands outward,
he imitated the sound traveling through the house.

"We heard it in the bathroom and went and got Mama," Brandon added from the doorway. Brandon, who often translated Brady's
sentences, had developed a habit of translating for Teddy, as well.

"Boys," Mary scolded. "Downstairs. Now." She turned back to
me apologetically. "We should probably go get you checked out." I
felt a stab of pain as she parted the hair on my left temple. "No."

I moved to sit up. Head reeling, I sank back against the pillows. "Just . . . just let me wait . . . a minute." Laying a hand over my eyes, I tried to think, tried to put together the chain of events that had left me on the bathroom floor. Did I get sick to my stomach again? I was sick in the morning. . . .

"Ifeoma called from work and told me what happened this afternoon." Mary's voice seemed far away. I wished she would be quiet so I could concentrate. "I know you must be upset . . . about the house, I mean. It has to be a mistake. Mr. Parker wouldn't sell this house. He loves it. He's always talking about growing up here, and showing Brady and Brandon little secret places where he liked to play. He'd never sell this house. It's a mistake, isn't it?"

The house . . . the house. . . .

I felt Teddy shift beside me, turn toward Mary. "This Daddy Ed house, Mary. Daddy Ed house."

Mary's look of apprehension brought everything back in a rush. The computer, the secret drawer in the gray metal desk, the safe-deposit box, the visit to Hanna Beth's room, the truth about Teddy, the truth about my mother, the house. "The papers . . ." I'd left the eviction papers on the bed.

"I put them on the desk." Mary pointed.

The papers . . . the pregnancy test. The pregnancy test was still on the bathroom counter. I sat up, turned toward the door, tried to swing my legs around, but Teddy was in the way.

"I cleaned up in the bathroom." Mary averted her gaze, embarrassed, then laid a hand on Teddy's shoulder. "I think she's all right now, Teddy. I'll stay with her another minute or two if you'll go down and watch the boys for me."

Teddy pressed his lips together in a rare frown, the bottom one pursing out. "You ohh-kay, A-becca?"

"I'm all right, Teddy."

He blinked hard, his eyes growing moist.

"I'm all right, Teddy," I said, a bit more emphatically. "I just . . . slipped on the tile. It's a good thing you were there to pick me up."

Normally, the comment would have won a honk-laugh, or at least one of his broad grins, but his lips trembled downward instead. "Don't go way like Mama, A-becca. Don't go way like Mama."

My heart constricted, fell into his worried gaze. Finding me crumpled on the floor must have been like finding Hanna Beth the day of her stroke. "I'm not going away, Teddy." I reached out and hugged him to me and was filled with a rush of love that was deep, instinctive, warm like his body against mine. Teddy, my brother, who knew how to nurture fragile things, to believe in the potential of tiny seeds. "I'm not going anywhere."

"You a good girl, A-becca," Teddy sniffled.

"I love you, Teddy," I said, and I felt the words down deep.

The embrace ended as spontaneously as it began, and Teddy left to go entertain the boys.

Mary picked up a damp washcloth from the nightstand and folded it absently, listening as Teddy disappeared down the hall. "I'm sorry he got so scared. He cares about you a lot."

"I know he does."

Mary turned her attention back to the washcloth, unfolded it, then folded it again, as if she had something on her mind but was debating whether to say it. "You're lucky . . . to have a family, I mean. I know it seems like a lot to handle right now, but you're lucky."

I realized I didn't know much about Mary, except that she and her husband had recently split. Watching her, I'd tried to imagine being in her shoes, left alone with two young children, ongoing expenses, medical bills, day-care charges, and a nurse's aide job that probably didn't pay nearly enough to cover everything. Another reality struck me as she shook out the washcloth and twisted it around her finger. My father, Hanna Beth, and Teddy weren't the only ones dependent on this house. Mary's future, at least for now, was wrapped up here, too. It was becoming increasingly clear that she and the boys didn't have anywhere else to go.

"Don't worry about the eviction papers," I said. "There's no way anyone's getting this house. You'll still have a job here for however long you want it."

The nervous movement of her hands stopped. "Don't feel like you have to . . . I know you think we're desperate." Cheeks reddening, she fluttered a glance my way.

"That has nothing to do with it. You're wonderful with my father. Teddy adores the boys and you know Hanna Beth loves you. We'll make it work, all right?"

Her lips parted in a long, slow sigh. "It feels good to be someplace like this—around a family, I mean. It's been just Joshua and me since I got pregnant with Brandon. I keep thinking Joshua will come back, and things'll be easier. He loves us . . . it just . . . it was harder than he thought it would be, leaving community, getting a place to live, trying to pay for everything. You don't learn how to do any of those things in community."

"In community?" I repeated, sensing that we might be entering a long discussion for which I didn't have time. Even so, I sat waiting for Mary's answer.

"In community, everyone lives and works together—like a family, kind of. We have separate houses, but they're all part of the community. The believers raise pecans and organic crops, operate a gristmill and produce whole-grain flour, do handmade crafts and things like that. It's all for sale in the store. People come off the highway to buy things, and then the store supports the community."

"Like a commune?" I felt as if we'd entered an episode of *48 Hours*, an exposé on strange, alternative ways of living.

Mary drew back at the word. "They don't call it that. Members are free to come and go. Joshua and I left"—snapping her lips closed, she swallowed hard, thought carefully about her next words—"before Brandon came."

"Do people ever go back?"

"I can't go back." A flush painted Mary's cheeks, and she tilted her face away. "It wouldn't be a good place for me, or the boys."

"Did your husband go back?"

"I don't know," she admitted. "I don't think so. The apartment rent came due, and then he was just . . . gone. He left the van with the keys in it and a note that said he was sorry he'd messed up our lives." Her gaze lifted, met mine, and I felt the weight of yet another crushing set of expectations, another complicated mishmash of needs.

"I'm sorry," I muttered, shuddering at this glimpse into Mary's background. It was a wonder she seemed so well adjusted.

"Other things happen in community," she added simply. "I don't want Brandon and Brady to know those things. That's why I can't go back."

"You won't have to," I promised. "We'll find a way."

Mary nodded and turned to leave. "Thanks, Mrs. Macklin. If I can do anything to help, just tell me."

"Mary?" I stopped her before she could get out the door.

"Yes?"

"What you saw in the bathroom . . ." The heat of embarrassment rushed over me. "I don't want anyone to know."

Inclining her head, she considered me for a moment. "It's not my business to tell anyone."

"It's just . . . it wasn't planned."

Mary nodded again, her ear turning to the sound of Brandon and Brady coming up the stairs on all fours, Teddy thumping behind them. From somewhere in the living room, my father hollered, "What's that? Someone's turned loose a pack of elephants in my house again. They'd better not come stick their trunks in my popcorn bowl."

The boys squealed, and the ruckus receded down the stairs.

Mary turned back to me. "Brandon wasn't planned. When I did the pregnancy test, I sat on the bathroom floor and cried for two hours."

Raking the hair away from my face, I let my head fall back. "Yeah."

Laughter from the living room echoed up the stairs.

Mary smiled slightly. "The funny thing is that now, even with all that's happened, there are things I'd change, but my little boy isn't one of them. Every time he brings me something he found in the yard, or when I watch him sleeping at night, I think that if it hadn't happened when it did, he wouldn't be who he is. He wouldn't be my Brandon."

I sat staring at the lengthening shadows on the ceiling as Mary's footsteps disappeared down the hall. Through the floor, I heard the vibrations of the children's laughter, my father's voice, Teddy's reply. The sounds of family.

I picked up my phone from the nightstand and dialed Kyle's cell. My heart rose into my throat before the first ring. Pulling the phone away from my ear, I considered hanging up, then pressed it to my ear again, and waited. When he answered, I couldn't think of anything to say at first.

"Rebecca?" His voice floated through the ether.

"Yes . . . sorry. I was distracted." In my mind, words and thoughts whirled on an invisible wind of fear. Taking a deep breath, I tried to bring everything into focus.

"Rebecca?"

"I need you to come here, Kyle." The request was out of my mouth before I had time to consider the ramifications. I couldn't tell him about the pregnancy long-distance on the phone. I needed him here, to help sort out the situation with the house, stop the eviction order, file injunctions, whatever it took. Kyle would know what to do.

If he were here, would I be able to say the things that hovered unspoken?

"Come again?" Kyle was noticeably stunned.

"Something's happened." The next thing I knew, I was rushing through the story of the desk, the computer, the safe-deposit box, my conversation with Hanna Beth, the eviction order. Strangely enough, those were the easy things to discuss. It felt good to share the day with him, to unload everything while he listened.

"All right, read me the paperwork," he said, when I finished. "Give me everything you've got. I can work on it from my office and hire someone in Dallas to handle the legal legwork locally."

"I need you here, Kyle." I felt my heart sinking, the warmth inside me cooling.

"Rebecca, I can't just drop everything and wing off to Texas."

You'd do it for a client. You'd do it for a client in a heartbeat. "It's the weekend, Kyle. The office is closed."

"What about Macey?" Kyle was grasping at straws. Macey never entered into his plans for travel. Was he using her as an excuse, a reason not to leave California—not to leave whoever was in California?

"Bring Macey. It's time she met her grandfather. If the worst happens with this eviction notice, if we have to move him, there's no telling how well he'll do in a new location. I want her to see him the way he is now, and I want her to see the house. I just . . ." Emotion choked the words, and I cleared it from my throat. "I need both of you here, Kyle. I just . . . need you here." I felt weak and pathetic, begging for his attention.

What if he won't come? a voice whispered in my ear. *If he refuses, what then?* I waited for his answer, breathless, rigid, struggling to prepare myself for the worst. If he wouldn't come when I needed him most, what hope was there for the future?

"We'll leave in the morning," he said, and everything inside me went limp, exhausted by the day.

"Thanks," I said, my throat clogged with a confusing mix of emotions. For a moment, neither of us spoke.

"Rebecca?" Kyle said finally. "Is everything all right?"

Is everything all right? Is it? Such a simple question, so hard to answer. "I don't know," I said, and even though I couldn't bring myself to address anything that really mattered, I wanted to keep him on the phone. "How was Macey's day?"

"Pretty good, it sounds like." He seemed content not to delve into the deeper meanings of *I don't know*. In a way, that disappointed me. "Mace's outside picking leaves for a science project. She had some kind of minor girl trauma at school today—something about 'I'm her friend, but I'm not your friend. . . .' She can probably tell you much better than I can. Want me to go get her?"

"No," I said. "You can just give me the short version."

"You want *me* to tell you about Macey's girl trauma?"

"Yeah," I said. "I just need to . . . talk for a while, okay?" Letting my eyes fall closed, I leaned against the headboard, let the cool wood soothe my skin.

"All right," Kyle answered tentatively, then launched into a reluctant description of Macey's on-again, off-again friendship.

I sat and listened, relaxing in the comfortable humdrum of fourth-grade social trauma. By tomorrow, it would all be over and the girls would move on to something new, as always.

My call waiting started beeping as Kyle finished. "I have a call coming in," I admitted. "I'd better go."

"Sounds good. I'll let you know once we've booked a flight."

We exchanged good nights and I answered the other line. It was Ifeoma, calling to apologize again for signing the foreclosure paperwork and to let me know that she'd seen Hanna Beth's name on the nursing center's birthday list for tomorrow. "I have been asked to double my shift tonight, so if you like, I would be available to purchase a card for you and bring it to her in the morning," she offered.

"Let me think about it and call you back later," I said, unable to imagine what the card would say. In view of everything that was happening, now hardly seemed like the time for a celebration.

CHAPTER 26
Hanna Beth Parker

Even though Rebecca had Ifeoma tell me I shouldn't worry about the situation with the house, I fretted about it most of the night. In spite of a sleeping medication, I was awake when Ifeoma came to my room in the morning. I was thinking of Blue Sky Hill, of the house and the garden. I imagined sitting in a patio chair, in the calm of morning, nothing to disturb the leaves and the flowers but a slight breeze.

Ifeoma was in a surprisingly good humor as she helped me into the wheelchair and took me to the bathroom to wash up. I didn't feel like going through all those ministrations, but Ifeoma was insistent.

She only smiled at me when I complained. "You must be washed and dressed by eight o'clock," she said, her rolling accent echoing against the bathroom walls, making her voice deep and resonant. "Do you not know today is your birthday, Hanna Beth Parker?"

"Umm-my bird-day." Suddenly, the morning rush made sense. Volunteers from the local hair salon, whom the staff called "the birthday ladies," came to the nursing center weekly and treated all the birthday girls to hairstyles, makeup, and manicures. While it was a sweet tradition, I wasn't in the mood today.

Ifeoma moved efficiently about her work, as if this process of washing and dressing another person were perfectly normal. "Rebecca has sent clothing for you from home. A woman should wear her favorite outfit on her birthday. I have it in my cart."

"Rebecca?" I'd expected the nursing center staff to know it was my birthday—their computer would remind them—but I hadn't thought Rebecca would be aware of it. Why would she bother with such a frivolity, considering everything going on at home? Then again, if Rebecca had time for picking out clothes to send me, perhaps I was fretting too much.

Another thought came on the heels of that one. Perhaps there was a reason I was being gussied up. Perhaps I would be entertaining some special visitors today. "Ed-ward com-eeeng?"

Ifeoma's lips twisted slyly. "It could be so."

"Teddy com-eeeng?"

"Perhaps."

The whiff of a good secret tickled my senses like a freshly baked spice cake. Edward had learned early on to double wrap my Christmas gifts. He knew I'd go peeking if I could. "Wwwhen com-eeeng?"

Ifeoma tutted her tongue against her teeth. "I cannot say." What she meant was, she *wouldn't* say. There was a twinkle in her eye. "Teddy has grown flowers for your birthday. Many, many flowers."

A shadow of guilt slid over my burgeoning curiosity. To bring the flowers here, Teddy would have to cut them. Teddy didn't like to cut his flowers. He felt sad for the plants. "Nnn-no. No flll-oors."

Ifeoma frowned at me as she hung the washcloth in the shower, then helped me towel off and dress in the blue summer pantsuit Edward had given me last year on my birthday. I didn't think I'd like the outfit when I opened it, but Edward said I looked like a vision in it. I loved it after that. I wore it often in the yard, because the thin nylon was airy and easy to wash. As Ifeoma slipped the jacket over my blouse, I took a deep breath and imagined I could smell my garden.

"It is time for you in the salon," Ifeoma said, and wheeled me down the hall to where the birthday ladies performed their magic.

As I got the treatment, the ladies giggled and joked, and told me how lovely I was. When they were finished, they turned me toward the mirror. I might have cried, but I didn't want to muss my makeup. In my own clothes, with my hair fixed and my face clean, I felt like myself again. The woman in the mirror, but for the slight sag on one side of her face, was Hanna Beth Parker. Even with the sag, she was Hanna Beth Parker.

I hugged each of the beauty ladies before they wheeled me into the commons room, where I could parade with other birthday girls, showing off the new-old me.

"Why, Birdie, look at you!" Claude was quickly at my table. "I'd offer to match you in a game of chess, but you're such a peach today, I think I wouldn't be able to keep my mind on the game."

I shook a finger at him and gave a playful *tsk-tsk*.

"Now, Birdie, you know I wasn't bein' untoward," he protested. "I understand you're a married woman." We laughed together, then sat in silence for a while, neither of us thinking of much to say.

"Things are goin' good at my house," Claude offered finally. You could always depend on Claude to come up with some way to start a conversation.

"Ummm?"

"Sure thing. We made a lot of decisions yesterday. Sure was good to spend a little time at the old place again. I almost told 'em, just leave me there in my woodshop—I wasn't comin' back here after all." His mood sobered, and he patted the arm of his wheelchair, then took a breath and straightened his shoulders, checking the front door. "Ouita Mae and Doc Barnhill think it'll do them just fine. Doc's gonna leave the old shop buildin' like it was, let all the stuff from my trains and all my old tools stay out there. He said he thought it'd be all right if my little neighbor girl wanted to bring me over there once in a while, and I could piddle with my woodworkin' stuff. He don't have time to do anythin' out there anyhow."

"Good," I said, but, really, I felt sorry for Claude. I reached out and patted his hand, which probably I shouldn't have done, because now that I was up and about, I'd discovered that the old ladies in the nursing center relished gossip.

"It's a little tough, things changin'," he admitted.

"Wee-da . . . gu-rl pooool," I said, even though by now I knew it was surely hopeless. I'd tried at least a hundred times, and I couldn't make such a complicated concept understood. By the time I finally gained enough language to accomplish it, there was no telling where Claude and Ouita Mae would be.

Claude quirked a brow at me. "No, the house don't have a pool. I don't know why you keep askin' me that, Birdie."

I huffed and rolled my eyes.

"I wasn't meaning it in a cross way," Claude said apologetically. "I might of told you the house had a pool. I forget what I'm sayin' sometimes. They changed my medicines around, though, and my mind's better. There's a wet-weather crick runnin' through the back, but no pool."

"Innn yerrr umm-mind?" I motioned to his head.

Claude grinned. "Well, there's probably a wet-weather crick in my mind, too, but I was meanin' at the house." We laughed together, and he said, "Ah, Birdie, it'll be a long day without ya."

I couldn't imagine what he was talking about. "I'mmm here."

Claude checked the door again, then smiled and nodded to steer my attention in that direction. "Happy birthday, by the way. You don't look a minute over twenty-five, twenty-six at the most."

Laughing, I pushed against the table to turn myself toward the main entrance. Rebecca was standing on the welcome mat waiting for Teddy to come through the wheelchair door with a bundle of helium balloons. He was inching up the ramp one step at a time, carefully watching to see when the door would swish open. Finally, it did, and he rushed past with the balloons, lumbering into the lobby in a clatter of stomping shoes and bouncing cellophane. Everyone turned to look.

"Happy bird-day, Mama!" Teddy's greeting burst into the room, filling the empty space. Suddenly, it felt like my birthday. I couldn't have imagined a better gift than Teddy coming through the door in a flash of bright colors.

"Ted-dy ubb-boy!"

"Happy bird-day, Mama!" Teddy said again, and a moment later, he was in my arms, his body curled over the wheelchair. I held on, and we rocked back and forth with balloons bouncing everywhere. Teddy's love filled every corner of me.

When I finally looked over Teddy's shoulder, Rebecca was sniffling and wiping her eyes. "Happy birthday, Hanna Beth," she said as Teddy stood up and presented the balloons. I couldn't clutch them well enough, so Teddy tied them around my chair.

Beside me, Claude began clapping, and pretty soon everyone in the room was cheering for me, the birthday girl. It was a bit embarrassing, but I felt like a celebrity. Teddy began singing "Happy Birthday," and everyone joined in. The administrator came out of her office and reminded us that we had several birthday girls and a birthday boy in the room. Teddy spread the balloons around, and we sang "Happy Birthday" again. I did my best to sing along. Between laughing, crying, and singing, I was out of breath by the time we were done.

Rebecca hugged me as Teddy took a balloon down the hall to a woman who was bedfast. "I'm sorry I didn't know earlier about your birthday. Ifeoma called last night to tell me. We do have a little surprise for you, though."

"So sssweet." I looked around, expecting that perhaps now they would bring Edward in the door as my surprise, but I didn't see him.

"Are you ready for a little trip?" Rebecca leaned close to my ear, as if she had a secret. "We're busting you out of here."

I jerked back against the chair. "Wwwhat?"

"We're busting you out for the day," she repeated, smiling broadly. "Your walking papers are in the works. Just as soon as Dr. Barnhill shows up, we'll be headed home."

"We gone get party, Mama," Teddy added, crossing the room. "Someone comin' on air-pane." Eyes flying wide, he slapped a hand over his mouth. "Oop! Don' tell." He snickered behind his hand, and I tried to imagine what he could possibly be talking about. Who would be flying in on an airplane to see me?

Dr. Barnhill came in the front door and joined us before I could ask any questions.

Claude quickly observed that Ouita Mae wasn't with him. In spite of her lack of interest in Claude, he was certainly interested in her. "Where'd you leave your grandmother at, Doc?"

Dr. Barnhill cast a chagrinned look over his shoulder. "She's out there taking cuttings off the bushes. She wants to try to root them at your place. I thought I'd better come in before we got arrested. She'll be along in a minute."

"That gal's got a mind of her own," Claude observed.

"She does that," the doctor agreed, then turned his attention to me. "So, you're headed for your first home visit a little early."

"Yes," I said, and felt a smile all over my body.

My jubilation was short-lived. "Gonna be lonesome around here," Claude commented, and made an effort to smile through the melancholy, so as not to rain on my parade. "I'll have to show Herb my book some more. I think he likes it when I do that."

Poor Claude, I thought. Herb didn't even know he was there. An idea formed in my head so suddenly it was startling. "Yerrr book," I said, and patted the table, then waved toward his room. "Yerrr book." I waved empathically again.

Claude's eyebrows knotted as he followed the motions, then scanned the circle of people around us. "I think they already seen my book."

"Yer book," I insisted, slapping the table so loudly the domino players in the corner turned to look.

Rebecca frowned at me. She probably didn't want Claude to get started on one of his stories. "I don't think . . ."

I slapped the table again, again, again, fully determined. Any minute now, Ouita Mae would come in the door, and we'd be all together in one place. All I needed was the picture of the boy on the yellow horse. "Yerrr book."

Claude pedaled his wheelchair backward. "Well . . . I can go get it, if ya really want. . . ."

"Yesss." I nodded, and he turned his chair toward the hallway with a confounded look.

Rebecca scratched the back of her head, squinting as Claude disappeared down the corridor, and Dr. Barnhill began giving instructions for my care and medication. I barely heard the conversation. I kept watching the hallway, willing Claude to come back.

Hurry up, hurry up, I thought, as the conversation began winding down. Ouita Mae strolled in the door, the basket on her walker filled with cuttings she'd pilfered from the front bushes. Dr. Barnhill blanched, seeming eager to finish the conversation so that he could usher Ouita Mae and her cuttings out of the building. *"Grandma,"* he complained when she started grooming the cuttings and laying cast-off pieces on the table.

"Oh, for heaven's sake," she answered. "All the extra work you put in here, I think we can take a few cuttings. It doesn't hurt the bushes any. I'll need some water to put them in."

"There's a cup in the car. Let's go see Miss Hanna Beth out, and grab the cup." He used his foot to nudge Ouita Mae's walker toward the front door.

I reached out and caught her arm. "No."

"Well, heaven's sake." She looked down at me and smiled. "You'd think a birthday girl headed home for a visit would be in more of a hurry than that. Now, don't you let us slow you down. I need to get these plants in some water, anyhow." She turned to her grandson with a purposeful look. "I'll walk Hanna Beth out and wait on the bench."

Dr. Barnhill nodded indulgently. "I'm not sure why I bother to make plans. . . ."

"Oh, hush up, now," Ouita Mae chided. "I can still turn you over my knee, young man."

Dr. Barnhill shook his head.

"Better get on, Hanna Beth," Ouita Mae urged. "You don't want to spend your birthday sitting here."

"Wwwait!" I said, but Ouita Mae just shrugged helplessly and turned her walker from the table. "Come on, sweetie. You've got a big day ahead of you." She glanced at Rebecca and smiled as Rebecca took my wheelchair handles and pulled me back.

I looked down the hall, checking for Claude. "Wwwait," I said again.

"We'd better get going, Hanna Beth," Rebecca protested gently.

"We gone home, Mama!" Teddy cheered.

Suddenly desperate, I pitched forward, grabbed Ouita Mae's walker with one hand. I expected the wheelchair belt to stop me, but the buckle snapped open, and I was tumbling toward the floor. Flailing my free arm, I caught a chair. It buckled under my weight and hit the tiles with a resounding clang.

"Hanna Beth!" Rebecca jumped forward to grab me.

"Mama, no!" Teddy joined her, the two of them holding me suspended, my legs tangled in the footrests, my hand clutching Ouita Mae's walker. The moment seemed to stretch out forever. I imagined myself falling, breaking a hip, a leg.

"We've got you." Rebecca was breathless. "Let go. We've got you."

I held on, my heart pounding, my pulse racing, a fine sweat

breaking over my skin. *You'll ruin your makeup.* The thought seemed comical, considering. In the slice of open air between Teddy and Rebecca, I could see Claude coming up the hall. Catching sight of the commotion, he sped up, pulling his chair across the floor in double time.

Hurry, I thought as someone's hand closed over mine, loosening my grip on the walker. After this display, they'd probably revoke my furlough and tie me to a bed.

"Mama, leg-go," Teddy pleaded.

"Hanna Beth . . ." Rebecca's arms were around my middle, trying to lift me back into the wheelchair.

"Everyone hold on a minute," I heard Dr. Barnhill right behind my ear. His arms encircled me. "All right, Hanna Beth. I'm going to lift you back into the chair now. It's all right. Just let go of the walker."

I held on, but my hand was sweaty. Someone was prying my fingers, pulling me loose inch by inch.

"What in tarnation?" I heard Claude say just as my grip failed, sending all of us stumbling backward. Teddy caught Rebecca, and Dr. Barnhill ended up sprawled over my chair and me.

"Good gravy!" Ouita Mae gasped, bumping her walker into Claude's chair. "What in the name a Pete?" She turned around and gave Claude an irritated look for being in the way.

Claude apologized and started backing up.

Dr. Barnhill buckled me into my seat again. "No more sudden maneuvers, young lady," he ordered, then brushed the hair out of his face as he turned to Rebecca. "Looks like we'd better get this birthday girl to the car before she tries a handspring."

Catching her breath, Rebecca moved behind my chair to take the handles, but Teddy was quicker, since he never missed the chance to operate anything with wheels. "I gone push Mama." Laying claim to the handles and me, he maneuvered around the fallen chair.

"Ate!" The word was out of my mouth before I had time to form it clearly. "Wwwait! Wwwait!"

"Hanna Beth, what in the world has got into you?" Ouita Mae gave me a frown of complete consternation. "You're finally goin' to your house, darlin'. It's all right."

"Sssee Cl-ud!" I slapped the table, then swirled my hand in the air, trying to bring Claude closer. It was now or never. No telling when, or if, I'd ever have the two of them in one place again. "Ubbb-book." I pounded the tabletop again. "Yer ubbb-book."

Rubbing his stubbly gray chin, Claude flushed, suddenly bashful of all things. "I don't think anyone wants to see my book right this minute, Birdie. You go on, now. You have a big birthday."

"Ubbb-book!"

"Now, Birdie . . ."

"Ubbb-book!" My voice reverberated around the room, so that everyone froze. "Hhh-here."

Claude drew back like he thought I might slap him. "Well-well-well, all right." He pedaled forward a few steps and set the book on the table.

"Ummm-ulll," I tried, but my heart was beating fast, my mind racing. I couldn't think clearly, couldn't piece the words together. Below the picture of the mules was the one of the boy on the yellow horse. I slid my hand to the book, pushed open the cover, nodded over my shoulder at Ouita Mae. "Ulll-look, Www-eeda. See?" Teddy, now interested in the pictures, leaned over to help me turn the pages. The photos in front were the most recent—his house, various cars, vacations, his wife, a picnic with neighborhood kids, Claude standing in his vegetable garden, proudly holding a bushel basket of freshly picked corn.

"Yup, that's a real nice book," Ouita Mae said obligingly. "I bet a lot of the folks here would enjoy lookin' at it, Hanna Beth, but you better get on to your birthday."

"Ulll-look . . . look," I insisted, the words coming more easily now.

"All right, hon." Ouita Mae sighed. She passed a glance at Claude, and he shrugged as if he were apologizing for taking up her time.

I couldn't find the picture of the white mules. Perhaps this was the wrong book. Perhaps he had more than one. "Ummm-ools . . . mmmm-ools." *Please, God, if you never give me another grand accomplishment in my life, let me have this little one. Let me help them understand, then go home and have my birthday. And take care of Teddy. That's all I ask. Just three things.* "Mmm . . .ools."

"Oh, them old mules?" Claude laughed, the realization finally striking him. "You want me to show that picture of the mules?"

"Yes!" I gasped. *Finally.*

"It's back here." Claude flipped to the end of the book. "Some of them last pictures fell out the other day, and I hadn't gone after any tape to put 'em back. Can't filch tape off the bulletin board." He winked at me.

Squinting through her bifocals, Ouita Mae leaned closer to the book, showing some interest. Overhead, everyone else did too. "She knows my daddy raised horses," Ouita Mae said, trying to put some method to my madness about Claude's book and the pictures.

"Oh," Rebecca murmured, moving around the table. Pressing her hands against her thighs, she said, "Hanna Beth, we really need get out of everyone's way." She was trying her best to be patient, but I could tell she was frustrated with the delays. As usual, she looked like she hadn't slept a wink all night and had been rushing all day. She probably thought I wasn't the least bit grateful for the birthday plans she'd made.

"Yes," I said, and held up a finger. *One more moment. Just one.* Claude was pulling out the picture of the white mules from beneath the endpaper in the back of the book. The picture was loose, no longer taped to the page with the yellow horse.

"Here's them old mules," Claude said. "My daddy won many a contest with them two. Funny thing was, one was blind, and one was deaf. . . ."

Claude prattled on about the mules, and Ouita Mae turned the picture around, then traced the edge with her finger.

"I think one of your pictures has fallen, old rooster." Ifeoma was suddenly above us. "I have discovered it in the corridor, just now." On the table, she laid the faded sepia photo of the smiling young cowboy on the tall yellow horse.

Ouita Mae touched the face of the boy, blinked hard. Nudging her glasses higher onto her nose, she stared deep into the image.

Claude went on with his story. "Darned near kilt my daddy to have to sell that team. He couldn't even do it hisself. He sent me off to the auction sale with 'em. Said he didn't want to know where they went, nor what happened after. My sister was down with polio, and he knew them mules would bring the money we needed, and that was that. I never did know what become of the mules, but many was the time I thought about the day of that auction sale. It's funny how there's whole parts of your life you don't remember, and then there'll be a day where every moment's as clear as if you'd just lived it."

A tear traced the creases of Ouita Mae's cheek, trickled downward, like the beginnings of a river coming to life again after a long dry season. "I think we've met before," she whispered, turning from the picture to Claude, from the boy to the man. "I think we met a long, long time ago. Do you remember a girl riding a brown and white paint horse? You gave her a first kiss out behind the barn."

Claude looked up, took in her expression, blinked in confusion, in surprise and disbelief.

"The girl didn't tell another soul about that kiss," she whispered. "Except the white mules who lived on the lane by her school. She often fed them carrots, so they wouldn't reveal her secret."

Claude's eyes widened, grew moist. His lips parted, trembled upward, and all at once, I knew he saw the girl from long ago.

I patted Teddy's hand and motioned for him to move me back from the table. Neither Claude nor Ouita Mae seemed to notice as we slipped away with Dr. Barnhill, leaving them alone to finish the story that had been interrupted so many years ago. They didn't need me any longer, and besides, I was on my way home.

CHAPTER 27

Rebecca Macklin

I was determined that no matter what happened afterward, we would give Hanna Beth a perfect birthday. She would be home with my father and Teddy, and for the first time in a long while the house on Blue Sky Hill would be filled with family. Even if this was the last good day, the only good day before the world caved in around us, I wanted our family to have that much.

Perhaps throwing it all together—readying the garden, picking up a cake, contacting Dr. Barnhill about taking Hanna Beth home for her birthday, stopping by the little white church to invite Pastor Al and any other friends or neighbors Hanna Beth might have been close to—were only desperate distractions. The idea of celebrating Hanna Beth's birthday was a tiny bright spot amid the cloud of looming reality. Planning the party felt like something manageable. Something I could do, other than wait for Kyle and Macey to arrive, wait for someone from the constable's office to show up and throw us out of the house, wait for my mind to cycle repeatedly through the unavoidable questions. Hanna Beth? The house? Teddy? My father? Kyle? Susan Sewell? The bank accounts? Kenita Kendal? Pregnancy?

None of it seemed real. Hanna Beth's party was real, a tangible accomplishment. Her expression when we told her she was going home for the day made all the effort worthwhile. Her smile was one of pure elation. As we put her in the car and drove through the city streets, she thanked me over and over, then turned her attention to noting familiar landmarks and pointing out antique roses growing in front of various houses and businesses, which, apparently, Teddy had rooted from cuttings and given away over the years.

"So goo-duh, so good!" Hanna Beth reached across the seat and held my hand, squeezed hard. "So happy birrr-day my howt."

I laughed. "You may change your mind before we actually get there. I have a few stops to make—dry cleaners, post office, grocery store for milk." In the backseat, Teddy started to say we had plenty of milk, but I quickly shushed him. "It's okay, Teddy. Your mom knows it might take *a little while* for us to get home." I shot him a pointed look in the rearview mirror, and his mouth dropped open in a silent O as he remembered the top-secret birthday plan, which included stalling Hanna Beth's arrival until a call from the house informed us that all the partygoers were in place.

Folding her hands patiently in her lap, Hanna Beth sat gazing out the window, occasionally noting flowering plants, or snorting at new condominium construction, and commenting on old buildings being converted into luxurious loft apartments.

"The neighborhood's really changing," I commented, then was immediately sorry I'd brought it up. My stomach clenched at this reminder of the eviction notice. I imagined our house on Blue Sky Hill being torn down, the old-growth trees and antique roses plowed under to make room for cookie-cutter condos or zero-lot-line mini-mansions. The idea was sickening. There had to be a way to prevent my father and Hanna Beth from being robbed of their home.

Kyle would figure out something. I might question his commitment as a husband and father, but I had no doubt about his skills as a lawyer. If a loophole existed in a real estate deal, Kyle could dig it up. He knew exactly where to look. He would find a way.

Would *we*? Was there a way for us?

I pictured Macey watching our belongings being divided, just as I had all those years ago. I imagined that kind of pain inside her, imagined it living within her like a damaged organ undergoing a slow bleed for the rest of her life. I would do almost anything to prevent that. To save her, to save this new baby. Our son. Our daughter.

Ours. In my heart, I knew I wanted to raise this baby with Kyle. I wanted the two of us to come together, to be the way we were when Macey was young. Back then it was us against the world, working together to start a business, to buy a house, to begin a family, to build a life. Seventeen years later, there was so much history between us, so many memories. How could we let it go?

Would I stay with a man who'd been unfaithful to me? If he admitted it, would I stay with him?

If he denied it, would I trust him?

Things aren't always what they seem. I looked at Hanna Beth, next to me in the seat. *She isn't what you thought she was. You could have discovered that long ago. You could have had years with her, with Dad, with Teddy, but you chose to believe the worst. You chose to be angry. You chose not to forgive. You chose the pain.*

The phone rang, vibrating against the console. The noise took a moment to register.

"Phone, phone, phone!" Teddy cheered, leaning into the space between the seats.

I flipped open the phone and answered. Macey was on the other end. "Mom, we're here." Her greeting echoed through the earpiece, then she lowered her voice. "We, like, went right to the backyard, the way you said. This place is totally awesome. I like the little greenhouse thing. Mary said I could go in it, so I'm here with the plants right now. Everybody else is ready on the patio, and Mary just went inside to wake up Grandpa Parker. She said he probably won't come out here for the party, though. He's, like, afraid of the backyard?"

"We'll see how that goes," I answered.

The plan was to give my father and Hanna Beth a moment to reunite in the privacy of the living room first, then see if he would go into the yard with her. So far, even with the new medication, he never ventured beyond the house and the garage, but he'd awakened particularly clearheaded and happy today. When I showed him the calendar and told him it was Hanna Beth's birthday, he smiled at me and said, "Of course it is. You didn't know?" He'd helped with the preparations by blowing up balloons, his hands shaking as he went through the painstaking process of tying each one, then giving them to Brandon and Brady, so they could dash out and decorate the patio furniture.

I wondered if he would enjoy Macey's company as much as he relished the companionship of Mary's boys. It would be nice for her to have another grandfather, one who had hours and hours to sit and tie balloons, play marbles on the floor, engage in domino games, or figure out how to put broken tires back on toy cars. Macey would enjoy that unqualified attention.

"So, how long until you get here?" Macey asked. I heard the greenhouse windows squeal as she cranked them open. "I can't wait to see the inside of the house. This place is so cool. Who grows all these plants and stuff?"

"I'll talk to you all about that in a little while," I answered, deliberately vague because, beside me, Hanna Beth had tuned into my end of the conversation.

" 'Kay." Macey paused. "Some more people just came. A dude in a preacher suit and a lady."

"Thanks for the update, Mace, I'd better go now." I hoped Hanna Beth couldn't hear Macey chattering on.

"Oh, sorry," Macey whispered.

"Love you," I said, as if she weren't just a few blocks away. It was hard to believe she was so close, and in just a few moments I'd have her in my arms.

"Love you, too, Mom. Hurry, okay?"

"I will."

Hanna Beth watched me suspiciously as I hung up the phone.

"What Matey say?" Teddy asked.

"She said to tell you hi," I hedged. If this conversation went on much longer, Teddy would give away the big secret we'd been working all morning to conceal. "Listen, I bet Hanna Beth is getting tired. Why don't we head on home for now, and we can do our errands later?"

"Hooo-kay," Teddy replied absently. Our gazes met in the mirror, and he clued in. "Ohhh." Slapping a hand over his mouth, he hid a conspiratorial grin. "We gone home. See Daddy Ed. Daddy Ed home all-lone. It jus' Daddy Ed."

"Right." Laughter pressed my throat and I pretended to cough. As we sat waiting to make the left turn onto Vista Street, I pointed out the freshly planted flower bed by the new boutiques. "Hey, Teddy, look at those pink flowers, aren't those beautiful?"

"Di-an-is." Teddy named the Dianthus very carefully. "Good plant. Lot sun, not too lotsa water."

"We should buy some of those." I was glad to have sidetracked the conversation to something safe.

The rest of the way home, we talked about flowers. As we passed the construction sites, Teddy rolled down the window, stuck out his arm, and hollered. From one of the upstairs windows, Rusty waved.

Hanna Beth scoffed and turned her face away from the condominiums. "More connn-dozzz," she observed sadly.

"I know," I commiserated. "I miss the old houses, especially the blue one with the gingerbread. When I was little, I always knew we were almost home when I saw the blue house."

Hanna Beth smiled. "Me, too."

We rounded the corner onto Blue Sky Hill Court, and I pointed out how well the big pecan trees were doing. The party guests had parked up the street by the garage house where the guy with the art portfolio lived. I didn't want Hanna Beth to notice the cars and get suspicious. Fortunately, she was too busy taking in the house. The trim in front was freshly painted, thanks to Sy and our construction crew, and Teddy had meticulously groomed the bushes. Compared to the way it had looked when I first arrived, the house was a showplace.

Resting a hand on the dashboard, Hanna Beth leaned closer to the car window, the light falling softly on her face, reflecting against the sparkle in her eyes. "Oh . . . hhhome," she breathed.

"Don't cry." I handed her a Sonic napkin from the stack of leftovers stuffed in the console. "You'll make your mascara run."

Hanna Beth sniffled and laughed, then tried to dab her eyes.

Popping the trunk latch, I asked Teddy to lift out the wheelchair, then I took the napkin from Hanna Beth. "Here," I whispered, leaning over to wipe away the tears. "The birthday girl should make her grand entrance looking beautiful, right?"

Hanna Beth nodded. "Hap-eee teee-rs."

"I know," I said, and then I hugged her. It felt like the most natural thing in the world. "Let's go in. There's someone waiting to see you." Outside the door, Teddy was struggling to unfold the wheelchair. I hurried around to help him, and, together, we lifted Hanna Beth out of the car. She was stronger than I'd anticipated, able to support herself partially, but, even so, it was a clumsy process. By the time we'd accomplished it, all three of us were laughing.

"Su-pi-ise!" Teddy exclaimed as the garage door opened. For a moment, I thought he'd grown overzealous about the party, but actually, he was doing a big reveal on the wheelchair ramp, which the crew had painted only yesterday. "Sy make the steps gone way, see?" Teddy added the sound of a motor and screeching brakes as he steered Hanna Beth through the garage, then hung a one-eighty and pushed her up the ramp.

"Weeee!" Hanna Beth threw her hands in the air, her head snapping backward as they topped the ramp and bounced into the cloakroom.

"We're home!" I called as we motored up the hallway. My chest fluttered with the unfettered anticipation I always felt when I heard Macey running down the stairs on Christmas morning.

When Teddy turned the corner into the living room, my father was standing in the long stream of sunlight from the windows. The sight of him took me aback. In contrast to his usual rumpled polyester pants and undershirt, he was dressed in a light gray suit. His thick silver hair, normally askew, was neatly combed, his face clean-shaven, his eyes bright and alive.

He looked like the father I remembered—a tall, strong, straight man, larger than life.

"There are my girls," he said, crossing the room. Leaning over Hanna Beth's chair, he kissed me on the cheek, then took Hanna Beth's hand, bowed forward, and brought it to his lips. "Hello, sweetheart," he whispered. "Welcome home." Still clasping her hand in his, he shared with her the tender kiss of reunion, of a life spent together, of remembrance.

Standing against the glass doors to block the view of the garden, Mary and Ifeoma smiled. Teddy circled me with his arms and crushed me in an exuberant hug. I hung on, and we rocked back and forth, my brother and I.

Something crashed outside on the patio, and Teddy jerked away, his eyes wide.

My father stood upright and moved to the side of Hanna Beth's chair, offering his elbow like a king about to escort his queen to the ball. "Come outside, my dear. You won't believe the roses this spring."

I glanced at Mary by the door, and she nodded. As Teddy pushed the wheelchair forward, Mary and Ifeoma threw open the doors, flooding the room with sunlight, the scents of early summer, the sweet perfume of honeysuckle.

Closing her eyes, Hanna Beth drew a long breath as Teddy pushed her over the threshold.

"Su-pi-ise!" Teddy's cheer broke the silence, and our small gathering of guests—Pastor Al and his church secretary, Brandon and Brady, Mary and Ifeoma, Dr. Barnhill with Ouita Mae and Claude—joined in the cheer. Kyle stepped from behind the garden house, looking slightly out of place but clapping obligingly, and Macey rushed from inside, soft tendrils of honey-colored hair floating behind her like ribbons as she hop-dashed unevenly across the lawn in her walking cast. In her hands, she carried bouquets of roses in iridescent silver wrappings. Stopping in front of Hanna Beth's chair she presented the larger bouquet to her. "Happy birthday, Grandma Parker."

Hanna Beth, still stunned, motioned her close and kissed her on the cheek. "Ma-cee," she said, smiling up at my daughter. "Hello, Ma-cee." She paused to smell the roses. "So beauuu-ti-fool."

Macey beamed.

"My heavens, that can't be Macey!" my father exclaimed. "That's too big to be Macey. Macey's no bigger than this." He leveled a palm close to his hip.

Macey rolled her eyes playfully and smiled. "I'm nine years old."

"Nine years old?" my father repeated with exaggerated amazement. "How in heaven's name did that happen?"

Macey quirked a brow, shrugging her slim shoulders upward. "I grew up."

My father laughed. "Little girls do that," he observed. Giving me a long, sideways look, he smiled, then turned back to Macey. "And, look at this, you've brought me pink roses."

Macey's nose crinkled, and she giggled, then sidestepped and held the roses out to me. "A lady had them two for one at the airport," she joked, her blue eyes rounding upward, mirroring her smile.

"Come here, you." Bending low, I lifted her and the roses into my arms, closed my eyes as she draped over my shoulders, the walking cast bumping my thigh. As she nestled her head against my cheek, I breathed in the scent of her hair, felt the warmth of her closeness, felt her sink into me like water, like a part of my body, separated and now returned. There were no words to explain the completeness of holding my daughter in my arms.

My mind opened a door, took in the soft white light of the moment. *It will be like this with the new baby,* I thought. *It'll be just like this.* The baby wasn't a line on a pregnancy test, an inconvenience, a mistake, an unwanted sea change knocking me off course at forty-something. This baby was Macey, nine years ago, a tiny hint of life, a mysterious combining of body and soul that would grow within me for only a little while, and then become separate. My son. My daughter. Macey's brother or sister.

In my arms, Macey started to wiggle. "Mom, let go," she whispered. "We have to get the cake and the presents."

Emotion welled in my chest. Swallowing hard, I lowered her to the ground, and waited for her to catch her balance on the cast. "I'll get the cake," I said. "Why don't you help Grandma Parker start opening her gifts?" Taking my bouquet from Macey's hand, I turned and slipped through the doors into the house. I needed a moment to compose myself before going on with the party.

The kitchen was quiet, save for the muffled hum of voices outside. An occasional outbreak of raucous laughter rose above the white noise, and I stood listening, enjoying the sounds of the celebration, the high-pitched giggles of Macey and the boys, the deep resonance of my father's laugh, the gravelly voice of Claude Fisher calling out to the boys, telling them which gift to give to Hanna Beth. The gifts weren't much—all of them having been purchased hastily that morning—but it wouldn't matter. The point was that this was a real birthday party, a day to remember, a day to begin a new year.

Many happy returns.

Would there be many happy returns?

What changes would this coming year bring? Would we come back here for holidays, birthdays, family celebrations?

Just focus on today, I told myself. *Just focus on this moment.*

The door opened, and I reached for the box of candles. "I'll be ready in a minute. I just need to finish the cake."

"Don't rush. The little boys made a mud pie in their sandbox for Hanna Beth. They've all gone on a tour to see it." Kyle's voice caused the air to solidify in my lungs. I wasn't ready to face him yet. After weeks of drifting, of supposition and uncertainty, of hope and then hopelessness, the idea of bringing everything into the open was still terrifying. It could be the end of everything. It was so much easier to let things continue in limbo.

My hands felt stiff and unresponsive as I pulled the box top. The cardboard ripped, and birthday candles spilled onto the counter, tiny slashes of color rolling across the jade green tile, then falling toward the floor.

Kyle caught a blue one in midair, picked up several from the floor. "They don't make boxes like they used to."

Another candle rolled to the edge of the counter and toppled off as he stood up. I watched it fall, hit the floor, and break into three pieces. "No, they don't," I muttered absently.

Kyle pushed the rest of the candles away from the drop-off. I didn't look at him, but at his hand. His wedding ring caught the sunlight, glinted. I remembered the day we picked out our rings. We had so many plans, so many things we wanted to see, and do, and experience together. Every time he walked into a room, my heart sped up. When we were apart during the day while he went to his job clerking at a law firm and I went to class, I thought of him. I couldn't wait for the moment we would be together again. What had happened? When had we lost sight of each other and become focused, instead,

on houses, cars, career goals, schedules, Macey's activities, and every
commitment except our commitment to each other? How had we
become just two people who kept their stuff in the same house?

His ring caught the sunlight again. Did he ever take it off? Did he
slip it from his finger under the table and tuck it in his pocket like an
actor in some made-for-TV movie about a marriage gone wrong?

"Rebecca?"

I was suddenly aware that he'd been talking. I picked up a candle,
robotically stuck it in the cake. "Hmmm?"

"I said, I had Dan Canter do some research about the sale of the
house."

"The house?" *Focus, Rebecca. Focus. The house. The reason you
asked Kyle to come here. Dan Canter, Kyle's favorite private investigator—
the man who can track down delinquent property owners, prior judg-
ments, and wild deeds, anytime, anywhere.* It occurred to me that, in
Kyle's mind, the house was the only ongoing issue. "Did Dan find
anything?"

"Kenita Kendal has an employment history with various nursing
centers and home health agencies in Florida, usually only for a few
months here and a few months there before moving on. In Florida, she
was Kenita Kendal-Dawson, but Dan did a little digging and found
out she dropped the married name after pleading out of a charge of
illegal sale of prescription drugs in Florida. Her LVN was pulled after
that, which was probably why she moved to another state. She was
working for an agency here, so your parents most likely felt that they
could trust her. If the agency performed a basic background check on
Kenita Kendal, they wouldn't have found anything. LMK Limited,
the company that's been taking automatic drafts from your father's accounts, is hers. No telling, really, how she convinced him to allow the
drafts. It may have been as simple as getting his online passwords, or
as complicated as convincing him that the money was needed to pay
bills, or was being transferred into investments, but it's been going

on for over a year, and there's quite a bit of money involved—at least seventy thousand dollars that Dan could track."

"My God," I whispered. "How could that happen here?"

Kyle's eyes narrowed, as in, *Don't be naive, Rebecca.* "Your father and Hanna Beth probably looked like prime targets. Hanna Beth was in a desperate situation with your father's medical problems, he was in a state of mental decline, they own a big house in a location that's hot with developers who would jump at the opportunity to snap up this house. No doubt this Kenita Kendal-slash-Dawson thought she'd hit the jackpot when Hanna Beth had the stroke. With Hanna Beth out of the way, she could get your father to sign over the house, then she could turn a quick sale to a development company and be gone before anyone questioned it. According to Dan, Kenita Kendal has a deed, signed by your father and notarized three weeks before you got here. I informed the Constable's Office of the situation with the house, and they've agreed to stand down on the eviction order until we can get to court on Monday."

I imagined my father's home embroiled in a long legal battle, one that could spoil these final years, when my father and Hanna Beth should be enjoying their lives in peace. "Could this woman really end up with the house?"

Kyle shook his head. "The good news is that your father's a smart man. He must have had some concern when his original diagnosis was made, because he set up a Blue Sky Real Estate Trust and transferred the bulk of his assets, as well as the house, into the trust—hence his reason for putting the name of his lawyer in the safe-deposit box he left for you. He knew they would have all the paperwork. The trust was never filed with the courthouse, but it's all in safekeeping with the firm—Elliston, Hatch, and Williams, here in Dallas. I talked with Elliston this morning—he's a Pepperdine man, by the way. Good lawyer. Blue Sky Trust is solid, and it predates Kenita Kendal's deed. Nothing can come out of Blue Sky Trust without the approval of Hanna

Beth, and in the event Hanna Beth is incapacitated, the trust reverts in equal shares to you and Teddy, with Elliston seeing to Teddy's interests. Any sale of properties in the trust would have to be approved both by you and by your father's lawyer."

I was momentarily stunned. "My father left an equal share of the trust to me?" The idea touched me like a fresh breeze. My father had been thinking of me all along. Even after all the years that had passed, all the times I'd refused contact with him, he'd believed that Blue Sky Hill was still my home.

Kyle gave a confident smile. In Kyle's world, things always worked out the way he wanted them to. "Monday morning, I'm set to meet with Elliston. We'll be filing a motion in J.P. Court for a declaratory judgment that the Kenita Kendal claim constitutes a wild deed, and legal ownership of the house rests with the Blue Sky Trust. If Kenita Kendal does show up to contest it, or makes contact about the eviction over the weekend, there will be an arrest warrant waiting for her. Aside from the fraudulent claim to the house, there's the issue of the money she's bilked from your father's checking accounts, so the police are involved now. But the truth is, given her history and the cash missing from his bank account, my guess is that she'll take what she's got and run. Whether we'll ever recover any of the seventy thousand is anybody's guess, but the bulk of your father's estate is safe."

The knots that had been tightening in my spine since yesterday began to loosen. Letting my head roll forward, I rubbed the back of my neck. "Thanks for doing this, Kyle. Thanks for coming."

He frowned, seeming confused. "Did you think I wouldn't?" He reached for me, and I jerked away without meaning to.

The distance separating us was suddenly, painfully clear. A few feet, yet miles. "I wasn't sure." *How can I be sure of anything?* "I thought you might have . . . other plans." The words took on a sharp edge, a dark color, spilled hot and squalid onto the floor. I wanted to mop them up, reabsorb the animosity, hide the mess until later. Now wasn't the time for it.

Jerking his chin up, he appraised me narrowly. "What's that supposed to mean?"

Clutching a hand over the racing pulse in my throat, I shook my head. "Nothing. I'm sorry. I'm just stressed. It's been a busy day."

"Yeah, sure," he muttered.

"We'd better take the cake outside."

"They're walking around the yard, remember?" He stiffened, his cheek going tight, twitching slightly. "I hate it when you're like this."

"Like what, Kyle?" The corrosive mixture of supposition and unspoken accusations boiled higher inside me, hissed like a pressure cooker coming up to steam. "What am I like?" *How am I different from Susan Sewell?*

"Like your mother," he ground out. "She's still right here, even though she's gone." Kyle's dislike for my mother, and my mother's dislike for Kyle, had always been a thinly veiled secret. In his view, she interfered consistently and purposefully in our marriage. In her view, he was a man, after all. She'd always made known her opinion that he was a little too smooth, too friendly, too quick to strike up conversations with other women.

"This has nothing to do with my mother," I hissed, trying to control the volume of my voice, to keep it from pressing through the walls and entering the garden.

"This? This what?" Kyle's hands flailed in the air, demanding an answer. "I thought we were doing better. We took the anniversary trip. I came home for family movie night. I skipped golf, went to three of Macey's gymnastic meets. . . ."

"You had your face in your PalmPilot the whole time, Kyle. How does that help?" I shot back, even though the arguments about Macey had played out between us a dozen times before. It was easier to stay in familiar territory instead of opening up something new. "Macey needs you to be present, to be focused on her once in a while. She's growing up, and most of the time, you're not there."

He coughed in disbelief. "And you're so much better? You're at that stupid boutique six hours a day after you leave the office, and by the way, you never wanted to take over the shop—or have you forgotten? Our whole lives, you've been letting your mom reel you in—with her illness, with the shop, with her issues. You want to complain about my letting *my* job take me away from the family? What about you?"

"This isn't about me, Kyle. This isn't about my mother, and it's not about the shop. It's about . . ." I could feel the accusation on the tip of my tongue, so close, ready to rush out and shatter our lives into a million small pieces.

"About *what?*" he finished, his chin jutting toward me. His eyes flashed a challenge. "About *what?* Why don't you just say what you mean, Rebecca? Why don't you just get it out? There's been something going on with you ever since you left California."

"This isn't the time." I turned away from him and braced my hands on the edge of the counter, closed my eyes and tried to calm down. *Breathe, breathe. You can't do this now—not with birthday guests in the backyard and Macey close enough to walk in any minute.*

"It is the time. It's past time," Kyle pressed, fiercely determined, a skillful debater as usual. "You asked me to come here, I came. I try to touch you, you're hostile. Last night, we're talking on the phone like everything's fine, and today you're all over me. What's going on?"

Something inside me broke through the restraints, rushed toward daylight. "I *saw* you, Kyle. The morning I left, I saw you at the café with Susan Sewell, all right?" There it was, the truth, the facts of the case laid out on the table.

Kyle stumbled backward, stunned silent, his eyes blinking rapidly, as if I'd just thrown a punch and he was struggling to recover from it. "I don't know what you think you saw, but . . ."

I wheeled toward him. My hand caught the cake knife and sent it skittering onto the floor. "I *know* what I saw, Kyle. I saw the two of you holding hands. I saw her leaning across the table, gazing into your eyes. I saw you leaning close, like it wasn't the first time. I'm not stupid, Kyle. I know what a romantic interlude looks like. For heaven's sake, I had Macey in the car with me. She could have seen! What were you thinking?"

"A what? A romantic interlude?" He had the audacity to punctuate the question with an indignant cough. His mouth dropped open, and he shook his head. "Rebecca, are you serious? What you saw was me meeting with a *client*. Talking about real estate."

"Do you always hold hands when you talk about real estate?" I spat out, the anger, the frustration, the weeks of wounded uncertainty spewing from me.

Kyle's eyebrows shot up. He slapped a hand over them. "That was thirty seconds. Thirty seconds of misguided affection in an hour-long conversation about separation of real estate assets. She's lonely. That's all. She's forty, divorced, and insecure about the future."

Forty, divorced, and insecure. . . . The description could apply to me soon enough. Was that what I wanted? What if Kyle was telling the truth? What if I'd misconstrued what I saw, built it up into more than it was?

Don't be gullible, my mother's voice whispered in my head. *A woman can't afford to be pie-in-the-sky these days. You think you know somebody. You think you're a good wife, and you're doing all the things a good wife should, and then boom. . . .*

"You *gave* her Macey's *au pair*, Kyle. You want me to believe you did that for a business relationship and thirty seconds of flirtation?" *A woman has to be practical, watchful. Watch yourself, that's all I can say. . . .*

Kyle's hand flew into the air, slammed to the counter in a fist, bouncing the cake platter. "I didn't *give* her Macey's au pair. I found a solution that was best for everyone. I wanted Macey's au pair out of the house. That's it. End of story."

"Interesting how all these women are pursuing you, completely without encouragement on your part." That was something my mother would have said. *He's far too conversational with other women, Rebecca. Men don't do that without a reason. . . .*

Kyle's arms stiffened at his sides. Cursing under his breath, he turned away, paced to the door and came back. "All right, I'll admit it. I was flattered. Is that what you wanted to hear? The big bad husband goes wrong, just like your mother warned you about? Just like your father did?" He spread his arms wide, as if he were offering an open shot, as if he were through defending himself.

"This has nothing to do with my mother," I countered, but deep inside, I knew it did. There was a part of me that always heard her voice, that was always defensive, careful to maintain my independence.

"Come on, Rebecca. It has everything to do with your mother," Kyle insisted, his voice suddenly calm, making the words seem logical. "Haven't we been working up to this point for years? Ever since the day we got married, it's been you, your mother, your father, and me. Even when they're not there, they're there. Our whole lives have been a holding pattern, waiting for history to repeat itself."

"I don't want history to repeat itself," I protested, searching his face, groping for the truth. "All I want . . . all I ever wanted was a family, a normal life, the three of us spending time together, but you're never there, Kyle."

"I'm never there for whom, Rebecca?" Encompassing the kitchen with a sweeping gesture, he looked around, indicating the absence of anyone else in the room. "Who's there to come home to—you? Macey? Yes, I'll admit I'm driven. I work. I love what I do. I love it when a deal pays off. I get caught up in it more than I probably should. But there's no one to come home to, Rebecca.

You're gone to the shop. Macey's gone to her activities. You make it home at bedtime, and then you're so tired, there's nothing left. We sleep on opposite sides of the same bed. You don't want me. You don't need me. You're so busy trying to make sure you're not leaning on anybody, that you're ready to go it alone, I'm on the outside, all the time. So, is it any wonder that when an attractive woman offered to let me in, even for thirty seconds, I was tempted? I'm human, Rebecca."

Our gazes tangled, held fast. I felt sick inside, hollow. I felt like the twelve-year-old girl deciding whether to stay or go as Teddy ran across the lawn. Open up, take a chance? Get in the car, and hide behind the door?

Was Kyle telling the truth? There was no way to answer the question, except to trust.

Trust. Such a simple word. Such a hard thing to accomplish after a lifetime of self-defense. Was Kyle right? Had I spent our years casting him in my father's role and myself in my mother's?

But I was wrong about my mother's role. She wasn't the helpless victim of a philandering man. She was the person who purposefully kept my father from his child, who kept me from my brother, who hid the truth, even to her dying breath. All these years, I'd let her maintain a stranglehold on my life. All these years, she'd been trying to edge out my father. She'd used me to punish him, to punish Hanna Beth and Teddy. Even when she lay terminally ill, when she knew she would be leaving us, she had been trying to push Kyle out of my life, out of Macey's. She'd said she was leaving me the shop, so I would have something of my own, so I could take care of myself and Macey . . . in case . . .

Did she realize what she was doing, or was she only trying to protect me from the marital collapse she considered inevitable?

Were her choices acts of misguided love, or of selfishness?

I would never know for sure. There was no one to ask. There was nothing to do but go on from here, to stop listening to her voice and listen to my own. My heart wanted Kyle, still loved him. In the end, that was truth. It was my truth. Kyle loved me. He always had. All these years, he'd remained patiently on the outside, waiting for me to break free from the damage done the summer I left Blue Sky Hill, to leave the past behind, to stop living my mother's life and live my own, throw open the door and let him in.

Why would he have done that? Why would he be here now if he didn't love me?

Outside the window, my father laughed. Squinting through the wavy glass, I watched him strolling across the lawn, hand in hand with Hanna Beth as Teddy pushed the chair. How had they come back together, all those years ago? Who had been the first to believe, to bridge the gap between them, to open up and become vulnerable? How many years would they have missed if they hadn't mustered the courage to turn away from the past and step into the present?

A lifetime. A long and wonderful lifetime that began with an instant of trust.

Outside, Hanna Beth smiled at my father, placed her free hand over their intertwined fingers. He gazed down at her, his eyes filled with adoration, with need, with happiness, even now, when the road ahead seemed so difficult.

"I want our marriage," I whispered, turning back to my husband. "I want our family. I want us to spend more time together—do things. Being here, watching my father and Hanna Beth . . . I realize how fast a life goes by, Kyle. In the end, the only thing that matters is the people you love, the time you spend together. When we look back someday, I don't want it all to be a blur of meaningless activity. I want our life back. I want *us* back."

Kyle sighed, as if he'd been holding the breath inside of himself, waiting. "I was never gone. I've always been here. I love you, Rebecca. I love you, and I love Macey. I may not always show it as much as I should, but there was never a time I was looking for anything else. We have everything we need."

We have everything we need. We had more than he knew. I scraped together my courage, tried to find the right words to tell him about the baby. What would he think? What would he say? Would he wonder? Would he question?

"I'm . . . I'm pregnant." The truth shivered into the air and hovered there. Kyle blinked hard, as if he were trying to focus.

"Wha . . . how?"

"The anniversary trip."

"But . . ."

"Vasectomies fail, Kyle. Your father's did."

He gaped at me in stunned silence, his body rounding forward, his arms hanging limp. He opened his mouth, closed it, opened it again, staggered backward a step and sank into a chair. "I don't know . . . a baby?" I searched for intonation in the words, some indication. Happiness? Anger? Fear? Disappointment? Doubt? Something.

"I took a test yesterday. For obvious reasons, pregnancy was the furthest thing from my mind."

"Yeah," he muttered, swaying sideways, his gaze sweeping the floor. "Are you . . . well . . . sure?"

"The tests are pretty accurate," I answered, still trying to read his reaction. "I've been having symptoms."

He lifted his hands, let them fall to his lap, stared at the floor. I waited for him to take in the idea. Finally, he squinted up at me, his eyebrows knotted in his forehead. "How do you think Mace's going to feel about this?"

The tension in my chest began to dissipate, growing lighter. "We could wait a while to tell her. I don't even know how I feel about it yet."

"Yeah," Kyle muttered, nodding, his gaze unfocused.

The door to the garden opened, and both of us jerked upright. "We're ready for the cake," Mary called.

"Coming," I answered, wiping the tear trails from my cheeks. I picked up Hanna Beth's birthday cake and balanced it between my hands, stared down at the icing words, but couldn't comprehend them. "We'd better go out there."

"I'll . . . I'll get . . . the door," Kyle muttered. He stood and followed me, his steps slow and wooden. "I'll be in my sixties when the baby graduates from high school," he muttered as he reached for the doorknob.

"I know," I said, and in spite of everything, his bemused look made me smile as we went out the door.

On the patio, the celebration was proceeding, the partygoers oblivious to the moment of truth in the kitchen. I placed the cake on a white iron table in front of Hanna Beth. Ifeoma lit the candles and Teddy helped my father into a chair. Together we sang "Happy Birthday," our voices blending together, young and old. When the song was over, my father leaned across, cupped Hanna Beth's face in his hand and kissed her, then sang, "May I call you sweetheart, I'm in love with you," as he handed her one of Macey's roses.

Hanna Beth smiled and rested her head on his shoulder. Together, they watched the birthday flames sway in the wind.

"Blow da candle, Mama," Teddy cheered, waving his hands over the cake.

"Let the children," my father suggested, and laid his cheek atop Hanna Beth's silver hair.

"Yes, let the children," Ouita Mae echoed, maneuvering her walker toward the table as she motioned the children in. "Gather round, now. There's a hungry old man waiting for some cake." She winked over her shoulder at Claude, and he blushed, then grinned tenderly in reply. "Phillip." She motioned to her grandson as Brady clasped the edge of the table, tipping it to one side. "Lift up the little guy so he can help."

Dr. Barnhill awkwardly picked up Mary's younger son, and, together with Macey, the boys blew out the candles.

"Happy birf-day to Hanna Bet!" Brady cheered, and everyone laughed.

Pastor Al suggested we say a prayer over the food, and we bowed our heads. As his voice resonated in the damp, still air, blessing the food and our gathering, I felt Kyle's arms slip around me—tentatively at first, then tighter, circling my stomach, cupping the tiny life we'd created and would nurture together as the years went by. He pulled me into him and held me close. I leaned against his chest, turned in his arms and rested my head there, heard his heartbeat beneath my ear, slow and familiar. After weeks of fighting for air, I felt as if I could finally breathe.

My senses filled with the earthy scents of Teddy's garden, the faint traces of smoke from Hanna Beth's birthday candles, the radiant glow of light, the slight stirrings of people all around me. A family. As the prayer ended, I listened to the voices—my father presenting the first slice of cake to his birthday girl. Hanna Beth laughing. Macey struggling to lift Brady to the table again so he could watch the cake being cut. The old house yawning and crackling, radiating warmth as the afternoon sun pressed through the canopy of slumbering branches.

The breath of summer stirred the trees overhead, and I opened my eyes, looked up. A leaf pulled free, sailed on invisible currents, swirling and diving, dancing and spinning like the dragonfly lights in my bedroom upstairs. I felt the spirit of the girl who once lived there, now standing close, watching the leaf drift toward earth.

It floated downward.

Circling . . .

Circling . . .

Until it touched the ground and rested silent among the grass-green waves of my father's lawn.

I thought of the Japanese gardener, far away on the waterfront in San Diego, shaded beneath his wide straw hat, carefully combing seas of gravel to reflect the invisible tides that swell from hidden places deep within the soul.

The tides swirled around me, whispered with a completeness that spilled warmth into all the spaces that had been empty, that had searched and wondered, waited and struggled to find peace.

The little-girl spirit left the patio, dashed over the grass on light, silent feet, paused to smile at what had fallen there. And suddenly I understood how the gardener knew that the leaf was meant to stay.

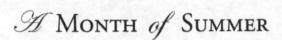

A Month *of* Summer

LISA WINGATE

This Conversation Guide is intended to enrich the
individual reading experience, as well as encourage us
to explore these topics together—because books,
and life, are meant for sharing.

A CONVERSATION
WITH LISA WINGATE

Q. A Month of Summer *is your ninth novel. Has your writing process changed over the years?*

A. For me, the writing process has remained much the same. I still begin with characters and an initial situation. From there, the process of writing the novel becomes a journey of discovering the characters from the outside in. Each story is a quest to understand the hearts and minds of several individuals—the ways in which each is a product of a specific set of experiences. As the story develops, the needs of the characters begin to mesh, and the potential for connection becomes more evident. While I'm working on the first part of the novel, the threads seem to be traveling in a dozen different directions. About halfway through, the threads develop a weave, and the larger picture becomes clear. The story grows in a sense of plan and purpose, gaining a personality of its own.

If anything has changed about my writing process over the years it is that it's easier not to panic when the threads seem to be scattered all over the loom. These days, I can (usually) be more patient in allowing the process to work, in letting the story move at its own pace until the larger canvas takes shape.

Q. The books in your Tending Roses series have largely employed rural settings. What inspired you to create Rebecca and Hanna Beth's story in an urban setting?

A. Living within proximity of Dallas, I've been aware for quite some time of the revitalization of historic areas near downtown. While it is wonderful to see once-abandoned neighborhoods undergoing reclamation and again becoming vital living spaces for families, these changes sometimes take place at the expense of historic structures and longtime residents, who are often priced out of their own neighborhoods by rising property values and higher taxes. Such situations also provide fertile ground for the victimization of disadvantaged families and elderly home owners, such as Edward and Hanna Beth. Often these home owners have few resources available. As neighborhoods change, family members and old friends have sold out and moved away, and the remaining original residents become islands unto themselves as new and old struggle to cohabitate. Such a situation seemed like an ideal location in which to mesh the stories of several characters who need one another to survive.

Q. Your story depicts a complicated family situation that is tragic but also realistic, particularly in today's world of fractured family ties. Are any parts of the story based on real life?

A. In every story there are some bits of real life, some nibblets of sheer invention, and a sprinkle of serendipity. Writers are always the people slyly turning an ear to the tiny human dramas in restaurants, department store checkout lines, cell phone conversations in the next bathroom stall. The past trauma in Edward and Hanna

Beth's family is largely a combination of eavesdropping and fiction, but I do feel that the story could apply to any family, particularly in a world where so many families are separated by distance and various types of emotional and physical estrangement.

The issue of Alzheimer's care is one to which I was able to contribute personally. Having experienced the ravages of this disease within my own family, I understand the difficulty of caring for a loved one who is physically able but facing slow mental decline. While these changes are very individual, the continuum of emotions and the challenges of caretaking are, in some ways, constant. Caretaking is very often a lonely occupation. Even friends and family members who would like to help frequently don't know how to contribute. My hope is that Rebecca and Hanna Beth's story will help to build bridges and create dialogue between primary caretakers and surrounding friends and family members. Sometimes just a few hours out of the house, while a friend or family member takes over the duties, can be an incredible gift.

Q. Through extraordinary circumstances, Rebecca is compelled to behave in a heroic manner, even though she often struggles with her own resentments. Do you think all of us have the capacity for such self-sacrifice?

A. I believe that within each of us there is the potential to transcend ordinary fears and inhibitions. Many of us may never encounter the situation that would require a heroic act. We go through life watching the heroic acts of others and wondering if, faced with the same set of circumstances, we would be compelled to take action, to do the right thing.

True heroism doesn't manifest itself only in those who run into burning buildings or cross battlefields to save the wounded. Heroism exists in those who spend weekends building Habitat homes, who care for children in need of parents or mentors, who provide for parents who have become dependent themselves. To my mind, each character in the novel is heroic in some way, whether that heroism manifests itself in something as complex as traveling across the country to see to an estranged relative, or as simple as stretching upward from a wheelchair to raise a window blind and let in the sunlight. By each doing what is possible, we should be ultimately achieve the impossible.

Q. Like so many contemporary women, Rebecca packs long days with seemingly endless responsibilities, and her daughter's after-school hours are tightly scheduled as well. You yourself are married, raising two boys on a horse ranch, writing two novels a year, and speaking to groups on a continuing basis. Is Rebecca's situation inspired in any way by your own? Do you have any advice for readers about how to maintain a sense of balance while keeping up with their busy lives?

A. Certainly as a mom, writer, daughter, and member of a busy community of friends and readers, I can relate to the push and pull of Rebecca's situation. Our days are often filled with activities and the family calendar sometimes looks like the Scrabble board after a long game—everything intertwined and not a space empty. Fortunately, I am not the type who needs a quiet space to work. I can write anywhere, anytime, and no matter what's going on. Over the years, I've packed my laptop along and sat typing on the sidelines of soccer practices, between baseball games, in the car on family trips, in the living room while the guys are hollering at football games on TV.

In terms of maintaining a sense of peace and connection at home, I still believe in the family dinner. Sometimes, it's so tempting to serve off the counter and let everyone wander back to various TVs or whatever. In defiance of the whines and the "But, Mom, the game's on!" I just insist. We sit, we say grace, we eat together. We talk.

Q. You speak to booksellers and readers at events all year. What do people say about your books? Are there any surprising or gratifying responses you'd like to share?

A. I love spending time with readers and booksellers. The most, most, most wonderful part of writing a story is knowing that someone else enjoyed reading it, and found it a source of entertainment, courage for change, a greater appreciation of life, or just a few hours of peace. Over the years, I've treasured letters from readers who were encouraged in difficult times, inspired to make life changes, to reunite with family members, to finally document the stories of older family members, to look at life with new eyes, to appreciate the gifts of the moment. I'm amazed and humbled that a story can be a catalyst for action, but at the same time, I recall the stories that have moved me over the years. Once, a reader who'd finished my novel *Texas Cooking* and had been inspired to relocate back to the hometown she'd always missed, ended an e-mail to me by writing, "Did you ever imagine that your humorous book about Texas would affect someone this way?"

What a wonderful and complicated question! I always hope the books will produce good fruit, but I never know what it will be, or where it will land, or what will grow from the seeds within. So much of that remains in God's hands, which is as it should be.

Q. What's next?

A. In addition to the continuation of the small-town Texas series that began with *Talk of the Town*, published by Bethany House, I plan to continue stories of life in the houses on Blue Sky Hill, published by New American Library. As with the books in the Tending Roses series, the ending of each character's story often marks the beginning of another journey. Because I never know where a story might lead, or how it will end, or what may happen to the characters after the final page, the only way to find the next image in the canvas is to get out the loom and let the threads start moving again. Eventually, it'll all start to make sense, and after it does, there will be another thread that seems to continue beyond the picture, raising the question, What happens now?

QUESTIONS
FOR DISCUSSION

1. Today, Alzheimer's disease remains one of the most prevalent, difficult, and costly diseases of aging. Has your family been affected by Alzheimer's disease? In what ways? How have your experiences been like or unlike those in the book?

2. After seeing her husband with Susan at the café, Rebecca is quick to assume infidelity. Do you think she is justified in her lack of trust? How do our past experiences affect our present relationships?

3. As Hanna Beth watches Teddy and Rebecca interact, she begins to wonder if, in her efforts to protect Teddy and keep him safe, she might have also thwarted his ability to become more independent. Do you think this is true? Why or why not? Do you think Hanna Beth would have imagined that Teddy could navigate several miles through the neighborhood streets to find food and keep the household afloat?

4. Claude Fisher takes an active interest in Hanna Beth, even when she is not able to physically respond to his companionship. Why do you think he does so?

5. When Rebecca finds Edward's letter, she feels cheated and betrayed by Marilyn's refusal to tell her the truth about her father, the past, and Teddy. What motivated Marilyn to take the truth to her deathbed? Was it a decision of misguided love or a final act of retaliation against Edward and Hanna Beth?

6. Rebecca's growing affection for Teddy is often hampered by a lingering resentment of the fact that Edward chose to actively nurture Teddy while allowing Rebecca to be permanently taken away by her mother. Have you seen or experienced situations in which adult sibling relationships are hampered by feelings that one sibling was favored over another in childhood? Are these feelings normal? How do we overcome this as adults?

7. The author describes this as a story of an ordinary person compelled by extraordinary circumstances. How do you think you would react if your humanity compelled you to actively sacrifice for someone you feel injured you in the past?

8. How do you think the future will be different for Teddy, Rebecca, and Hanna Beth? For Mary and Ifeoma? For Ouita Mae and Claude?

9. Some of the most heroic characters in the novel are also the most helpless. How do Teddy, Claude, and Mary manage to contribute to the people around them despite a lack of personal resources?

10. Late in the story, Hanna Beth realizes that the combined tragedy of her stroke and Edward's illness has been the driving force in reuniting the family. Have you experienced times when a tragic event caused distanced family or friends to come together?

Can anything go right in this tumbleweed town?

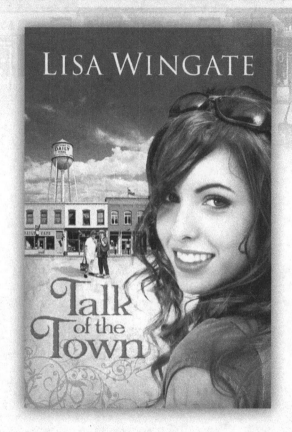

LISA WINGATE

Talk of the Town

When her glamorous job lands her in the off-the-map town of Daily, Texas, Mandalay Florentino finds she needs more than just her Hollywood charm to survive…